TO Barb:

TO LOVE WITH HATE

Best wishes
and good health

[illegible]

S.R. Carson

outskirtspress
DENVER, COLORADO

To Love With Hate

v2.0

Outskirts Press, Inc.
http://www.outskirtspress.com

ISBN: 978-1-4787-2984-6

PRINTED IN THE UNITED STATES OF AMERICA

"All is Caprice.
They love without measure those whom
they will soon hate without reason."

—Thomas Sydenham, 17th-century physician

CHAPTER 1

Wyatt Barton, M.D., saved a pregnant woman struggling for her life as well as the life of her unborn baby, but he failed to save what he valued the most: the children he loved. Despite the admiration he received from patients and families for his medical successes, he saw himself in light of this failure, a heavy load he carried in the lonely outposts of his soul. But she was always there for him, a loyal friend who had repaired the gaping holes in his wounded heart.

"Oh, hello, honey." Even through the phone her voice was sultry, radiating her exotic European upbringing. "Is it not amazing—I was just getting ready to punch in your numbers! It's like we feel each other at the same moment, and we call simultaneously more often than not. God, I've missed you. After last night, I just can't stop thinking of you—and well, us."

"Sweetie, I can't believe how lucky I am to have met such a beautiful woman after you came to this country, alone and without anyone, and now I feel empty if I don't see you every day somehow."

"You always find such beautiful words, Wyatt. They tickle me somewhere that I can't really describe, or at least not in public—ooh la la. How was your day?"

"I'm exhausted really. Sprawled out watching mindless TV."

"What is 'sprawled'? Sorry, I haven't learned that word yet."

Wyatt laughed gently. "It means lying down with one leg on the couch and another hanging down to the floor."

She chuckled. "Oh I see. Now tell me, was it worse than usual today?"

Wyatt carefully rubbed the jagged scar on his forehead that partially severed his heavy left eyebrow. After all these years, it still irritated him when he was stressed. "One of the obstetricians panicked because this young pregnant woman went cyanotic on him—you know, turning blue due to lack of oxygen. He was worried as hell about her as well as the baby. Quite a high-strung guy at the best of times—probably should've never gone into obstetrics. These pregnant ladies need reassurance with calm confidence. Anyway he finally called me in for a third opinion."

"They should've called you first, you brilliant, sexy man. You're kinda like that Dr. House guy I saw on TV, diagnosing all those weird problems, although you're not as nasty as he is." She laughed. "You do have your moments, though."

"Yeah, right. I just get lucky sometimes. Well maybe it's my relentless persistence. 'Stubborn' is what my mother called it, God rest her soul. Turns out it was the platypnea-orthodeoxia syndrome. My ultrasound bubble test confirmed it. I asked her to cough while she sat up from the exam table, and that exposed a hole in her upper heart chambers that was shunting oxygen—depleted venous blood back to her arterial circulation. Not enough oxygen for her, and definitely not good for the baby."

"Sounds amazing! I'm not sure I understand your medical lingo but the more time we spend together, the easier it will become, I suppose. Anyway, you're my hero, you know. Did you fix the poor thing?"

"No hero, honey. And I promise to talk about my patients only on rare occasions, maybe lunch because we won't have many of those together. Yeah, I rushed her to the catheterization lab and closed the hole. They're both doing fine now."

"Wyatt, my sweet doctor, I appreciate you for what you do in this nasty world. But please go to bed now so you can be fresh for your patients and, well, especially for me."

"Now you're talking, babe. I'll always be ready for you. In fact, I'll call you early tomorrow morning as soon as I'm out of the shower so you can imagine my wet, dripping body that you could've had the night before. By the way, I can't get enough of you."

"Exactly what I'm thinking. I can't wait to run my hand through your hair. All of it. Then pull you close and let my hands slide down over the small of your back and then up and down the curve of your muscular butt. Best butt I've ever seen."

"Ah, you've seen a lot of those?"

"Well, not really but I've seen enough to know what I like, so I'm not, as you say, 'horngreen.'"

Wyatt laughed. "You mean 'greenhorn,' honey."

"Whatever. You know what I mean, babe."

"Honey, you can run your hands up and down my wet body any time you want. Hey, don't take it personally if I'm late calling tomorrow—I'm on call tonight."

Wyatt grunted while he slowly rousted himself off the couch for the bedroom.

He had barely sunk into sleep when he was startled awake. The November wind flapped the metal oven vents on the roof and vibrated the windowpanes, threatening to shatter them. He was used to being alone in the spacious house, jerking awake when the phone rang at all hours. The neighbors often let their dogs out during the night, but tonight their usual howling ended abruptly with some sharp whimpers. He knew his neighbor was not the kind of guy to beat his dogs; in fact, they controlled him. Curiosity compelled Wyatt toward the bank of windows facing the neighbor's house across the street. Swirling snow covered the almost bare trees, but no dogs in Brad's yard. Partially hidden by the trees at the lot's boundary was a junky pickup parked at an odd angle. Maybe Brad's son was home early from college for Thanksgiving. That kid was snarly and could easily beat the dogs.

Surprised that the hospital hadn't called, he checked his cell and beeper: both working fine. Reassured that it was an unusually quiet night on call, he drifted back off to sleep.

An hour later he was alert once more. The lashing of the wind had intensified yet again. But the wind didn't bother him; in fact, it was kind of a natural nuisance that reminded him of how warm and well built his house was. The neighborhood break-ins briefly crossed his mind now, although it would be rare that a single man would be a target. He had no worries because he really had nothing worth stealing anyway. Either way, he reminded himself that his Remington short barrel "home protector" lay beneath the bed, within his reach and loaded, although he knew it didn't need to be that close to him or even in his bedroom. In a way, though, it was reassuring to have the gun in the house, and he looked forward to actually shooting it someday at a target range. Ron, the presently enthusiastic gun salesman, a former army sergeant, had instructed him to snatch the gun, chamber a round, and release the safety. "Ready for anything, man."

"After I put on my glasses," he'd quipped without mentioning his civilian relationship to Special Forces teams.

Ron also assured him that the sound of the classic pump action would be enough to scare most bad guys away. To liven up the conversation, Wyatt chatted about a burglary down the block during his cash exchange.

"No one was at home fortunately. With my kids gone five years already, I'm finally comfortable having a shotgun in the house now, although it's unlikely I'll ever be in a position to use it."

Ron gave him his change and some advice: "You need to have a plan, specific for your home, or the bad guys fucking win. What's your plan, Dr. Rambo?"

Wyatt smiled at him and left the gun store, as happy as a young boy with a new toy.

His mind let go of the memories and he fell comfortably into a sleep trance, light as the snowfall outside.

The violent shatter of glass onto the foyer's marble floor hurled him off the bed. His bad knee slammed onto the frigid stone floor and his yell reverberated through the house like a loud siren in a deep cavern.

He cursed at himself for the screw-up. Probably was the damn wind, but if there was an intruder, he'd given away his precise location. He knew he was in danger of becoming a victim if it was the latter. He felt around the bedside table for his glasses and searched desperately below the bed unsuccessfully. The unmistakable squeaks of rubber soles on polished floors reminded him of the noises made by players running on basketball courts, and they accelerated towards the bedroom. It wasn't the wind. His neck arteries pounded from the pumping adrenaline surge. He fumbled under the bed again for his shotgun and furiously chambered a shell.

A sledgehammer kick blew open the bedroom door. Wyatt whirled around in the darkness to face a barely discernible hulk bearing down upon him and pulled the trigger, aiming in the general direction of the menace. The intruder screamed when the shotgun blast missed the main target but shattered his knee instead. His scream was overcome by Wyatt's primal howl after a bullet ripped through the tender flesh of his upper abdomen.

Writhing in pain, Wyatt crawled to his bedside table and his bloody hand slapped weakly for his cell phone, blood dripping onto the slippery floor while he lost strength. Then everything went dark. The intruder dragged his angulated leg into the blizzard outside, leaving a trail of warm blood like red flames scattered on the white marble.

"St. Anthony Hospital operator. May I help you?"

"This is the charge nurse in the ER. We need Dr. Barton now!"

"Ma'am, we've been paging him and calling for over an hour now, with no answer."

"Then do it again damn it, and keep doing it till you get him. I have patients down here with heart attacks and chest pain. The chief of the ER isn't happy!"

"Okay, okay, I'll keep trying!"

The bossy charge nurse had had enough. "He better not be boinking some hot nursing student 'cause I'll cut off his love tool for this!"

It was an often-repeated joke that senior nursing administrators could easily "eat their young." They were not taken lightly.

The operator's face turned red and she shuddered. After her tenth attempt, she called back the ER supervisor. "Sorry, ma'am, I can't reach him. Tried ten times. I don't know what else to do."

"I'll fix that."

Dr. Burlington, the chief of emergency services, requested that police be summoned to Wyatt's home.

Patrol officer Carl Jenkins received the call during a quiet night on duty, deep in reverie over a doughnut and orange juice at Dunkin Donuts.

"Two Adam 23, proceed to 1401 Sunnyside Rd. Welfare check at the residence of on-call doctor hospital can't reach."

Jenkins ran out the door with the half-eaten jelly doughnut stuck in his mouth. He drove without a siren to fetch the wayward doctor because it was three am, but he drove as fast as the streets allowed. Evanston was relatively quiet on Tuesday nights, and Jenkins was looking forward to the end of his shift. This would be an easy assignment before heading home to his warm bed. He really hoped that his shift would be topped off by finding Dr. Barton's wife or girlfriend standing in the doorway in sexy lingerie.

Officer Jenkins rang Wyatt's booming doorbell twice, then he knocked as hard as he dared. A few remaining glass shards from the front window dropped from the force of the wind and shattered onto the stone walkway near the porch. The officer jumped. Then he saw that the front window had been completely smashed. A frigid sweat streaked down his spine and he leaped through the window frame. The blood trail stopped him cold and his breath quickened in small gasps. He cocked his weapon and held it in front of him with both hands, following the blood trail directly to Wyatt's bedroom. Dr. Wyatt Barton was lying in a pool of blood on the floor next to his bed with his shotgun several feet away. Jenkins surveyed the bedroom and hallway, saw no threats, and then knelt by Barton's quivering body.

"Say something to me, Dr. Barton!"

His gurgling was almost unintelligible. "C-call D-Dr. M-Moore."

Jenkins radioed dispatch. "2 Adam 23, step up cover!"

"Dispatch, 2 Adam 51, I'm near the scene and rolling."

Another call. "Roll medical."

The police academy CPR training had been deeply ingrained into his neurons. Weak pulse, critically wounded, shallow breaths at forty per minute. No chest compressions needed; he knew that much. Jenkins wiped the sweat from his face before checking Barton's wounds. His hands trembled when he saw the blood soaking Barton's shorts and the right half of his chest.

"Dr. Barton, talk to me."

No response. Jenkins shook his shoulder. "Dr. Barton! Dr. Barton!"

He applied pressure on the wound while implementing his best first responder aid, elevating the legs to increase central blood volume and pulling the bed comforter over the quaking body. There was nothing more he could do until the medics and backup arrived. The two minutes alone with the critically wounded doctor dragged on like decades for Jenkins.

Wyatt knew he was dying. He saw the beckoning light, then darkness, then back and forth with the light drawing him closer and closer to peaceful bliss. He suddenly opened his eyes and gurgled a few words: "Where are Spencer and Colby? Must save them."

Jenkins put his ear up to Wyatt's mouth. "Are there others in the house? Who are Spencer and Colby?"

Wyatt had lost consciousness. If there were others in the house, they could be shot too, but he couldn't leave Wyatt before help arrived.

"Carl, what the hell happened here?" asked the second officer.

"Got a doc down, shot but barely alive with a weapon on the floor.

He said something about Spencer and Colby so there might be other victims in the house. Make sure no one else is hit."

"You stay with him while I clear the rest of the house to see if the perp is still here."

No medics were allowed in until the scene was safely cleared of potential violence.

Jenkins tried again to talk to the doc, but he wasn't good with small talk, especially with a dying man. The house was clear, so Spencer and Colby would remain a mystery. When the medics took over the emergency care, Jenkins stepped away and prayed that Barton would awaken, but there was no response—just the persistent raging wind, the metal clanging on the roof, Jenkins' pounding temporal pulse, and Wyatt's fast and desperate gasps for air.

Dr. Wyatt Barton started the evening satisfied that he had saved the life of a pregnant woman and her unborn child, blissfully thinking about his lover, but ended the evening fighting for his own life.

CHAPTER 2

FIFTEEN YEARS EARLIER:

You were lonely and it was just sex. Only known her maybe two months. High school education, and that's it. Okay, she's pretty with flashy red hair and green eyes. Now she drops the pregnancy bomb? She said she was on the pill that night. Don't be naïve. No one will blame you if you walk away now. But the child will need a dad and a family.

Dr. Wyatt Barton was almost twenty-nine years old and had a few months left in his Internal Medicine residency at Northwestern University, to be followed in the fall by a cardiology fellowship at Northwestern as well. He and Katherine had been married for about a month, living frugally in a tiny one-bedroom apartment, surviving on his meager resident's salary. The apartment was furnished in classic apple-crate style. Katherine spent her days preparing the apartment for the arrival of their son Spencer, who was due in six months. Although ridiculously busy at the hospital, he didn't mind the long hours, but his thoughts frequently drifted.

She says she loves me, but will I ever fall in love with her?

Another shock hit Wyatt broadside soon after he came home from the hospital to relax. He plopped on his favorite couch and read the paper with his stocking feet resting up on the garage sale coffee table, finally relaxing after a difficult day as chief resident, keeping the green interns and medical students from screwing up and causing harm to patients.

"Don't sit there, Wyatt!"

"Why? I don't see a reserved sign sitting on the couch."

Katherine glared at him with a blank face. "Tina and Italy are lying there. I finally got them to sleep. If you sit there, I know you'll wake them."

"Funny, I don't see anybody sitting here. Who are Tina and Italy by the way? Little invisible friends of yours?"

She continued to stare at him without emotion. He thought she was a good joker and continued to play along. "Italy is kind of a funny name, don't you think? How 'bout you name him Curly or Moe or something?"

He took his feet off the coffee table and tapped them nervously on the floor. Sensing something ominous creeping into his rapidly changing life, he hoped that Katherine was playing a game with him.

"I can't believe you didn't see them, Wyatt."

He stared at her. Her eyes were distant with a glassy grayness.

"Keep your voice down, Wyatt. If you wake them up, they will cause hell, trust me. Earlier this afternoon I had to clean up after they pooped all over the bedroom carpet. Then they made a nasty mess in the bathroom. But after all, they're just wild monkeys and they don't know any better. I hope they get sleepy soon so I can get some rest."

Wyatt laughed loudly. "Katherine, you're quite a comedienne. After I finish reading the sports page I'll head out to the porch and burn some burgers, whattya say?"

"No. Don't wake up the monkeys!" She grabbed Wyatt's arm and pulled him off the couch with a violent yank.

Wyatt stood there, frozen. A trembling motion took over his insides; his stomach lurched and fell like a free-fall roller coaster when it sunk in that something definitely was wrong with his wife. She was clearly experiencing visual hallucinations.

They began to occur nightly, and the pattern that he detected was that they occurred just after the start of a migraine headache. She'd never told him that she had a medical or maybe a psychiatric problem.

But then, she didn't tell him much at all before they married. During her episodes of hallucinations, he struggled with her, trying to keep her from injuring herself, and sometimes he even had to help her go to the bathroom because of her fear of the monkeys. Getting her to the bedroom and eventually asleep was his only hope for peace. He noticed that the next morning she was always back to normal, and it seemed she had no recollection of the events the night before. She displayed a sweet attitude when she wasn't hallucinating, and her warmth soothed him, albeit only in the mornings. He hoped it was just stress from the pregnancy and marriage and it would be a temporary phenomenon, never to be experienced again.

He arranged for her to see a neurologist, who ordered CT scans, MRI's, and EEG tests of her brain, all of which were normal. The neurologist said the hallucinations were simply unusual manifestations of a severe migraine, and all he could do was treat the migraine with pain medications and hope for the best. But Wyatt struggled with the realization that the medications didn't help the hallucinations directly.

One evening he came home to their apartment and found newspapers and blankets spread all around the family room carpeting and the floors of the kitchen, bathroom, and bedroom.

"Who are you?" asked Katherine.

She looked normal to Wyatt, so he played along. Maybe this time it was a role-play erotic thing she was trying. He hoped this would be fun.

"Oh, hi; I'm the plumber coming to fix your leaky faucet, ma'am."

There was her distant stare again. Her glassy gaze shot straight through him as if he weren't there, and he wondered if anyone in the world was in the same position as he was.

"Katherine, I'm your husband Wyatt."

"Bullshit. You've come to give the monkeys their shots. I know. But be careful, Italy and Tina are sick, and I had to cover the floors because they were puking."

He felt the shock stab deeply in his spine when he realized the hallucinations weren't going away, and he would have to live with them and protect her from injury while he searched for an answer. He scoured the medical literature on migraines, and came across a case report in a medical journal showing how nasal oxygen can sometimes resolve severe vascular headaches. He asked his friend at the local medical supply company to deliver a tank of oxygen over that evening and he put Katherine to bed with oxygen. It worked. The hallucinations resolved and she fell asleep without a struggle. But the days slowed like a barely dripping faucet for Wyatt, and soon he learned to detect the first sign of her migraines and immediately put her to bed with oxygen. He was able to stop the hallucinations, but for how long?

Before the marriage, Wyatt looked forward to contact with his parents. But now he had to be careful, because he knew that his mother was familiar with his tone of voice and what it meant. He couldn't let her know what was happening to his new wife, and he worked hard to demonstrate to his parents that his marriage was normal and going well. But then, what is a normal marriage? He could tell Mom was already suspicious because of the quick marriage without much of a courtship.

"Hello, honey. How are things with you and your new bride? We haven't heard from you in a while."

"Hey, Mom. Thanks for calling. Sorry, I've been busy at work, but you know, things are great here. Couldn't be better."

"I'm happy for you. How's Katherine doing with the pregnancy? No morning sickness?"

"She's doing quite well. Not having any morning sickness or swelling. Thanks for asking."

"Put her on the phone. I need to talk to her about your birthday coming up, and I also had some ideas on having the nursery ready for baby Spencer."

"She stepped out to get some groceries. I'll tell her you called as soon as she comes back."

"Tell her I'll be home all day if she wants to call back. You take care now, hon. Dad sends his best too. Love ya."

"Love ya too."

She needs me. The child will need me. Seems I'm the only one who can help her and I can't leave this poor woman in her time of need. What would people think of me leaving a pregnant wife after a few months of marriage? Just wouldn't be right to leave now. Maybe her problem is just stress. It'll resolve soon, and we can make this marriage work.

The migraines and secondary hallucinations resolved after two months of struggle for Wyatt, never to return, vanishing without a clear explanation. The newly married couple welcomed Spencer into the world and Wyatt grew confident that his family was healthy now, and the baby safe with Katherine. He immersed himself in the joy of Spencer, and the thoughts of leaving Katherine to find a woman that he actually fell in love with and chose deleted themselves from his memory bank.

CHAPTER 3

Colby Barton arrived into the world two years after Spencer. During the early years with his young sons, Wyatt absorbed himself into family life, and he cherished the time he had with his sons. He affectionately called Spencer "Bubba" and Colby "Boogie" when they were infants and young children. Of course now that Spencer was fifteen and Colby just turned thirteen, they no longer appreciated the nicknames Wyatt gave them, although he did it just to get a reaction at times. Spencer was almost six feet tall, only slightly shorter than his father, and he'd inherited his father's blue eyes and blond hair. Red-haired Colby had inherited most features from his mother, including her green eyes and slightly heavier build.

But it was the small jagged scar across Wyatt's left eyebrow that separated his facial features the most from his sons. It was a scar that made people curious about its origin, but not a topic of open conversation. Keenly aware that Katherine always made sure the house remained immaculate, despite being lived in by three males, those males made sure they walked carefully around her just vacuumed carpet or polished floors. They would hear about it if others messed up her dream house, and loudly. It was late on a Sunday afternoon, and the two teenagers remained holed up in their room, avoiding contact with their parents.

"Wyatt, I'm taking the kids shopping for some new jeans and school clothes. We'll be back in a few hours. I'm not even going to ask you to go."

"Good move. And by the way, I'm sure the boys are excited about this golden opportunity. Or perhaps you made them an offer they couldn't refuse: have the two of them clean the deck with a toothbrush?"

"You think you're pretty funny, don't you? They need clothes. Maybe we can meet somewhere for dinner later if you're not called in to the hospital immediately when your on-call starts at 4:30?"

"Can't promise anything. You know how unpredictable my on-call nights can be. But I may play some golf with the guys while you're gone. Haven't played in over a year, and I've turned Tom and Ed down too many times. May have my physician's license taken away if I don't make an appearance on the course."

"Yeah, right, you poor thing. You better get going then. This is your chance to play when we're gone. It's 9:30 now and you may not be able to finish 18 holes in time for your hospital duties if you don't leave soon."

"It'll take us about four hours or less depending on who's playing in front of us, so I should be home around three or so."

"I'll put a pot roast in the Crock-Pot so it'll be warm and ready for us before you're on call. That's a better idea than going out to eat and taking the risk of you leaving us alone at the table."

"Yum, my favorite meal before I start work. You're the best, babe."

The boys finally came downstairs when they heard bits of the parental conversation about golf and shopping. Teenage ears are tuned selectively for pleasure activities.

"I'm going with Dad," said Spencer.

"Yeah, me too, Mom," said Colby. "You know our sizes and we can try the stuff on when you bring it home."

"Sounds like a done deal to me," said Wyatt. "Let's go smack some golf balls, guys." He loved taking the boys to the golf course to teach them the gentlemen's sport, although he knew he wasn't much of a teacher.

"No dice. Won't happen. I need you to come with me so I can see the clothes on you, and then I won't have to take them back if they don't fit. You can play with your father some other time."

"Well, sorry about that, guys. Looks like we're not going to win this one. I'll take you out another time—maybe on a Saturday when I'm off."

The brisk wind partially neutralized the intense sunshine, keeping them reasonably comfortable, although it was brutal on Wyatt's already perfect slice into the woods, way out of bounds. He was, as expected, the worst player of the threesome, but the sunny afternoon on the course felt good because he didn't really fret about his score. They were on the ninth hole green, and it was just reaching 1:30 because of slow play all day in front of them. He knew he had to stop at nine holes because of his upcoming on-call duties in three hours.

"You guys can play on, but I need to stop here. Taught you guys enough today as it is."

"Whatever," said Tom. "You make us look good, Wyatt. Right, Ed?"

"That's not saying much. How about calling it a day, and stop at the clubhouse for lunch before Earp has to leave?"

"Sounds like a plan. But you forgot to add the beer to that sentence," said Tom, smiling ear to ear.

"Perfect. I could use a sandwich, but no beer for me," said Wyatt.

The trio ordered the basic clubhouse fare of sandwiches, chips, and pickles. Tom ordered three beers.

"Thanks, Tom, but you guys drink the beer. You know I don't drink when I'm going to be on call," said Wyatt.

"Yeah, we know," said Tom. "But you're not on call for another what, two hours from now? C'mon, you can have at least one beer, you wuss. It'll be out of your system way before your duties for the hospital start. Not only that; you probably won't be called in to the hospital until later, if at all, and you're so good at what you do you could probably do your procedures in your sleep. No worries."

Wyatt hesitated and looked at his watch at least three times in a period of a minute. The cold brews were more than tempting, and Tom convinced him that it was probably harmless this one time. "Okay, then, bring on the brew."

Wyatt arrived home about three thirty after the golf outing and one pint at lunch. Katherine called to say she and the boys would be late, but that he could go ahead and help himself to the beef roast, which he did. He then fell asleep on the couch with his beeper next to his head. Exactly at 4:30, sure enough, the beeper sounded off, awakening Wyatt from a nice slumber on the soft leather couch.

Damn. It's almost as if the ER is waiting, watching the clock until I'm on call so they can immediately hammer me hard.

"Hello, Dr. Barton. This is the answering service. We have Doctor Evans in the emergency department who would like to speak to you."

"Patch him through."

Wyatt was an avid cyclist and his resting pulse rate was a forty-five. But not now. He felt the rapid pounding and checked his pulse quickly. It catapulted up to one hundred while he waited for the emergency department doctor to be patched through.

C'mon Wyatt, you moron. You know better than to drink before on-call. But there's no problem. You've got all your faculties and that was over two hours ago and only one beer.

"Well whaddya know? The big dog's on call tonight; we're in luck. Hey. Wyatt, I'm glad you've got the duty for interventional tonight. We can count on you to always call back quickly and take care of business without throwing roadblocks at us."

"Yeah, Rick, I know you. You just want a cardiologist that you can punt to. What'ya got?"

"Got a seventy-five-year-old VIP lawyer here having a heart attack. He's unstable and he worries me. Gave him blood thinners, aspirin, and beta blockers to slow his heart rate. Got nitroglycerin in the field and some morphine here in the department. Still with some pain—about a two out of ten. Blood pressure hundred-fifteen over sixty with an irregular pulse. Apparently, he was on the golf course today when he had his attack. Oh, yeah, and you need to know that he apparently has more money than the state of Illinois and is the senior partner of a major international law firm downtown."

Wyatt's mind shifted into turbo mode. "You know me, Rick. I don't care if he digs ditches for a living; I treat all patients the same. I might make an exception for an Al Qaeda operative, though, because then I would have to give him the really special treatment, if you know what I mean."

"Ha ha. Clint Eastwood Barton. Make my day. What do you want me to do now?"

"Call a cardiac alert and I'll notify the catheterization team and see him in the cardiac lab. Does he have any family with him?"

"No, but he has his company doctor named Freeman and his company lawyer with him too, forgot his name. Lots of initials before his name. Freeman said they were all golfing together today at the country club and the old boy had too many Cubans and martinis in the clubhouse. Guess his son is a hotshot lawyer with the firm too, and he's on his way."

"I know a guy named Larry Freeman. He used to work in the ER years ago. Good doc. Looks like he found himself a nice cushy job. I'm on my way." Wyatt felt relief they were at a different course earlier. Probably couldn't afford the country club the Flanagan clan frequented anyway.

His confidence soared when he realized his words were clearly not slurred, and his mind was engaged completely. But he couldn't get that VIP lawyer statement out of his head. He threw on his shoes and socks, pounded down a glass of orange juice, brushed his teeth, gargled, and loaded up on breath mints. He knew he was perfectly fine, but he had never had a drink when he was on call before, and knew he shouldn't have listened to Tom.

Wyatt arrived in the interventional cardiac catheterization lab to find the patient, Sean Flanagan, on the procedure table, still conscious and talking. Cigar smoke permeated Sean's polo shirt and nearly filled the room with stench. Nurses and technicians scurried around organizing the equipment and gathering the sterile drapes and medications for the procedure. Multiple wide-screen video monitors surrounded the operating table, lights blinking and ready for action. He quickly reviewed the electrocardiogram tracing and labs, and then went to see the patient.

"Hello, Mr. Flanagan. My name is Wyatt Barton."They shook hands warmly. "I'll be performing an emergency cardiac catheterization on you because you're having what we call an 'acute anterior myocardial infarction' or 'heart attack,' and I need to open up the blockage in your coronary arteries to allow good blood flow again."

"Nice to meet you, Dr. Barton, and here's my older son, Gavin."

He smiled while he and Gavin shook hands, but Gavin showed no emotion. Wyatt felt a cold chill during the handshake, but decided the son must be nervous about his father's condition.

"Mr. Flanagan, I need you to sign the consent before we proceed, and we don't have the luxury of time. It's good that your son is here, because he may have to sign the consent for you because you've already received a significant amount of morphine and you won't understand the procedure and risks very well."

"I understand perfectly well, doc. What are the risks?"

"Severe heart arrhythmias, rupture of the coronary artery, shock from worsened coronary blood flow, emergency open-heart surgery, and death. I won't know what's wrong with your coronary artery anatomy until I actually look into your arteries using a catheter tube and X-ray dye. I may have to open up the culprit artery with a balloon and then place a stent in to keep it open. If I'm unsuccessful, you may need emergency open-heart surgery."

"No, I will not have open-heart surgery."

"Even if it's the only procedure available to save your life?"

"I don't want a heart butcher near me."

Gavin took command of matters with his ailing father for the first time in his life. "Dad, you're being unreasonable. Sign the consent and I'll cosign it. For God's sakes don't tie the doc's hands behind his back. Give him a chance to save you."

"Fine, Dr. Barton," said Sean. "Fix me with your damn magic stent, and if it becomes necessary, I'll have open-heart surgery. Sean's pain roared back and he clutched his chest with his fist while motioning with the other hand for Gavin to sign for him. After signing the consent, Gavin said good-bye to his father and went to the waiting room to join Dr. Freeman and E. David Carson, the firm's corporate counsel.

"Larry, do you know this Barton guy?" asked Gavin.

"Yeah, I remember him when I worked in the ER a few years ago, before I retired. He's a respected cardiologist and top-notch interventionalist. Sean's in excellent hands. They call him a cowboy though."

"Why? Does he wear boots and a cowboy hat? If so, I don't want him near Dad."

"No, it's because he has a reputation for taking the worst cases and diving in without fear and he ends up winning, unscathed. Kinda like a medical bull rider I guess."

"Cowboy or not, he damn well better be stellar or he won't know what hit him."

CHAPTER 4

Assisting Dr. Barton during the procedure were several catheterization lab technicians and Amy Adams, RN, an experienced emergency department nurse who had learned the specialized skills required in the catheterization lab. When Dr. Barton entered the room, respect flowed both ways. The procedure he was about to perform was one that he had accomplished successfully a thousand times before, and he knew that the cardiac catheterization lab staff felt confident in his technical skill. Yet, he never allowed himself to take that confidence for granted, never put his guard down.

After Amy injected the sedation medications, he applied local anesthesia and took control, easily inserting the introducer sheath into the right femoral artery, allowing him to advance the pigtail catheter up into the artery in Sean's heart.

Amy glanced quickly at him, and they made eye contact, their silent smiles hidden securely beneath their surgical masks. He was pleased that, as requested, smooth jazz played during the operation. The music calmed him and he was accomplished at not showing his feelings of stress to the people around him who looked up to him.

While deftly examining the coronary arteries displayed on the monitor across from him, he found the left anterior descending artery had a ninety percent blockage near the take-off from the aorta. The other arteries he examined showed smaller, less significant obstructions. He then tried to pre-open the artery with a balloon, but the lesion proved to be difficult. The complexity of the task ejected sweat onto his forehead and slowly moistened the scar on his eyebrow. Hoping that Amy and the other staff would not see this rare pronouncement of his stress, he reviewed in his mind quickly that all the steps had been done correctly. He then carefully placed a guide wire through the obstructed lesion and deployed the stent into the artery to keep it open.

Amy monitored Sean's vital signs and her voice grew louder. "Dr. Barton, he's having increasing ventricular arrhythmias, and his oxygen saturation is dropping!"

Wyatt's breathing accelerated, and his calm voice displayed a slight crackle. "Okay, thanks, Amy. He has bad lungs from smoking, probably emphysema. Increase his oxygen flow, please, and keep watching his rhythm, let me know if it worsens."

The circulating technician paced the room while humming nervously, loud enough for Wyatt to hear, but he didn't pay attention. Amy stayed by his side watching the monitors, and her warmth and familiar scent soothed him.

"Dr. Barton," Amy yelled suddenly, shattering the quiet, "we're losing his pressure!"

"Start him on a dopamine drip and bring me the heart ultrasound machine stat!" Wyatt immediately terminated the procedure. Sean, the VIP lawyer, was dying, and he had to work quickly. He tried to insert a tube into Sean's trachea to breathe for him, but due to the patient's obese neck, the breathing tube couldn't be placed on the first attempt. He had no time to call pulmonary medicine or anesthesia for help, but he knew his technicians had already pulled the emergency code resuscitation alarm so the emergency code team would run to assist them. He could hear the staff sigh with relief when he successfully placed the tube into the trachea on the second attempt, just as the emergency code team arrived.

He reviewed the cardiac ultrasound images that proved his worst fear: there was a large collection of blood in the membranous sac around the heart, causing the heart essentially to drown. His guide wire had most likely perforated the fragile left anterior descending artery and was leaking blood into the sac surrounding the heart—the pericardium.

"Get the cardiac surgeon on call here stat," commanded Dr. Barton. "In the meantime get me a pericardial needle so I can drain this blood under pressure from the pericardial sac." He prepped the bottom of Sean's sternum with sterile cleansing solution, and then, using the heart ultrasound machine to guide him, placed a needle directly into the sac around Sean's heart. He then advanced a guide wire through the needle over which he placed a pigtail catheter into position, confirmed by the ultrasound machine. Blood drained immediately out of the pigtail catheter, successfully deflating the sac of blood around the heart, allowing the heart to pump more effectively without the constriction of the blood-filled pericardial sac.

Dr. Ron Parker, the on-call cardiac surgeon, arrived breathless. "Wyatt, what's the problem?"

"Acute tamponade. Probably ruptured left anterior descending artery during an attempted stent. He's in shock despite a catheter in the pericardium. He needs you to crack his chest."

Dr. Parker responded almost before the words left Wyatt's mouth. "The OR and the surgical team are ready. Roll him down to the OR now!"

The cath lab team flew into action and raced Flanagan to the OR at the highest speed possible without crashing into walls and unsuspecting hospital workers. As soon as they arrived in the operating suite, Flanagan lost his pulse and suffered a ventricular fibrillation cardiac arrest. The team, under Dr. Barton's supervision, with Dr. Parker assisting, started immediate CPR, applying electrical shocks to terminate the lethal cardiac rhythm—first two hundred joules of energy, then three hundred. The rhythm changed to flat line, and a mixture of epinephrine and other heart-stimulating drugs proved unsuccessful in bringing Sean Flanagan back to life. They lost him before they could even transfer him to the operating-room table for Dr. Parker to begin the desperate operation.

Chicago's most successful and powerful law firm senior partner was now dead.

Wyatt looked at Amy and they connected again. Her once bright green eyes now seemed almost a reddish gray. He was a doctor who took every patient's death with significant introspection and wondered: Could he have done something differently, even though he knew the patient was lucky to have made it alive to the hospital? He reasoned that he couldn't have done anything differently except immediate open-heart surgery, which the patient had refused.

"You did everything you could, Wyatt," said Dr. Parker, answering Wyatt's silent question. "He had a nasty lesion in a ratty artery with bad lungs to boot. No way were we going to save this guy, no matter what we did. You want me to go talk to the family with you?"

"No thanks, Ron; that's okay. I'll do it myself. You have to go back to the operating room."

Amy hugged Wyatt before he walked to the waiting room to talk to the Flanagan gathering. Her silky perfume and warm smile boosted his strength. He hoped she didn't detect any residual alcohol on his breath when she was close, but he was sure that was long gone, and it was only one pint five hours ago now.

At the family waiting room door Wyatt hesitated, drew a deep breath, threw some more mints in his mouth for safety, and walked in. The three men followed him with their eyes closely, and to Wyatt, the walk down the hall to the far end of the waiting room seemed like a marathon, the last twenty feet being the longest of the journey. He knew he had to be direct, rubbed his throbbing scar as was his habit, then went to Gavin and looked him directly in the eyes. "I'm sorry to say this, but we have lost your father."

There was a grave silence, and then anguish engulfed the previously quiet waiting room. "No, it can't be!" Gavin shouted. "It was just a simple cardiac catheterization. How could he die? He was brought to this hospital alive. Why didn't you save him? We were confident in you, and look what you've done!"

"I'm sorry. I can't tell you how sorry I am, Gavin."

E. David Carson put his hand on Gavin's shoulder to give him support.

After a few minutes, Gavin calmed down enough to participate in a discussion. "What happened, Dr. Barton?"

"He had a massive heart attack before he arrived to the hospital, and we tried to open his occluded left anterior descending artery under emergency conditions and place a stent in the artery to save his life. Unfortunately, his heart failed during the procedure, and he went into cardiac arrest and we couldn't resuscitate him. We did all that we possibly could."

"Yes, I'm sure you did, Dr. Barton," said Gavin, almost too quietly.

Wyatt knew it was useless to say any more, and he left the waiting room to continue rounds. He bristled when rich families showed demanding and unreasonable attitudes. It was an entitlement society to some. He would have rather spent all night working for free trying to save a poor person who had a family that appreciated his efforts. But then, each person received the same treatment from Wyatt. He made sure of that.

"Is there anything I can do?" E. David Carson asked, putting his hand on Gavin's shoulder again to comfort him.

"Hell, yes, there is. A couple things. One, did you notice the mints in Barton's mouth? It's almost as if he was hiding something on his breath. Seemed inappropriate. It reminded me of some of my college fraternity friends hiding their alcohol breath when their parents visited the frat house. Just seemed a little inappropriate, don't you think?"

"I did notice the mints, but I didn't smell alcohol, if that's what you mean. Nothing seemed out of the ordinary to me," said Carson. "Understandably, you're too emotional now to make rational observations."

"You're right, I've lost my mind, but either way I would like you to notify our firm's best plaintiff's malpractice attorney that he has himself a case to investigate, and that case is his boss, now deceased, killed by a damn quack cardiologist!"

CHAPTER 5

"Wyatt, it's seven pm. Where have you been? The kids are starving and I needed to delay supper for you." Katherine's hands gripped her hips so firmly that her fingertips blanched and her eyes glared at him. The boys were sitting at the glass kitchen table eating, and as usual, the house was glistening clean. She stood between Wyatt and the kitchen table, not allowing him to join them until she was satisfied with his response to her interrogation.

"Where do you think I've been? Playing golf under the lights? Some VIP lawyer died in the cath lab today. It was a hell of a challenging day."

She smiled playfully. "I see. I'm sure there was probably a pretty nurse involved too, right?"

He figured it was safe to play along. "Yes you're right. There was a pretty nurse involved and I must be honest. We had nasty sex on the catheterization lab table while everyone watched, and then they clapped afterwards. It was unbelievable!"

Wyatt figured he was far enough away from the boys to be out of listening range, but when he saw the boys' eyes, clearly he'd made a mistake. He couldn't protect them from everything in life, but he never used foul language in front of them.

She glared at him, then walked over to talk to the boys. "He's kidding, guys; right, Wyatt?"

"Of course I was! C'mon, lighten up and smile a little." He motioned to her to come and talk to him privately. "Now that was a nice romantic prelude to what I was going to say, but here it is anyway: I have tickets for us to go on a cruise to the Mexican Riviera. Kids are getting older and I thought it would be nice for us to get away for a while and have some fun together, just you and I. We've got young teenagers now and it's time you left them for a while."

"Wyatt, I told you before; I hate leaving the kids. They need me, I mean us. We've never taken a vacation together because they were too young."

"That's my point. You always say no. I've already called my parents and they've agreed to come and stay with the boys for a while during the trip. What's your answer, honey?"

She looked at the kids first, then back at Wyatt. "Okay. Why not?"

The "Ocean Goddess" boarded at the Port of Los Angeles, and the next two full days would be at sea until the first scheduled port of call, Puerto Vallarta. Katherine remained hard to convince to travel without the kids, but he loved to travel and immerse himself in local culture and history. In his book, Europe loomed higher on his list of fun destinations than the Mexican Riviera, but the cruise was certainly an easier sell to her.

In the cabin, Katherine told Wyatt to go somewhere so she could fix up the place, unpack, and make her little nest. He gladly obliged, and found himself at the bar downing several beers and a plate of nachos. But there was one cocktail waitress who caught his eye; long legs that went on and on and the way she bent over to serve drinks made him hope she would serve him personally in the near future, and heck, they had four days on the ship. Katherine found him at the bar and they went to a more comfortable place to relax.

Warm Pacific breezes and calm waves greeted the couple while they lounged on their deck chairs in the bright sun. "It's amazing how the ancient Mayan Indians were able to construct such an accurate calendar using mathematics and knowledge of astronomy, don't you think?" Wyatt asked, hoping to engage Katherine in a conversation unrelated to the kids.

"I don't know who the Mayans are, Wyatt. Do they live on a reservation in Arizona?"

Wyatt paused, and then forced a smile and a respectful response. "No, they were an advanced ancient civilization that lived on the Yucatan Peninsula in Mexico."

"There you go again, trying to make me look like I don't have a brain. Just because I didn't go to medical school like you doesn't mean I don't have street smarts. And no, I just tried to study a little high school Spanish, and didn't master Arabic and Pasha or whatever it's called."

"Actually it's Pashto. Spoken by the Pashtun people in Afghanistan and some parts of Pakistan. C'mon, I was just trying to make conversation. Don't be so sensitive."

There was lifeless silence in the baking sun, and Wyatt gazed pensively over the undulating ocean waves. *It seems like forever since I've enjoyed some stimulating conversation with an adult.*

That young cocktail server sauntered gracefully to their table. She wore a short yellow sundress and black halter-top that barely had enough material to hold her "Tropical Cruise Lines" host badge. She looked briefly at Katherine and smiled politely, then concentrated her efforts on Wyatt. His blues met her browns and his heart fluttered when he recognized those long legs, and he briefly devoured the view of the server's full red lips and soft dark skin. She purposely bent way down to Wyatt to show him her well-filled halter-top and asked, "What may I get you two to drink today?"

Katherine stared intensely at him and he pulled his eyes painfully away from the feminine paradise and said, "Honey, what would you like?"

She hesitated, looked at Wyatt, and said, "I don't know, maybe a Tom Collins."

The sultry server interjected, "Ma'am, may I suggest the Tropical Cruise Paradise? It's a fruity, rum-based drink that women like."

"Okay, sounds good," said Katherine.

He couldn't help but take a video of the woman's legs with his eyes while Katherine ordered.

She smiled at Katherine respectfully, then broadened her smile and bent over gracefully to obtain Wyatt's order. His busy life studying had kept him generally naïve about women, but apparently, he finally figured out that his blue eyes and wide smile attracted women.

"I'll have a Sam Adams lager."

"Sorry, sir. We don't have Sam Adams, but we have lots of Corona and tons of limes."

"Sounds perfect." Wyatt loved talking to people from different cultures, engaging them to learn about geography and travel. Problem was, this girl was stunning and by definition, ridiculously dangerous.

"By the way, where are you from?" He was hypnotized with her and tried to keep from drooling when he talked.

Katherine stared at him. He didn't notice the quiver in her twine-tight lips until it was too late.

"Columbia. I'm working on this ship to earn some money for my second year in architectural design school at the Pratt Institute in New York."

He hoped Katherine would engage in the conversation for the both of them. When it was clear she wasn't going to, he continued, "Interesting. Your English is excellent, by the way."

"Thanks. In school I loved to study it. Always wanted to travel to the United States or England, and I am lucky that I can study in New York in the fall."

"Good luck." After she brought them their drinks, Wyatt paid the server with a good tip and she left to serve some other guests. Wyatt sensed the danger and maybe he'd had too many drinks, but he had to watch her walk away, shaking all her stuff with such a tasty rhythm.

"Your tongue was hanging out of your mouth and you were panting like a dog in heat when that server was here. I'm surprised you didn't slip her your phone number too!"

"Lighten up, honey. I don't see what's wrong in having a little innocent conversation to keep the atmosphere around here alive enough to have a palpable pulse. Thought it was interesting she was in architectural school. Do you want me to stare at the table and be mute when people talk to me?"

"You're full of shit, Wyatt."

"Right, and that's why you love me."

After dinner and maybe five words exchanged between them, the couple walked around the ship and he noticed there was a band playing a variety of island music on one of the decks. "Would you like to have a few drinks and enjoy the music, maybe some dancing?" asked Wyatt.

"No, thanks. I'd rather go to the casino. Maybe later."

"Sure honey, I'll go with you to give you some good luck on the machines by massaging your back while you play."

In the casino, Katherine lost all but ten dollars of the one hundred she dribbled into the quarter slots.

"Well, Katherine, maybe it's time you walked away from this money drain. Let's go dancing and enjoy the night."

"No. I'm going to bed. It's ten o'clock here, but midnight back home, so I'm beat."

In their cabin they kissed quickly and she turned on her side away from him. He caressed her smooth behind and yearned for more. She was asleep too easily. His eyes remained wide open because his mind wanted to move to the rhythm of the music he was still hearing and explore life, but he was the only one in the room who could feel the rhythm.

The next morning they arrived in Puerto Vallarta.

Katherine arranged for them to ride the tour bus to the city and later La Playa, and Wyatt found the inspiration to try his broken Spanish on the bus drivers, who courteously smiled and played along. When they arrived at the beach, she waited for him to go get some drinks and snacks and then called the kids.

"Hello, Spencer. Are you kids doing okay?" asked Katherine.

"Hey Mom. How 'bout you and Dad? Havin' fun in the sun?"

"Sure, we're doing great. Are you enjoying your Grandma and Grandpa?"

"Totally. We're having a great time and wish you would've let us do this before. It's cool."

"Really? Well you know, your dad actually didn't want to go on this vacation and I had to drag him kicking and screaming here. I think he would rather be working. Spencer, honey, why don't you get Colby on the phone so I can talk to him."

"Yeah. But where's Dad? One of those Krav Maga moves he taught me I think I've mastered. It's the single leg sweep. I wanted to tell him thanks for teaching me. It's cool that my friends want to learn from him too, but I told them he only instructs police and army guys when he has time. He's a cool dad."

"Honey, he's busy now. I can't find him. Congratulations on that stuff you mentioned though."

"Yeah. Mom, that's strange that you can't find him. Will you tell him?"

"Sure honey, you know I will. Now get Colby on the phone."

"Hey, Mom. You guys surfing the waves? Cowabunga!"

"Hi Colby. No not yet, but I think I'll just lie on the beach while your father goes snorkeling or something."

"Sick! Hey, tell Dad I threw some curve balls today when the coach let me pitch at the game. Struck out four players! Can I talk to Dad?"

"Oh, he'd love to talk to you I'm sure, but he's busy right now. I think he's trying to talk to one of the servers at the bar in Spanish to impress her, I don't know. We'll call again."

"Okay, you and Dad have fun, and make sure you tell him about my curve balls."

"Of course. I love you, Colby. I miss you boys."

Wyatt arrived at the beach chairs carrying food and drinks in time to see Katherine put her phone back into the beach bag.

"So, you called the kids? How are they?"

"They're doing great, having a good time with your parents."

"See, I told you they would. I'd like to call them." He reached into Katherine's bag to pick up the phone.

"Wyatt, the kids said they're busy now, so they may not answer."

"I'll call them later maybe when they're home. Did they have anything else to say? How was Colby's baseball game?"

"Oh they were running out the door when I called." She stared at the food he brought, smiled, and said, "Those enchiladas smell fantastic. I'm famished!"

On the last day of the cruise, they went to the late-night show after dinner. After a comedian and a decent magician, the dancing girls came on stage to provide the grand finale. Obviously, they were hired for their long legs and smiling faces, wearing glittery outfits accented by their fishnet hose. Wyatt and Katherine sat in the back of the large auditorium, much to his chagrin, but his two martinis put him in a playful mood. He would've much preferred a closer seating to enjoy the dancers a little more, but as it was, he was able to concentrate completely on their dancing and the bodies that couldn't be hidden by the skimpy outfits.

When the show was over, she left immediately, giving Wyatt the silent treatment.

"What's wrong?"

"You know what's wrong."

"No, I don't. I bet I said something wrong at dinner. Something about the joke I told about the dead gynecologist at the dinner table. Right?"

"You want to be with that blonde, don't you?"

"What blonde?"

"Don't play dumb. The blonde you kept staring at during the show. I saw your eyes light up when you watched her display herself. You really want her, don't you?"

"I don't know what blonde you're referring to or how you were able to imagine my field of vision from the back of the auditorium, but I think you're imagining things, Katherine. I took you on this cruise to have fun with you alone, and try to inject some life into our marriage, but you won't let it happen, will you?"

She put on her best pout and his words hit their mark. "I guess you're right, Wyatt. I'm sorry and I love you. I know I've been a little hard on you, but I'd like to make it up to you if you know what I mean."

She effectively softened his mood, hugged him, and gave him a surprisingly passionate kiss, causing him to pick her up and throw her on the bed in their cabin.

Wyatt immersed himself in an uncontrollable testosterone surge that he unleashed on Katherine, and they had their first and only intimacy during the entire cruise. But his surge was also fueled by the image of fishnet stockings and perfect dancing legs, while he elevated her to sexual paradise multiple times.

Perfect ending to a tropical cruise vacation. Life is good.

CHAPTER 6

Blake Flanagan enjoyed some rare Christmas leave from Marine sniper scout school, where he was an instructor. It was the first time that he had been back to Chicago since his father's funeral six months earlier. Like his brother Gavin, Blake was moving on with his life. Gavin and his latest lover, a French brunette, invited Blake to Gavin's twelve thousand square foot mansion for a Christmas dinner and get-together.

The heavily muscled Marine walked into the entry, quickly scanning the expansive family room: the huge Christmas tree, a crackling fire, and, especially, the beautiful brunette sitting elegantly on a lucky couch.

"Congratulations, little bro; you rock!"

"What the hell you mean, you lawyer puke?"

"As always, you still have a way with words. I heard you won the Marine middleweight boxing championship, and I wanted to congratulate you. At least that allows you to release your violence in a sanctioned way, rather than on the streets or at a bar here at home when you're not deployed to some secret location."

Blake wasn't sure whether this was a compliment, but he responded to Gavin in his usual style. "Thanks, I think, but now that you're the official CEO of Dad's firm, you think your shit is hotter than ever. Remember, though, I can kick your ass with one hand tied behind my back and one leg in a cast any time I want to. Not too bad for a guy who wasn't smart enough to go to 'Pussyversity' like you did. By the way, I had no problem getting some despite not going to 'Pussyversity.'"

Blake smirked while he watched his brother smile nervously at his new lover, Delphine, who was giggling at Blake's statement and trying to hide her pleasure with her dainty hand. He also noticed that she didn't attempt to hide her slender legs that were barely covered by her tiny skirt, and so he stared at her legs while they talked.

"Funny, Blake. You have about as much class as I do patience, and yeah, I guess that is one of the advantages of higher education. Too bad you don't realize that brains are more important than muscles in this world, unless you're a caveman I guess."

"Whatever. By the way, Gavin, are you going to introduce me to this beautiful lady or are you going to keep yapping your mouth? If she were my girl, I would've introduced her first thing. I'd be proud as hell."

"Oh yeah, sorry. Blake, this is Delphine."

She stretched out her hand adorned by fake fingernails to Blake and smiled, but instead of shaking it, he kissed it. She blushed in pleasant surprise.

"I met her in Bordeaux when I was providing legal advice to the St. Emilion wine consortium a few months ago. She's a model who works in both Paris and New York, and, well, we hit it off pretty well. So I invited her here to visit me in the windy city for a while before she has to go back to New York for a photo shoot. I wish she could stay longer. C'est vrai?"

"Oui, et ton frère est très intéressant et très beau!"

"Chicago will never be the same with her here, that's for sure," said Blake. "I don't know what she said but I damn sure loved the way it sounded."

"She said that you seem like a nice boy but a little rough around the edges."

Delphine glared at Gavin because of the fabricated translation.

"Tell me, Delphine, I know you must speak English fairly well."

"Oui. I mean yes, of course."

"Is that really what you said to me, the way Gavin interpreted it? He is my brother, but I don't trust him when it comes to women."

Delphine looked for guidance from Gavin, who smiled nervously. "Well, I think Gavin doesn't understand French as much as he thinks he does. I don't know what 'rough' means, but basically I meant to say that you are an interesting and handsome man."

"Thanks, and you can bet I'll need some time with you later to learn some more special French words in private," said Blake.

"Let's go to the living room and have some drinks before the chef brings us dinner," Gavin said, intervening quickly.

"Sounds good to me," said Blake. He watched Delphine saunter gracefully and he soaked her in while Gavin resumed the conversation on the couch.

"So tell us about your exploits in the Marines, Blake. We haven't heard much from you over the years."

"That sounds damn boring. I'd much rather talk about Delphine."

"No, please, Monsieur Blake, please tell me, I mean us, of your valor."

"Ah well, if you insist. Unlike your lover who went to Harvard Law School and travels to the Caribbean every year to play with the girls on the beach, I served my country. It started in Marine basic training, of course. I shot expert on the rifle range early on, and that's why they noticed me. After I scored maximum on the first-class PFT, the corps began to separate me out for certain specialty training."

"PFT. What is that?" asked Gavin.

"Physical Fitness Test. A maximum score includes a three-mile run in under eighteen minutes, twenty dead-hang pull-ups, one hundred sit-ups in fewer than two minutes, and finally a fifty-meter swim holding a weight out of the water and then treading water for thirty seconds while holding the weight."

"Impressive," said Gavin.

Gavin opened a bottle of Chateau Meraux for both Delphine and himself, but Blake was happy with his bottle of Corona and lime. He was even more pleased that he was sitting across from Delphine on the opposite couch, taking in the spectacular view she presented. He alternated quick glances at her legs and thin ankles, then her full lips while she swirled the wine deftly inside her delicate mouth. He could feel her staring back at his bulging biceps outlined by large veins. Blake had seen that gaze before, and he understood that it usually meant that she admired his hard physique and secretly wanted him to ravish her aggressively. At least that's what he hoped she was thinking. Gavin had shared with him on the phone previously that although he had known her only a few weeks, she seemed to constantly want sex with him, any time, any place. Blake figured that Delphine would only satisfy Gavin's needs briefly, then as usual, he would dump her and look for new conquests, allowing his brother to move in for the kill.

No, Blake thought, this hottie may have enjoyed Gavin's movie-star looks, but it was his wealth and future financial security as CEO of the firm that most likely attracted her to his gene pool. He reasoned that what she desired to taste for the moment was completely different from what she wanted for a lifetime. He knew she wanted him for the moment more than she wanted his brother, and he would make sure they ended up in bed.

"I knew that I had aptitude, so I volunteered for Force Recon and became Recon qualified, then went to sniper school." Blake continued the best he could despite the gorgeous distraction sitting across from him. "After sniper school I deployed for several tours in Iraq and Afghanistan, and a few other places that I can't talk about."

"You know, Blake, Dad told me he was proud of you, and so am I. We just wished that you would've communicated with us more than once a year when you deployed. We were worried about you, and Dad started smoking and drinking more because of that."

"Bullshit. I do what I'm trained to do. I do my job to perfection with no emotion and without need for attention. There's a shitload of bad people out there who want to kill Americans everywhere, but I'm one of the guys who has the skills to stop them. I don't need you to worry about that stuff. You need men like me to fight for you so you can eat caviar and drink champagne at the damn country club."

Gavin shifted on the couch and tapped his feet on the ground. "You know I appreciate your service, Blake. But listen, when you get out of the Marines, you can always get a job at the firm working with me. Dad, as you know, left me in control. But I understand that with your share of the inheritance you won't really need to work."

Delphine eagerly chimed in. "You are an American hero."

"Thanks, I appreciate that, sweetie. Yeah, the inheritance is great, but I'm a career Marine. Can't think of another career that would suit me right now, and I'm not the kind of guy to sit on his ass and drink froufrou drinks all day."

"Well, Blake, on another subject, you'll be happy to know that our firm's best malpractice attorney is filing a malpractice suit against this Dr. Barton."

"Good. Is he the best you could find?"

"Best at the firm, and probably in the state, with a high success rate in the cases he selects."

"He's not a wuss who will back down when things go bad, is he? I want this doc taken down for killing Dad."

"As I said, he's experienced and never quits when he sees blood or money. In this case, there are lots of both. Our firm will pay him well for his efforts. And I don't want to comment about your last statement. We're both angry at this quack, but we need to be smart."

"How long will the legal proceedings take?"

"Well that depends on what the defense throws up against us during the discovery and deposition phase. But first, our team will investigate to see if we have a legitimate case against him, and if not, at least we will dig up some dirt on him. I'd say it would take at least a year to get to a jury trial. Nothing we can do now anyway, our legal team is on it. Having said that, you need to know I'm going to France and Germany for business next week, but I'll stay in touch about the legal proceedings against Barton."

Satisfied, Blake got up to leave. "I'll see you when I see you, bro. Merry Christmas to you both. And Delphine, it was pure pleasure to meet you."

"Enchanté, Monsieur Blake." She smiled so warmly Blake was immediately aroused.

Gavin and Blake shook hands, and then Blake hugged Delphine and inhaled her French perfume deeply into the bottom of his lungs. He pulled her close to his body and he loved that she didn't pull away. She seemed to stick to him. Although he didn't see her look back when he walked down the lighted sidewalk to his car, he could feel Delphine studying the back of his tight jeans, even with Gavin standing next to her. His training gave him a sixth sense.

Gavin pulled her away from the doorway and they walked into the house hand in hand towards the bedroom upstairs. "Sweetie, what do you think of my little brother?"

She smiled. "Well, he's definitely not little and he is certainly an interesting man."

CHAPTER 7

Both teens grew quickly during the next year. Colby landed the lead in the school production of *A Midsummer Night's Dream*. At fourteen, he was the youngest in school history to have the lead in the fall play. His stage presence was unusual for his age. The classic Shakespearean comedy was quite a production for the school and drew a decent crowd of parents and some from the community as well. Like his older brother, Colby was an excellent student and athlete, but seemed to excel in the liberal arts rather than his brother who preferred math and science. Wyatt, Katherine, and Spencer arrived at the school auditorium and took their seats for the Saturday afternoon performance. Wyatt made sure his call schedule was clear so he could attend. As usual, he put himself in charge of photography and family videos. He insisted on capturing the memories that his children would enjoy looking back on when they grew up. His parents had done that for him, and he wanted to do the same for his kids.

They sat about ten rows back of the stage with Spencer in the middle aisle seat, Katherine next to him, then Wyatt. Next to him was the mother of one of Colby's hockey friends. She whispered to him that the lady was divorced, but he just shrugged his shoulders in a non-caring way. She had an athletic body but her teeth were crooked and her face displayed premature wrinkling, possibly from smoking. He smiled at her and politely asked about her son, but that was the extent of the conversation.

When the play began, the man in front of Wyatt blocked his view of Colby, so he moved his chair an inch away from Katherine, towards the divorced mother, to take photos of Colby unobstructed. For the remainder of the play, Katherine continued to glance at Wyatt coldly.

He smiled at her at prideful moments during Colby's performance, but her smile remained fixed at Colby, not Wyatt.

After the play, they congratulated Colby, and Wyatt took pictures of him with other cast members.

"How 'bout I take the boys to Dave and Buster's for some fun while you go shopping or have some time for yourself?"

"Great idea. I'm in the mood for shopping, and I hate video arcades anyway."

Wyatt and the boys always ate up Dave and Busters. Since father and sons were golfers, they thought it was especially cool to play the simulated Pebble Beach course with real clubs to measure their swing and distance. But the real competition between the three was to see who could win the most tickets at the video arcades and basketball shootouts. And as usual, the winners were: Spencer in basketball accuracy, Colby in video arcades, and Wyatt in golf simulation. His kids were teenagers, but they still enjoyed activities with their father, at least for a while.

Later that evening they all met at their favorite pizza restaurant. Katherine laughed and smiled with the boys, obviously refreshed from some therapeutic shopping, and the boys stuffed themselves with pizza while ogling at the girls at the table across from them. Wyatt gave Spencer the thumbs-up when he saw that he and a cute cheerleader were making eyes at each other. Spencer's face turned crimson and he stopped gazing at her after that.

"So, you think Jenny is hot, huh?" asked Katherine, wanting attention.

"What are you talking about, Katherine?"

"You know—Colby's friend's mom you sat next to. You were almost trying to sit in her lap."

"Oh really? I hadn't thought of that, but it sounds like a good idea. It would've given me a nicer vantage point to watch Colby and certainly would've added some excitement."

The boys, adorned by ear buds, looked up briefly from iPod reverie, then continued on, ignoring their parents.

"You're nuts, Katherine." Wyatt glared at her, hoping to convince her to stop this adult talk in front of the boys. They didn't need that in their lives. He wanted them to experience life to the fullest with parental support and nurturing, but without parental drama.

She stopped the attack.

He continued. "But even if you are nuts, you're ten times hotter than Jenny and you also have all your teeth, and that's a plus." Wyatt smiled at her and lifted his scarred eyebrow, causing her to melt like a Snickers bar in the desert.

At home, Wyatt told the kids good night and they went upstairs. Katherine followed them upstairs about ten minutes later to "debrief" them. He stayed downstairs trying to catch up on some medical journal reading and to have a drink. Hell, he thought, he deserved several. So he proceeded to enjoy the company of his friends Jack Daniels and Johnny Walker.

Katherine asked Colby to join her in Spencer's room. "Colby, we're proud of you and your performance tonight. And Spencer, thanks for being a good sport."

"Yeah Mom, plays aren't my thing."

"That's because you probably couldn't remember your lines anyway," said Colby.

"C'mon boys, that's enough. I think it was real special that Dad came tonight to the play and spent time with you kids."

"What does that mean, Mom?" asked Spencer. "Dad always spends time with us."

"Yeah," said Colby.

"Well you know I love you kids very much and I've spent twenty-four/seven with you since you were babies. I'm happy Dad was able to come tonight, you know, he isn't around much as he should be because the hospital patients seem to come first. Anyway, seems you kids had a good time."

Colby answered quickly. "Don't know about that but it's cool when he's here."

"Whatever, Mom, no worries," said Spencer. "He's a good dad."

"You're right. He's a good dad and he does his best for us. Guys, you need to get some sleep. Good night."

After two drinks Wyatt left his desk, went to the couch by the fireplace and thought of the sultry cruise-ship server from Columbia, her long brown legs, full lips, and charming smile. Choosing a woman of his preference was a right he had relinquished years before. He felt the marriage was almost going through the motions now, and he couldn't remember the last time they had sex. He hoped he could provide the best he could for his sons and give them as happy a home as he could fake. He would never let them see him drink alone, though.

Downstairs, Katherine found Wyatt in the den reading his journals and enjoying his bourbon.

"I see you're drinking again, Wyatt. You need to slow it down. That's not a good example for the boys, and it's going to get you in trouble. You know I care about you."

"Yeah, you're right. There's a lot I need to do, in fact, but this helps ease the pain a little."

"What pain?"

"Whatever. What've you been doing?"

"Oh I was doing some laundry and making a grocery list out. Why do you ask?"

"Nothing. Just wondering. Seemed awful quiet upstairs."

"I'm going to bed, Wyatt."

He looked at Katherine; her red hair and pouty lips reminded him of the times she was warm and loving, rather than insecure and jealous. He yearned for that warmth again, and his hormones took over his brain.

"Instead of going upstairs to bed, how 'bout you join me here on the couch. I'm cold and your warm body on top of me is exactly what I need right now."

He pulled her down on top of him, kissing her while his hands explored her eager body, loosening her belt while crazily searching for the feminine treasure his manhood needed so badly. He took her and she gave herself to him, and her loud screaming forced him to place his hand over her quivering mouth so the kids wouldn't think there was a violent intruder in the den.

When they were finished Katherine quickly put her skirt back on, smiled at Wyatt, then went upstairs. He stayed motionless on the couch in his boxers, smiled back, and blew her a kiss before following her a few minutes later.

Maybe things aren't so bad after all.

CHAPTER 8

Gavin Flanagan usually stayed at the Amarante Beau Manoir Hotel when he was in Paris to do business, but he was equally happy on this trip to Bordeaux to stay at the exclusive Bordeaux Regent Hotel. Its luxury and proximity to the beautiful French women who shopped the high-end stores downtown was an added bonus. Only problem was the elevators were a bit too small. He thought the French women were slightly more difficult to seduce than other European women, but he loved their accents and his charm with his broken French was enough to get them to bed and keep him from being alone at night. His firm had been hired to represent the Bordeaux Vineyards of Medoc and St. Emilion in their efforts to reduce or eliminate the high tariffs imposed on their wines by the United States, which gave them trouble competing with California wines. But what he looked forward to the most was going to St. Emilion, 15 Rue Port Bouqueyre, where he would find his friends at Bordeaux Classique, Marchand de Vins. The owners of the shop allowed him to taste the best wines in Bordeaux, providing their expertise, and this often resulted in his shipping some wine home to enjoy and impress his women.

After he left his meetings in the Bordeaux area, he flew to Frankfurt to meet with Mercedes Benz on American product liability protection issues. That wasn't much of a problem because the German-made cars required very little maintenance and rarely had mechanical failures that caused injury or death. Walking through Frankfurt Airport to fly back to Chicago, he was wearing a casual outfit that was popular in Europe: jeans, white dress shirt with one button open, a camel-colored sports jacket, and casual loafers. He enjoyed the smiles he received from women when he walked. He smiled back, and made sure his walk was purposeful but not hurried, for their viewing pleasure. He was thinking about Delphine. When would he see and touch her again? But the scent of the Narcisse Noir perfume worn by the Bordeaux goddess he had been with the night before lingered on his clothes and allowed him to soothe his mind temporarily away from Delphine. He had French women on his mind wherever he went.

"Now boarding passengers in first class and those requiring special assistance."

Gavin was pleased, as usual, to board early because he was always flying first class. He smiled and swaggered confidently past the long line of coach passengers looking at their boarding passes to see when their section would be called. He would soon be sitting in a comfortable seat reading *The Wall Street Journal* while others struggled to find their seats and stow their bags. He didn't care about them. As he passed adjacent to the line of coach passengers, he immediately caught sight of a stunning blond, statuesque and confident, smiling and laughing with the others waiting to board. The smell of her perfume was just enough for him to imagine a soft summer breeze on the beach. Her silken hair cascaded over her shoulders, and her blue eyes glittered when she laughed. She was definitely a bouncy blonde, yet elegant and refined. He slowed his walk down to more of a prowl so that he could delay his entry into the plane and devour her image a little more, and perhaps prove lucky enough to have her eyes meet his. Luckily for him, she dropped her boarding pass, and he lunged forward, picking it up from the floor and quickly handing it to her. "Here you go. You may need this." Their eyes met.

"Oh, thank you, sir! You are so kind."

"No problem, have a good flight and I hope to talk to you more before we land in Chicago."

Her genuine smile and warmth made him thank God that she

dropped her ticket near him. His heart pounded and his face remained flushed when he took his seat in first class. He knew he had to become closer to her and to strike up a real conversation that would charm her enough to get her to hand over her phone number. His many previous conquests of beautiful women had taught him that a few seemingly innocent words and a spontaneous act of kindness or generosity would effectively put him in position for the kill. Fortunately, his sharp brown eyes found her seat number after he looked at her dropped boarding pass: section 1, seat 1b. Problem was, he was in first class and she was in the front of the coach section, and he needed a quick plan to get a seat next to her.

"Now boarding section four, please. All passengers with section four on their boarding passes may board now."

He spied an elderly woman with her cane dropped in front of her seat, sitting in the coach section, seat 1a directly behind first class. She had been seated early because of her age. While the other passengers boarded the back of the plane, he jumped out of his seat and approached the elderly woman.

"Excuse me, ma'am, but I wanted to ask if you would like to sit in first class."

"Why of course, young man, but I didn't buy a ticket for first class. Too expensive."

"Yes, of course, but I would like you to take my seat so you can be more comfortable. I need a change, since I fly first class all the time, and the people up there are too stuffy sometimes."

"Well, I couldn't, I..."

"Yes you can. Here's my ticket stub and I'll help you to my seat and inform the flight attendant of our switch."

She reluctantly agreed, and Gavin helped her navigate without incident through the aisle that was filling with boarding passengers and escorted her to his first-class seat. She smiled and thanked him as she settled in, and a cute flight attendant took a practiced notice.

"What a generous man you are!"

"Ah, not really, but thanks, hon." He gave her a wide grin, flashing his bright teeth.

The attendant walked closer to him so their conversation would be more private. "My name is Amanda. If you need anything at all, anything, you let me know."

"Thanks, Amanda, I'm Gavin."

He studied her straight teeth and bright smile, and noted that she'd had some surgery up front, but that never really mattered to him as long as it looked good. She then deftly slipped her card into his side coat pocket, and they smiled at each other while he quickly ran to seat 1a in coach. He had a box full of cards from businesswomen and flight attendants at home in Chicago, but hadn't had the time to call most of them. Some day he would transfer all the numbers from the hottest ones to his cell phone. The present plan came to fruition so quickly that he felt his heart fluttering, and he measured his pulse rate at one hundred, fully forty beats above his resting heart rate. He was a distance runner and frequently checked his pulse during runs, and this frenetic fifteen minutes of seat-changing felt similar to a mile race on the track. He was ecstatic thinking about the eventual arrival of the blonde who dropped her ticket, and pleased that his skills pertaining to the hunt of feminine beauty were as sharp as ever. It reminded him of some techniques he'd used in the past to meet attractive flight attendants and then sleep with them if their final stop was the same. You had to act fast and efficiently in these situations, or you lost out. Hopefully, his luck would continue.

He detected her perfume first, and his nervous system geared up immediately because of her imminent arrival, and just like that, she was standing next to him.

"Oh, hi again, sir, but I think you are in the wrong seat."

"Really? I'm sorry. I'll move for you; no problem."

He could see that the flaxen-haired beauty wanted the aisle seat.

Maybe window seats made her nervous. The window seat was 1b, and he moved graciously for her, allowing her to think she had the correct seat assignment. He couldn't help but be amused by this, even though he was originally in the correct seat occupied by the old woman. He didn't care what seat she had, as long as he was lucky enough to sit next to her on this long international flight. He was accustomed to accomplishing whatever he wanted in life, influencing people with his charm and intelligence, and he was certainly feeling confident about his chances with her now. Yet he decided to push the issue to keep the conversation going.

"Would you please just recheck your boarding pass? Perhaps you just misread it."

She held her head up high and stated her case firmly. "I would like you to take a pawsa and find your stub, sir. Maybe it is you that have misread yours."

"Excuse me. What is a 'pawsa'?" Her European accent fascinated him.

"You know, like to stop and think. Am I not correct? Sorry I am not so good to speaking English." She looked into her generous purse, found that she had her stub and that on second glance it did say 1a.

"Oi, I am very embarrassed, sir! I am wrong. You will take my aisle seat please."

She stood up, and this allowed him to enjoy a closer examination of her tight leggings that provided a smooth road map up the hemline to her black sweater dress, accented by the snug belt that divided her body in a heavenly way. The tight sweater was easy to notice too. After he'd completely absorbed the image, he answered. "No of course not. Sit down and stay where you are."

"That is wonderful. You are nice man."

"So what is your name?"

"Marta. And yours?"

"Gavin." He quickly realized that he wasn't as eloquent as he usually was with women. Her presence and the way she held herself seemed to suck the air right out of his lungs.

He wanted to guess her nationality, but couldn't quite place it from her charming accent, so he stalled and didn't ask. He knew she was probably asked that question hundreds of times per week, and he forced himself to show her he was different.

They shared a few more pleasantries, exchanged business cards as a formality, and the conversation faded. He read that she was a PhD and a professor at Northwestern University.

Gavin was stunned at his circumstances and soon lost himself in his thoughts. So much for the dumb blonde stereotype. But he had already figured that one out. He was never attracted to bimbos for anything other than quick hot sex, and the more intelligent and classy a woman was, the easier it was to communicate. Especially in bed. He knew he could have sex with beautiful women whenever he wanted to or needed it, simply by picking up one of the business cards in his box, or just by smiling at a pretty girl. No woman ever said "no" to him, and he averaged at least two women per week, depending on his work schedule and if Delphine was in town. But he saw that this blond was different. She had a brain and was educated and charming, and this, he knew, was what he was missing in his relationships.

He turned away from her and grinned when he noticed she had no wedding ring on her smooth fingers. Not that he would be stopped by a ring anyway. Just made things easier.

Marta nodded off, and eventually fell asleep. Her head tilted automatically to the left onto Gavin's broad shoulder. He didn't move. At first he felt awkward but then relished the fact that her warmth and natural beauty lured his shoulder even closer to her. Her scent, maybe Palermo Picasso, completely erased his immediate memory of those French women. He hoped his new desire would be consummated soon but never fully quenched. She slept on his shoulder for about two hours, and this made the long flight seem like milliseconds according to Gavin's inner body clock.

Marta startled when she woke up and realized her head was on his shoulder. "Oi, I am sorry."

"It's quite all right, my pleasure. I couldn't sleep anyway. Too much coffee I think."

The plane landed at O'Hare and the two seatmates said their good-byes and went their separate ways.

After he found his black Jaguar in the long-term parking lot, he sat in his car and thought a few minutes about Marta and how she seemed to have it all: beauty, intelligence, and elegant charm. He knew she would have quite a few suitors, but he figured that he would easily destroy the competition when he set his mind to it. He always did. Now, however, his mind quickly jumped to the voluptuous flight attendant, Amanda, whom he knew would fulfill his immediate physical needs. He reached into his coat pocket and called the cell number she wrote for him on a business card.

"Hello," said Amanda in a silky voice.

"Is this Amanda?"

"Yes it is. Who is this?"

"It's Gavin. We met on the plane and you were kind enough to leave me your number in my coat pocket."

"Oh, yes of course! Wow. Thanks for calling, darling. Did you enjoy your flight?"

"Boring and uneventful until I saw you, then things changed for the better. But I guess that's what you want when flying, right?"

Amanda giggled. "Yes of course. Listen, Gavin. I'm on the shuttle bus with the other crewmembers on the way to our hotel. I would love it if you would come and join me for a drink in the lobby bar. I need to unwind after work. You look like the perfect guy to unwind with, if you know what I mean. Meet me at The Drake in thirty minutes if you would like. If I'm not at the bar, you can come to room three twenty-five."

"Be there in fifteen, babe."

Amanda was not at the bar when he arrived at the hotel, so he took a seat that had an empty stool next to him and ordered a vodka martini. He knew this conquest would be an easy one, but the alcohol would help erase his very recent memories of Marta so that he could concentrate on Amanda. He needed a woman now. He saw Amanda strut down the stairs then across the smooth marble towards the bar, and his eyes devoured the image of her bouncing within her tight-fitting sweater. She had a classic runway walk that boldly announced her merciless hips. Her short leather skirt clung to her shapely hips, sending his imagination to naughty places. He was already inside her clothes with his hungry eyes.

"Excuse me, sir, are you alone?" she whispered into his ear.

His smile revealed teeth that required sunglasses to view. "No, I am not alone. I'm waiting to meet a hot flight attendant, but I think you'll do in a pinch."

"Hmm. Be careful where you pinch a girl. She might moan uncontrollably if you hit the right spot. And by the way, I have my own bar in my room, and I'd love you to join me there—that is unless you really want to wait for this flight attendant bitch you mentioned."

He laughed. "You've convinced me to dump her. Take my hand, sweetie, so that I don't fall from dizziness while I watch you walk."

Her spacious room was nicely decorated, but Gavin was only interested in one piece of furniture, and it didn't really matter if the sheet thread count was two hundred fifty or one thousand, pima or muslin. He figured that he probably wouldn't notice if the sheets were made of medium-grit sandpaper.

Amanda spoke first. "Darling, go ahead and open the champagne bottle I see sitting on the table, and make yourself comfortable for a while, if you can. I'm going to take a shower and freshen up. It was a long flight."

She walked toward the bathroom; her skirt dropped to the floor several feet in front of the doorway, as did her sweater and bra. Only her panties remained. Her backside reminded him of the smoothness of his favorite winter toboggan run when he was a kid. Before she entered the bathroom, she looked back at Gavin, knowing he was watching, and smiled seductively before she closed the bathroom door behind her. But she didn't close it completely. Gavin quickly threw her black roller travel bag off the bed and pulled back the covers in preparation for his passion, then stopped, thought better of it, and walked to the bathroom. He never touched the champagne.

The steam slowly rose, and this allowed him to watch her through the glass doors of the shower. He enjoyed the view of her washing herself while he drank in her shapely silhouette through the now partially steamed shower door. When she bent over, he couldn't take it any longer, and pulled off his jeans, but with difficulty due to his arousal. He forgot to take off his shirt and hurried into the shower, but it didn't matter because she immediately saw his excitement when he pulled her close to him and he kissed her quivering lips, neck, and finally her more sensitive aroused areas as well. He found her light and easy to pick up in the shower. She eagerly wrapped her tanned legs tightly around his waist and the slick shower wall served as their support while the muscular conqueror first made her moan, then scream so loudly that the next day her fellow flight attendants half-scolded her for disrupting their precious sleep with her nighttime activities.

CHAPTER 9

"Your wife is having a myocardial infarction or heart attack. I assume you know how the system works. We have an on call cardiologist for the emergency department, or we can call a physician of your choice and see if he is available at this time of day," said the emergency-room doctor. "Since you're the hospital CEO some exceptions could be made I suppose."

It was six pm and the CEO of St. Anthony Hospital sat by his wife in the Emergency Room cardiac bed. She was connected to heart monitors, an automatic blood pressure cuff, and a pulse oximeter to measure her oxygen level. An erasable writing board at the foot of her bed on the wall provided patient orientation: *This is the St. Anthony Emergency Cardiac monitoring unit. It is Wednesday, and Julie is your nurse.*

The CEO did not hesitate with his response. "Call Wyatt Barton, please. I know him and have heard that he's definitely the one you want for difficult cases."

"I can try, but he's not on call. He may be home by now."

"Hey Wyatt, it's Jim Thornton down in the ER. You still in house?"

"Yeah Jim. Just finished a procedure and heading home to see my son play basketball. He's perfected his three-point shot and it's a thing of beauty to watch. What's going on?"

"Got the CEO's wife down here, she's got an abnormal ECG with chest pain and I think she's having an MI. Family wants you, even though I told them you're not on call. Yes or no?"

Wyatt's pause lingered longer than expected. ER docs need immediate answers. He agonized about Spencer and the game, and how much he loved seeing him play, especially now that this was his last season before graduating from high school and he was the starting forward.

"No problem, Jim. I'm coming down there now. I'll call the catheterization lab and get them ready."

Wyatt examined the CEO's wife, did a quick cardiac ultrasound, and reviewed her ECG and labs. It looked like an acute anterior infarction, but he was suspicious due to the ultrasound that it could be something else. He performed a diagnostic catheterization with Amy and the crew, and the patient's coronary arteries were completely open with no obstruction or plaque. But he observed that the shape of the heart was clearly abnormal.

Wyatt met the family in the waiting room. "The good news is that she is not having a heart attack per se, from blockages of her heart arteries. But she does have what we call 'takotsubo cardiomyopathy.' Basically, in times of stress, the heart can fail from temporary weakening of the heart muscle, and it can mimic a heart attack on ECG. The ultrasound I did proves that the bottom of her heart is shaped like a balloon and it's causing her to have low blood pressure and fluid on her lungs."

The CEO felt relieved that it wasn't a true heart attack, but nervous about this unusual diagnosis. "I've never heard of that. I guess she's been under stress lately because our daughter eloped with some guy we don't know."

"Well, then that might have been the trigger. We don't know exactly what causes the temporary heart damage, but it is also aptly named 'Broken Heart Syndrome,'" said Wyatt. "We'll admit her into the Intensive Care Unit and treat her with medications and supportive care. She'll be fine."

"Thanks, Wyatt. We really appreciate your helping, even though you weren't on call and we kept you from your family tonight. You're a rare breed nowadays. Some docs seem to care about their lifestyle more than the patient, but you're different. Don't change."

"No problem, my pleasure."

Katherine wished Spencer good luck before she and Colby took their seats in the basketball arena.

"Thanks, Mom. Gotta go warm up."

"By the way, I don't know if your dad will make it tonight, you know, hospital duties happen at the most inconvenient times."

"Yeah, whatever," said Spencer.

Katherine sat in the hometown seats next to another player's parents while Colby ran off with his friends far from the adults.

"So, Katherine, is Wyatt coming?" asked the other mother. She chuckled. "We've got extra room here because he always jumps and yells when Spencer scores."

Katherine produced a half smile. "I don't know. Hope he comes. The boys need more time with him."

"I'm sure you expected that when you married a busy cardiologist. It's not like he's a family doc without on-call hospital responsibilities or one of those shift-work docs who have figured out that life-and-death decisions are for someone else to worry about when their shift is over."

Katherine looked straight ahead while she spoke. "Yeah, you're right. It's almost like the hospital is his mistress."

The game started and the noise level rose several decibels. Wyatt arrived from the hospital after the first half of play was finished. He tried to get Spencer's eye during time-outs, but he wasn't sure if Spencer saw him. Wyatt looked into the stands to find Katherine and went up to join her at the half-time break. He sat down next to her, received her glare, and a bright smile from the other mother.

"I'm sorry I'm late. What did I miss?"

"Spencer hit a couple threes and had a few rebounds. What were you doing, Wyatt, that was so important?"

"CEO's wife had some problems that I needed to take care of. The family requested me."

"Yeah, I'm sure you took care of her problems very nicely, Wyatt, but that's why you have partners to take your call. Our family needs you too."

Perplexed, Wyatt looked at her briefly and said no more to her the rest of the game or the evening. In fact, even the boys didn't seem to want to talk to him anymore. *Maybe they're just acting like normal teenagers.*

After the game, Colby had some friends drive him home and Spencer said the coach would drive him and some other players home after a team meeting. Wyatt talked briefly with the other parents after the game, then drove home, found himself alone, and enjoyed some soothing liquid refreshment from Kentucky.

Gavin met John Willoughby, Esquire, his firm's chief malpractice plaintiff's attorney, in his plush office. He sat behind a cherry desk with an enlarged photograph of himself and his father standing next to Bill Clinton back in the nineties, all three with golf clubs and Cuban cigars. "Morning, John. What do you have for me?"

"Well, I had our boys do some background detective work on this Dr. Barton as you requested, and also some preliminary work on the case involving your father's death."

"I hired you because of your courtroom talents as well as your twenty-year FBI counterterrorism work. I know you'll have interesting information for me."

"Of course, but you must keep in mind that since you have not formally decided to file suit, we can't legally obtain the actual hospital chart entries for review and discovery."

"Right, but I know you, John. You have ways of getting enough information to make good decisions, right?"

"Money talks so information flows."

"That's my boy."

"Dr. Barton is board certified in cardiology and specializes in interventional cardiology—you know, stents and balloons in clogged heart arteries, etc. He was past president of the county medical society, and clearly is well respected by his peers in the community with regard to his medical knowledge and technical skills."

"Yeah, okay, that's putting me to sleep. Damn it, tell me if there's anything juicy for us to sink our teeth into."

"He's married with two sons, but is somewhat of a loner, and he and his wife aren't known in the usual social circles for some reason. Seems he was busted for DUI years ago, apparently just after he was accepted to medical school. What's more, he apparently got in a bar fight that night and the police report described a bloody laceration on his forehead when they pulled him over. I guess that explains his scar."

"Really? I'm surprised they didn't kick his ass out of medical school."

"Maybe the school never found out. Anyway, his medical school grades were top of his class and he had an exemplary record as a resident and cardiology fellow at Northwestern."

"John, I need to know if you have evidence that he's got an alcohol problem."

"We have no evidence of that presently. You know, Gavin, we've looked briefly at the facts of the case, unofficially of course, and it seems he did everything correctly with no major screwups. But we've learned something interesting about him. He's fluent in Arabic and Pashto and is an expert in Krav Maga fighting technique. Seems he takes trips overseas once or twice a year and doesn't usually take his wife and kids."

"That's an unusual background for a doctor, or for that matter anyone outside of the military. Sounds like kind of a tough guy doctor who does some traveling to exotic places."

"We don't know the purpose of these trips, but it may be medical missionary work."

Gavin snorted. "Almost sounds clandestine. Really, I don't give a shit. But hell, John, do we have a case or not?"

"I'm sure if we received complete discovery, we could find a few minor slipups that we could scare him with in deposition or in court, but he seems like Mr. Clean. It also appears to me that he isn't the kind of man who scares easily or backs away from challenges. Let me know if you want to file a malpractice suit against this doc. We have a two-year window before the statute of limitations runs out."

"I see. What do you recommend, John?"

"I recommend we leave him alone. There seems to be no negligence."

"Okay, let's not file suit. Blake and I certainly don't need the money, and you know my father smoked, drank, and had a bad heart that probably couldn't be fixed by anyone. I'm surprised he didn't die of a heart attack in bed with one of our young law clerks."

"Yeah, he was a character; that's for sure. Gavin, it's been nice talking to you as usual, and I wish you and Blake the best."

"Thanks John, but you know I still don't like the guy, even if you think he's clean."

"Your call."

CHAPTER 10

Wyatt finished a procedure in the cath lab and walked down the hall to complete rounds on the cardiology floor. Amy Adams, RN, followed close behind with her surgical shoe covers still on, scrub top tucked tightly to accent her fit shape.

"Dr. Barton, wait."

"Wyatt turned around and smiled when he saw her. "Amy—good job today and thanks for your help as always."

"No problem. It's always a pleasure working with my favorite doctor."

Wyatt's laugh was louder than he wanted. "Sure that's what you tell all the cardiologists."

She shrugged off the comment. "Dr. Barton, do you have time to join me for some coffee at the Starbucks downstairs? I could really use a jolt of caffeine and wanted to talk to you about the lab."

"Don't know. I still have some patients to see."

"C'mon, doc. Just a few minutes."

Wyatt looked briefly at his watch. "Why not? Let's go."

They sat down at the Starbucks, Amy slurping a peppermint mocha and Wyatt drinking a red eye. He tried to avoid Amy's brown eyes and full lips, but it proved difficult. She constantly smiled at him and he soaked it in.

"So tell me, Amy, what was on your mind about the cath lab?"

"Well, it wasn't really the cath lab, but I knew you wouldn't come here to meet me without a specific work-related issue. You always have your mind buried in your work."

Wyatt smirked while she played with her flowing blond hair. "Go on, Amy; spill it out."

"You know my friend Julie is an oncology nurse and we were going to let off some steam at Rick's Bar for happy hour after work. I would love it if you would join us for a drink and a little conversation. It's harmless. You can just tell your wife you went out with the guys for a little while."

"Heh. I'm flattered that you would ask me, but you know I really have to get home early tonight. I need to spend some time with my kids. That is, if they're not too busy."

Amy purred. "Not just for a little while?"

"No, sorry, not even for a little while, Amy."

She displayed her most coquettish pout. "Okay. You know a girl has to try. You look lonely at times and your mind seems distant. Thought you needed to talk. Maybe some other time?"

Wyatt smiled. "I have to finish rounds. Thanks for the invitation and coffee. Maybe some other time. Have a great day."

He watched her walk away, and the rhythmic choreography of her feminine motion forced him to hold his chair arms for stability. He took a deep breath, then looked at his watch and concentrated on his next procedure.

Amy and Julie met at Rick's Bar, an institution that was famous for its happy hour, and the effect it had on facilitating the testosterone-estrogen interaction. They both wore short skirts and heels because they could, and they looked good especially when they posed at the front on high bar stools.

"Kinda quiet here," said Julie.

"Don't worry. It'll pick up. Especially if we're here." They both giggled simultaneously.

"Classic crossed-leg man bait," said Julie. "Works every time."

Julie slurped a margarita while Amy sucked on her vodka martini.

"So, Amy, what hot guy are you with now? Or are you trying to sink your nails into someone with more long-term potential?"

"You know, Julie, sometimes I just take a hunky lover for fun, but when I find a good man with money and power, he won't get away—ever."

Julie almost meowed. "Poor guy won't know how to escape once your nails are inside his naïve skin. What will it be tonight?"

"Depends on what rolls in the door. But seriously, there is someone that I think might be the one."

"Do tell."

"Okay. He's about six-two, blue eyes, nice body with a scar over his left eyebrow that I find easy to ignore. Oh yeah, nice smile too." Amy beamed. She played with her silky hair and re-crossed her legs while scanning the male occupants of the room. "But the problem is, he's a doctor and married. Good family man."

"That's a dangerous situation. Well, now that I think about it, more dangerous for him than you. So who is this guy?"

"I don't kiss and tell."

"Right. I believe that as much as I do politicians. By the way is this kissing a fantasy of yours, or have you actually done it with him?"

"No I haven't tasted his lips yet, but that will happen. Don't worry about that because when I'm on the hunt, I never stop till I have the kill."

"Are you kidding? I never worry about you because it seems you always get what you want when you set your mind to it. But Amy, I won't let you leave without telling me who it is."

She grinned and looked directly at Julie. "Dr. Wyatt Barton."

"Oh my God!" said Julie. "He's a real catch, but the word is he's untouchable and of course, married to boot."

"Yeah, but every man has his weakness that I will exploit."

"Katherine, I've got a four-day weekend coming up in a few weeks and the boys said they don't have any sports competitions, so I thought

I'd take them on a fishing trip in Wyoming. You want to join us?"

"You know I hate fishing. It's dirty and I don't particularly enjoy baiting hooks and handling slimy fish. What got you into this?"

"I haven't taken them on any father-son adventures since they were young and we went to that dude ranch in Colorado, so I thought before they considered it uncool to vacation with parents I'd spend some quality time with them. Good to get out of the city and enjoy the fresh mountain air, catch a few trout in the streams, and maybe teach them some target shooting at the same time."

"Shooting? I hate guns and no, I don't need them doing that. Fishing's okay but my little babies don't need to be around guns, just because you've been trained."

"So, let me get this right. You don't want your boys to be boys? Maybe instead you could take them to a gardening class in the suburbs somewhere, or maybe a class on crochet and fashion design? C'mon, they're boys, soon to be flying from your comfy nest, and fishing is a sport that they can enjoy the rest of their lives and besides, learning proper firearm use and safety is something that everyone needs to know, even you. Let 'em get dirty and spit on the ground a little."

"I don't know, not so sure about this idea."

"Gonna happen whether you like it or not, Katherine. It'll give you some free time by yourself to clean the house without us around like you've always wanted, or just have some time by yourself to catch up on reading."

"You know I don't like to read. But I'll miss my babies—I'm with them 24/7."

"My point exactly."

"Guess the house is a mess and this'll give me some time to do some good deep-down cleaning and polish the floors without everyone walking on them and tracking filth around."

Wyatt and the boys arrived at their cabin near the North Platte River in Wyoming late in the evening Wednesday, and they planned to stay until Sunday. The weather forecast showed sunny and warm the whole time, and the guide told them the water flow would allow wading in certain areas. Although Wyatt had taught the boys some basic fly rod casting techniques and knot tying before they left, he reserved the next morning for some professional fly-fishing education with the guide, leaving the afternoon for an introduction to the sport of clay shooting. Spencer proved to be the better shooter early on, but Colby was much better at tying the basic line knots, even though the guides would make sure everyone had effective and safe equipment.

It was 4:30 am on Friday, in a cabin near the Grey Reef Tailwaters of the North Platte, and Wyatt roused his two teenage sons out of their sleep, but found that it may have been easier to awaken two rocks.

"Time to get dressed, get some breakfast, and hit the river. Daylight's burning."

"What daylight? It's dark – o'clock, Dad!" said Spencer.

"Yeah, good point. But the sun'll be up soon enough, and we need to get a jump on those unsuspecting fish. Guide's going to be at the boat launch at 5:30 am."

Colby finally succeeded in prying his dry lips open to speak. "Problem is, Dad, the fish are probably smarter than we are."

The three Barton men spent all day on the North Platte, and with help from the guide who steered the boat to the best places to fish, they were able to catch cutthroat, rainbows, and a few browns. Both kids were excited that they were able to best their father in the total fish count. They went to bed early after dinner, with plans to fish with their waders in the river Saturday morning.

Wyatt was up early again, cooking his signature cheese omelettes for breakfast while letting the kids sleep a little later. He figured they deserved it after all. He didn't want them to think they were at boot camp.

After receiving tips from the guide on the best wading spots and proper flies to attract the trout, he led his sons to the river to wade in, cast for fish, and enjoy the peaceful surroundings, listening to the gurgle of the water flowing past their waders. There were two other anglers out in the water, about 50 yards upstream. Wyatt could see the long hair of a woman with her son, both of whom were superbly better fly-casters than Wyatt, and therefore looked comfortable in the river. But Wyatt noticed the water flow surged faster than he'd expected, so he instructed his sons to wade out only about six feet into the water, keeping the water line about mid-thigh at the highest.

Between his long casts, Wyatt glanced upstream intermittently at the woman and her son, concerned because they were casting in the middle of the rushing stream, just about navel level in the water. That seems a little risky, he thought, but then they must know what they're doing. He didn't want his sons to fall in and take water into their waders, potentially dragging them underwater. Suddenly Spencer yells, "Got one!"

Wyatt smiled and watched Spencer gently reel the fish to him like he was taught, net at the ready, but at the same time he heard a high-pitched scream, forcing his head to turn directly upstream.

"Help me, my son!"

Quickly scanning upriver, he saw the boy's arms flailing, bobbing up and down, controlled by the strong current quickly taking him downstream in the middle of the river. He saw the top of a boulder, mostly hidden underwater, looming between himself and the floundering boy—clearly a danger if he hit it with his head traveling downstream. He threw his rod toward the shore, pushed into the middle of the stream, and dove in front of the boulder, placing his body between the boy and the boulder, grabbing the boy in a cross-chest arm hold, yanking him away from danger while kicking hard against the current to the shore. He carried the still-conscious boy to shore and laid him down so they both could catch their breath. While the boy heaved with exhaustion, he checked his head and found no injuries; the kid was okay but just shook up. He thought he looked to be about Colby's age and size.

"Thanks, uh Mister. That was close!"

Wyatt smiled generously. "No problem. That current's pretty strong today and your waders must've filled up, huh?"

"Yeah, hey, is my mom okay?"

Before Wyatt could answer, the frantic mother arrived, sloshing with her water-filled waders. "Eric my baby, are you okay?" The two hugged for about a minute.

"Just fine, Mom." He looked at Wyatt. "Good thing this man was here to save me."

His mother smiled warmly at Wyatt and hugged him. "Thanks for saving my son! I'm Linda."

"Wyatt. And here's my two boys Spencer and Colby."

All five sat on the riverbank for about an hour, resting and drying out while admiring the trout caught by Spencer and Colby.

"You know, Wyatt, I've got some extra sandwiches and fruit in my car, and I'd like to share with you and your sons—that is, if you don't have any plans."

"Thanks, that's kind of you, but the boys and I were planning on going into town to get something later. I appreciate the offer, but we're fine." Colby gave Spencer a quizzical look, and they both shook their heads and started a conversation with Eric while the adults talked.

"No, I insist. It's the least I could do, you know."

Wyatt hesitated, looked out toward the water, and then agreed. The group ate lunch together on the riverbank, then Spencer and Colby both got up to go fishing again.

"You coming, Eric?" asked Colby.

Eric looked at his mother with imploring eyes.

"No, we need to go now. There's been enough excitement for one day," said Linda.

Linda got up and Wyatt went to join his sons in the river. "Thanks for the lunch. You two have a nice day now and it's been nice to meet you."

She followed Wyatt to the water. "Wait, I have something to say to you."

He stopped and looked at her with a pleasant smile.

"I want you to know how much I appreciate what you did, and it's good to know that there are heroes in this world where you least expect them. You're a brave man to risk your life for my son."

His face reddened, turned away briefly, then looked back at her. "No big deal, Linda. It's what anyone would do if they were in the situation. Just try to stay safe next time. That water can be unforgiving."

She rolled her eyes, then smiled meekly. "We're both experienced so we should've known better, but we'll be back. You guys take care now."

At the dinner table, Katherine's smile wouldn't stop now that her boys came home to her nest. The house was immaculate, almost sterile from all her work when they were gone. She looked at Spencer, then Colby. "Who wants to tell me about the great fishing expedition first?"

"It was fantastic! Best vacation yet," said Spencer.

"Yeah, Mom. Too bad you didn't come, but you probably wouldn't have liked shooting the clays," said Colby.

"Right, but I missed you guys so much."

Colby continued. "But there's something you need to know, Mom. Dad's a hero. He saved some kid who almost drowned in the river."

She looked at Wyatt with a surprised look. "Oh really?"

"Yeah, some lady was fishing with her son nearby and he fell in, went downstream with the current, and Dad jumped in after him before he hit a boulder. She was real happy."

Katherine's wide smile faded quickly to more of a forced grin. She looked at Wyatt. "How happy was she, Wyatt?"

Wyatt blushed and his scar turned more scarlet than the rest of his face. "I don't know. No big deal, honey."

Spencer interrupted. "She was so happy she gave Dad a big hug and thanked him, then we all had lunch together. Her son's pretty cool."

"Lunch too? Didn't you bring lunch for my babies, Wyatt? She shouldn't have had to do that for you."

"We were hungry and she offered us some sandwiches. Thought that was pretty nice."

"She sounds like a nice woman. What did she look like, Wyatt?"

"Didn't notice really except she was soaking wet."

Katherine turned her attention back to the kids, smiling again. "Time for you guys to go upstairs and get cleaned up. I need some time to talk to your father the hero."

Wyatt and Katherine were now alone at the table and she smiled at Wyatt. "So did you get her phone number, my hero husband?"

CHAPTER 11

Gavin couldn't keep his mind on his work.

Marta seemed so different, beautiful and elegant with intelligence and sophistication. He found her business card and called her at work.

"Northwestern University Microbiology Department. How may I help you?"

"Uh, yes, I need to talk to Dr. Liepa. Is she available?"

"Not sure. I think she's finished with her lecture to the medical students. I'll ring her lab. May I tell her who's calling?"

"Sure. Gavin Flanagan."

After about a minute, the receptionist came back on the phone with Gavin. "Mr. Flanagan, I will connect you with Dr. Liepa."

A PhD at a major university medical center. Impressive. Flanagan, you've got it made now. But maybe since she didn't put her cell phone on the card she has someone else and isn't interested in me. Doesn't matter.

"Hello. This is Dr. Liepa."

"I'm sorry to bother you at work, Dr. Liepa, but this is Gavin Flanagan. We sat next to each other on the flight from Frankfurt to Chicago a few weeks ago. I hope you remember me."

The brief silence caused Gavin to twitch nervously. "Oh, yes, you're the nice man who let me fall asleep on your shoulder on the airplane. That was embarrassing. What can I do for you today?"

"I guess I'll get right to the point. I would be very honored if you would join me for dinner some night … that is, if you are single and able to date."

"Oh, that is so nice of you to ask. And yes, I am single, but I don't date much. I'm just too busy it seems."

"That's a relief that you don't have a man in your life. But I won't ask for much of your time, just a dinner and some conversation and some nice wine."

She hesitated. "Okay, why not? Here's my cell phone number. I'm busy for the next week with some projects, but call me sometime after."

"It will be my honor, Dr. Liepa. You can expect my call."

"It's Marta, remember? Have a good day, Gavin."

It was several weeks before Gavin called Marta. He picked her up in his Jaguar and they drove to the Rumba restaurant on West Hubbard Street for dinner. Gavin liked to dance, and hoped he would be able to get Marta to dance with him after dinner, especially since it would be Latin dancing.

"Such a nice place, Gavin," said Marta. "Thanks for taking me here. I don't get out much and really enjoy learning about America and its culture."

"Definitely my pleasure to show some of America to you. However, this is a Latin-themed restaurant."

"I see that, but I must say that I've never been to a place like this, with all this spicy food and lively music. I don't experience it much where I'm from."

They enjoyed their dinner and wine. "So I have to ask now; where are you from? I was going to guess Germany, but I can't really place your accent."

"Yes, most people say Germany. But I'm from Riga Latvia."

"Ah, the Baltics. Eastern European women are so beautiful."

She smiled. "Thanks. You're kind."

"How long have you been living in the United States?"

"One year. I wrote my PhD in molecular biology and virology and then was recruited to come to the United States to work."

"How did you end up deciding to get a job here in the U.S., Marta?"

"I was recruited by the U.S. Department of Homeland Security after the horrible 2001 attacks in New York. They were looking for experts in the field of bioterrorism. Right now, I'm teaching virology and molecular biology at Northwestern Medical School. Once or twice a year, I travel to Atlanta to the CDC where I do some work for the government."

"Impressive. What do you do at the CDC?"

"That's all I have to say about that right now."

"Of course, I apologize for asking so many questions, but you fascinate me. Where do you live in Chicago, Marta?"

"North suburbs. I live with my son who is in high school."

"Oh, I see. You're divorced."

"Yes, for several years now."

"Is your ex still living in Latvia?"

"That's enough about me. Tell me what you do. I see that your card says you work for the Flanagan law firm. What type of law do you practice?"

"I'm the senior partner and CEO of the Flanagan law firm."

"You don't look very senior to me to be so successful. You must've inherited that position."

He was taken aback by her astute comment and her desire to protect her personal life.

"You're direct, I like that. My father died earlier in the year, and I inherited the company, along with my brother."

The conversation faded and they both looked out on the dance floor. Some couples were doing the Salsa and Cha-Cha. They watched quietly and drank margaritas. Then the tango music started.

"Do you know how to tango, Marta?"

"I love it! It's rare to find a man who knows the tango. Let's go."

They danced the tango and there were only two other couples on the floor. He beamed because he was able to feel Marta's graceful body while he led her in the sensual dance. Her lively movements told him that they were comfortable together, at least on the dance floor, and the more they danced, the more he hoped they would be even more comfortable in his bed.

When they returned to the table, Gavin received several phone calls, and he answered them while Marta remained cordial. "Oh hi Amanda. No, I'm busy right now. Maybe we can talk later. I'll call you when I get a chance."

"I'm sorry, Gavin," said Marta. "Perhaps I should go freshen up while you make your calls in private."

"No, that's not necessary. I mean, only if you need to. I want to spend time with you, Marta. That was just my office assistant. She thinks I work all day and night. I wish she would leave me alone."

Marta smiled knowingly and played along. "Everyone needs time off. You should teach your office staff to respect your free time though. I'm sure you rarely have time for a social life, right?" Her bright smile faded gently, then she turned to look towards the dance floor.

"Yes, of course. You're right."

An attractive woman came up to their table. "Gavin, it's so great to see you! It's been so long. I'm out with the girls tonight since my hubby is out of town on business. May I have the next dance?"

"Kerry! Nice to see you too. This is Marta, my date for this evening."

The two women exchanged brief pleasantries.

"Gavin, it's okay. You can dance with her," said Marta. But beware; there may be some men who may want to dance with me as well when you are gone."

Kerry was one of the married women Gavin met at social events, and she was usually with her oblivious husband. She liked to cling to him. It was difficult for him to avoid staring at her physical charms and he was tempted to add her to his list of conquests, but tonight, he knew better. He knew that Marta was the type of woman who wouldn't be trifled with. She had the rare qualities he was looking for in a woman, and there was so much more he wanted to know about her.

"Kerry, it's nice to see you tonight, but there are a lot of nice men sitting alone on the other side of the room who would love to dance with you. Say hello to Randy for me and have fun."

"Thanks for the kind words, but you know I wouldn't have minded at all if you danced with her," said Marta. "We're here just to have fun. I wouldn't be offended." After they finished their dinner and wine, he showed his eagerness to leave. "If you'd like we can drink some French wine at my place and talk a little more while listening to some good music."

"Yes, it's time to go now, but I would rather go to my home now. I had a great evening."

Gavin drove her home and he walked her to her front door. He leaned to kiss her and she turned so he would kiss her cheek.

"I would love to see you again, Marta. I'll call you next week."

"Thanks, Gavin. It'll be better if I call you though. Good night."

Gavin drove home and couldn't stop thinking about Marta.

No woman tells me that it's better that she call me. However, she is an amazing woman. I'll do whatever is necessary to have her as mine. Anything.

CHAPTER 12

"Sorry I'm running late. You'll have to start dinner without me. I've got an unstable patient in the CCU. Hopefully I can resolve the problem quickly."

As usual, the kids prowled around in the kitchen snacking before dinner while Katherine cooked. During the phone conversation, she initially walked away, then returned to the kitchen while talking, pacing the floor.

"That's unfortunate, honey. We understand you're busy. Hopefully tomorrow you can finally come home early. Too bad you can't be here now. Spencer really wanted to talk to you about his college applications."

"Tell him we'll talk when I come home, okay?"

She looked at Spencer with a concerned look, then changed to a smile. "Of course, honey."

"Well, boys, your dad's going to be late again, so let's eat without him."

"Where is he?" said Colby.

"Says he's stuck at the hospital and doesn't know when he'll be home. But you know, he's a good doctor and always does what is best for his patients."

At the dinner table, Katherine smiled at the boys while they plowed through their food, but continued to touch her left forearm, caressing a small bruise.

Spencer noticed her constant playing with the bruise. "Where'd you get that bruise, Mom? Looks like it hurts."

"Yeah, it's a little painful, but it's nothing. I fell down a couple steps in the garage because your dad left a paint can on the step."

"Careless of him. He should be more careful," said Spencer.

Colby scowled at his brother briefly, and then continued to eat.

"Like I said, guys, it's no big deal. These things happen. It looks bad I guess, but it'll heal."

"Dr. Liepa, sorry to bother you, but there's a doctor here in the front office here to see you. Says he doesn't have an appointment."

"That's bold. Is it customary for doctors in the United States to just come to the workplace unannounced and expect to be seen?"

"No, not usually, but he says he has some research to show you."

"What's his name?"

"Dr. Flanagan."

"Doesn't sound familiar. Okay, I'm working in the laminar flow hood now on a viral cell culture preparation. Tell him it'll take me about 15 to 30 minutes if he's lucky."

The microbiology department receptionist didn't tell her he had a vase with a dozen red roses waiting for her. She smiled at him and he flashed his bright whites at her and patiently took a seat in the waiting room. Every now and then the receptionist looked at him, then glanced at the business card he'd handed her with his cell phone handwritten and circled up top, placing it in her purse.

Marta finally entered the reception area wearing her white lab coat open in front, a white blouse, and tight-fitting jeans that naturally hugged her hips.

"Oh, it's you, Gavin!" She avoided scolding him in front of the receptionist for his lie about being a research doctor. The red roses she saw, however, softened her tone.

"Are those for me?"

"Of course they are. They don't compare to your beauty, but I hope they brighten your day."

He gently placed his hand on her back and guided her out the door into the hallway for privacy.

"I've been thinking about you since our last date last month and well, needed to see you again. You said you'd call, but I figured you were shy and I couldn't wait any longer."

"You're pretty sure of yourself, aren't you? I'm not shy, but I do have a busy life. What was so important to tell me that you had to lie about being a doctor at my lab? But then, I guess it's easy for some lawyers to lie to get what they want, right?"

Gavin wasn't accustomed to women putting up barriers to his advances, but strong women in the top echelons of their field could be forgiven. "I do what I have to do to succeed in my goals, and my goal is to take you to dinner tonight. No dancing this time though."

"A lofty goal indeed, Gavin. Thanks for the offer and flowers, but no dinner date tonight. I've got an early meeting tomorrow morning with the dean."

"Okay then, how 'bout a drink and some conversation at the bar a few blocks down the street?"

She looked at his brown eyes and solid shoulders, and figured a drink might be nice after a long day and she might as well enjoy it with a handsome guy.

"Sure. Give me a few minutes to close the lab and we're on our way."

They sat at the bar, Bears game on the wide screen, but Marta had no concept of how the game of American football was played. She liked the uniforms though, and how they hugged the players' butts. She knew he was studying her blouse and jeans, but his stares were a bit too long. He was certainly handsome, but she longed for a man who could match her in conversation, or at least inspire her mind with some respect instead of undressing her with his eyes. The cabernet was smooth and it loosened her tongue more than she'd expected.

"So, you told me you were suddenly handed the job of CEO of your dad's company. How's that gift going for ya?"

"I uh, haven't heard it put that way before, but it's going well.

Large firms require a tight rein so that all the employees and attorneys understand the culture of the organization."

She smiled knowingly. "Culture, I see. Perhaps what you mean is the overlying principle of making money no matter whom or what you have to push out of the way to do it, right?"

"I must admit you're a confident woman with your opinions. I like that, but you're making the mistake of wrong assumptions, my dear. We don't compromise principles of fairness and we are a benevolent organization, giving money to charities such as the boys and girls clubs, homeless shelters, etc. In fact, there was a news clip of me last year working at the soup kitchen on Thanksgiving. Got tons of publicity for our firm."

"Ah, yes, that's good for marketing, right?"

"Well of course, because a firm with 40 attorneys in multiple fields requires a good name to stay strong with a large pipeline of clients. We do family law, contract law, bankruptcy, corporate law, real estate, and of course, my specialty—international business. So because I travel a lot, I don't have time to meet quality ladies, so that's why I had to be aggressive with you."

"A real jet-setter, so they say. But Gavin, I'm not naïve enough to think you don't meet women if you travel around the world on an unlimited expense account."

He hadn't blushed in quite a few years, but he came perilously close. "I'm just too busy for a relationship now. Mostly casual acquaintances because it's too difficult to find a quality woman who fulfills my sexual needs but also stimulates my brain. Last time my brain was stimulated was Harvard law. But heck, the brain doesn't always need stimulation and the ladies enjoy my company."

Marta laughed loudly because she realized how easily his mouth put him on the ropes in the corner with no means of escape from himself. But she enjoyed his honesty.

"Sounds like you have quite a few needs and desires that are mostly controlled with your brain down below, Mr. CEO Attorney, and men like you think with that brain more than you should. Personally, I like a man who is confident in himself and admires a woman and her views on the world and inspirations about life without having to spout off about his sexual prowess."

"Oh my, I guess I've been convicted without a trial. I'm guilty as charged when it comes to my social life, but with you, my dear, perhaps things could change."

She knew she had full control of the moment. "And how's that, Mr. Player?Your lower brain doesn't find me as attractive as your other conquests?"

"No, er, I meant you're very attractive physically but there's something about your personality that I can't seem to get enough of. Anyway, I'm sorry this conversation hasn't gone so well tonight, it seems. Perhaps I've been under too much stress at the office."

She could see how insecure he was, immersed in himself and not in her, but she decided to take it easy on him and give him a breather. "It's probably my accent that has you talking in ways you're not accustomed to. Anyway, what's bothering you at your office?"

"Remember I told you my father died of a heart attack about six months ago. Well, I really don't like the doc that was involved, don't like his attitude. I wonder if he could've saved my dad, but made some mistakes in his care. We're going to look into it, and if we think there's a case, then I'll have my guys go after him hard with a suit. We're the best law firm in Chicago, possibly the country, and we never lose a case."

She got up, retrieved her purse, and looked at Gavin curiously, wondering why a man so attractive could be so confused about life. "Thanks for the drink and the conversation. You're an interesting man, but you harbor some seething anger inside. I hope that you're able to find some peace in your life. You must think hard about doing the right thing. Where I come from, physicians are respected and lawsuits are much more difficult to achieve, and when they are without merit, in fact, they just aren't allowed. When a malpractice suit is allowed against the doctor, the losing party pays the opponent's legal costs. Cuts down on frivolous suits and makes the plaintiff's attorneys honest. Seems much more fair than the way it is in your country."

He walked her to her car in the parking garage, then moved forward for the kiss, but once again, she turned her head slightly so his kiss would land on her cheek, not lips.

She drove away and he was still standing there, shaking his head.

CHAPTER 13

March rolled around and as usual, Wyatt attended the annual meeting of the American College of Cardiology, this time in Philadelphia. After the first day of seminars, scientific sessions, and reviews of new stent technology, he plopped onto his hotel room bed and made his nightly call to his sons. He realized that the summer would arrive after a few months, and it was time to plan for another father-son trip with the boys.

"Spence, how're you doing?"

"Hey, Dad. Doin' fine. How's the conference in the city of brotherly love?"

"Not bad, but then I've been to better ones. Listen, would you get Colby on the other phone? I need to talk to you guys together."

When Colby picked up the other phone, he continued.

"Listen, guys. Summer's coming and we need to plan another trip. Thought maybe we'd have another guy trip before Spence goes to college. Right, Bubba?"

"Yeah, Dad. Thought we deleted the Bubba thing a few years ago. But heck yeah, I'm all in!"

"Let's go," said Colby.

"So where do you want to go this year? Fishing trip again or a rafting/camping trip out west?"

"I vote for a fishing trip again. Loved it last time," said Spencer.

"Gotta say my vote is rafting and camping. We can do a little fishing in between," said Colby.

"Well you boys think about it for the next few days, and then we'll decide when I get back."

"Good night, guys; love ya."

"Yeah; night, Dad."

"We'll see ya when we see ya."

"Was that your dad on the phone?"

Spencer took over as the spokesperson. "Yeah, he's talking about our next summer trip. Pretty cool this year, it's either fishing or rafting down some white water."

"You guys are talking about that already? Let's see, it's been about what, eight months since your Wyoming trip and you're still talking about it? Are you sure he wants to plan a trip with you again this year?"

"What do you mean?" said Spencer. "Why wouldn't he? We go somewhere every year and that's cool. Lot of my friends don't get to do that with their dad and heck, eight months seems like a long time ago."

"Well you know I miss you kids when you're gone. I've spent the most time with you since your dad wasn't able to over the years and you know, it's hard on me."

Colby interjected. "Mom, what did you mean when you said 'are you sure' that dad wants to make plans with us again this summer? That sounded kinda weird."

She played with her hair and looked down at the floor. "I just find it surprising you know, considering what he said recently."

"What did he say?" both kids said together.

"He said that he was growing a little tired of his trips with you guys and that sometimes you're more trouble than it's worth."

Colby drew silent. "Really?" said Spencer. "He actually said that?"

"You know I would never lie to you kids. I love you too much to do that. I'm sure what he really meant was that his work was taking a lot of his energy and he wanted to make sure he made arrangements in advance for the time off."

She again started to play with her bruise, which now was fading somewhat, but still visible.

"Does that bruise still hurt, Mom?" asked Spencer. "You told us about that a month ago and said it was nothing to worry about."

"Yeah, it hurts more than I told you before. I hope I don't have a greenstick fracture or something. Your dad said I didn't need it X-rayed, so I trust him, even though he's a cardiologist and not an orthopedist."

"So tell us, Mom, what happened again? You said you fell down the steps and hit your arm on the garage floor?"

Katherine hesitated, looked at her arm again, and then smiled. "Kinda like that I guess."

Then she winced in pain and moaned a little and the kids' faces grew more concerned.

"Mom, maybe you need to go to the emergency room and have that looked at," said Spencer.

"No that's not necessary."

"I'll drive you. It's no problem. We'll call Dad on our way to the hospital."

"No, you guys have school early tomorrow and you know, it could be embarrassing you know, in the ER."

"Why would it be embarrassing?" said Spencer.

Katherine looked away from her two sons on the couch and tried to hide a tear that was suddenly forming. "I didn't want to tell you kids this before since he's your dad and he's got an important job."

"Go ahead," said Spencer.

"Your dad punched me then pushed me down the stairs. That's actually how it happened."

"No way," said Colby. "Dad would never do that!"

Spencer was speechless for a few minutes, then he started in. "Are you sure this is true, Mom?"

"Definitely. He was angry at me that night, I'm not sure why. You know me; I always care about him and want him to be happy."

Both boys looked at each other, expressionless, then got up to go to their rooms.

"Guys, he's a good father and I love him. Please don't be angry at him. He just lost control a little that night."

CHAPTER 14

Wyatt arrived home at five, the earliest he'd been home in months. It was nice to come home and eat a relaxed dinner with his family. Katherine was cheerful, and she cooked his favorite beef pot roast dinner. She even had the gas logs burning in the family room fireplace. The boys interacted a little, but mostly just scarfed down massive quantities of food. But Wyatt wasn't far behind in the food consumption category. His wife was an incredibly good cook.

"Spencer, how's the college application process going?" asked Wyatt. He wanted to wait till later to tell the kids about the reservations he'd made for their rafting expedition on the Colorado River.

"Okay."

"Just okay? Which ones did you send so far?"

"Northwestern, Stanford, and Illinois."

"I guess you didn't need any help."

"No, I didn't, but it wasn't bad. They're done. Hey listen, I gotta go do some homework." Spencer excused himself from the table.

Wyatt thought he was still acting strange. Couldn't put his finger on it. So he tried to engage Colby. "So Colby, how's hockey practice going?"

"Okay."

"Do you like your new coach?"

"He's okay. Mom and Dad, I need to go upstairs too. Term paper due tomorrow. Thanks, Mom, for the dinner."

"You're welcome, honey. Study hard."

"Wait guys, before you go, I need to tell you I made the reservations for our rafting trip. We're going down the Colorado and camping!"

Both boys turned, kept walking towards the stairs, and each said

"Cool" then continued on.

Wyatt felt his heart free-fall straight into his belly. The boys had been acting a little cold to him for the last few months and he couldn't figure it out. He tried his best but seemed to be fighting a losing battle. He remembered the minor incident at Colby's play and his late appearance to Spencer's game. But the reason for his sons' their change in behavior toward him was a mystery. Teenage boys are foreigners from a strange land. Now it was just him and Katherine at the table. She seemed talkative and warm this evening and surprisingly loving.

"Thanks for coming home early tonight. I appreciate it. You know how much I love you. Do you love me, Wyatt?"

"Of course." He welcomed her soothing words; it was finally a night without stress, and he thought about a drink in front of the fireplace with her. It felt good to be home.

"How was your day, Wyatt? You know I'm proud of you for what you do."

He flashed his wide grin. "Thanks, no major disasters today. Did you start your home decorator company like I suggested?"

"C'mon now. You know I need a degree for that. I just have street smarts. Cleaned the house and went grocery shopping. Washed the dog and bought some clothes for the kids."

They ate quietly and smiled at each other, but during the cleanup of supper dishes, her expression suddenly changed from bright to sullen, like a light switch. "Why have you been coming home so late recently? You always say it's because you're working late, but the paychecks you bring home don't seem to reflect all that work you say you're doing."

He stared at her as if he were looking at a stranger. "What happened to your loving wife personality? You need to flip the switch back to warm."

She displayed her tight lips again. "Whatever, I'm smarter than you think."

"So, you actually examine my paychecks and try to correlate it with my work schedule? That isn't logical because it's not a one-to-one relationship. Sometimes I work for hours on a patient and don't get paid at all!" Clearly, the female Jekyll and Hyde was now in the Hyde mode.

"It's obvious you must have some hot woman there at the hospital or something. Is she blonde or brunette?"

He hesitated and his face flushed with adrenaline-powered blood. There she went again. He decided he would antagonize her. "Of course I do. She's a brunette this time and hot as hell. Love how her hair bounces when she walks."

"I thought so. I told my friends at the women's church fellowship how you always found a way to come home late. They all told me that I should be suspicious that you are playing around on me. Of course, I told them they were wrong and you would never do such a thing. But it's hard to defend you when my friends tell me they heard many bad things about you."

"Is that so? You're delusional. I don't care what your friends say. In fact, I didn't even think you had friends. And no, I don't have a woman friend, but maybe I should. What do you think?"

She chuckled dismissively. "They've all heard that you have a reputation for flirting with women and having affairs, but again, I stick up for you. Now, be the good father and husband I know you can be."

He walked away to his study to do some reading. The thoughts of warm and cozy smooching by the fireplace vanished into a pit of vipers deep underground, directed by his wife, the snake charmer. He wondered whether one of the intelligent, attractive women around him could make him happy and fill the deep void he'd had inside ever since their marriage. He thought it would be wonderful to actually court and choose a woman for the qualities that he desired in a mate, one who wouldn't erupt from warm to frigid in thirty seconds. He prayed that he was providing a calm home for his boys, but it was slowly progressing to the point that he was more often than not turning the heat off the simmering pot to avoid a boiling overflow.

Suddenly the door to his study crashed open from Katherine's kick and she threw a dinner plate directly at him at his desk. He ducked and it missed his head and crashed to the floor. The loud shatter of ceramic on the stone floor behind him made him jump, and he looked at Katherine, her face crimson and eyes glazed.

"Get out of this house now, Wyatt, or next time I won't miss, you fucking bastard."

Exhaustion engulfed his body. All he wanted was peace, a drink of bourbon, and some nice rejuvenating sleep. But her continued irrational screaming made sleep impossible. He escaped to the basement to try to sleep on the couch, hoping she would calm down and revert to her softer personality. He lay on the cold leather couch with no blanket, and he again worried about his boys and how they would turn out in life, having experienced this bizarre family life. It had not occurred to him that he would be involved in such a caustic, unstable marriage. But then, there was a lot he didn't know when he married Katherine.

He drifted off to sleep on the frigid couch in the basement, immersed in the memories of his boys, how he'd delivered them both at birth, and how much he loved spending precious time with them.

Upstairs, Katherine rushed up to talk to the boys—another of her secret "debriefings" that she usually initiated after one of her explosions. "I'm sorry about our fight tonight, guys. You know that I love you both so much, and you two mean everything to me."

"I know," said Spencer.

Colby then added, "I love you, Mom."

The boys had learned that it was best to agree with their mother on most occasions; otherwise, she would make their young lives miserable, devoid of any semblance of calm.

"You see, your father slapped me in the face tonight after you left the table."

"What?" said Spencer. "You're kidding me, Mom. Right? He did it again? Are you okay? We heard some crashing noises downstairs and didn't know what was happening."

"A little scared, but I'm fine. But I'm not kidding. I found out he was having an affair with a young nurse tonight, so he became angry with me when I asked him about it innocently, and then he hit me."

Spencer began exerting his almost 17-year-old manliness. "A husband should never hit his wife ever, especially when he is guilty of sinning."

Colby quickly joined the dad bashing. "He may be my biological father, but I'm not sure if he is a dad anymore. I remember you said he didn't want to go to my play. That was really weird. But now he's hit you twice?"

"Yeah," said Spencer. "Mom, we've heard a ton of stuff from you about him and his problems. You told me he forgot my basketball game and that was selfish. I just couldn't believe it at first, but it seems you just keep telling us about bad things he does, so maybe it is true. I know you don't want to tell these things to us, but we're glad you did."

With a wide smile, she finished the conversation. "Now, boys, he's a good man, and you shouldn't talk about him like that. Even though he hurt me tonight, I love him."

"Mom, I can't believe Dad is so bad, but maybe he is," said Colby. "He was a cool dad before and I didn't think dads could change. It seems you're sweet to him, though. I wanna go to bed. This whole thing weirds me out like a bad dream. Night, Mom."

"Night, boys."

Satisfied, she left the two boys, and then quickly ran downstairs to the dark basement to find Wyatt. He was in a deep refreshing sleep, unaware of the conversation upstairs. She put her hand on his shoulder and in a soothing voice she said, "Come upstairs to bed, honey. I love you." She heard no response from him, smiled, and went upstairs to bed.

CHAPTER 15

It was about a week before Christmas. Wyatt had already made sure he bought the kids' gifts early. He enjoyed Christmas with his family, but things seemed to be getting increasingly tense at home for some reason. Why would Katherine refuse to go to his office holiday party? It didn't make sense.

"I already told you last month that I wouldn't go to your office party. I don't like any of your partners at Premier Cardiology, and the office staff would see quickly that the two of us are smiling fake smiles when we're together. And here you are getting ready to go alone to the party tonight."

"Hell yes. Of course. I'm a partner and I need to be there but you refuse to go. Now you're angry with me for going without you. You can't have it both ways."

"Wyatt, you have no idea how many men would be lucky to go with me to a Christmas party."

He stared at her in disbelief at this incongruous statement. He then walked away to the bedroom to change his clothes for the party, and Katherine followed behind him. She cornered him at the doorway to his walk-in closet, barring his exit.

"I still can't believe you're getting dressed to go alone. You should respect me, and refuse to go because I don't feel comfortable. I am your wife and you said your marriage vows to God and me. Since you're going without me, you are once again proving that you don't love me. I tell you, Wyatt Barton, it's me or the party, which is it?"

"Stop playing games with my mind. You're being irrational. I am going to the damn office party, either with you or without you. I appreciate my partners and office staff, and I don't really need you giving me this stress right before I get dressed to leave. And by the way, I reserved two tickets for us just in case you changed your mind, as is your usual pattern."

"I'll have you know that I bought a new dress just for this party, but now the party is in fifteen minutes, and it's too late to get ready."

"Really? If that's the case then why are you fighting with me and manipulating me and not getting dressed if you've now changed your mind?"

"Because you don't deserve me. At least that's what the kids told me, and I finally agree with them. In fact, Spencer's hockey coach told him that he thinks I'm hot, and you know, he's right. I'm a good-looking woman and the kids and I will make a good package for some man some day since you don't want us."

Wyatt no longer knew when Katherine was lying about the kids and their private words she claimed they said to her. Either way, the brutal words ripped sharply into his gut.

"Okay, good. If that's how you feel, then go for it." He took a white shirt and a red and green Christmas tie, laid them neatly on a chair, and prepared to dress for the party. "If you don't mind, I need to put on my dress shirt and tie and go."

Katherine placed herself between Wyatt and his hangered and pressed white shirt. He took the shirt off the hangar, and she grabbed her nearby glass of orange juice and threw it on the shirt, ruining it. Wyatt was stunned, and she stood in his way, blocking his path to find another shirt. She would not budge, and he stopped to avoid a physical confrontation. He was in control but his muscles tightened like an elevator cable carrying a heavy load of passengers. He stared at her. She slapped him in the face and the strike echoed throughout the house.

He turned and glared at her, grabbed a basic polo shirt that was within reach, and went to the garage to drive away to the party. Spencer and Colby were watching TV quietly in the family room. They were 17 and 15 respectively, trying to lead typical teenage lives and avoid adult issues.

Katherine saw her opportunity and seized it. "Your father refused to take me to the Christmas party because he says he doesn't love me, and then he hit me in the face!"

Drawn into the fray, the kids reacted.

"Bastard!" said Colby.

"Our coach Mark is a better man than he is," Spencer added, "and he would never hurt you, Mom."

"I'm sure you're right, Colby. Mark sounds like a good man. I just wish your father would love me the way I deserve to be loved."

At the Christmas party, Wyatt's face remained cherry colored, although not as bright as it had been thirty minutes earlier at home. He knew she was becoming progressively more difficult, but he figured the kids would survive it and take his side because that seemed most logical. He tried gallantly to sing songs with the office staff and smiled courageously to show no evidence of the struggle that was raging inside his soul. He bid Merry Christmas and Happy Hanukkah to the staff and his partners, and then realized he needed sleep for his on-call duties the next day. His patients needed him. But it was becoming clearer to him that he could no longer live with her and still maintain his physical health and sanity.

Wyatt stayed overnight at the hospital on-call room, but continued to receive pestering calls throughout the long night from a wife boiling in irrational rage.

"Where are you, Wyatt? Why didn't you come home? The kids and I are waiting for you, and I miss you. But again, I think you must have a girl with you, and that's why you won't come home to your loving family."

Katherine deftly morphed from rage to kindness, back and forth seamlessly as if nothing happened. But then, he found that to be her standard operating procedure now.

"I'm not coming home tonight and you know why, so leave me alone so I can get some sleep."

"Yeah, I know. The woman you are with won't let you come home, now will she? I bet her legs are wrapped around you and you can't escape."

He hung up and turned off his cell phone and beeper since he was not on call. His brain needed a vacation from her bizarre absurdity.

The next day, Wyatt made rounds in the hospital Cardiac Care Unit, performed a smooth cardiac catheterization, and then decided to call Katherine and tell her his plans so there wouldn't be any explosive surprises waiting for him at home. When she answered his call on her cell phone, she purposely didn't tell him she was in the car with the two boys. Spencer was driving, Katherine was in the front passenger seat, and Colby was in the back seat. They were going to Colby's hockey game. The boys couldn't hear Wyatt's voice on Katherine's cell phone, but she made her voice loud enough for people in other cars to hear.

"Where are you, and when are you coming home, Wyatt?"

"I've rented an apartment and I'm coming home tonight to pick up my clothes after I go to Colby's game. We need to separate for a while until we both figure this marriage out, but we need to keep the kids out of our marriage problems. I'm going early so I can have a good seat to take some movies of the game."

"Really?" said Katherine, loudly for the kids to hear. "I can't believe you said you don't love the kids, and you have no intention of going to the hockey game to see Colby! A good father would never say that."

He was shocked at the horrible words he'd just heard. "It disgusts me that you're such a low-life bitch that you would tell that lie to the kids."

"What did you call me, Wyatt? A bitch?" She gave the phone to

Colby. "I hate you, Dad. Clean up your life, and don't cry to me. Stay away from me!" Colby then angrily threw the phone to his older brother.

"You're not a good man, and you're a deadbeat dad. You are an idiot and unchristian. Mom's friend Mark is a better man than you, and you don't deserve the three of us. Leave us alone, you jerk. Bye."

Wyatt couldn't respond. His cell phone dropped from his trembling hands. The taste of salty blood flooded his mouth while his chest heaved to keep pace with the hammering of his heart. He could no longer see the road signs clearly, so he pulled over. Tears welled up in his eyes for the first time in years, and he felt as though a baseball was solidly lodged in his throat. This kind of hatred and disrespect was foreign to him, and he knew he had to resist the urge to lash out against their words, because he knew there was no way to stop this raging firestorm. Any words to his children would simply fuel the fire started by their mother.

Later that evening, Wyatt came to the house to pick up his clothes. Colby lurked downstairs in the lower level trying to avoid further drama, but Katherine called him upstairs anyway. Spencer was already busy throwing some of Wyatt's clothes randomly into old suitcases. The kids were doing what she told them to do in order to avoid the screaming she would rain down upon them at a moment's notice. He desperately wanted to say good-bye to his kids and tell them he loved them, but he knew the atmosphere was so charged he could not display what was in his heart, unless it involved ripping his heart out for them to step on with boots covered with excrement.

He watched in disbelief while his oldest son packed some of his dad's toiletry articles in bags and handed them to him with no comment, helping to facilitate the separation. He couldn't believe what he saw.

"Step back, Spencer. I don't care if your mother told you to pack my things; it's not your business!"

Katherine stood near them, arms folded and scowling.

"And Katherine," said Wyatt. "You get out of my way too. You disgust me. If you want to kick me out of my own house and make my sons participate in your stinking garbage then don't come near me."

Spencer's intelligence forced him to walk away. His father was a master at Krav Maga but was never violent. His voice demanded respect in an instinctive, animal way that Spencer sensed.

While Wyatt loaded his car with his few belongings, she yelled out so all could hear: "Wyatt, give me the garage-door opener and our house keys since you have decided to leave our loving family home and abandon us."

Incensed at the request and twisted words designed to manipulate the kids, Wyatt shot back. "No way. I pay the damn mortgage, your food, the car, the kids' private schools, and the ridiculously expensive crap you buy for yourself. Wait till the divorce is processed, then you'll get my keys and the garage-door opener that I own!"

At that point, she dispatched her protector Spencer out to the driveway to retrieve the house keys and garage-door opener from his uncooperative father. She knew that Wyatt had a soft spot for his kids and her ploy would likely work. Spencer ran to Wyatt's car, then tripped and fell on the porch step and gashed his head; the blood was dripping down his face.

Wyatt ran to his aid instinctively. "Are you okay, Spencer? You took quite a fall. Let me take you inside and dress your wound."

"Don't worry about me. Mom wants your keys and garage-door opener. Give them to me now!"

Wyatt hesitated, staring at the red in Spencer's eyes with the blood dripping down from his forehead onto his nose and realized it was of no use. He wouldn't be coming back, and the disrespect he was seeing sucked the energy from him. He knew he had to avoid a confrontation with Spencer before it escalated, so he gave the keys and opener to Spencer, then started the car, hesitating to drive away because he knew he would never return to the family home. He prayed that somehow he could repair his broken relationship with the kids he loved, and that despite the parental separation, the father-son relationship would remain intact, as it should.

Spencer walked back into the house.

Katherine saw the small abrasion on his forehead and the bleeding, became enraged, then grabbed her cell phone and took multiple pictures of his bloody forehead. She then yelled out to Wyatt, who was sitting in his car stupefied, the door still open. "I'm going to file child abuse charges against you, Wyatt. We now have proof with these pictures. I don't care if this causes you to lose your job and your medical license. By the way, my boyfriend, Mark, will take care of the kids and me much better than you ever did. Now that you have abandoned us, I will call him to take Spencer to the emergency department to get help, and that is where your career will probably end. You are clearly an abusive father and husband, abusing me physically as well as Spencer. You will pay! And if you come back to us, I will kill myself and the kids too!"

Wyatt drove away. He thought about calling the police due to her comment about killing herself and the kids too, and then realized that she had made similar false threats over the years, and that further drama wouldn't be necessary. Empty threats. He was a respected physician and didn't want the whole community to know his family was blowing up in front of him. But then, what was the correct thing to do? The whole thing was confusing. His stomach churned and knifelike pain seared the center of his sternum as if it was scalded by a branding iron while he drove to the cheap apartment he'd rented to retreat from the horror.

Abuse was a word he didn't understand and was incapable of performing. He didn't remember driving the fifteen-minute trip to his apartment because of the swirling turmoil in his brain. He wondered if he would survive this brutal situation, but he knew he needed to get some sleep in order to be fresh and professional for his patients the next day.

He lay in bed that night counting the dust balls flying off the ceiling fan, his mind in turmoil. He didn't want to lose the kids he loved, or at least the kids he thought he knew. They seemed no longer to have a genetic connection to him. It was bizarre to him that Katherine wanted to frame him for an abuse he hadn't committed, because that would hurt her financially if somehow she would be able to convince the courts to take her seriously. Sleep was impossible; he hoped he didn't make any mistakes with his patients the next day due to his family stress.

Katherine looked at Spencer, and she told him to sit next to Colby on the couch in the family room for another of her mind-washing sessions. The bleeding had stopped and only required a Band-Aid for the minor abrasion that had nevertheless caused a lot of excitement.

"Spencer, I know your father hit you, didn't he?"

"Well I..."

"Of course he did. It hurts, doesn't it?You're the man of the house, now that your father has abandoned us, Spencer. I love you, and I'm confident that you will take care of me and your brother."

"I'll do my best, Mom. I guess we don't have a father anymore. We will have to get used to it."

"Yeah, he threw out a great family."

CHAPTER 16

Diane, the office nurse, knocked on Wyatt's office door gently at first, then louder when there was no answer. "Dr. Barton, Mrs. Kline has been waiting in the exam room for you for 30 minutes. Will you see her shortly? She's getting frustrated."

Wyatt woke up from a brief micro sleep, his head snapping back up from his chest with Mrs. Kline's chart open in front of him. "Uh, yes Diane, I'm just finishing up some things, I'll be right there. Thank you."

When he walked into Mrs. Kline's room, his tie was only partly tied and his hair disheveled. Mrs. Kline was recently hospitalized for an MI and she had ten questions written down for Wyatt to answer.

Embarrassed that he was late, he knew he had to figure out something to say to Mrs. Kline, a nice patient that he'd followed for years. "I'm sorry I was so late, Linda. My last case was kinda complicated and well, took a lot of time."

"Sure doc, I understand, but you're worth the wait. Perhaps you'll give me some extra time in return."

Wyatt covered his mouth to try to hide the cavernous yawn. "Definitely I'll do that. I see you have a list of questions for me. I'll be happy to review them." He took the list of ten questions she'd meticulously written down for him to answer and stared at them, rubbing his eyes to focus on her cursive.

"I've known you for a long time, Dr. Barton, so I'm sure you don't mind me saying that you really look tired today. Your eyes are bloodshot. Are you okay?"

Wyatt smiled. "No I don't mind at all, and you're right. I am a little tired. You know, long night on call at the hospital, but you have my undivided attention."

He listened to her medical complaints, asked about whether she had any recurrent chest pain or shortness of breath, and examined her. He then answered her questions about diet, exercise limitations, salt intake, symptoms to expect in the future, and whether it was safe to fly to Europe. Satisfied, she agreed to make an appointment in three months for a stress test, and just before she left the room, she turned around and looked at Wyatt. "Dr. Barton, I called the on-call service last night to get a refill on my nitroglycerin, and you weren't on call. It's none of my business about what's going on with you, but I hope you're okay and can get it resolved."

He blushed with embarrassment, and knew there wasn't anything to say anymore to his perceptive patient with a motherly instinct. "Thanks Linda, everything's okay. Have a nice trip to Europe and I'll see you when you get back."

Wyatt dragged through the rest of the day as best he could, wishing he could be doing procedures instead. He desperately needed a coffee-driven energy pump to keep his mind focused away from the recent bizarre events at home.

At lunchtime, his receptionist came to his office, ignored the clutter of papers and coffee cups, and said, "Dr. Barton, we weren't going to have lunch brought in today, but we had a surprise delivery of a hot lunch today, courtesy of the hospital catheterization lab."

"Well, that's good news. Since when did they start sending us lunches? Heck, we should be buying them lunches for all the work they do for us. Oh well, this will save me a trip to the sandwich cart across the street."

After enjoying his hot lunch, he returned to his office refreshed and found Amy Adams sitting in front of his desk.

"This is a surprise! What are you doing here, Amy? Is there a case you wanted to talk about?"

"No, Dr. Barton, and nice to see you too. I arranged the lunch for you today and for your office staff, as a gesture of appreciation for what you and your partners do for the hospital cardiac service line. But at the same time, I have something special for you."

She handed him a card and asked him to open it in front of her.

"Now Amy, this is completely unnecessary. You know we..."

"Don't say anything more. Just open the card, Wyatt, I mean Dr. Barton."

He reluctantly opened the card, smelled the perfume she must've impregnated into the seal, and read it: *What an honor it is to work with you, Wyatt. The lunch is only a small sample of what you deserve. I hope our working relationship continues, and if you need anything at all, anything, here's my number. Let's have coffee again! Best regards, Amy.*

He looked at her and smiled, trying to avoid looking at how she crossed her lean legs and bounced her heels up and down while pointing them to accent her calf muscles. "This is all very kind of you, and I hope you have a good rest of the day in the lab. You must excuse me though, I have a one o'clock patient and I need to try to be on time now."

"No problem, Dr. Barton, you know where to find me if you need me."

He closed the door after she left, and put his head into both hands to try to figure all this out. *Nice to look at, but lethal to touch.*

CHAPTER 17

It was a Monday, and Wyatt's exhaustion had extracted its toll. A full morning awaited him in the catheterization lab, followed by a busy office load. Then the calls came in from Katherine. He took the calls because his heart ached for information from the kids, especially information that had some civility and truth. He would never extinguish his hope for a relationship with them.

"I'm taking the kids to Texas to stay with my mom for awhile and we will be looking for schools. I'm going to move the kids there."

"Like hell you are! You can't take the kids anywhere without a court order, and there hasn't even been a divorce yet. You do that and it's kidnapping."

"Just try me. You know, you caused all this, Wyatt. You and your fucking bimbos and lame excuses. Why are you so fucking rude? If you don't love me, just free me. Spencer even told me that he wants me to find someone else to be his dad."

Wyatt stopped and caught his breath. Whenever she talked about the kids, he somehow believed what she said. He felt in his heart that his kids just couldn't lie. The muscles in his neck spasmed like a frozen steak.

She continued while Wyatt maintained silence. "And you must know that I'll put a restraining order on you to keep you from the kids. I'll change the locks in case you have a hidden key to the house and I'm changing our home phone number to protect us from you. You abandoned us and abused us."

"You're insane. You can't take the kids away from me. I'm their father and have done nothing wrong except allow them to listen to your conniving lies!"

"Wyatt, I'm a good catch with some amazing sons and lots of men would love to have us. In fact, my friend Dave is happy as hell now that we're separated, and says I'm hot and he calls me 'sweetie.' He's going to take the three of us to his condo on Lake Michigan next weekend. So don't try to find us."

"Interesting. I thought Mark was your new hot boyfriend. Did he get smart and dump you already?"

She chuckled derisively. "When a good-looking woman is on the market, she receives tons of attention."

"Leave me alone. I've got to get back to my patients." Wyatt walked around the hospital corridor, trying to find a private place so no one could hear. "I'm sick and tired of you and all your bullshit."

"Have it your way, Wyatt, but I need to tell you one more thing before I hang up and cook dinner for our precious kids. My left saline breast implant is leaking ever since you beat me up the night of the Christmas party. I need to go to a plastic surgeon today and it may be that the left one needs replacing. Could you come over and watch the kids for me?"

"Well first of all I never beat you and you know it! Second, the kids are teenagers now and certainly don't need a babysitter, unless something has changed since I left."

"Oh, so you don't care about the kids? You won't come over and check on them while I'm gone? If that's how you feel, I'll have Mark come over and spend time with them."

Wyatt didn't know what she had planned, but his pride as a father would not allow another man to intervene; he needed to see them and talk.

"Okay, I will," said Wyatt.

He drove up to the front door of the house and rang the door-bell but no one answered. After waiting five minutes, he drove away and looked back to see Colby briefly steal a glance out of his upstairs bedroom window. Wyatt wondered if the kids really were alone and if

Katherine truly was at the surgeon's office for some other reason. He called the house, and Spencer answered.

"Hello Spence. Are you two okay?"

"Don't come near us, you idiot, or I'll call the police."

Wyatt's insides whipped like an upside-down roller-coaster ride and he realized he had been duped again, but worst of all, his love for his children was the weakness they easily preyed upon again.

The next day, a heavy load in the office crushed Wyatt again and he needed to stay focused on his patients and not his chaotic personal life. Between patients, he tried to make a quick call to see if Katherine actually had been at the plastic surgeon's office the day before.

"Esthetic Plastic Surgery Consultants," answered the cheery receptionist.

"Hello, this is Dr. Wyatt Barton. If it's possible, I would like to talk to the doctor about my wife's visit yesterday and the results of the findings." Wyatt was unsure if she would give out any information, but he was kind to her.

The receptionist hesitated, and then responded. "What is your wife's name?"

"Katherine Barton."

"Okay, I'll check to see when her appointment was and then I'll see if the doctor has a moment to talk to you. Will you be able to wait on hold for a few minutes, sir?"

"Sure. No problem."

Several minutes later, she returned to the phone. "I'm sorry, Doctor, but we have no record of your wife being here yesterday. In fact, we don't have her in our system as ever being a patient."

"I see. I must've been mistaken. I'm sorry. Thank you for your time and have a good day." His suspicions were true.

Wyatt went home to his apartment exhausted, mentally and

physically. He didn't have a couch, just one battered easy chair, and he fell asleep about seven pm. The phone next to him rang. Startled, he answered instinctively, thinking it was the hospital. "Hello, Dr. Barton."

"Of course I know who you are, Wyatt," answered Katherine.

Wyatt cursed at himself for not putting caller ID on. "What do you want now, Katherine? I need some sleep."

"Poor baby. I'm here taking care of our amazing children twenty-four/seven and you are in your little bachelor pad having fun without a care in the world. By the way, so many people tell me how wonderful our children are, and how horrible it is that you abandoned them. No father abandons his children. I want you to know that Colby was hurt at his hockey game tonight, but how would you know? You don't care or want to go."

"You know damn well Colby doesn't want me near him anymore. He told me that and that makes you happy, I'm sure. Now how did he get hurt?"

"He suffered a laceration to his hand during a body check when he didn't have his glove on. He has blood on his shirt, but he's okay now I think. Mark is here with Spencer and me and his assistant coach has given him wonderful first aid. Colby wants to talk to you and I'll hand the phone over."

Wyatt took a cavernous breath, preparing for the searing words from his son that would soon follow.

"I just want you to know that I told my coaches that my dad hurt my brother Spencer and me worse and bloodier at home than at the hockey game. I don't want to see you again, you deadbeat dad! Stay away from us."

"What?" Wyatt responded in shock. "I never hurt..."

Colby hung up before Wyatt could finish. His kids had mastered their lessons from Professor Katherine quite well. About an hour later, Spencer decided to call Wyatt back on Katherine's cell phone.

"What is it now, another contrived emergency?"

"Yeah, well, lots of the men at my school are better Christians and role models than you. I don't respect you and don't want to see you anymore. Yes, you're one of the perfect Bartons who don't care about us, only yourself. Mom is right."

Wyatt had had enough of the hateful words from his sons. "That's a nasty thing to say to your father, Spencer, and I won't tolerate that kind of language from you or your brother. If you can't talk to me in a civil way, then don't talk to me at all."

"Well then get used to it. You screwed up and so screw you," said Spencer. He hung up.

Colby took Spencer aside, out of earshot of Katherine who was engaged in a deep conversation with Mark. "Spence, I think we've been hitting Dad too hard lately. I feel bad. I know Mom says he's messed up a lot, but maybe we're too hard on him. We never hear him defend himself. I'm really pissed at him and all, but you know, something doesn't feel right. Everything is weird."

"You're cracked, Colby! He doesn't care about either of us and he doesn't love Mom. He runs around with bimbos. He hits her. C'mon, she needs better, and so do we. Let him live his life and leave us alone."

Colby walked away to the locker room, head down, biting his lip.

Wyatt's energy sucked away like a sinkhole on a sand dune. He sat in his chair for hours, unable to sleep because he had absolutely no idea what Katherine had put into their minds to turn them from him so harshly. He also wanted to knock some sense into his kids for their words. They needed a good old-fashioned ass kicking to straighten out their mommy-mimicking attitudes. He finally realized it was hopeless, and he decided to make an appointment with a lawyer to file for divorce. He had previously called him for advice and his advice was, "Stop the bleeding." Three months had passed since the separation and now it was time to end it with as much distance as possible between him and the evil bitch. At least that's what he hoped would happen.

The next day he arrived in his office early to do paperwork and found a postal letter on his desk. The return address was from a man he didn't recognize with a strange address that didn't make sense. The greeting read: "Dear Wyatt, from Pastor T." He then went on to read the rest of the strange letter:

I am the pastor for your wife and two lovely boys. They have received counseling from me at the church multiple times during your family crisis. I know that Katherine is a sweet, God-fearing woman and your two kids are brilliant with such spirit and love inside. Katherine so much wants to have a loving, warm family; yet you decided to throw this treasure of a family away. She is with them twenty-four / seven but wouldn't give them up for the world. You have failed your children, and there are many Godly men around to take your place. She blames herself for this separation, but clearly you are the one who has thrown away so much. I hope you can come to your senses and find some peace in your life.

Bizarre, Wyatt thought. Katherine never even went to church until he convinced her to. It's not Katherine's style of writing, so someone else wrote it, but clearly no pastor would ever write such a thing or he would be excommunicated from the church. He knew it was bogus but still effective in scrambling his mind a little more.

He then turned on his computer and opened another barrage of e-mails. He had been sending the kids some gentle e-mails telling them he loved them. In response, he opened up e-mails from the kids, sometimes using Katherine's address, and sometimes he believed Katherine wrote them using the kids' individual e-mail addresses:

You are a Jerk. Leave us alone. I hope you find happiness somewhere. Sorry you are so bad. Colby.

Stop e-mailing me and saying you love me or Happy Birthday. Go be with your blonde. Spencer.

One was written on Spencer's e-mail address, yet signed by Katherine: *Wyatt, your partners' wives are telling me that you need to come back on your knees to me. They all say they hate you for what you did and how you abandoned us. By the way, I am going to my lawyer's office tomorrow to file abuse charges against you. So be prepared.*

And another e-mail, also using Katherine's address: *I am Dave S., Katherine's sweetie. I've read some of your horrible e-mails to Katherine and the boys, and you should be ashamed of yourself. I've reviewed her financial records. She needs more money, and you are bleeding her.You have no idea how sweet Katherine is and how great your sons are. I'll be happy to take care of them.*

Wyatt turned off the computer and went about his day the best he could, his brain in a haze from the bizarre calls and e-mails. He had no idea who was writing what, and whether Katherine was writing all of them using the kids' accounts to fake their words into his head.

Later that evening, he prepared himself for an afternoon appointment with his lawyer. When he finally collapsed into bed, he received another call from her.

"What is it now, Katherine?The entire Chicago Bears team is coming to beat me up because they are in love with you?"

"Funny, you asshole. The kids told me to file abuse charges against you, Wyatt. Right, kids?"

"Yeah, do it," they both yelled into the receiver so Wyatt could hear.

"You're going to suffer some difficult days and years, mourning the loss of your two wonderful children," said Katherine. Wyatt could feel the almost giddy happiness in her voice when she uttered those horrible words no father should ever hear.

"Wyatt, if you come back to our circle of three, I won't file abuse charges, but if you don't come back, I will kill myself and the kids too."

There she goes again. Previously she said that if I do come back she would kill herself. She's confused with her story. She won't kill the boys; they are her weapon. Without them she is, in fact, nothing. This is all skillful manipulation. He wondered what a circle of three is. *Sounds more like devil's triangle.*

"First of all, Katherine, no man will come back home during a separation if his wife uses abuse as a weapon to get him back. If, in fact, I am as bad as you say I am and how you describe me to your friends, why would you say that you want me back? Second, you damn well won't kill yourself or the kids, because they are all you have, and they're powerful weapons you use to manipulate me. Maybe I should finally call the police on you for your threatening words. What do you think?"

"Well if you do, I will show them pictures of Spencer's wound and how you beat him. That will bury you. Anyway, you do what you have to do and you will suffer the consequences. I told you your choices. Anyway, I want you to know I love you though."

She slammed that word "love" into a nasty place. That was not the definition of love that he understood. But he would never stop in his quest to find real love that could obliterate the hate. He filed for divorce the first thing when the law offices opened the next day.

R. David Palmer had a small office. An older lawyer, he had seen many strange cases before and he was ready to warn and prepare Wyatt for the future.

"We're going to analyze your personal finances and business finances and Katherine's going to take an especially large chunk of both. Especially since she has no job skills and just a high school education. And, since Spencer is 17 and Colby is 15, they're going to pose a problem with regard to custody. At this age, we can't force them to live with you even though you may, in fact, be the more stable parent. They seem to have a lot of hatred from what you have described."

"That's for sure. But tell me; is she going to file for abuse even though it's bogus? That worries me not only because it's a lie, but also because of my reputation in the community. Will a court believe her?"

"No, she won't file. I see this all the time with some of these parents who try to alienate their spouses. Professionals will sniff through false charges easily. That's why I'll recommend that both counsel employ

Dr. Randolph Turner, a forensic psychologist, to make recommendations with regard to a parenting plan. This is going to be a rocky road for you, Wyatt, so be prepared."

"I understand. I look forward to meeting with Dr. Turner, and believe me, I'm prepared for anything so that I can be away from this woman. I can lose all my money, but it's killing me that I feel I have lost or am losing the kids whom I love. No amount of money can replace the loss of your children and contact with them. I'm nervous about filing for divorce and losing daily contact with my boys, but I'm sure I'll get co-custody or at least see them every other weekend and every other holiday.

"Yeah, I'm with you on that. Leave me your five thousand dollar retainer and I'll keep in touch."

Wyatt sent the psychologist a five thousand dollar deposit as well, hoping for a positive outcome in this parenting matter, and during the next six months, meetings with the psychologist and the Barton family occurred. Dr. Turner interviewed the kids first, then the parents separately. Wyatt remained hopeful that this professional would be able to sort out a positive plan for him and his kids, but the beleaguered cardiologist had no idea what was in store for him.

CHAPTER 18

Wyatt arrived to his appointment at Dr. Turner's office fifteen minutes early, and filled out extensive background forms, intelligence tests, and finally the MMPI personality inventory. Turner told him to come back the next day after he'd analyzed the material. He was his first client the next morning.

"Hello Wyatt. I'm pleased that we're finally able to meet. May I get you some water or soda?"

"Sure. I'll have bottled water if you don't mind." Wyatt chuckled. "I think I'll need it."

Dr. Turner walked over to the small refrigerator in his office and retrieved cold bottled water for Wyatt, but didn't respond to his comment. He then began the interview.

"By the way, you can call me 'Randy.' I know this separation and divorce process has been difficult on you, especially with your lack of contact with your boys," said Dr. Turner. "I'm told you haven't seen your boys since the separation four months ago."

"That's true. It's been a challenge to say the least—more severe than I could ever have imagined."

"I've already interviewed your soon-to-be ex-wife as well as your kids. I have also reviewed your MMPI and the other mental status tools you filled out. I know a significant amount about the situation already, but I saved you for my last interview. As you know, the court has asked me, at your expense, to formulate a parenting plan and also to investigate certain claims that your wife has made against you."

"Understood."

"Let me ask you directly. Did you abuse your wife physically, or your kids physically or sexually at any time?"

"Absolutely not! Never." Wyatt jumped up from the couch, paced a few steps around Randy's cramped office, then sat back down on the couch. "You've got to be kidding, Randy! This lie she produced is ripping me apart."

"Katherine has accused you of physically abusing her and also physically abusing Spencer. She's also suggested sexual abuse of the kids as well. I won't go into the details of the conversations, but I have absolutely no question that these are fabricated charges made by her to gain some advantage against you with the kids. I just needed to hear it from you. Unfortunately I see this all the time in cases of severe parental alienation created by one spouse against the other, but this is a severe case, perhaps the worst case I've seen in my practice since I started 20 years ago."

Wyatt didn't comment, just looked at Randy without emotion.

"There's something more I must tell you."

"Go ahead. Nothing surprises me anymore."

"Your ex has severe Borderline Personality Disorder. Are you aware of this disorder, Wyatt?"

Wyatt shifted his body uncomfortably on the three-cushion couch; a feeling of dark anticipation was creeping up his straight spine. "No, I must admit I am not familiar with that disorder. Psych was obviously not my best rotation in medical school."

"I try to limit my practice with Borderlines because they are so difficult to treat, and there are unfortunately no medications to help them. Furthermore, they tend to try to manipulate the therapist and are very resistant to treatment. I recommend the book *I Hate You; Don't Leave Me* by Kreisman and Straus. But today I want to give you a brief overview so that you can understand what you are dealing with and why you are in the position you are in."

Wyatt listened intently to Dr. Turner, and felt relieved and vindicated that finally a professional had diagnosed Katherine as having a personality disorder. This would give him an advantage with regard to custody. He knew her behavior over the years had been abnormal and difficult to tolerate, but he was not able to classify it himself. It did remind him of the distant hallucinations about monkeys she had had when they were first married. It appears the neurologists were wrong about the migraines as the cause. "Okay, I'm ready to hear it, but it feels like I'm about to receive a lecture from the psych professor; I'm like an anxious second-year medical student hoping to hear a *One Flew over the Cuckoo's Nest*–type story."

Randy forced a weak smirk but continued unfazed. "It may be that between fifteen and twenty-five percent of patients who go to psychiatrists are afflicted with BPD, and it is the most common of all personality disorders. Interestingly, despite its prevalence it's relatively unknown to the public. Borderlines can be sicker than neurotic patients, but perhaps less sick than psychotic patients. It is a very difficult illness for the professional to define adequately, treat, or explain to the patient."

"I wish I had known this before I married her. But then, I should've known."

"What do you mean?"

"Never mind. Go on. I need to know more about this. What criteria do you use to make the diagnosis?"

"When you read Kreisman and Straus and a couple other journal articles I'll give you, you'll see there are eight criteria. I'll read them for you: 1) Unstable and intense interpersonal relationships. 2) Impulsiveness in potentially self-damaging behaviors such as sex, substance abuse, shoplifting, and binge drinking. 3) Severe mood shifts. 4) Frequent and inappropriate displays of anger. 5) Recurrent suicidal threats or gestures or self-mutilating behaviors. 6) Lack of a clear sense of identity. 7) Chronic feelings of emptiness or boredom. 8) Frantic efforts to avoid real or imagined abandonment." (1)

"I can see that Katherine had almost all of these criteria," said Wyatt with quiet resignation. "Go on, Professor, I'm soaking it all in."

"Severe case."

"Did you tell her the diagnosis?"

"Yes, I did, and I told her that she needed treatment by a well-trained psychologist or therapist, but she blew up and said the problem was not hers, but yours. Therefore, it is unlikely she will get help on her own or accept it. I would like to touch on a few major points that you need to know about BPD before we conclude our session today. Is that okay?"

"Sure, go ahead. I'm learning a lot. But you know, Randy, I need to take a breather because this is all difficult to take in at once, especially for a man who lived with this so many years, hoping it would improve and love would take over somehow."

"Of course. There's a public restroom in the hallway outside and some vending machines by the elevator. Let's meet back in five minutes."

Flooding nausea burst up from his stomach, and he splashed cold water on his face in the restroom in an attempt to clear his head. To his relief, no one else was in the restroom to witness his angst. He left after a few minutes, bought a Sprite to calm his shaking stomach, and returned to Randy's office to resume the painful but educational session.

"One of the major components of BPD is that of identity diffusion. This means that patients cannot answer these questions: 'Who am I?' 'What do I want?' 'How can I be differentiated from everyone else?' They essentially don't know who they are and have an unstable and fragile sense of self. The other major component is that of unstable relationships. They are dependent and clingy and prone to manipulation, hypochondriasis and suicidal threats to gain attention, and helplessness." (2)

"Unbelievable to hear this. This has been my life with her. Should've gotten rid of her a long time ago."

"I see. Do you know what 'splitting' is?"

"Obviously you mean something different than splitting hairs."

"It's central to BPD. It means the BPD patient believes a person is either good or evil, but there is no in-between zone. For example, the afflicted individual may adore someone one day and completely dismiss him or her as evil the next day. It is the main defense mechanism for these patients." (1)

"Well, that explains why she says she loves me after she tells me she wants me gone because I'm evil. But tell me, will my children be at risk for this disorder also, or is there some hope that they can put up a defense against it and live their lives in reality?"

"I wish it was a simple virus like the flu and we could vaccinate the children against it. But yes, unfortunately, the boys are at risk and it seems they're already showing some of these traits cultivated within them by their mother. The data is clear that children of mothers with BPD are at greater risk of emotional, behavioral, and somatic problems. They need early treatment to prevent them from developing significant psychopathology later in life." (3)

"Now that you've brought this to my attention and I think about some of her behavior, she seems psychotic at times. Worse than just a personality disorder. Is that a separate process or part of the disorder?"

"BPD may be associated with another disorder such as schizophrenia or depression. Like a patient with schizophrenia, a patient with BPD can demonstrate agitated, psychotic episodes, but these are less common over time in BPD. Both disorders can cause self-destructive behaviors. But it's important to know that a Borderline usually can function quite well in society, while the schizophrenic is much more likely to be impaired socially." (1)

"Randy, this is much more information than I can handle right now. The main thing is I am away from this woman, and I need to be as far away as possible from this evil snake."

Dr. Turner's receptionist opened the door and interrupted. "Excuse me, Dr. Turner, but I must tell you that Mrs. Barton is holding on the phone. She called to say there's a family emergency."

Dr. Turner frowned and looked at Wyatt. "You see, she's up to her tricks now. She knew we were in session."

"Tell your staff the only way to handle the witch is to hang up on her immediately."

"Annie," said Dr. Turner, "please ask her what the nature of the emergency is."

After a few minutes Annie came back, obviously nervous about what she'd just heard from Katherine on the phone. "She says their son Colby got hurt today at school."

Wyatt rolled his eyes. "Not this crap again."

Dr. Turner responded immediately. "You tell her to take him to the emergency room or primary physician and seek medical help the best way possible. Dr. Barton is unavailable right now. If this is a real emergency we will hear about it later."

"Thanks, Randy. Now you see her in action with her manipulations. She frequently tries the 'kids are hurt' ploy, and they're hardly ever hurt when she plays the game. I assume you're going to tell the court she's an unfit mother, right? Clearly I deserve complete custody of those kids!"

"No I won't say that."

"Wyatt's face flushed. "You're kidding me! I think she should be in jail for what she's done to those kids! C'mon, Randy, go to bat for me. She makes evil she-devils look like schoolgirls. There's an avalanche roaring down the mountain straight at me, and I need some help to either stop it or sidestep it before it causes a disaster."

"I'll tell the court that there is no evidence of abuse by you on your family, and that your children absolutely need contact with you in their life, but unfortunately, they're obviously not ready. They will live with their mother while I work with you to get your relationships with your kids back. You are clearly a positive influence on their lives, but that has been taken away from them by their mother."

"This whole thing smells and makes me nauseous." He stood up and started for the door. "I've had enough, and I need to go."

"Wait, Wyatt, you must understand that there is no evidence she did anything illegal or that she physically abused the kids. The kids have expressed to me their hatred of you, misplaced as it is. If I recommend that the court take the kids away from her, they would have no place to stay except in a home somewhere decided by the state. They are both over fourteen, and can make their choice of what parent to live with. Not only that, if I told the court the details of my findings, they would potentially declare her disabled, and you would have to pay for her the rest of her life. You don't want that now, do you?"

"Wasn't aware of that part."

"The kids say they love their mother and want to live with her, so that's how we will leave it. I will also recommend she get mental-health treatment and the kids absolutely will need it too. I will make it optional for you, only because I think you will need counseling and support to get through this. I have some names of some good counselors for you to see. And finally, I want to try a technique to get your kids to talk to you, but this will be relatively gentle on them but difficult on you."

"Yeah, it always falls on me, doesn't it? Seems I'm always the guilty one. But it's okay, Randy; people tell me my shoulders can carry heavy loads when they need to. Now I feel what Ayn Rand meant with the title *Atlas Shrugged*."

Randy smiled graciously. "Nice analogy. The kids told me they can't talk to you because apparently they believe that you don't listen to them; right or wrong, I must hear them out. So, I'll arrange for Katherine to leave your marital house for several hours, and then you and I will come and meet the kids. I'll allow them to vent all of their concerns and angst towards you, but you will not be allowed to speak at all or respond to their accusations. You must simply sit and listen. I'll be the monitor so that they don't overstep the boundaries I set."

"With all due respect, this sounds like a draconian plan, almost like an interrogation of a prisoner of war in his own home. Better yet, why don't you just tie my hands and legs up and lay me on the couch and let them beat me with their fists; physical pain seems to me to be more tolerable than this mental abuse you're considering letting them smother me with. Tell me, have you put anyone else through this hell?"

"No, not really, but I think it's the best way to take a step forward with your kids and improve your relationship eventually down the road. It'll be tough for you. Are you willing to give it a try?"

"Not sure. I'll have to think about it. But then, you're the expert. I know about heart disease but this is way out of my field. I'll try just about anything, I guess, if there's hope I can save my kids and repair my relationship with them. I'll let you know once I make my decision. Have a good day."

Wyatt felt some relief that he now had a diagnosis for Katherine, but completely frustrated by the bizarre solution that now confronted him. *If I agree to this, it will be like agreeing to have my fingernails pulled out one by one by needle-nose pliers while being forbidden to scream out in pain.*

CHAPTER 19

The date arrived for Wyatt and Dr. Turner to meet the kids with their father remaining mute while they grilled him with their concerns and gripes. The prisoner was soon to be tortured officially with the blessing of the court-appointed psychologist/executioner. It was going to be a Saturday morning when he was not on call. That was a week away, but the onslaught from the kids continued like a breakaway dam explosion. The harsh words now erupted almost exclusively from the mouth of Spencer. It had been almost six months since he filed for divorce officially, and Katherine, the boys, Mark, and his children were all allegedly on vacation on some island in the Caribbean. Wyatt learned of this from an e-mail he received, supposedly sent by "Colby's and Spencer's buds."

We're all down here in the Virgin Islands having a great time. Mom's boyfriend, Mark, is cool, and he's taking us all sailing. You never did that. Hope you're feeling sad, Wyatt, cause you really screwed up and threw away a cool family. Remember the late Terri Schiavo who was on the TV? Her parents wanted to hold her close and cherish every moment, but you, Wyatt, will never do that with us. You're probably at home playing with yourself. Signed, Colby and Spencer.

As usual, he couldn't verify who wrote these bizarre e-mails. It could've been Katherine masquerading as the kids, or the kids writing for themselves. Each time he read the hateful e-mails his hopes of a kind word vanished, and his heart ripped once more with a sharp arrow imbedded with poisonous venom. After they returned from the islands, Wyatt received a phone call from Spencer. He hadn't heard the word "Dad" in a long time and figured he never would again.

"Wyatt, Mom showed me her diary where she entered that you told her you wanted to abort me as a fetus! This shows you are an evil man, and Colby and I do not ever want to see you again. I have her diary entry as proof. You are a bastard, and we no longer want to keep the Barton name."

"You've got to be kidding! I never said the word 'abort' to your mother. That's a nasty lie that should never be told to a child! In fact, I delivered you two kids and I love you both. Your mom fabricated that entry and is a liar, my son."

"Whatever. I no longer believe anything you say, and don't use the word 'love' with us. You're the liar. In fact, stop sending us cards or calling us during birthdays and holidays. Leave us alone forever, and let us live our lives happily without you."

Wyatt sighed slowly and deeply. His voice turned quiet and distant. "I'm sorry you feel that way, Son. Good-bye."

He stared angrily at the phone as if it were a snarling dog that had just bitten his hand after he gave it his favorite food. His control evaporated. He grabbed the phone and threw it against the wall, splitting the plaster. *It's hopeless. The kids are gone and I doubt that Turner's plan will be of any benefit at all. You slimy bitch, Katherine! You destroyed them and took their innocent little hearts and minds from me.*

Wyatt arrived at the home he'd previously lived in and built for Katherine, and immediately felt like a stranger. The house reminded him of a cold funeral parlor. Turner met him in the driveway, and the two walked up the steps, rang the chiming doorbell, and Spencer answered the door and allowed them into the spacious foyer. Wyatt said hello, but Spencer said nothing. Wyatt remembered the black leather furniture, the sterile smell, and the grandiosity of Katherine's expensive Greek column décor topped off with massive chandeliers. Dr. Turner and Wyatt sat on one sofa that directly faced Colby and Spencer sitting on the opposite facing couch eight feet away. It felt like dueling couches: one couch was loaded with cannons and howitzers and the other couch fired back with forced silence. Wyatt said hello to Colby and, like Spencer, he didn't return the greeting. Dr. Turner then took control and began the session promptly.

"Spencer, is your mother gone?"

"Yeah, she went to a friend's house for two hours."

"Good. Let's begin. Here are the rules. You boys can take turns making statements to your father about your concerns with him and his actions as a father when he lived with you. I told your father that he is not to respond verbally to you at all. I ask that you refrain from using foul language or degrading comments to your father or I will terminate this session. Is that clear, boys?"

"Yes," they said in unison.

Spencer went first. "Wyatt, you never think we're good enough. I was in a state history contest and got fifth place, but you thought it was not good enough. So then, you helped me find study techniques that would help me on the next competition. But I didn't ask for that. When I played baseball, you would always teach me and give me pointers on how to swing the bat effectively after a game, if I didn't get a hit. You made me look bad."

Wyatt looked at him directly and shook his head.

"Worse than that," Colby interjected, interrupting his brother, "you don't love Mom and you never did. You hit her in the face several times, and that means you're not a good man or father. No man should do that to his wife. Not only that, Mom says you were not paying us child support or alimony for us to live on. You should be ashamed. She loved you so much and now you have destroyed your family."

"Colby, those are very serious accusations to make against your father. Did you see him hit your mother?" asked Turner.

Colby looked down to the floor to avoid Wyatt's eyes. "Well no, but Mom told us several times. So, you know, it must be true. She's a good mother who cares for us and does everything possible for us. She wouldn't lie."

"You also had an affair," Spencer chimed in. "We know it. We know why you came home late sometimes. One of our friends even saw you at a coffee shop with a blonde recently after you moved out of the house. I even heard you on the phone sometimes talking to someone when you were at our games, and that must've been a woman, I'm sure. That means you are guilty of adultery and thus you ruined your marriage to a perfect loving wife. Dr. Turner, I would like to read some scripture for Wyatt to hear. Is that okay, Dr. Turner?"

"I suppose so, but make it quick. And don't you boys call him 'Dad' or 'father' anymore? Just Wyatt?"

"No, he doesn't deserve to be called 'Dad.' Spencer pulled out a small Bible from his backpack. There were yellow pieces of paper marking the scriptures he wanted to read. "Now I will read Matthew 5:27 and 28. 'You have heard that it was said, *Do not commit adultery*. But I tell you that anyone who looks at a woman lustfully has already committed adultery in his heart.' How many times have you done this, Wyatt?"

Wyatt stared at him, unflinchingly, as instructed.

"I will now finish with verse 32. 'But I tell you that anyone who divorces his wife except for marital unfaithfulness causes her to become an adulteress, and anyone who marries the divorced woman commits adultery.' Okay, now I have one more passage about divorce. Luke 16:18: 'Anyone who divorces his wife and marries another woman commits adultery, and the man who marries a divorced woman commits adultery.' So look, you jerk, what you have done to Mom! By the way, you are unchristian, even though you took us to church when we were younger. You don't even know any Bible verses, do you?"

"Now that's enough, Spencer," said Turner. "I told you not to use degrading words. I'm wrapping this session up now. Do either one of you have anything more to say to your father?"

"No," said Colby as he continued to look down at the floor, avoiding his father's eyes, unlike the piercing stare Spencer was giving his father. "Enough's been said already."

"Yes, I have something more," said Spencer. "You're an evil man for telling Mom that she needed to abort me when I was a fetus. Why would she write that in her journal if it wasn't true? I really don't have any love for you and don't care for you at all."

Wyatt looked at him, but the boiling that he was controlling in his stomach the whole session was about to explode and he felt he would lose control of his emotions, so he looked away from the children he loved so they couldn't see his face. He recovered quickly, and Turner ended the session, walking out with Wyatt who walked quickly with eyes fixed sullenly towards the ground.

In the driveway, standing next to their cars, Turner tried to comfort him.

"'Honor your father and your mother, so that you may live long in the land the Lord your God has given you.' Exodus, chapter twenty, the Ten Commandments," said Wyatt. "That's the Bible verse I wanted to recite in response to Spencer's ridiculous tirade if I you would've allowed it. Difference is I would've cut out the 'mother' part. Those kids have become like their mother, and I no longer believe that my flesh and blood could act that way and say those things about me. That was the nastiest ordeal I've had to endure in my life, to maintain control of my mouth and my emotions in that trash-talking, shit-flinging session from my sons that you created."

"Of course it was difficult to not be able to respond. I don't know how effective it was in making progress with the kids, though."

"I would say that it was at best, brutal, and the worst words a father could imagine hearing from his children. I'm outta here."

"Do you want us to schedule another session, maybe gradually allowing you to make comments while the kids become more comfortable?"

"No way. I really have no stomach for this crap you came up with.

I think the only solution that the kids will understand is for me to kick their spoiled mommy-boy asses. Too bad the court won't sanction that, Randy! I've laid down and let them hit me and kick me, hoping they will come back to reality but it won't work, Turner, and you know it. I'm beginning to wonder if they're not my kids genetically at all and Katherine enjoyed a nighttime tryst with a visitor from the prison early-release program years ago."

The judge finalized the divorce after nearly two years of separation. Spencer had just graduated from high school, and Colby finished his junior year. Due to Katherine's lack of education and training after high school and poor employability coupled with Wyatt's success as a physician, she received a larger than normal alimony award per month—half as much per month as most families earn per year and twice the Illinois allowance. Wyatt was to pay the mortgage on the house while he lived in a small one-bedroom apartment partially furnished with ragged used furniture.

As far as the kids, Dr. Turner told the court there was no evidence at all that Wyatt committed spousal or child abuse and the boys would live with their mother, as their strong preference. All efforts would be made to allow the kids contact with the father, as this was felt to be important to Dr. Turner. However, since they weren't ready, he advised that Katherine receive professional mental-health services and the kids receive counseling as well, all at Wyatt's expense.

Struggling both emotionally and financially, he took Dr. Turner's advice and sought help from both a different psychologist and a counselor to help him deal with his devastating loss.

The counselor proved helpful but direct and realistic. "Dr. Barton, I reviewed your case with Dr. Turner, and here's my recommendation: you may or may not ever see your kids again and I believe theoretically there is perhaps a fifty percent lifetime chance you'll ever have a relationship again with your sons, but realistically they're too far gone for you to have any hope, sad to say. They're completely under the influence of their mother."

"That's for sure. Their previously innocent young minds have been rewired with mommy-built zombie neurons, bathed in Katherine's homemade witch's nutrients. Too bad there's no law to protect the kids from her brainwashing. The only solution is that she needs to be a prison princess, or better yet, shipped off to some gulag in Siberia enduring forced labor the rest of her life."

The counselor enjoyed a good chuckle. "She has refused psychological help or counseling, and after one session with the kids, she pulled them out of therapy. The only way I see for this to improve is for them to go to a deprogramming camp for about a month. You would have to attend with them, but the problem is the rule that you must have custody in order to qualify for the camp. Unfortunately, you don't have custody so that's not an option for you. I worry for you, though. You are letting them destroy you emotionally by constantly allowing them to contact you either by e-mail or phone. You need to stop all contact to protect your mental health."

"Really? What if they need my help in some way?"

"You've got to stop thinking like that, Wyatt. They don't want your help. In fact, I'm sure you're not going to want to hear this, but your kids don't care about you at all. If there is an emergency, they will know how to find you and inform you, but again, I want you to stop the contact, for your own health. You absolutely must block their e-mails and phone calls completely, and try to live your life without them. Find a good woman, and hopefully you now have better judgment with women. Fall in love and enjoy life the best you can, but be prepared that you may not ever have your children again. I want you to travel or maybe play more golf or something. It's time for you now, not them."

He felt a heavy boulder drop away from his shoulders.

CHAPTER 20

Wyatt read the poster announcing a lecture outside the hospital auditorium: *Virology and the Potential for Biological Terrorism, by M. Liepa, PhD*. Unfortunately, he rarely had the time to listen to a lecture and was even less likely to eat lunch sitting down. He welcomed the momentary lull in his hectic schedule and ate a provided box lunch while waiting impatiently for the lecture to begin.

Dr. Liepa strolled from her seat up front to the podium and when he saw her, Wyatt studied her carefully, putting down his sandwich so he wouldn't drop it on his white coat. She walked with the grace of a prima ballerina while maintaining the poise of an Olympic diver moving calmly to the edge of the ten-meter platform.

He stared at her the entire lecture, focused on her lecture completely, ignoring her European accent because her knowledge of the subject was impressive. She awoke within him such a strong desire to learn more about her that he completely forgot to eat lunch, and only occasionally would try to put the sandwich in his mouth, but he missed and his lunch ended up in his lap; his nutrition fell victim to his eyes, mesmerized by a speaker the staff was so lucky to hear. When Dr. Liepa stepped down from the stage, the usually shy Dr. Barton couldn't help but rush up to meet her before others surrounded her to ask questions.

"Excuse me, Dr. Liepa, but I just wanted to say that I enjoyed your lecture very much. Very impressive," said Wyatt. *Although I don't remember anything you said because you completely hypnotized me.*

"Thank you, sir. I am happy that you liked it. You must be a physician here at St. Anthony. And you are...?"

"Wyatt Barton." They shook hands, and he forced himself not to linger too long in her hand.

"Nice to meet you." She laughed easily. "I hope my lecture didn't last too long. I know it's hard to concentrate during lunch."

"Well, let's just say you had my complete attention. By the way, I love your accent. It must be Eastern European but I just can't pin it down."

"I understand. I hear that all the time. I am from Latvia. Riga, Latvia."

Wyatt smiled. "You are the first person from Latvia that I've met. I heard during your introduction that you are a professor here at the Medical School. That's impressive, Dr. Liepa."

"Call me Marta and yes, thank you. I was lucky that the U.S. invited me here to accept the position. Today I was quite nervous because this is my first large lecture in English. You see, when I came here I didn't know any English, and it has taken me a long time to learn enough English at evening community college classes so that I can communicate effectively. Problem is that I think the mice in my lab only understood English and they wouldn't cooperate when I spoke Latvian."

He laughed loudly. "Yeah, our mice here are not multilingual. Typical Americans. Do you have time to join me for coffee?" He had work to do, but his fascination for Marta couldn't be controlled. It had been a long time since he'd so aggressively pursued a woman, but his actions just flowed naturally.

"Yes, that would be great!" said Marta. "It is unusual that I would turn down good coffee."

The two walked across the street from the hospital to Starbucks, and Wyatt felt the stares of men watching Marta walking with him, and he felt proud to be with her. He ordered a double shot espresso for Marta and a red eye for himself, while Marta captured a cozy table near the window by the street.

"What type of physician are you?"

"I'm a cardiologist with Premier Cardiology."

"I see. That means you can fix broken hearts."

He chuckled. "I guess, in a manner of speaking." He enjoyed her quick wit, wide smile, and the way she looked him straight in the eye.

"Speaking of heart disease, seems we have a connection there, Wyatt. Some years ago my lab was one of the first to isolate the possible connection between Chlamydia Pneumoniae infection and vascular disease. Fascinating subject really."

"Yes, I've read some of the studies on that. Where was your lab?"

"At that time I was doing my post-doctoral fellowship at the University of Cambridge. We found Chlamydia Pneumoniae in atherosclerotic lesions by both electron microscopy and immunocytochemical staining in coronary lesions as well as in other areas of vasculature."

"Interesting, but it's a complex issue isn't it? You've got lots of bad guys in the mix causing these plaques: family history, HDL, LDL, C-reactive protein, homocysteine, inflammation, and now you say infection?"

"Well, as you know, the data isn't strong and causative right now, but yes, it's a field that fascinated me for some time, but now, my real love is virology as I mentioned in my lecture. I'm monitoring outbreaks of avian flu throughout the world because those are the potential worldwide epidemics that we need to control because they can spread so fast and kill easily."

He immersed himself in her scientific background and forgot to drink his coffee.

"I'm just a cardiologist working the front lines of patient care, saving lives when we can, but prevention is key. We need dedicated scientists like you to bring the research to us and apply it to daily patient care."

"Thanks. Someday, if you don't mind, I'd like to round with you in the hospital to see how a practicing physician applies some of the science we do in the lab."

Wyatt's smile now almost hurt it was so wide. "Well sure, anytime just call me and I'll show you around the cardiac intensive care unit and the catheterization lab." Then he hesitated, looked away, then back at her. "Are you single?"

Marta laughed. "You don't see a wedding ring, do you?"

"No. Excellent point. Have you ever been married?"

"Yes, divorced several years ago. I have one son, Linas, who is 15."

"Does he enjoy the United States, or is he finding it a difficult transition?"

"Oh no, he loves it here. In fact, he's beginning to find American girls interesting, and loves how they dress!"

"Yes, it's too bad girls didn't dress like that when I was his age," said Wyatt.

"Too bad? And you are saying that you were deprived of feminine charms because of that? Somehow I find it hard to believe you were in a Puritan society."

"Well, no, you got me there I guess."

"You know, I can't help but notice that you have blue eyes to match the color of your scrub shirt, only your eyes are a brighter blue," said Marta. "But I seem to detect some pain in your soul that is deep inside."

Wyatt was amazed at how easy Marta was to talk to. For some reason the two newly acquainted professionals easily dropped their guards enough to talk comfortably about their lives, even though they had just met. "Really? That's interesting. How did you know that?"

"I have an ability to read people and understand them quickly."

He sighed. "Yes, I have pain, you're right, but that's a story that I won't bore you with."

"Okay. But I don't mind hearing about your life some time, Wyatt. You seem like a nice man in a good profession, smart and educated. I am alone here in America and I need to have some educated friends if I can. You know, someone to talk about politics or life issues with. I've met some interesting men here in America, but they are too aggressive to me. You know, they want intimacy so quickly. You seem to have some rare qualities that I haven't seen very often."

Flashing bordeaux as fast as a light switch, his face displayed a sheepish smile. "What do you mean?"

"I think you are honest, with a good heart, it seems."

"I don't know what to say now," said Wyatt. "You didn't mention my bulging muscles!"

Marta giggled. "Well you know I didn't want to stare. You are single, no?"

"Well, yes. I am divorced now too."

"I see. Was it difficult?"

"Yes, extremely brutal."

"I am sorry, Wyatt. Really. Do you have children?"

"Thanks but don't feel sorry for me. I escaped from hell. And yes, two boys."

"Thankfully you at least have your sons to spend some fun time with. I think in America you people play baseball with them in the summer, eat hotdogs, and then American football in the winter. That is important, right?"

"No, my children are gone, for years now. Do we really have to talk about this? There are so much more pleasant subjects to discuss."

"I am sorry. When did they die?"

Wyatt paused, took a deep breath before responding. "No, that's the difficult part. They're alive, but I've had no contact with them for several years now except when they send me words of anger and rejection. I never thought I would lose my kids while they were still alive. I loved them very much, but they were purposefully alienated from me by their evil mother, and therefore, they have rejected me completely and send me only words of hate."

Marta squirmed in her seat. "Well, most kids who are victims of a divorce spend some time with both parents. I've heard of some parents who are in prison, but still have their kids visit them. I don't know how to say this, and I know we just met, but it seems to someone on the outside that you may have done bad things to your children, or maybe you ran away and didn't pay child support or alimony."

Wyatt found himself taken aback by her direct and honest statement and his face turned pale as beach sand while he quickly shot back, "No, nothing could be further from the truth! I suppose people who don't know me could easily be led to believe I was a bad father or husband, and that was Katherine's method to destroy me. Maybe it worked, I don't know. But people who know me understand that I could never abuse the kids or my ex-wife. On the contrary, she abused me with her machinations and manipulations. As far as money goes, I'm paying her ridiculous amounts of money for alimony and child support. It's been a struggle for me financially, but the financial burden doesn't in any way compare to the loss of my children's love. All I receive from Katherine and the kids is hatred and bizarre manipulations despite all the money I send them. So, no, I am not a deadbeat dad, and I did not abuse or abandon my family. Really Marta, I don't want to talk about this anymore."

"Oh my. I believe you. I'm sorry and I wish you the strength to survive, Wyatt. Be strong. I believe you are a good person, though. It is refreshing to meet a man with your background and kindness."

Wyatt recovered from his offense at her innocent opinion. He understood she was stating the obvious from an outsider's viewpoint, and it wasn't her fault. "Thanks Marta. I'm honored to have met you, and thanks for sharing your time with me after your lecture."

"As I said, I can look into your eyes and see good things. I don't spend time with men who are not good inside."

Just as they were ending their conversation, Marta received a call on her cell phone. "Oh, hi, Gavin. Yes, you're right. It's been a long time. No, I'm busy right now, but we can talk later. Thanks for the call."

Wyatt found himself immersed in thought while they walked out of Starbucks. She clearly is an example of how Europeans easily conquered the American continent years ago. They both agreed to meet for coffee again sometime when their schedules allowed, and maybe after coffee a day of rounding together in the hospital. The phone call showed Wyatt he had competition for Marta's affection, but he was not surprised. Wyatt was not a man to back away from competition, especially when the prize was such a rare diamond.

Gavin is a name that sounds familiar, but I can't place it.

CHAPTER 21

Six years after the divorce became finalized, Spencer Barton was in his senior year at the University of Illinois, and his brother, Colby, was in his sophomore year at Northwestern. Colby lived in a dormitory, and once or twice a week, the brothers enjoyed a hamburger cookout at Spencer's on-campus apartment. Katherine still expected them to come home most weekends, and they complied the best they could to avoid stress. The boys always came home during the holidays, birthdays, and especially Mother's Day. Father's Day was the only named holiday that they didn't observe because they still would not acknowledge to anyone that they had a father. They never called or had contact with their father.

Father's Day, at least for him personally, was the holiday Wyatt learned to avoid and ignore almost entirely, except he did treat his father quite well on that day. However, because he was no longer treated as a father himself, he felt a complete disconnect when he watched the sweet Father's Day commercials on TV and radio ads honoring families and kids and what Father's Day gifts were the best to go with baseball and apple pie. It had been at least four years since he'd received a call or a card from his kids, and that single Father's Day card he received remained painfully etched in his memory forever: a nice picture of a father and his two young sons fishing on a dock on a blue lake surrounded by a dense forest, but inside, the words "Happy Father's Day" were crossed out by a pen. Below it was the cursive writing of Spencer: *You may be our biological father but you are not our Dad. Signed, Spencer and Colby.* His heart endured the searing pain he was experiencing all too often. He ripped the card into pieces. That night, Wyatt immersed himself in large quantities of the liquid pleasures provided by his old friend Jack. J.D. was a friend that was always there for him, and although he eased his pain only temporarily, and only added to his problems, Jack continued to demand more and more of his attention, and he obliged him frequently, sometimes culminating in passing out on the couch, numb from any pain.

Spencer used crack cocaine and Ecstasy on occasion, but he didn't consider himself an addict. He seemed to be able to control his cravings for the powerful drugs, but he used amphetamines to stay up all night and cram for exams. He enjoyed the heightened sense of arousal and clearness of mind that the drugs provided him. Occasionally he would hallucinate while on them, but they were usually sexual hallucinations that he craved. He never told Colby about his drug use, and certainly he would never tell Katherine, because he didn't want to hurt her of all people. However, in spite of his crack use, he was in the top one percent of his class. His friends and instructors considered him a model student; he was polite and intelligent and had a sharp mind. Lisa, his girlfriend, thought he was a good man that maybe had potential for marriage, especially because it seemed he was a shoe-in for law school. He thought Lisa was special, but neither one of them was sure that love was what they had together. Spencer hid much below the surface that Lisa couldn't see. A phone call woke him up in his apartment.

"Yeah."

"Hey, Spence, haven't seen or heard from you in a while," said his friend Jerry Thompson.

"Been studying for the LSAT exam to get into law school. What's goin' on?"

"Well, I should study too, but I might not take the LSAT until next year. My after-school business is doing well now, and I'm in no hurry. Life is good."

"Must be nice. I'm not independently wealthy like you are. My dad has money, but my mom says he didn't give her any after the divorce. He's a selfish jerk who sure as hell didn't care about us."

Jerry laughed. "Are you sure, Spence? Doesn't quite make sense to me that he would throw the relationship with his two sons away so easily. Matter of fact, I'm sure the court probably made sure he paid lots of money to your mother in alimony and child support after the divorce, and I'll bet the check your mother sends you for tuition comes from his support to her. By the way, where do you get the money to pay me for your shit if it didn't come from your dad's alimony and child support?"

"I asked Mom for extra allowance money. She never asked why and I never thought of where she got the money. I just tell her that I need lots of new clothes and suits and stuff to prepare for my eventual acceptance into law school. As far as my dad, yeah, I'm sure he's a dud 'cause my mom tells me that."

"You're a smart guy, Spence, but that's the dumbest thing I've heard come from you. There you go with your mother again. You are sure a momma's boy but you'll never listen to me. I may not have your brains and good grades, but I'm 'world smart.' I don't really understand your family situation, but I think in some ways you're far from reality and might as well be on another planet. Tell me, would you jump off a cliff if your beloved mommy told you to?"

"Of course not. I don't want to talk about this shit."

"Okay, let's forget that. Listen, I'm throwing a party at my parents' house in New Buffalo, Michigan, on the lake this weekend since they are out of town. It's a five-bedroom house and we'll have plenty of room for some wild fun. I only invite the hottest women in the area and my best and most trusted clients, and you are one of them, as you know. In fact, I am inviting you because you really helped me in my law school preparation when I was having trouble with my grades. I'll never forget how you wrote some of those long papers for me so I could pass

European history and classical Greek literature. That's why I let you in my inner circle. It's a difficult circle to enter, but congratulations, you're in. If you come, you'll probably get lucky with some babe, and I'll even throw in some free crack for your additional pleasure."

Spencer hesitated before answering. "No thanks, Jerry. Gotta study some more this weekend 'cause Lisa wants me to take her dancing somewhere. Maybe some other time."

"Damn. Can't believe you're saying no to me. Do you know people would kill to come to this party? You've done a lot for me, Spence, but I've helped you a lot as well, haven't I? Gave you some free shit when your momma's check was late. You might need me again sometime. Not only that, there are lots of people that will come to the party you will want to meet—powerful people who can get you what you want."

"Okay, you've convinced me. I'll be there."

"Damn right! There you go. It'll be a great time. See you there, buddy."

Spencer kept their relationship because Jerry was able to get him drugs secretly when he needed them, and protected him from dark characters and Lisa's watchful eyes. He knew that Jerry had some clients and associates who were either running from the law or had previous criminal records. Some were ex-cons according to Jerry, but Spencer didn't want to hear about that. He just wanted his speed on occasion for exam cramming, and didn't want to hear about anything else. All he wanted was to stay above the dirt a little, since he believed he was a good person with a future as a corporate lawyer and that Jerry would protect him as a trusted client. He just needed a little help sometimes, since he believed he didn't really have a father for guidance. He remembered when he and Colby sent a Father's Day card to Wyatt, writing that he was simply their biological father, but not their dad. He felt good after he sent that Father's Day card to hurt Wyatt, and remembered the smile on his mom's face when she witnessed the two brothers signing the card before mailing it. His love for his mother would not allow him to see her hurt or angry.

When he drove up to Jerry's childhood home, he could hear the music wailing out of the open windows facing the breakers on the lakeshore. He smelled weed smoke billowing out as well. Spencer never liked weed. It didn't do much for him. When he entered the party, he couldn't believe what he saw.

"Hey Spence! Glad you could grace us with your presence. Let me introduce you to some of my good friends," said Jerry.

"Sure, sounds good."

Spencer quickly surveyed the large entertainment room. All of the girls looked like lingerie models, skinny legs and boob jobs, shiny teeth, and smooth skin. It seemed to Spencer that short skirts and revealing tops was the female uniform of the evening. Jerry brought two of these women to meet Spencer, and he thought that as they approached they all moved in lockstep like runway models.

Jerry introduced him to the girls. "This is Spencer Barton, ladies, my good friend, hero, and future lawyer. Spence, I would like to introduce Annie and Christie."

Spencer almost stuttered from the sight. "Nice to meet you, ladies, you both look um, damn hot!"

"Hmmm," they purred in unison and looked at him, longingly devouring the vision of his tall athletic figure from his pants to his straight teeth and blue eyes. The one with the shortest skirt and longest legs, Christie, made the first move and her friend followed willingly.

"You're a real cutie," said Christie. "You wanna party with us?"

Spencer's testosterone levels pulsed to red line while he reviewed her pleasing curves and tiny waistline, overwhelmed by the smorgasbord laid out for him.

"Hmm that sounds tasty. Party on."

"We'll be in the bedroom on the far left at the top of the stairs. No need to knock. We'll be waiting for you." They giggled and strutted upstairs, looking back at the two men on their way up.

Before Spencer could follow the duet of feminine honey upstairs, Jerry grabbed him by the shoulder to introduce him to a client and friend of his.

"Spence, this is Brock Lawson. He's a friend of mine you need to know."

They shook hands. Brock's grip was like a pair of vise grips. "Nice to meet you, Brock."

Brock was a man who was not easy to forget. He was as tall as an NBA forward, long red hair sporting a ponytail in back, and black dagger tattoos on the backs of his hands, sharp end pointing out.

"Likewise. I've heard a lot about you from Jerry. What are you into, Spencer?"

"Pardon?"

"I mean, you ever been in trouble with the law?"

"No, and I hope not to be."

Brock laughed. "Yeah, that's what they all say. However, you know Jerry says a lot of good things about you and he says he trusts you, and hell, if he trusts you then that means I trust you. When I got out of the pen last year, I swore I would never get into trouble with dope again and I want to stay clean. Problem is, trouble is in my blood I guess, and I can't help it. I like guns more than drugs now because guns give you power over people." He opened his jacket and showed Spencer the shoulder-holstered .357 Smith and Wesson with pride. "Mr. Smokey here demands respect, don't you agree, Spencer?"

Spencer stepped back a few feet. "Yeah, I guess so. I don't know much about handguns, except for the time my dad took us clay shooting with a shotgun."

"Not much you need to know, except always be on the correct side of the gun. Let me tell you this, since you are a friend of mine now. It's like if you ever need anything you'll know who to call. If anybody gives you shit, you can call me and I'll take care of the problem. Just don't fuck with me and you and I will have no problem. Understand?"

Spencer's face turned pale. "Yeah, I think so. Listen Brock, it's been nice to meet you, and thanks for showing me Mr. Smokey. I have to go upstairs now to meet some people. Talk to you later."

"See you when I see you," said Brock.

He didn't know exactly what Brock meant, but he seemed to be a shady character with a past he didn't care to know about. He was not the kind of man Spencer wanted as a friend, and so he wanted to leave quickly to join the girls upstairs. Although he knew he wouldn't hang around with Brock, he understood that he was the kind of guy you wanted on your side when there was trouble.

Spencer knocked on the door to the bedroom on the far left and heard girls laughing and kissing.

"Come in, honey," said Annie.

He rushed in to find the women in their revealing lingerie, lying on the king-size bed.

Christie took control. "Annie, here's our honey, Spencer. Get him some shit and let's party."

After he smoked the crack, he began to feed ravenously on the feminine feast laid before him. Spencer's lean body and defined muscles provided the eager centerpiece for a frenzied tangle of four tanned female legs and 20 exploring manicured fingers, their meow-like moaning and screaming drowned out by the pounding music down below.

He woke up the next morning to find two naked women in bed with him and a scatter of bras and panties on the floor. He didn't quite remember what happened the night before, but thought it must've been good. All he could think of was Lisa and what she would think of him. He also had a flash of memory of what his father had told him and Colby during a fishing trip when they were young: "Work hard, study hard, love unselfishly, and most of all don't do drugs." But what did Wyatt know? He didn't grow up in a broken home with a deadbeat dad and a poor but loving mother. At least he could take comfort in knowing that his friend Jerry would protect him and keep this little thing away from Lisa. That was his fervent hope, because Lisa was his strength. Just like his mother.

CHAPTER 22

"Let's start rounding in the CCU first, and then you can observe me doing a cardiac catheterization, finished by rounding up on the wards. Depending on how you feel after that, you can come to my office to watch me in the outpatient arena in the afternoon. Depends on your energy level of course," said Wyatt.

"I'm a doctor, you know, PhD, but I'm not a medical doctor and didn't sign up for a marathon ordeal, you know. I prefer a relaxed cup of good coffee first, some easy rounding without stress, then a simple lunch. This afternoon I have to return to my lab to finish some writing up one of my research projects. My lab rats miss me, you know."

"Of course. I tend to get carried away at times. Let's head to the coffee shop to fuel up for our morning events."

She wore a long white coat, red dress with heels. Wyatt felt proud of the stares they received while they walked around the hospital, because of her. At the coffee shop, she carefully sipped her Doppio espresso as if it were a glass of fine wine. He gulped his coffee fast, occasionally checking his watch, worried about getting his work done, but at the same time trying not to rush Marta. Clearly, she refused to shorten the experience of a good cup of coffee in the morning and he hadn't yet learned how to relax in the hospital.

The first patient they visited in the CCU was a 70-year-old ex–Air Force fighter pilot who was on life support. "Marta, this gentleman had an acute inferior M.I. or heart attack and he was in shock. Last night, I took him to the cath lab and pulled out the clot from his right coronary artery, then placed two stents to keep the artery open. Kept him on the ventilator overnight because he had fluid on his lungs from heart failure. Should be ready to come off the ventilator today, but I'll leave that up to the Pulmonary/Critical Care team."

Marta watched while he examined the patient, reviewed some X-rays, and discussed medication changes with the nurse. "Once you get him off the ventilator machine and he makes his acute recovery, what will be his long-term care and prognosis?"

"He should make a full recovery, but that will require supervised exercise in the cardiac rehabilitation center, anti-cholesterol drugs, Beta Blocker medications, lifelong aspirin, and powerful anti-platelet drugs to keep the stents from clogging up. Although this is early, I think the quick intervention and lack of cardiac muscle damage should give him a good long-term prognosis as long as he makes lifestyle changes. Heck, I've had patients who dig ditches for the street department go back to work in about six to eight weeks and do well with this same type of lesion."

"Amazing what you can do with your procedures and medications. I'm sure you've saved some lives with your skill."

"I guess, Marta, but it's just my job. I don't know how to do anything else very well, that's for sure."

The public address system shattered their quiet reverie and caused Marta to jump. "Code Blue, CCU, room 3456. Code Blue, CCU, room 3456." Wyatt broke out in a run down the CCU corridor to room 3456, the first physician to arrive. Two nurses and a respiratory therapist were already initiating CPR after quickly placing a backboard under the patient. Wyatt saw the lethal rhythm torsade de pointes on the cardiac monitor and took control of the resuscitation of the dying patient.

"Prepare for defibrillation with 200 joules and continue CPR. Do we have a line?"

"Internal jugular central line," said the nurse, who wasn't doing CPR but was placing the electrode pads for the upcoming shock.

"Everyone clear!" said Wyatt. When he was sure everyone was away from the bed, he pressed the discharge button on the defibrillator and it successfully delivered 200 joules, causing the patient's body to jump slightly in the bed.

"What was his mag and K today?" he asked anyone who would answer.

"We don't have a mag today but his K was 4."

"Give two grams of mag sulfate and one amp epinephrine, then after 2 minutes of CPR we'll check pulses."

After two minutes, Wyatt commanded, "Stop CPR and check pulses."

He saw the rhythm revert to a normal sinus, and relief filled the room when a respiratory therapist and a nurse yelled out simultaneously, "Got strong pulses!"

"Check a pressure."

"One hundred ten over seventy, heart rate 120."

"Good job, everyone, you're the best."Then he looked at the nurse who had the patient that day and asked, "Who's this man's physician?"

"Kline. We called him and he said he's in his office and can be here in thirty minutes or so. He said he appreciates your help."

"No problem, I'll stay as long as you need me."Wyatt looked at the ECG tracing and noticed a prolonged QT interval, putting the patient at risk for further lethal torsade electrical rhythms. "What medicines is this patient on? Any quinolones, macrolides, anti-psychotics, or antiarrhythmics?"

"Let's see, Dr. Barton. He's on Amiodarone, Clarithromycin, Pepcid, Lovenox, and Lopressor."

"Stop the Amiodarone and the Clarithromycin now, and recheck a mag, potassium, and another ECG after the infusion. Those two drugs can, in certain situations, prolong the QT interval and this could happen again. He's stable now, thanks to all of you, and if you need me, I'm on beeper in house."

During the emergency, Marta sat in the nurses' station, observing the controlled chaos but staying out of the way of the staff. Wyatt came to her and smiled while escorting her out of the CCU. "Sorry Marta, that's probably not something you wanted to see today."

"No problem, that's out of your control and something I've never seen before, and congratulations for saving him! By the way, you forgot to wash your hands after that. I work with dangerous microbes every day and I am a fanatic about infection control."

A sheepish grin crept over his face. "Thanks, you're right. By the way, it's time for me to do that cardiac catheterization; we need to go down to the second floor."

"Thanks for the offer, but I've really had enough excitement for one morning. Maybe some other day."

"Or better yet, how about a real date next time, you know, dinner and movie, no blood and guts, death and dying?"

"I'd love that. Call me."

"You can count on it." Wyatt could barely contain his excitement the rest of the day, anticipating the moment in the evening when he would call Marta to discuss the date.

CHAPTER 23

"Wyatt, nice to hear from you. Great job today during rounds! I saw a hero in action, a doctor with a good heart who mends broken ones."

"No hero at all. And you—the foreign scientist here in America to break men's hearts that I've already fixed."

"How did you guess that so quickly? I'm a secret agent from Latvia, or at least that's my cover. Who would suspect someone like me, especially a dumb blond?"

"Well, dumb blondes are the most dangerous, that's for sure. I've read enough spy novels to know that if you were Russian, you'd be a perfect spy. You know, blonde, beautiful, and super smart. But then, if you are a spy then you make it easy for me to switch to the other side."

"I'll never tell."

"So, Marta, as I mentioned while you were running away from me at the hospital earlier today, I would like to take you to dinner, then a movie."

"Really? That would be great. I've never gone to an American movie theater. I do love buttered popcorn though, messier the better of course."

"You're my kind of woman. A blond, messy, popcorn-eating microbiologist who could be a spy. How 'bout I pick you up at six this Friday?"

"Can't do it at six. My son has a soccer game in the late afternoon, then the coach is having a small—how do you say, picky-nick—with food after the game. I'll meet you afterward at the theater at seven. We'll drive separately."

Wyatt laughed. "It's picnic actually. You'll enjoy that piece of American culture, but I'll be disappointed that I won't be taking you to dinner. Just a movie seems kinda..."

"Don't worry about it. I'm looking forward to it, especially since I can use this opportunity to learn more secrets for my spy job. Something inside me tells me you may be working for the other side. See you there."

Although Wyatt planned to change over his patients to his on-call partner at five pm, it was rare that he would actually have all his hospital work and patients "tucked in" early enough to achieve that goal. Hopefully that would happen today—especially today.

Mrs. Fraley suddenly went into shock at 4:50 pm with an acute heart attack, and he rushed her to the cath lab after putting her on the life-support machine and placing a large-bore central line for powerful resuscitation medications and an arterial line to measure blood pressure continuously. The catheterization procedure itself proved difficult due to her dangerously low blood pressure, but he was able to place several stents successfully, allowing her heart muscle to again enjoy precious oxygen from life-saving blood flow. He could've called his partner and asked him to start his call duties a little early so he could go home, but he was not the type of doctor who ran away from a patient who needed him at that moment.

After the successful completion of the life-saving procedures, he explained the events to ten nervous family members clinging to his every word. But he directed his responses mostly to Mrs. Fraley's worried husband.

"Will she make it through the night, Doctor? Is her heart damaged by this heart attack? When can we visit her?"

"I placed her on the ventilator or life-support machine to breathe for her now and give her heart a rest, so I'll keep her on the machine overnight. She had minimal heart muscle damage because I was able to open her culprit artery quickly and place two stents. She's regaining a normal blood pressure and I anticipate removing the breathing tube tomorrow morning if all goes well. She's going to be all right. The worst is over."

"Thanks, Dr. Barton. We appreciate your skills, saving my sweetheart's life tonight. We've been married 50 years now and I'm not ready to lose my bride."

"No problem at all. Are there any other questions tonight?"

"Yeah, doc, there is. It's getting late. You need to get home to your family."

Wyatt immediately glanced at his watch and saw that it was eight pm. His face lost all its color when he saw the cell-phone message from Marta, recorded at 7:15. He quickly left the family conference room to call her, frantic that he had missed the date because he'd immersed himself in Mrs. Fraley's emergency.

"Marta, I'm sorry I missed our date. I had an emergency and I..."

"I waited at the movie theater entrance until 7:45, and you never called or answered my voicemail, so I went home. You could've called, you know."

"Yes, you're right. So sorry, this is horrible. May I make it up to you soon and try this again?"

"I don't know, I'll have to think about it. Seems you're quite busy in your life and I guess I am too. I have to go now and pick up my son. Good-bye."

He walked out of the hospital, face drained of any emotion. *You really blew it now, you idiot. You can't do that to a high-quality woman.*

While driving to pick up Linas, she didn't want to answer the phone that was ringing on the passenger seat because she predicted it would be Wyatt again. When she saw it was Gavin, she picked it up.

"Gavin, nice to hear from you. You sure are persistent, aren't you? Sure, tomorrow will be great. I could use a strong drink."

CHAPTER 24

Ever since the death of Sean Flanagan, Amy Adams, RN, felt closer to Dr. Barton. She still cherished the memory of his strong arms and the scent of his cologne that day they hugged each other after the unsuccessful resuscitation of Sean Flanagan. She yearned to take it farther with him somehow. But why did he always avoid her advances after the divorce? She knew she needed to take the initiative.

With the last cardiac catheterization of the day completed, Wyatt walked down the hallway, and she ran after him.

"Dr. Barton, may I talk to you for a minute?"

Wyatt smiled graciously. "Why, sure, Amy. What's up?"

She blushed. "Listen, my parents brought me some St. Emilion Chateau Soutard when they were in France. Since you mentioned you like wine, I would like to share it with you while I burn some steaks at my place."

"Sounds great, but I don't usually make a habit of going on dates with hospital staff that I work with. You know, it can make things a little awkward at work, but I'm flattered, though, believe me."

"I suppose, but this will be as friends, with no expectations at all. Good friends and good wine is a rare treat in life that we can cherish as our little secret." She laughed. "I won't kiss and tell, you know."

Wyatt rubbed his dimpled chin, deep in thought. "Well, I guess there's a first time for everything, but it's rare that I'll turn down St. Emilion Bordeaux, a good steak, and a pretty lady."

"I'm relieved that you added the part about the pretty lady, because if you hadn't I would have saved the Chateau Soutard for myself and given you the Two Buck Chuck's."

"You're sure a tough woman who knows what she wants and then goes after it. I like that."

Amy handed him a card. "Here's my address and cell phone, how 'bout seven tonight?"

"Sounds okay now, but I'll have to check my social calendar to see if there are any conflicts," laughed Wyatt. "Especially female conflicts, the most dangerous kind you know."

"You're damn right, and this female will expect you at my house at seven. See you then."

The humidity dripped that summer evening, and Amy greeted Wyatt at the door of her single-level home wearing a light yellow summer dress with slits on the side and a V-neck front. She loved the wind blowing her dress so glimpses of her naked thighs were presented easily into his view; she could see by the way he looked at her that he enjoyed the view she had carefully prepared for him. She opened the bottle of Soutard and sipped the wine on her back porch, occasionally licking the wine off her lips slowly.

Wyatt insisted on grilling the steaks himself, even though he was a guest. After they each finished a glass of the smooth wine, they sat down to eat; the wine and conversation seemed to loosen them up, allowing them to shed their work lingo and carefully touch on their personal lives. Amy observed Wyatt stealing furtive glances at her smooth runner's legs and curvy front; she grew satisfied that her body was successfully opening the spigot of testosterone that he couldn't control voluntarily. He was a man, virile and confident in himself, but it was his soft blue eyes and rugged, toned body that propelled her to think about him under her sheets. Who cared about the scar over his eyebrow? She would learn about how it happened some day.

They cleaned up the dishes, and Wyatt's six-foot two-inch frame brushed by her body gently in the small kitchen and she felt an uncontrollable sensation of a light feather tickling her gently from her toes all the way to the back of her neck. She felt an urge to go up on her tippy toes and smell the cologne on his neck and bury her head in his muscular chest. She thought better of acting on her natural desires.

But after she rinsed dishes, Wyatt walked to the front door. "Thanks, Amy, for the nice evening. I enjoyed your wonderful hospitality. It's getting late, and I've got an early case tomorrow and I need my beauty sleep, you know."

"You're already beautiful, my dear, but so soon? You'll miss dessert!" She was hoping for at least a romantic kiss, but all she received from Wyatt was a hug, and when he walked away, she resisted the powerful urge to put her arms out to call him back.

"Again, thanks for the excellent wine and steaks, my friend. I'll have to take a rain check on the dessert; you know I have to watch my girlish figure."

"Bullshit. Anyway, it was my pleasure tonight. Maybe next time you can reciprocate at your man cave."

"Perhaps. We'll have to see if the stars align themselves, my schedule's tight. In the meantime, I'll see you at the hospital."

Amy watched him walk down the sidewalk to his car. She knew he was attracted to her, but he was still reserved and for some lame reason not interested in romance now. Maybe he had another woman he was dating, or maybe it was the unwritten hospital dating rule, but either way, she would not give up on snagging Dr. Wyatt Barton; she would not lose him to another woman, even if that woman was called St. Anthony Hospital.

Wyatt sped away, not knowing specifically where he would go but knowing it wasn't directly home. The XM radio was playing some '70s classics, now Harry Chapin's "The Cat's in the Cradle," and the words sent his mind rushing to his kids and the family he once had years ago: "My child arrived just the other day, came into the world in the usual way, but there were planes to catch and bills to pay. And he was walking before I knew it, and as he grew he said 'I'm gonna be like you, Dad, you know I'm gonna be like you.'"

The dull ache inside his chest reached a crescendo and he turned the radio off quickly, unable to listen to the rest of it, knowing the truth it would tell. He had cared deeply that his boys would grow up to respect him and share his legacy of love and strength, but it was now obvious that all of that fell into a smoldering pile of stinging memories. His sons had no intention of "being like him." His eyes misted over, and he completely forgot to heed the red light, passing through it obliviously, causing honking and screeching tires. He narrowly missed being T-boned in the intersection and drove, looking back through his mirror making sure no one was hurt. His heart pummeled his rib cage but he continued to drive until the flashing lights of the police cruiser pulled him over. In a way, he was thankful for that because he wanted the cruel memories to stop, and maybe this was the only way.

"Good evening. Show me your license and registration."

"Yes, Officer." Wyatt reached into his glove compartment and fiddled with the envelope trying to find his documents, all the while thankful that he only had one glass of wine at Amy's house.

The officer looked into the car and saw Wyatt's white coat and stethoscope on the passenger seat, then stepped away from the car with Wyatt's documents, did a computer check, found no prior record on Wyatt, and returned to the car. "You know you ran a red light at that intersection back there and nearly caused an accident."

"I know, Officer. Guess I just wasn't paying attention."

"Have you been drinking?"

"No sir, I haven't."

"Okay. Well, I'm going to believe you. I'm writing you a traffic citation for your violation. You can pay the fine or appear in court; it's your choice. Either way, you have a good night and be more careful from now on."

"Thanks, Officer."

The officer followed Wyatt closely from behind, observing his driving skills through two intersections, then turned away, satisfied that he wasn't impaired. But it wasn't long until Wyatt found himself in a zone of memories again, and they just wouldn't stop. This time it was the family dog, a yellow Labrador named Alphie. Wyatt loved Alphie. He would ride bikes with the boys, and Alphie would playfully follow them for as long as he could, always hoping they would stop and play ball retrieval with him. However, Wyatt would come home and walk him every day because the boys were too busy and lost interest, and during the walks, he would fling tennis balls for the dog to retrieve with glee. Wyatt affectionately called Alphie a "big dumb doggie," and damn, that dog loved Wyatt unconditionally. But after the separation and divorce, his former family never allowed him to see the dog he loved again, and he knew that begging them to allow him some time with Alphie would prompt statements like, "Oh, so you care about the dog more than your kids?"

Wyatt now realized that the only being in the family that really loved him no matter what was Alphie and that he would never see him again.

Got to send some flowers to Marta.

CHAPTER 25

The annual American Heart Association Ball occurred every February in Chicago, coinciding with Valentine's Day, at the Millennium Knickerbocker Hotel. This charity event was both a large moneymaker for the American Heart Association and a very prestigious evening that drew people from both the social elite and the medical community. The individual donation for a seat in the Crystal Ballroom was $500 per person or $950 per couple. Tables of four to twelve were also purchased by larger groups and companies for anywhere from $2,000 to $5,000. The Crystal Ballroom had a built-in illuminated dance floor with a balcony and stage, crystal chandeliers, and a gilded-dome ceiling.

Wyatt was on call the night before the event, and due to his usual post-call fatigue, had little desire to attend. He had not attended since his divorce was finalized and never really enjoyed himself with Katherine anyway when they had attended. This year, the keynote speaker was Dr. Kenyon T. Burrows, a famous cardiac surgeon and researcher who had contributed a large amount to the cardiac surgical field. Unfortunately, he became ill with the flu two days before the event and had to cancel. His choice as a replacement was Dr. Barton, and so he asked the American Heart Association Ball chairperson to call Wyatt to see if he would fill in.

"Well, sure I would. Kenyon is a good friend of mine and a colleague, but I haven't much time to prepare my address, do I?"

"No," said the chairperson, an energetic recent marketing graduate. "But we only need you to talk for fifteen minutes; just warm the audience up during the dinner and before the dancing begins."

"Okay, I'll give it a shot, but you know my credentials don't compare to Burrows."

"Nonsense. Dr. Burrows wouldn't have picked you to replace him if he didn't respect you. We are so thankful to you, Dr. Barton. I look forward to seeing you there."

Wyatt's first thought was that Marta would thoroughly enjoy the Knickerbocker Hotel and the Crystal Ballroom with its illuminated dance floor, crystal chandeliers, and gilded dome ceiling. He hoped the roses he sent her would help soften her up before he tried to ask her for a second chance date after his first colossal screw-up. Hopefully she would go with him to the Heart Ball. It was a risk he had to take.

"Hi Wyatt. Nice to hear from such a busy doctor."

"I do know how to keep track of time a little better now. Are you willing to give me a second chance?"

"Depends on what you're offering, Wyatt. Don't think I want to be left alone in front of a movie theater again, but I do believe in second chances. Maybe you should hire a personal assistant to make sure you honor your social obligations."

He felt a little soft humor creeping into her voice and he thought he had a chance. But she hadn't said anything about the roses yet. Maybe she didn't get them or if she did, maybe she didn't appreciate the gesture. "Listen, there's an American Heart Association charity ball on Valentine's Day at the Millenium Knickerbocker Hotel. The Heart Association has asked me to give the keynote address in the place of Dr. Burrows, who's apparently sick. There will be a nice dinner, champagne, and dancing. I would be honored if you would go with me as my date."

There was a brief silence on the other end and he dreaded it. "Thanks for the roses by the way, they were beautiful! You know, I would love to try it again and go with you, but unfortunately, I already accepted an invitation from someone else. I'm sorry, but I do look forward to seeing you there."

Wyatt sank deeply into his chair; his head slid down midway on the seat back and he nearly fell out. "I'm too late. Okay, well, at least let me buy you a drink or at least one dance when we meet there."

"You can count on that, Wyatt."

Wyatt did his best to hide his chagrin that Marta was going to the ball with someone else, but she was single and available, and she was on the market. He knew his previous mistake had created an opening wide enough to allow another man in. But then, he was single too and he didn't want to go to the ball alone. He decided to see if Amy was available. Probably a good chance she would say yes.

Blake Flanagan flew back into town and had to spend time at his brother's house until he bought a place of his own. His military assignments really didn't allow him to settle down anywhere for long. "So, Gavin, tell me how this malpractice case is going?" asked Blake as the brothers sat down in the spacious living room of their father's mansion and talked over beer and pizza. "I want to have this quack smacked around a little by your fancy black suits."

"I told our attorneys to wait and not file. Seems we don't have much of a case against him right now, so I think it's best to hold off. That doesn't mean I like him though."

"Figured you'd chicken out, you wuss. I still don't like the guy 'cause I think he killed Dad. Anyway, I'll change the subject. How's your love life? Any new hotties, or do you still only have eyes for Mademoiselle Delphine?"

"Haven't talked to Delphine in several months, but I do have an amazing woman who's going with me to the Heart Ball!"

"Who's that?"

"She's a blonde..."

"Stop right there. That's all I need to know."

"You're a real comedian, Blake. You know I don't discriminate with colors: blonde, brunette, black, or red. Sometimes the silver ones are hot too. Anyway, as I was trying to say, she's a PhD at Northwestern in some science field that I can't pronounce and she immigrated from

Latvia. Smart, sexy, and charming. I can't wait to go with her. I think all the men will drool when they stare at us dancing close to each other. By the way, will you be here Valentine's Day?"

"Yeah. Why? Do you want to date me instead, you pervert?"

"Of course. Seriously, I bought two extra seats at the ball and it would be great if you could come as well. You need to find a date though."

"That shouldn't be a problem. Girls love a Marine in dress uniform."

Gavin got up to go to the kitchen for a snack and then to bed, while Blake stayed up watching movies and gobbling popcorn with large quantities of beer. Later, after he was sure his brother was asleep, Blake found Gavin's date book in the drawer next to the living-room phone. He surveyed the hundreds of names and stopped at the one he needed. He smiled mischievously and downed another beer.

The stylish women in their elegant ballroom gowns accompanied by men in tuxedos and black bow ties flowed into the beautiful Crystal Ballroom at the Millennium Knickerbocker Hotel, and by seven pm, all sat in their assigned seats. Gavin and Marta were at the head table of 12 purchased by the firm, and Blake was far at the other end with Delphine. Marta smiled and talked to everyone, obviously enjoying the evening. Gavin stared at Blake, who was resplendent in his Marine dress uniform, kissing Delphine on her cheeks whenever he had the chance. Delphine occasionally allowed her eyes to meet Gavin's while smiling coquettishly for all to see.

Amy Adams sat at a table of eight at the front of the ballroom, sitting alone because Wyatt was up on the stage giving his keynote address.

After the dinner and Wyatt's address was over and the band began to play, Gavin motioned to Blake to join him for a private conversation at the side.

"Why the hell did you invite Delphine? You're a great brother, stealing my girl right after I introduce you two. I can't believe you did that! Why didn't you ask me if you could take her?"

Blake looked at him firmly. "Well, first of all if I asked you I am sure you would have said no. Second, you told me how head over heels you were about Marta, so why couldn't I call Delphine?"

"Where did you get her number? Did she give it to you that Christmas night when she was studying your biceps?"

"No, in your black book. Your fault for leaving it where I could find it."

Gavin took a deep breath. "Well, let's forget it and try to have a good time with our dates. But the damn thing that bothers me more is that we had to sit and listen to Dr. Whackjob Barton speak. He must be quite a hotshot, though, if he's the keynote speaker."

"Yeah, but he better not go to the bathroom when I'm there because he might not come out," said Blake. "I'll start his punishment by ripping his lips off, and then the fun will start. To hell with the courts."

Two courageous couples began the dancing, and it wasn't long before the whole illuminated floor teemed with people dancing, or at least attempting to. Style didn't matter because large amounts of champagne had been consumed, and no one cared about who was using the correct dance steps or form. Some women took their heels off and danced in their hose. Most of the men took off their bow ties and left them at the tables.

When the band took a break, many of the couples remained on the lighted dance floor talking and laughing. Marta went to the ladies' room and left Gavin alone. Blake took Delphine's order and went to the bar to get some drinks for the two of them. Delphine then saw Gavin alone and seized the opportunity to walk over and talk to him while Blake was busy. She told him he looked good and he said the same. She was always stunning, and he couldn't take his eyes off her.

Marta returned to the dance floor but couldn't find Gavin because he was with Delphine. Wyatt spied Marta alone and told Amy that he needed to go talk to a friend and he would be right back. She nodded and intently looked for more champagne at the table. He couldn't take his eyes off Marta's flowing blond hair while she walked, with dancer legs supported by delicate ankles. Her black dress clung eagerly to her lithe body, divided in the middle by a stylish belt, forcing his eyes to drink her in completely. He had to fight the urge to ski her mogul-like cheekbones gently with his sensitive fingertips.

Blake arrived at the bar; waiting in a long line, he struck up a conversation with Amy, who was now in line in front of him.

"Hello, lovely lady," said Blake. "Seems we've both been separated from our dates, but honestly I must say it's his error to leave you alone. My name's Blake Flanagan."

"Nice to meet you. Amy Adams." Her eyes glistened while she stared at Blake's Marine dress uniform—the dark blue coat adorned with service medals, light blue pants with red stripes on the side, and his white hat in his hand. The uniform fit his shape perfectly, accenting his wide shoulders in a diamond shape down to his waist.

Blake looked over to Delphine and saw her engaged intently in conversation with Gavin, so he felt free to continue with Amy. "So, Amy, are you a doctor at St. Anthony's?"

"Oh, no, I'm a nurse. I work with Dr. Wyatt Barton, the keynote speaker tonight."

"I see. I know of him. I've got to ask, why are you dating him? You can do better than that. I think he's a bad doc and we may pursue legal action against him."

Amy stepped back from him. "Oh really? That's a rude thing to say. What was your father's name anyway?"

"Sean Flanagan."

She thought for a moment. "Oh yes, I remember him and the procedure that Dr. Barton performed that day. I was there assisting. I'm a nurse, not a cardiologist so I can't comment on what happened, but I will say he's a good doctor, a gentleman, and you're wrong. I'm here to have fun and not talk about your problems. By the way, who is that blonde that my date is talking to right now? Seems that I saw her at your table with some handsome guy."

"Aren't you the curious one? The woman's name is Marta Liepa, and my brother Gavin is the handsome man you're referring to. He's wrapped in Marta completely and won't look at another woman, it seems, although he's now intent on talking to my date. Anyway, I appreciate your honesty, Amy, and you're certainly a woman who seems to know what information she wants and how to get it. I must let you know, however, that I can't stand the ground Dr. Barton walks on, and I want him to pay for what he did to my father, either in court or somewhere else if the courts don't do their job. I'm going to find my date now, and see if I can pry her away from my brother."

"Whatever, Blake. Stop the stupid crap! Like I said before, I don't know what your problem is with my Dr. Barton but I don't want to talk about it anymore. But before you go, do you know anything more about this Marta?"

"Not much except she's from somewhere in Europe and is a professor in one of the science departments at Northwestern. Anyway, I guess our conversation didn't start off that well, and I'm sorry about that, but I'd like to meet you under better circumstances. May I have your number?"

Amy hesitated and thought she would say no immediately, then studied Blake's handsome uniform and wide shoulders. She glanced over at Wyatt, who was talking with the blonde much longer than she thought he should. "Sure, why not."

Marta and Wyatt were engrossed in each other yet, still standing on the dance floor for all to see. "You know, Marta, you're dazzling everyone here with your looks."

"Thanks. You look great too, and I'm so proud of you for your speech. I know you didn't want to do it, but you did very well."

"Better be careful because you look like a Russian spy and they're watching you closely here. You never know who might be an FBI agent."

Marta laughed so loudly that most eyes in the crowd turned to look at them. Most importantly though, Gavin saw the couple and quickly excused himself from Delphine and nearly ran over.

"How did you know? I tried to hide that information but you figured me out. I am a Russian spy and you better be careful or I will drug your drink and kidnap you and take advantage of you."

"You promise?" Her brain ran like a greyhound right with his, and he enjoyed the intellectual chase. But he was sure that she was a woman who would never hear the phrase "dumb blonde" used in her presence.

Gavin arrived quickly and put his arm immediately around Marta, marking his territory. "Oh Gavin, I must introduce you to Dr. Wyatt Barton, he is—"

"Yeah, I know who he is." The two men looked at each other and nodded their heads in unemotional recognition.

Gavin wouldn't give up. "It seems you two have been having fun, laughing and enjoying the party. Where did you two meet?"

Marta said nothing and looked at Wyatt, hoping that he would support her by responding somehow.

Wyatt looked at him with an amused look. "Well, that's certainly a long story."

With his arm still protectively guarding Marta, Gavin then led her away back to safety at his table.

Wyatt thought to himself that certain overpaid lawyers who liked looking at themselves in mirrors were as useful as used toilet paper.

Blake left Amy with her number in his pocket and went to the men's room and next to him, two urinals down, was none other than Wyatt Barton.

At the sink, Wyatt introduced himself. "I'm Wyatt Barton. Thanks for serving our country in the Marine Corps."

"I'm Blake Flanagan and yes, you should be thankful that I am protecting pussies like you."

"What did you say?" said Wyatt.

"Yeah, you heard me. You're a well-educated pussy it seems, but a pussy nevertheless. You killed my father, Sean Flanagan."

"Now that's a ridiculous statement! Flanagan—yeah, I remember your father and I did my best to save him, and if you really had the brains to understand the situation, you would back off. But what's more, I'm surprised at you. You really have a bad attitude for a Marine."

"I'll show you a bad attitude!" Blake struck Wyatt in the chest with a sucker punch when he wasn't expecting violence, slamming the doctor against the bathroom wall. He then threw another punch at Wyatt's face, but it was a millisecond too slow. Wyatt caught his right arm mid-punch with a block using his left forearm, then did a pivot and simultaneously grabbed Blake's right elbow with his right arm and twisted it while he deftly tripped Blake with his leg and took him to the ground with a thud. Blake screamed in agony because Wyatt twisted Blake's elbow behind the Marine's back while he lay prone on the floor.

"Let me go, asshole!" Blake lay helpless, hyperventilating on the men's room floor, overcome by a gentleman of superior intellect and martial skill.

"Oh really? Why should I?" said Wyatt calmly. "You aren't showing much decorum for a Marine. You're a pathetic musclehead puke. I'm disappointed in you, Blake. Most Marines I know are much better men than you are and wouldn't put themselves in this position on the bathroom floor. You make me sick the way you dirty your proud uniform."

Several other men remained in the room and backed away from the scene. One asked, "Do you want us to call the police, Doctor? It seems to me you have this situation under control, though."

"No thanks; no need to call the police. Unfortunately this guy's sizable muscles are controlled with a brain lacking neurons and the few he has don't connect. We'll be done here in a minute, and Mr. Flanagan will apologize for causing a scene at this nice function."

"Fat chance, doc. Go to hell."

Wyatt bent Blake's elbow to an angle with an obtuse twist just short of the breaking point, causing Blake to scream.

"Okay. Okay. I apologize. Leave me alone."

"Good decision, Blake. I'm going to let you go now and rejoin the festivities. I respect the uniform of the Marines and the service. Believe me, many of my friends have served. I really don't know what your problem with me is. But if you so much as think about messing with me again, I won't be as nice and gentle, and you will be in the intensive care unit, recovering from multiple trauma from my hands. Do you understand me, brainless one, or do I need to talk slower?"

"Yes I do."

The men's room cleared and the main crowd was unaware of the events that occurred. Blake and Wyatt went their separate ways. Blake's uniform appeared dusty from the floor and wrinkles overcame the sharp creases, but he wiped it off the best he could. Wyatt's suit remained perfect because he stood upright the entire encounter. He went to find Amy, satisfied he'd silenced Blake.

If I was cursed with Blake's jumbled brain, I guess I might try to compensate by beating up as many people as I could also. Problem is, he picked on the wrong man tonight and he needs to be more careful who he decides to pick on. What a dumbass.

Blake found Delphine. "We need to go, honey. It's getting late."

"But it's only 10 o'clock. I want to do some more dancing." She looked closer at Blake. "What's wrong with you? You've got a red face and filthy uniform."

"Yeah, I slipped on some soap on the men's room floor. No big deal."

"You Americans are so strange. Are you hurt?"

Blake forced a smile. "No way. Can't hurt a Marine." He winced and massaged his arm gently when she wasn't looking.

When the evening ended Gavin and Marta, Blake and Delphine, Wyatt and Amy all left for home, but the only two wearing genuine smiles were Marta and Wyatt.

CHAPTER 26

Blake chugged his beers like a thirsty grizzly hunched over the only available water trough in the desert. He downed two bottles before Gavin could finish his first. Both had their shoes off, propped on a coffee table, watching the Bears play Denver at Gavin's house. It was the night after the Heart Ball, and neither brother uttered a word. Beer guzzling and potato chip crunching almost drowned out the play-by-play announcing of the game.

Gavin eventually broke the silence. "That was low of you to take Delphine to the ball. Some brother you are."

"Hell, you didn't want her anyway because you had your eyes on that new blond tail."

"Yeah but you really put it in my face. Tell me, did you two...?"

"C'mon, I don't want to talk about that. Drop it and go on."

The Bears were now ahead by a touchdown with Blake ahead in the beer race four to two.

Gavin moved to a chair farther away in case drunken violence erupted.

"You know, Gav; I really don't like this Dr. Barton guy."

"You don't say. I'm shocked and amazed."

"We both agreed to let this malpractice case rest because you said your fancy lawyer boys thought there wasn't a strong case against him and that he was clean. I don't like to sue people, but damn it, this guy pisses me off. Maybe your lawyers can dig deep into his past and find something ugly to scare him about."

Gavin shifted uncomfortably in his chair. "I know you think he could've saved Dad's nasty old heart and you're on his ass about that. But tell me; did something else go on between you and Barton at the ball? I remember you made the comment to me that you wanted to rip his lips off or something like that in the bathroom that night. Did something happen between you two?"

Blake stared at the TV while he gulped two large boluses of beer. "No. Nothing happened."

"I must admit I don't take kindly to him trying to move in on my girl."

"Damn right."

"I just leave for a few minutes to take a piss and then get some drinks, and there he is, laughing like a clown with Marta. I know he did that purposely to get to me. He says 'It's a long story' when I asked him how the two of them met. Bullshit. No one steals my girl in front of me and gets away with it."

The beer was clearly getting the best of Blake. "Hell no. Us two remaining Flanagans must stick together. Gotta ask though, ya sure she's yoursh, Gavin? Seems she's an independent lady and probably won't kiss your feet like your other women."

"Whatever. You're a drunk Marine."

"Kick your ass anytime, bro."

"Maybe, but you know, I think we both agree that Barton has pushed us around long enough and it's time to take him down."

"I told you before, Gavin, I can take care of it myself." He folded his tattooed arms and took a deep breath and his voice softened considerably. "But I think he'll be a tough one."

"I'm surprised you say that now because usually you say he's a pussy. Anyway, I've been thinking a lot about this malpractice case, and I changed my mind. I have the best plaintiff's attorney money can buy, John Willoughby, and he can take a fleck of dirt and make it into a landslide of boulders for the jury to see. He can make an innocent man look like Charles Manson if he doesn't tie his shoelaces correctly. I think we should go ahead and sue the bastard now. If nothing else, it will scare the hell out of him because doctors hate to get sued. What d'ya think?"

"Now you're talking. Let's do it. And if your way doesn't take him down, then I guarantee you that my way will."

CHAPTER 27

With business booming, Jerry Thompson's clueless parents expected him to go to law school, so he kept his grades up, largely with help from Spencer who wrote some of his papers. Jerry thought he needed a part-time job to polish his resume for law school, so he applied as an extern at a local law clinic that represented mostly indigent clients. Problem was, pre-interview drug tests remained in the way. He decided Spencer was the person who could help him. "You been clean, Spence?"

"Haven't done anything for several weeks now. Lisa's been watching me close."

"Women. Can't live with 'em and can't live without 'em," said Jerry. "Anyway, I need a favor from you. I'm going for a job interview tomorrow morning and I've been using every day for a while and I know I'll flunk a drug screen if they ask me to do one. Can't stay clean long enough. So, would you help me and do a piss bag for me?"

"What's a 'piss bag'?"

"You go with me the day of the drug screen, and I'll give you a bag that you piss into for me. Do it that morning so it's fresh, and then I'll tie it against my leg, under my pants, and go to the lab. It'll remain fresh and warm so it'll fool the lab."

"You've sure got it down, don't you?"

"I know the ropes. Then when they call my name, I have to go to the bathroom with a cup and I'm the only one allowed in for security reasons. The bottom of this specially designed urine bag has an injector port which will easily evacuate into the tamper-resistant urine cup the lab provides. And voila, I'm drug free."

"Okay, Jerry, I can do that for you. Doesn't sound like much of a problem."

Several days later, Jerry received notice of the random drug test and he immediately called Spencer, who mastered the piss bag technique flawlessly.

Spencer didn't want trouble so he treated Jerry as well as possible. That trouble could involve his mother, Lisa, the law school admissions board, or Brock Lawson. He knew that if he turned against Jerry, then Brock would soon become a dangerous enemy. It was also clear that he couldn't turn back now, and he had to keep things warm and friendly both with Jerry and Brock.

Several days later Jerry found out he was accepted for the job at the law clinic and so he gave Spencer a call.

"Spence, you da man! I got the job and it's definitely because of you. Now tell me is there anything I can do for you?"

"Well, nothing I can think of now, but thanks. I'm happy for you."

"Of course you are. When I'm happy, you're happy; right, man?"

"Yeah, right."

"Now you know, I want you to call me if anyone is hassling you or causing you trouble, 'cause no one messes with my man, Spence. If you feel like someone is coming down on you or your brother, let me know, and I'll have Brock handle it if I can't, okay?"

His pause hung in the air like a fully deployed parachute.

"Spencer, you there?"

"Yeah, sorry Jerry, must've been a bad connection. Appreciate your concern, and it's nice to know that you're available if I need help."

"Damn right it is. Listen, I gotta go. Talk to you later."

"Later."

That night, Spencer sprawled on his couch and thought about how he should've never become involved with drugs and especially with Jerry and Brock, but it was too late now. He could stop the coke and speed any time he wanted, but those lowlifes Jerry and Brock were now a part of his life. Katherine was the reason for more of his worry, though; he hoped she would never find out. She loved him, and he never wanted to lose his relationship with her, but Lisa—well, that was different. She was smart and seemed to understand life more than he did, and that's why he felt insecure about their relationship. At the same time, although Colby wasn't involved with drugs, he still worried about him back in Chicago, so he gave him a call.

"Hey little bro, how'ya doing?"

"Hey Spence. Maybe a little down I guess."

"What's got you down? Girl trouble? I'm an expert in women. Always tell them they're right even though they aren't, then buy them flowers when they least expect it."

"No, that's funny. It's Dad, I mean Wyatt. I kinda miss the good times we had with him, and I just think that maybe since it's been over six years since the divorce, maybe we, or I, should try to contact him. We haven't talked or had Christmas or birthdays together in years. I know we told him never to contact us, but maybe he's not so bad after all, I don't know. The whole thing seems a little one-sided, you know."

"What? I can't believe you're saying that, Colby. What's gotten into you? After he abandoned us, beat up Mom, and had affairs with bimbos? He doesn't care about us. Never did. We're better off without him and you know it. Now you straighten up, Colby, and remember that he has forgotten about you and me, and you need to go on with your life and let him go on without us."

There was a long silence between the two brothers. "Colby, you still there?"

"Yeah. I guess you're right. Probably we're better off. Mom has always been there for us."

"Good. Nice to talk to you, Colby, and say hi to Mom for me."

Before he drifted off to sleep, Spencer recalled a brief image of his father, and some words he had said to him and Colby when they were young: "Work hard, say your prayers, love unselfishly, and by all means don't ever get involved with drugs."

Colby collapsed on his dorm room bed and stared out the window at the streetlight outside. He had a new cell phone number since he'd last talked to his dad briefly three years ago, and Wyatt wouldn't recognize his number even if he gathered the courage to call him. He waited as long as he could, then picked up his cell phone and found his dad's old number. He called, let it ring twice, then lost his nerve and hung up before his father could answer.

The sound of crunching food and people talking with their mouths full filled the air at lunchtime in the doctor's lounge at St. Anthony's Hospital. The wide-screen TV set in the middle of the food fest was tuned to ESPN. Wyatt's colleagues, David Springer, a nephrologist, and Don Daly, a gregarious orthopedist, flanked him at their table.

"So Don, I heard your daughter got into medical school," Springer said. "Congratulations!"

"Thanks, Dave. We're proud of her, didn't think she would make it with a 3.8 GPA but her MCAT scores were off the charts, so that sealed the deal I guess. So, Suzy and I are taking her for our last family spring ski trip in Vail this weekend. I know we won't have time to see her much once she enters medical school."

Wyatt smiled at Don, congratulated him, and then looked away at the TV while he ate his lunch.

"Do you have any plans this weekend, Dave? I heard you're finally off call."

"Yeah we'll be going to my son John's basketball tournament in Springfield and then we'll drive back to Chicago to see my daughter perform her ballet recital. Apparently, the Joffrey Ballet is sending talent scouts to watch her performance. It's going to be a busy weekend."

Wyatt had had enough of the sweet family talk, jumped up, and looked at his watch. "Well, gotta get back to the salt mines. They're waiting for me in the cath lab. See you guys later."

"Later, Wyatt," they said, nearly in unison. They watched as he walked away, shoulders squared, and they looked at each other and shrugged their shoulders at his sudden departure.

CHAPTER 28

E. David Carson requested that John Willoughby, Esq., be the lead plaintiff's counsel in the malpractice case the Flanagan family filed against Dr. Wyatt Barton. Willoughby had been with the Flanagan firm for over fifteen years and had the best success rate of any malpractice plaintiff attorney in Chicago. He proved adept at all phases of malpractice plaintiff law, but especially the techniques that produced victory in cases with no merit: the intimidation of a defendant during deposition to extract words the defendant didn't mean to say, the manipulation of a jury's emotions, and the utilization of the firm's huge financial resources to buy the best expert witnesses. He knew how to find physicians who were hungry to receive his money and would testify the way he wanted. These were often doctors who were either retired or had unsuccessful practices and took courses around the country to teach them to be expert witnesses.

If Willoughby thought his case was without merit, he avoided using successful, knowledgeable physicians as experts. That could spell doom for a shaky case. He rarely made mistakes and was always prepared either for trial, or to force the defendant doctor to settle out of court to avoid a stressful trial. Both he and Drake Alston, Dr. Barton's attorney, were in the process of discovery for the case, and depositions were scheduled. The problem that Willoughby faced was that he couldn't find a believable expert witness to corroborate medical negligence on the part of Dr. Barton. Alston did not have that problem.

"Wyatt, may I get you something to drink?" Drake Alston asked.

"Black coffee please."

While Wyatt slurped his coffee and surveyed Alston's cherrywood consultation office, he found himself dwarfed by the large glass table surrounded by soundproof glass walls. He watched the law clerks and secretaries scurry about carrying briefcases and reams of paper to the other offices outside the glass walls. Why the glass-enclosed room? Maybe if things got nasty with opposing clients and the process deteriorated to fisticuffs, there'd be witnesses outside the room. Yeah, that was it.

"Here's the bottom line, Wyatt. We both know that this case has no merit and is a nuisance suit that does nothing but get me paid and increase healthcare costs in this country. Granted, there are bad physicians who need deletion from the profession or at least to be isolated from patient care. Every profession has these bad players, including the legal profession. However, Sean Flanagan was a man who had multiple risks for death from cardiac disease, and you tried to save his life, and he was going to die anyway, whether you did a procedure before his death or not. In addition, you performed a standard procedure on a high-risk patient. Do I have this right?"

"He even told me that he didn't want cardiac surgery unless it was last resort and my procedure failed to open his artery."

"But he signed consent for your cardiac catheterization and possible stent placement. I read the consent and his son Gavin agreed with the risks of death, perforation of the coronary artery, sudden cardiac arrhythmias, and emergency cardiac surgery. We have the consent forms to document that. Thankfully, you did a nice job of consenting the patient in an emergency situation."

"Took a class on consents from the hospital attorney. Guess I stayed awake during the important parts."

"So many of the doctors I represent have done no wrong. It seems that society expects perfect results from physicians, and no matter what the patient has done to destroy his body over the years, the public demands the physician to save him immediately, and with no complications. The problem is, good doctors can be harmed or even leave their practice in disgrace when named in a lawsuit, even if they have not been negligent. And that, Wyatt, is why I love being a defense attorney for medical malpractice. I want to protect innocent doctors from these meritless witch hunts."

"That's refreshing to hear. You sure you didn't receive an M.D. before your J.D.?"

"I just don't like society beating up on good docs. The problem I have with this case is that the family is not poor, and they are not filing a nuisance case for money only, the way many financially strapped families do. In fact, some families who are illegal aliens sue and win large sums of money in the U.S. The Flanagans have more money than they can count, but the sons still want to pursue this ridiculous case. I'm not sure what the motivation is here, but it seems the sons want you punished somehow or to derail your career for some reason."

"I think I know why. It seems that this Gavin guy is competing with me for the attention of a lady."

Alston cleared his throat while he pondered Wyatt's statement. "Oh I see. Well, that makes it more complicated because he's making it personal, but still winnable for us. I don't know much about his brother, Blake, though. Both signed the complaint filed in the court. I've talked to opposing counsel. They will depose you first, and after that, I've asked that we depose Dr. Ron Parker. If we don't have them beat by then, we'll depose Nurse Adams."

"Dr. Barton, how many cardiac catheterizations have you performed during your career?"

Wyatt hesitated. "I don't know, about two maybe three thousand."

"Please be exact, Dr. Barton. This is important."

"Objection," said Ashton.

"You can answer, Dr. Barton," said Willoughby.

"As I said, I don't know. I really don't care to count them anymore. I did when I was a brand new cardiologist, I suppose."

"I didn't ask you how you worked as a young doctor. How many?"

"Objection. The defendant has already answered the question," stated Ashton.

"My best guess is three per week for about twenty years of practice, so that's about three thousand."

"Okay, how many cardiac stent procedures did you do in your career?"

"I'm an invasive cardiologist, so I do more in my group than the other partners, because we each have different specialties and areas of expertise within the group. I happen to have the most exper..."

"That's not what I asked, Dr. Barton. How many stents have you placed in people's coronary arteries?"

Wyatt glared at Willoughby and stared him down, purposely delaying his answer. He was not going to let this shark lawyer intimidate him with his haughty manner. "I would say that probably forty percent of my catheterization procedures are stents or related procedures to open the artery. So, you can do the math."

Willoughby shifted his weight in his chair, then trained his best stare at Wyatt. "You knew you were going to kill Sean Flanagan during his procedure, but you didn't care to tell him, did you? You knew he was rich and you were trying to be a hero and snatch a nice financial reward with the procedure. Am I right?"

"Objection!" said Ashton.

Wyatt responded unflinchingly. "Wrong." *What a weenie son of a bitch.*

Willoughby continued. "If you had sent the deceased to emergency open-heart surgery he would still be alive today, wouldn't he, Dr. Barton?"

"Objection," again interjected Ashton.

"I was trying to save a dying man. He was suffering from a sudden, massive heart attack and needed me to open his closed artery as quickly and efficiently as possible. He was very high risk for immediate open-heart surgery due to his lung condition, and therefore catheterization with an attempt to open up the blockage quickly without surgery was the best option."

Willoughby shot back. "Did the deceased know that?"

"Yes he did," responded Barton "In fact, he told me in front of his son Gavin that he did not want to consider open-heart surgery at all unless it was his last chance and my procedure failed. He knew the risks including death during the procedure, and he wished to proceed. He had a very difficult anatomy and that made him high risk for complications during the procedure."

"Have you ever had a complication like this—a perforated artery during a stent procedure, Dr. Barton?"

"No, this is my first in twenty years."

"Right. Well, I noticed that during the cardiac arrest suffered by Mr. Flanagan on your catheterization table, it took you two attempts to intubate him, or put a breathing tube into his trachea. Is that correct?"

"Yes, it is."

"And when you don't intubate a patient the first time, that means oxygen levels can go down and the patient may suffer, is that correct, Doctor?"

"Well, not necessarily. I had the second tube in within thirty seconds of the first one, and we were using the ambu-bag to successfully ventilate…"

"That's not what I asked, Dr. Barton. Did his oxygen level suffer because you couldn't get the tube in immediately?"

"No, it did not."

"In many cases of cardiac arrest, or respiratory arrest, a cardiologist like you would request an anesthesiologist or a pulmonologist to help intubate the patient while you are resuscitating his heart. Am I correct, Barton?"

"Maybe, maybe not. Depends on the situation. He was obese with a thick neck and we had no time to waste. So…"

"Answer the question, Doctor. Yes or no?"

"Objection," said Ashton. "Baiting the witness."

Wyatt had had enough. "You know, Mr. Willoughby, law must be awfully easy to practice if everything comes down to 'yes' and 'no' in your world. Medicine is not so simple and complex cases are not black and white. I'm trying to answer your question and it does not come down to a 'yes' and 'no.' So if you want an answer, let me answer. Oh and by the way, you will address me as Dr. Barton."

"Your client is becoming somewhat hostile, Ashton."

"Off the record, please. Let my client answer the way he wants, John, or I'll sue you for legal malpractice."

"Very well then. Go ahead and answer."

"He was obese with a thick neck and even experienced anesthesiologists could struggle with that kind of emergency intubation. I knew I didn't have time to wait until the emergency code team arrived, and anesthesiologists may not be a part of that team. It was me or nobody, and I was successful on the second attempt, and his oxygen saturations did not drop."

"I see," said Willoughby. "How much do you drink, Dr. Barton?"

"Objection," said Ashton. "What relevance does this have to the case?"

"Let the doctor answer."

Wyatt tasted blood in his mouth while his heart pounded at a sprinter's pace. He knew he had to answer without hesitation and with confidence or he was cooked, although there was no way they would know he was drinking one stupid beer three hours before the procedure. "I'll be happy to answer that. I drink a glass of wine maybe two times per week socially. Red wine always, for the heart."

Willoughby laughed. "Of course, that keeps the heart healthy. But were you drinking the night you were on call and attending the late Mr. Flanagan?"

"Absolutely not."

"I see. Well that's all the questions I have. Thank you, Dr. Barton.

Drake, I yield to you now."

Drake Ashton stood up to stretch his legs and for emphasis. "Dr. Barton, who is Dr. Ron Parker?"

"He is a cardiac surgeon that I work with at St. Francis hospital."

"Are you friends with him? I mean, do you socialize with him?"

"No, I don't. I know nothing about his family or social situation."

Ashton continued the questioning, but in a much softer tone than Willoughby. "What was Dr. Parker's role in the treatment of the deceased?"

"After I discovered that I likely had a complication with Mr. Flanagan, I used the ultrasound machine to show me that blood was building up in the sac around his heart. I had my staff call Dr. Parker to prepare for open-heart surgery while I put a tube in the sac to drain the blood that was causing his heart to fail."

"Were you successful with that tube drainage procedure?"

"Yes, but his heart had already suffered severe damage before he arrived to the hospital, and it continued to fail quickly despite the tube draining the pericardial sac."

"So what did Dr. Parker do to help you?"

"He prepared the operating room for emergency surgery, but unfortunately, when the catheterization team and I wheeled Mr. Flanagan to the operating room, he suffered cardiac arrest in the room, and we were unable to resuscitate him. Dr. Parker was there to assist, but we could not bring Mr. Flanagan's heart back, no matter how we tried with CPR and drugs."

"I have no further questions," said Ashton. "The deposition is now terminated as all counsel has finished. I will have the court send a copy of your deposition to you for review and then sign it if there are no mistakes, Dr. Barton."

A week later, the same two attorneys deposed Dr. Ron Parker and Amy Adams, R.N., in the same day. Willoughby asked if he knew Dr. Barton as a friend, and he affirmed that they only knew each other professionally.

"I would have Dr. Barton treat me any time if I needed his help," said Dr. Parker.

"I didn't ask you a question, Dr. Parker. Please strike this from the record."

Willoughby was more persistent with Amy Adams during her deposition.

"Ms. Adams, do you know Dr. Barton socially or just professionally or both?"

"Professionally only. I assist him during his cardiac catheterization procedures but that's all. Nothing socially."

"But you would like to know him socially, right? He's handsome and available, right?"

Amy blushed and looked down. "I don't know, maybe, but I am probably not the only one who finds him attractive. Like I said, he doesn't socialize with hospital people."

"Did Dr. Barton intubate Mr. Flanagan quickly during the emergency?"

"Yes, second attempt slipped right in. Doubt anyone could've done it better. Mr. Flanagan had a very difficult anatomy to overcome."

"Does he drink, Nurse Adams?"

"Objection," said Ashton. He glanced at the court recorder and demanded off the record. "C'mon, John. Do you want me to tell your wife that you take some of your young lady law interns out for drinks then you sleep with them?"

"You're a tough foe there, Drake. I got it. We're done."

Willoughby and the firm offered large sums of money to various cardiologists across the country to testify on their behalf as expert witnesses, but they all refused after reviewing the case records. There were several retired family physicians and internal medicine physicians who agreed to serve as expert witnesses, but they did not have the credentials to be believable, so they didn't receive a call.

Ashton proceeded quickly and filed a motion for Summary Judgment with the court. Within his brief was a description of the discovery and excerpts of the depositions that showed that the plaintiff failed to obtain the required expert witness to support the claim of malpractice, and he wrote that there was no evidence of negligence or violation of the applicable standard of care. The judge agreed and dismissed the case with prejudice. Wyatt received a complete exoneration.

"You have got to be kidding me, Willoughby!" said Gavin. "I thought you were the best and you let some nobody lawyer from across the tracks beat us?"

"There was no case, Gavin. I couldn't find a credible expert witness. It wasn't going to happen. The guy is squeaky clean, I tell you. Or if he isn't, he's hiding pretty well. He's a good doctor that we won't take down this time. Can't stand docs like that. Hard to beat them."

"Well guess what, Willoughby? You're fired."

Blake blew his cool when he heard the news. "If this pussy Willoughby can't extract justice from this quack," he said, "then I will."

"Nobody takes my girl and kills my father," Gavin replied angrily. "He may have taken one from me, but he won't take both."

"It's going to get interesting now. Don't you think?"

"Perhaps. But right now I need some time to blow off some steam and forget about this for a while. I feel the need for some female company, so don't call me for the next few days. I'll be holed up in my house, hopefully just the bedroom."

"I know the feeling very well, in fact I'm feeling it now. I think I'm going to call Delphine."

"Go to hell. She's too good for you anyway, and you know it."

Blake laughed. "Maybe, but we certainly have one thing in common and it's not playing Scrabble."

CHAPTER 29

Gavin's cell phone rang and rang, but he ignored it because the young law clerk he was pounding was about to explode and her screaming drowned out the recurrent rings. Her powerful thighs clasped around him like a soft lobster claw, and he couldn't have gotten out of bed to answer anyway without dragging her with him. He was sure that she used the ThighMaster machine at the gym. Her bedroom enthusiasm was a sure bet to place her high on the list during hiring time at his firm.

Marta eventually gave up calling Gavin and called Wyatt instead. "I didn't want to call you this late but I'm scared. I think someone is either trying to get into my house or looking into the windows. I closed all the blinds the best I could. I thought I saw someone trying to peek in through my living-room window and heard noises in the bushes. I don't know if he's still here or not."

Wyatt immediately put on his pants and a t-shirt, grabbed the Glock 9 mm that he kept at home for backup home intrusion protection, and kept his cell phone next to his ear while he jumped in his car. "I'm on my way. Did you call the police?"

"Yes, but they said that since no one has broken in, they don't have enough officers to come by right now."

Bleary eyed after a difficult night on call, an adrenaline surge jolted every cell of his body into high alert. After ten minutes of speeding, he turned off his headlights and parked several houses away. "I'm in front of your house now. Are you okay?"

"Don't know. Someone is still making noise around my house, and I feel like someone is spying on me."

"Stay in your bedroom and lock the door."

"I'm already there."

He ran to the back of her house with his Glock at his side, and then quietly tiptoed in the darkness around the perimeter of the house. A quick survey showed no intruders in the backyard. Nothing on the east side either. He slowed his breathing down as much as he could until it hurt to breathe, hoping to avoid detection. He heard a noise and perceived a human form fall into a clump of bushes, and then start running from the opposite side of the house. The guy already had significant distance on him but he chased and quickly gained ground. His quarry wasn't very fast, and like a jaguar who knew he had his dinner, Wyatt kicked his legs high to gain sprint speed then sprang up to leap onto the intruder, but his foot caught awkwardly on a sprinkler head while he rose up into the air, and he fell to the wet ground, his ankle twisted. Searing pain bolted like lightning from his ankle, but he got up and continued to run with a limp; unfortunately, it was too late. The intruder jumped into a car down the street and it sped off. He tried to see the license plate but couldn't make out the numbers. He thought it looked like a jeep, but he wasn't sure. One thing he did know, this dude ran like a girl. In the darkness, all he could make out was a black baseball cap, black jeans, and a black sweatshirt.

Marta saw his limp when he entered the house and hugged him with all her strength, and he felt her tears on his cheeks while she kissed him warmly. He held her close until he felt her trembling cease. "Wyatt, I was so worried about you. You are neither a cowboy nor a police officer; you are a doctor. You could've been killed by whoever this was! You should've stayed with me in the room and waited for the police. And what happened to your leg?"

"Twisted my ankle when I tried to jump on the jerk. Damn, I almost had her. Do you have a ziplock bag so I can ice down my ankle before the swelling increases?"

"Sure, no problem. But what do you mean 'her'?"

"No offense to women intended but the intruder ran like a girl. That's all I could tell. And since she wasn't very fast I almost caught her, then I twisted my ankle on a lawn sprinkler head."

Marta started shaking again and this time he hugged her tightly, enjoying the curvy feel of her receptive body inside her warm robe. She gave him a passionate kiss, he kissed her back, and soon his hands were roaming gently up the sides for her legs and behind. It was a luxurious kiss filled with warmth and tender emotion. He could feel her heart through her soft lips and wanted to soak up all of her feminine beauty, and this would be the first of many kisses he hoped to enjoy with her. Eventually, their passionate grip broke away slightly to allow the couple to gulp some air.

"Oh my, that was amazing!" Marta gave him the largest smile he'd ever received from her, and she locked her hands around his neck in the way that only a woman knows how to do. "I'm so glad you came, but I'm sorry I woke you up. Well, I take that back. Now that I think about it, maybe I'm not so sorry at all."

Wyatt blushed. "You can call me anytime. I'll come running. Are you feeling better now?"

"Much better now, my hero. I'm certainly happy that Linas is at his friend's house tonight. It's so good that he wasn't here tonight because I wouldn't like to see him frightened."

"You're right. There are some bad people in America, so you must be careful. However, there are many more good people. Seems maybe someone knew you were alone and decided to spy on you or was trying to figure out a way to enter the house. We call that 'casing the joint.' I want to help you get an alarm system installed for your house and maybe buy you a gun to protect yourself. Of course, I'll teach you how to use it safely and effectively. Remember, though, if you have a gun in your house and there is an intruder, you must be ready to kill him or he'll kill you."

"Wyatt, that's kind of you, but not necessary. I'm okay. Don't worry about me. Not only that, I've never shot a gun before, so I'm afraid of them."

"No worries, I'll take care of you, so don't argue with me. Okay?"

"Okay." Marta quickly changed the subject. "Would you like to drink some tea with me on my couch? I know you're tired and need to get some sleep, but I would like you to stay here a while."

"Absolutely. Decaffeinated tea, please." Wyatt felt a little nervous in her house, having never been there before, but her gracious smile and their passionate connection increased his comfort quickly. He was surprised to notice that such a clean woman had large amounts of dishes piled up at the sink. She caught him staring at the pile.

"I'm sorry for the mess, but I don't have hot water today. I can't clean or take a bath without heating water on the stove. I will hire someone tomorrow to fix it."

"Is your hot water heater downstairs?"

"Um, I think so."

"Give me a flashlight and I'll see if the pilot light is out. I'm not much of a handyman, but I can light pilot lights without blowing myself up, I think." Wyatt went to the basement and relit the pilot light on the water heater, and after a while, Marta had hot water again. This was no major mechanical achievement, but Wyatt felt good that he was able to help Marta a little.

When he hurried upstairs, they sat on the sofa and talked. He confided about the emptiness he felt in his life and the loss of his sons.

"But you must protect yourself," she said when he finished. "You love your children, but it will tear you apart emotionally to keep thinking you can change them. Pray for them. Live your life, enjoy good people, and some day they will return to you."

He was slow to respond, but smiled because he could tell she cared. "You're right; I will never give up hope that things will change. I believe that the love of a father for his sons, or love in general, must rule the day. I'll see you at Starbucks for our morning coffee session," he said as he got up to leave.

"I can't wait. Drive safe."

They kissed again, and the tenderness of her lips made him not want to leave, but he knew he should. When he drove home with a sleepy haze in his eyes at three a.m., he noticed that a car followed him, but he was just too tired to care. Probably some kid coming home from a late-night party. He drove to his home and forgot about it, his mind completely on Marta.

"That was him. Illinois plate K25 4576. He left her house at precisely three a.m. and went home directly. He was there about 2 hours and I saw them kiss in the doorway.Yeah, I'm sure it was him. Funny thing is I think there may have been an attempted burglary. Looks like this Wyatt guy ran after someone and almost caught her but she got away.Yes, I am sure it was a girl, and no, I was not detected. Remember, you pay me lots of green for my services."

CHAPTER 30

Blake picked her up in a new red corvette with vanity plates, "Marine UNO." She wore a tight short skirt and heels with a light sweater that softly draped in front in folds, leaving plentiful fruit for the male imagination. Her hair draped softly over her shoulders, ending up in her face when she laughed. Blake wore tight jeans that accented his lower body, and his short-sleeved shirt was not tucked in, but fit tightly to his muscled chest and chiseled arms.

Initially they sat at the bar several feet away from each other, but it wasn't long before they moved to a cozy booth, sitting almost on top of each other, kissing and touching. Amy caressed his arms and felt his strength, imagining him holding her captive while he enjoyed ravenous sex with her helpless body. She wanted him now. She needed satisfaction by a man, to fill the void in her desire that had remained unquenched for too long. It didn't matter anymore about his attitude when she first met him, because her innate desire for a strong man was suffocating rational thought. She saw his eyes continually stealing glances at her hemline. She initially attempted to pull her skirt down, but it wasn't worth the effort and she gave up, enjoying his interest in her toned legs.

"I have a full bar at home, sound stereo and a movie theater. Don't you think that would be a better place than here at this bar?"

"Are you going to kidnap me, Mr. Blake, sir?"

"Only if you say no; then I will of course."

Amy laughed. "Well in that case, let's make it nonviolent. I say hell yeah, take me, you brute."

His right hand moved back and forth from Amy's leg to the gear-shift, giving her goose bumps. When they arrived at the front steps of the mansion, he fumbled for his keys while Amy kept her hand around his waist. Trembling with anticipation, the key insertion took way too long. Once inside, he almost put the wrong security code in to shut off the alarm because she wouldn't stop biting and kissing his neck. After walking a few feet inside the foyer, she turned him to face her, put both hands on his sculpted behind, and took control of his mouth with hers. She felt his excitement in front while his rough jeans creased her silky skirt. She made a brief little whine when he picked her up with one hand under her bottom and the other hand holding her head so their lips would not part, and then gently laid her on the couch in front of the fireplace. He then trapped her with iron arms on each side of her, commanding her to remove her skirt and panties while he watched like a lion preparing for the kill. Her vision at the bar of his strong arms and her sexual captivity was now real erotic frenzy. The lion completed his kill and his prey screamed in defenseless ecstasy.

"You know, Amy, I like you. I think we can develop a relationship with time. What do you think?"

"I like you too, but just as a sexual friend, you know, friends with benefits. Tonight was nothing more than animal sex, damn good sex, but I'm really only after one man. I don't want to offend you; you're great in bed, but you are not the one I want a relationship with."

He pulled away from her a little. "Damn, you're a straight shooter. You're stuck on asshole Barton. Have you had sex with him?"

"He may be an asshole to you, but he's a good man for my future. He's handsome, smart, and successful. Women don't tell about their sexual lives, dear, you should know that."

"Yeah well you know what I think about him. I think you're making a huge mistake, but if he ever hurts you, you call me and let me know; I'll go after him. And by the way, he's already got a woman that he's interested in, and my brother's going to take care of that."

"Old news, Blake. I have to go."

He drove her back home. They didn't kiss, but just said good-bye with no indication there would be a second encounter. Amy went to bed and stared at the fireplace mantel and the framed photo of Wyatt with her at the Heart Ball.

CHAPTER 31

"What a lovely birthday present, Wyatt! Of course I'll go."

"Perfect. I wanted to make it a special evening. I like the Goodman Theater. It's the oldest theater in Chicago and so it has lots of history. Before that, we're going to Catch 35, because I know you love seafood. I'll pick you up early so we can enjoy some wine and cheese and maybe spend some time in the hot tub before we leave."

"Sounds yummy, the earlier the better, but if it's okay I need to run some errands and buy some clothes for Linas, so I'll drive over to your house."

"It's a deal."

Marta arrived at Wyatt's house in an elegant red dress with tastefully cut slits on the sides, heels, and a wide smile. The dress accented her long blonde hair free-falling over her feminine shoulders. The cut of the top of the dress showed part of her left collarbone. Wyatt greeted her at the door and kissed her gently, and she could feel him breathe in her perfume with a deep, lingering breath.

"Happy birthday, honey! You look and smell great, and now I'm going to find out how you taste." He kissed her and nibbled on her neck. "Hmm, a delicious delicacy that I can't get enough of."

"Oh my, Wyatt, aren't you the romantic one tonight! If we keep going, I don't think we'll make the dinner and theater, but then I won't complain."

He controlled himself and led her to the kitchen table, poured two glasses of ten-year-old Chateau Lusseau St. Emilion Grand Cru, and pulled the chair out for her. "To my beautiful friend from Latvia," he toasted. "My gain, Latvia's loss." They drank and kissed again. Wyatt brought out a cake he'd bought, lit some candles, and sang the traditional American happy birthday song that Marta now heard for the first time. She beamed at Wyatt's soft blue eyes and straight white teeth.

They are in his house. They're both so naïve that they don't even think someone could be watching them from a car down the street. Surprise will be my advantage. How could that foreign bitch take him so quickly? I'm the only one who deserves him; she doesn't.

After some wine, cheese, and conversation, the happy couple got into the car and took off to Catch 35, Wyatt's left hand on the wheel and the right one holding Marta's left hand. She then followed them from behind, keeping a safe distance to avoid detection. They laughed and enjoyed each other's company, singing along with the XM radio. The windows and sunroof in his car were down, and the breeze blew their hair, especially Marta's, occasionally sucking it up above the car through the sunroof for all the other drivers to see.

She followed them from a distance, and the curvy roads protected her from detection. The two lovers stopped at their first stoplight, their torsos moving back and forth to the music, and he kissed her, his hand holding her head gently.

She grew incensed by the view of the two lovers kissing, and began to rev her engine loudly in anger.

Wyatt looked back to see who the motorhead was, but couldn't recognize anyone to his right or left. "Some kids must be trying to impress their girlfriends by revving their engines."

"Did you do that when you were younger?"

He laughed. "I couldn't afford a car during high school, so on the rare occasions I had my parents' car, I had to be careful, especially in a sexy station wagon. I tried to impress my dates in other, more subtle ways."

"And what would that be, my sexy friend?"

The light turned green and they proceeded on. "Well, would you believe my massive muscles and chiseled physique?"

"Funny, Wyatt. I think you can charm a woman just by being who you are."

She skillfully followed the couple, waiting for the best moment to make her move. She stayed one car behind the car next to Wyatt in the other lane. The car in front of her finally turned right on a side street and she accelerated up next to her quarry, rolling down her window, honking continuously.

Wyatt glanced to his right and saw Amy gesturing at him to roll down his passenger window. "My God," said Marta, who immediately recognized who it was screaming at them while they were driving in tandem down the road. "It's that woman you took to the Heart Ball!"

"Yeah, she's driving like a maniac. What is she doing?" Wyatt tried to escape from the menace, but she stayed up with him. He ignored her screams and kept driving down the road, not knowing what she would do next, caring only to keep his Marta safe.

"Don't respond to her, Marta; just look straight ahead."

Amy dropped behind his car, then sped up and again started yelling, this time at Marta directly. "You are fucking my man. You will pay, you slut!" Then, she glared at Wyatt. "I can't believe you're with that bitch! You know you're mine!"

Marta's body shook. "She's crazy, and I don't know what she'll do! We need to get away from her."

Wyatt rolled up the windows at the stoplight, but Amy kept yelling and driving next to them. Suddenly, she swerved over and almost hit his car. Quick reflexes prevented him from making contact with her car, but he did drive onto the shoulder of the road, and Marta screamed when he nearly collided with a light pole. When he recovered and got back onto the road, she sped off.

Wyatt pulled over into a gas-station parking lot to collect his thoughts. The two just stared straight ahead for what seemed an eternity. Finally, Marta said, "Thank God that crazy woman didn't kill us. What is your relationship to her? Still dating or was she a former lover? I know you took her to the Heart Ball, but maybe I should've asked more about her."

"She's a nurse who works at the hospital in the catheterization lab. I've known her professionally for three or four years, but no, we aren't dating. She invited me over to her house once for drinks and dinner and I went."

"Oh really. When was that?"

"Not long after you and I met at your lecture. She had asked me several times before, but I always made excuses and didn't go."

"Were you intimate?"

"No, as I said we didn't even kiss. I guess I just went out of curiosity and I was a little lonely. Now I realize it was a mistake because now she thinks I am hers for some insane reason. I had no idea she was off her rocker. She seemed like a nice person professionally."

"Interesting."

"Marta, I'm sorry this happened on your birthday. Let's try to enjoy the rest of the evening. I'll call the police and file a report tomorrow against her. It makes things difficult for us at the hospital, but I don't care, she's clearly dangerous and I want to protect us from her."

"File a report. I'll be a witness if they ask me, because it'll be your word against hers."

"Right, since there was no accident or traffic violation, I don't know if they can proceed with any action against her. She'll deny it."

Marta enjoyed the play and the atmosphere of the theater district of Chicago. She felt secure with Wyatt, and a connection that she had never felt before. She forgot about Amy and immersed herself in the pleasure of the moment. She could feel Wyatt's desire for her, and he made her feel like the only woman in the world. She believed in him.

They drove to his house after the theater, and they sat on his couch and talked, smooth jazz in the background. He poured her some more wine, took her hand, and pulled her close to him. They kissed, then got up and danced gently to the music, feeling each other's body and drinking in the closeness. He ran his fingers gently through her hair, kissing her lips softly then with more passion, followed by the soft nape of her neck then back to her lips again with more erotic eagerness. She responded by putting her arms around him and caressing his back and shoulders. She felt so wanted and feminine that she thought she would do anything he asked. He didn't ask. He took her wine glass out of her fingers and put it on the kitchen table, then gently held her hand and walked her to the bedroom.

They didn't say anything to each other; their absorption of each other's desire was complete and unstoppable. He continued to kiss her, and she eagerly allowed him to remove her dress and every other article of clothing that impeded skin-to-skin contact. They both fell to bed together, and he explored her entire body, gradually inducing her cry-like moans of blissful pleasure that undulated to the waves of his strong but rhythmic passion.

The two lovers lay on their sides, staring at each other, exhausted and satisfied. Finally, he broke the silence of the moment. "I love you, Marta."

"I love you too, Wyatt."

Wyatt lay completely relaxed next to his Marta, and he watched her sleep peacefully. What was wrong with Amy? Clearly unstable. He now had two crazy women in his life. Before he drifted off to sleep, he thought of Spencer and Colby. *God, help those boys and help me conquer this ridiculous hatred.*

CHAPTER 32

"What a surprise, Amy. Didn't think I would hear from you again," said Blake. "You must miss me."

She laughed. "I must admit that was a hot night we had together. But I'm calling for another reason, and I need your expertise."

"That's too bad, but fire away."

"I want to buy a gun, and you're an instructor in the Marine sniper scout school, so who would be better to go to for advice?"

"Guns are dangerous, pretty lady, if you don't know how to use them. Why do you want a gun?"

She paused. "Don't you think a single woman needs protection?"

"Sure I do."

"There have been some break-ins around town that I read about on the news and I thought it was about time for me to have a weapon at home in case there is an intruder. I think I'm a prime target because I live alone. I've always been afraid of handguns, but I thought maybe you could help me buy one and learn to shoot it."

"Not a problem, sweetie. Meet me at my house, and I'll drive you to the gun store then the firing range for a little lesson."

They looked at several weapons in the gun store. He thought a short-barrel shotgun would be the best for her, but he didn't think she could handle a gun that size. He showed her a Ruger 380 lightweight compact pistol. She liked the small size, but he ruled it out since it would only be effective at point-blank range. If she was that close to the attacker then she'd be in trouble. Hopefully she would be able to fire at a longer range. She liked the Smith-and-Wesson

.357 magnum and the Glock 19. She showed him that she was able to cock the Glock and it didn't require much strength. He noticed that she made her decision very quickly in the store and showed no emotion at all during the purchase, almost as if this was just a mundane job.

At the firing range he showed her the basics of gun safety, then had her try target shooting at close range and then at farther distances. After about fifty rounds, he was surprised to see that she could easily hit the human figure in the face and chest consistently at seven yards, and with a decent score at fifteen yards.

"It seems that you have a natural eye for shooting."

"Just lucky I guess. Thanks for teaching me and helping me get comfortable. I feel much safer now."

Before they got into his car, he stopped her and asked, "This idiot Barton isn't causing you trouble, is he?"

"No, of course not. Are you kidding? He's a gentleman. There aren't many real gentlemen left anymore it seems. But he's ignoring me because his mind's on that Euro chick and it's becoming too difficult to work with him at the hospital. So, I quit my hospital job and now I work for a visiting nurse service."

"Strikes me as odd that you would take a drastic step like that just because he's spurning you. Whatever you need to do, I guess. What's interesting, though, is that he's still dating my brother's dream girl so that's going to make things nice and complicated for you."

"Yeah, I saw them together sometimes at the hospital before I resigned. They seem to enjoy drinking coffee at Starbucks together."

"I'm surprised a woman of that quality would stay with a guy like that. I figured she would've dumped him by now. Gavin has a lot more money than this guy, and could make her a rich woman. He's really pissed, though. I know one thing about Gavin, and that is when he picks a woman, he gets her. What makes it worse is that he's the stupid doctor who also killed our dad. Now the courts say he's innocent and our case was dismissed because of no evidence of malpractice. That's bullshit. Gavin and I know he's guilty."

"You know, Blake, you're great in the sack, but you are way off base and have no idea what you're talking about. He's a good doctor and you two brothers have a warped vendetta against him. Just let it go. I'm sorry I have to say this but your late father was a fat, cigar-smoking, cardiac time bomb."

They got in the car and drove back to his house. After a few minutes of silence, he spoke up. "You know, I don't usually take kindly to someone who puts down my family, but I guess, in your case because of your fine body, I'll have to make an exception."

Amy didn't skip a beat after his comment. "You and your brother need to stop your ridiculous hatred against this innocent man. Just take out your misplaced anger instead on enemies of the United States; that's what you're trained to do. Stick to war and not innocent civilians who save lives."

"Damn, Amy. You got some spunk. But Flanagan family business is between myself and my brother, and we don't need your opinion. Now I need to change the subject to something more pleasant. I expect payment for my services today, sexy nurse Amy, and I don't mean money. I need a nice send-off to go back to base. Will you give it to me?"

Amy nodded and went into his house. She tolerated Blake because his bedroom skills forced her brain away from heavy thoughts to pure pleasure, starting as soon as he smiled and flexed his veiny biceps. To her, brawn was better than brains in bed, but only in bed. "Okay, but I can't stay long. I have some important work to do later tonight. Just a quickie."

They both achieved satisfaction quickly, but he noticed that her mind seemed distant. She showed no emotion in the bed, save for her primitive erotic reflexes, but he didn't care; he got what he wanted and so did she. He wondered, though, when or if she would be successful in her quest for her elusive man.

CHAPTER 33

Walking through the hospital, Wyatt's energy transformed his cadence to a strut. He couldn't get Marta off his mind. His life had changed completely because of her. People asked him why he was in such a good mood, but he just smiled and said that he felt great and life was good finally. Nothing else mattered right now but her. After his duties at the hospital were over, he went to the jewelry store and bought an expensive engagement ring that he thought would look good on her finger. While driving home, he sang along with the radio while it played the old song by Firefall: "You are the woman that I always dreamed of, I knew it from the start, I saw your face and that's the last I've seen of my heart." He was proud of the ring he bought, and proud of himself for finally finding real love in his life. He'd found a woman who was actually of his choosing, a woman who not only understood love and life, but also gave love unconditionally despite his problems. *She's a divine symphony of feminine perfection.*

It was about six p.m. Tuesday evening, and Wyatt had already left to pick up Marta for their dinner date when Spencer and Colby, staying at their mother's home for summer vacation, decided to drive by their old house, now their father's residence, just out of curiosity. They hoped to see Marta's car or some other interesting item to report to Katherine, but it was just the house as they knew it, with the outside lights on.

They drove home and sat down to a debriefing with Katherine at dinner. "Did you guys see her car? It's a silver Toyota Camry."

"No, Mom," they both answered in unison. "No cars."

"Yeah, well you can bet he's out with her somewhere. I'm lucky to have Mark, because he is so good to me and he loves you kids, don't you think so?"

"He's a better man than Wyatt ever was, that's for sure," Spencer said. "He's good to us."

"Yeah," said Colby. "Mark's nice, but I just wish Dad, I mean Wyatt, would've stayed with us."

"Right," said Spencer. "At least he's been consistent over the years. He's a selfish bastard. I think my life is much better without him. I know he called us many times, sent us cards on holidays, and asked to spend stupid time with us, but we told him to stick it because he blew it with us. I'm glad he finally started to listen to us and stopped calling us. I don't know about you, Colby, but I know we're better off without him. We have you, Mom, and Mark as a new father; that is if you get married—hint hint."

Colby couldn't hold his tongue. "I like Mark, but then I also liked David, your other boyfriend that you had when Wyatt left us, or as you say, Mom, 'abandoned' us. It doesn't matter to me who you're with. I just want you to be happy. As far as Wyatt, I hate him for what he did to us. But at the same time, I miss him a little, you know, the good times."

"Really? I'm surprised at you, Colby," said Spencer. "I want him as far from us as possible and you should feel the same way."

Katherine smiled and hugged her two sons. "You boys are my life, everything to me, and I will do anything for you. You're right; you don't need him and the three of us are happy now. He lost some great sons. I just don't know if I will ever recover, though, from what he has done to us. And as far as Mark, I saw him talking to a woman one day when I did a little surprise drive-by of his house, so, some men just can't be trusted, I guess."

"How often do you drive by his house, Mom?" asked Colby.

"Don't know, couple times a week maybe."

"Really? Maybe you should just give him some space. Probably just the neighbor lady he was talking to anyway."

"Never is. None of your business anyway."

Drinking on a weeknight was unusual for Gavin, but this was a rare time—he didn't have office work to do at home, and his brother was leaving the next day for Quantico. The brothers had not been close over the years, but after their father's death, they seemed to appreciate their time together, especially if it was beer night. Gavin cooked some steaks on the back patio grill and Blake brought the beer. As they drank more and more beer, their conversation became more animated.

"So who have you been hooking up with here in Chicago?"

"You remember that cute nurse that Barton took to the Heart Ball?"

"Yeah I remember. Her legs went on forever."

"We've spent some hot times together, but that's all. We only have one thing in common."

"What about Delphine? I thought you would be all over her since you went behind my back and brought her to the dance."

"No. Damn thing is that she's always unavailable. You know, jet-setting model flanked by lots of pretty boys. Doesn't matter, seems Amy and I have some kind of connection even though she's apparently hot for Barton."

"I don't care about Delphine, but I do care about Marta." Gavin raised his voice. "She's the best woman I've ever met, and I can't believe she's dating that guy; he stole her right from under my nose. No one has ever successfully done that to me, and I won't let him get away with it! Just so you know, I hired a top private detective to follow him, and I'm accumulating lots of damn good information on him."

"What kind of information?"

"The detective followed him, so we know where he lives. We know what his office hours are, when he usually arrives home, and we've been able to figure out that his usual on-call night is Tuesday, and he is on call every fourth weekend as well.

"That's boring stuff, but go on. I hope it gets better before I fall asleep."

"He drives a black Audi, and we know the license number. He goes to the grocery once a week and runs about 5 miles a day early in the morning about 5:30, and rides his bike long distances on the weekends when he's off."

"Does he have any other women over to his house besides Marta?"

"No, I was hoping for that but no dice. He only dates Marta. Seems they've been dating steady for the last six months or so, before that I don't know. That is a big problem. Huge. I really don't want him with her anymore, and I'm going to destroy him."

"I'm with you on that, Gavin. While I understand that you can't stand the jerk because he stole your girl, I think he's shit because of what he did to Dad, no matter what the courts say. Do you have any plans for resolving this problem?"

"Of course."

"Are you going to tell me what you're planning to do with this private detective information or is this a secret?"

Gavin looked down and thought for a while, then responded. "Some people who work in our firm know some prostitutes who work the streets and have gotten in trouble with the law, and some of our guys have bailed them out of trouble, you know."

"Yeah, okay. Go on."

"Well, I've asked our guys to pay a couple thousand to this hot prostitute and convince her that she's to go to Barton's office and pose as if she has chest pain or some cardiac problem. We'll tell her to wear decent clothes and present herself well so there would be no suspicion by Barton or his staff. Since cardiologists do examinations that don't require the patient to undress, it's unlikely that he will ask a nurse to assist him and stay in the room. That way there will be no witnesses to support his innocence. So, after the exam, we'll instruct her to walk out of the room and scream to the staff, 'He touched me inappropriately! I can't believe your Doctor Barton is a pervert. I'll call my lawyer and the state licensing board.'

"I'll then have her file a case of inappropriate sexual conduct with the licensing board, and that will cause him all kinds of trouble. He won't be able to prove his case and she won't be able to prove her case, but it'll cast suspicion of him with Marta, his staff, colleagues, and patients. My hope is he'll either quit or, better yet, lose his practice, but more importantly, lose Marta."

"That's certainly well planned out, but I think it's a damn wussy way of hurting him. Too many variables, too expensive, and it may not work. You know, maybe you need to let me take care of things my way, with finality, so there will be no way for him to wiggle out of it."

"I know what you're thinking, but I don't want to hear any more about it. I know violence is your way of life. You can do things the way you want without my knowledge. Count on me to extract justice my way, but it seems we both are on the same page."

"It's getting late, and I have things to do. By the way, I need to talk to your private detective. There's some information I need to get from him about Wyatt."

Gavin handed Blake the detective's cell phone number. "I'll see you when I see you. Have a good flight tomorrow."

Gazing deeply into each other's eyes, Marta and Wyatt laughed and smiled during the candlelight dinner. Marta loved her red wine, and Wyatt drank ice water because he was on call for the hospital.

"I wish you could enjoy the wine with me. It's excellent and smooth."

"Don't worry, honey, I'm intoxicated with the moment."

"What do you mean?" She could tell he was getting serious.

"There's something I want to ask you, sweetie."

"Okay, darling, my ears are eager."

Wyatt pulled out the ring box from his jacket pocket, kept it in his left hand, then reached across and, taking hold of Marta's dainty hand, dropped to his knees in front of her. He kissed her hand, and then said, "Here's a ring for my love, the woman I want to be with forever."

"Oh Wyatt, it's beautiful!" Without hesitation, she kissed Wyatt and with tears of joy said, "Yes, of course I'm yours! I could never be happier than right now! I love you too!"

The waiter saw what Wyatt did, and applauded loudly while the couple smiled and kissed each other. Soon the rest of the restaurant customers understood what was happening, and they joined the clapping and cheering as well. The couple stayed for hours and eventually left the restaurant at closing time.

They walked to their respective cars, kissed again, and then Marta said, "I've never been happier in my life. I am so lucky to have come to America and met you. I'll go home to tell Linas the good news, and we will see each other tomorrow morning before work at the coffee shop, okay?"

"I'll be there, Marta. Nothing and nobody can keep us from being together."

"Call me when you get home from the hospital."

"You can bet on that."

CHAPTER 34

BACK TO THE PRESENT:

When the medics rushed to the scene, they found Dr. Barton in shock with shallow breathing, and they immediately inserted large-bore intravenous lines to pour fluids in, while simultaneously inserting a breathing tube into his airway. They drew blood for labs and cross matching for the imminent transfusion that had to occur when they arrived at St. Anthony's. He was quickly loaded into the ambulance, and the neighbors watched on their comfortable porches in their pajamas, awakened by all the sirens, unable to speak due to their fear. The medics still felt Wyatt's pulse, but it was barely palpable. He was dying.

The chief medic radioed St. Anthony's Hospital emergency department requesting a full trauma alert to mobilize the appropriate nursing staff, respiratory therapists, lab and blood bank technicians, the operating room and trauma surgeons. The triage nurse had a steady voice and calmly handed the radio mike over to Dr. Brian Moore, one of the emergency physicians on duty, and a golfing buddy of Dr. Barton.

"What do you have?"

"Full trauma, gunshot wound to the upper right abdomen, severe shock, but we still have pulses. The airway's secure."

"What's your ETA?"

"Three minutes tops."

"Does he have a chest wound?"

"Affirmative. Looks like right chest and abdomen."

Ready for action, Moore's voice was steel-steady. "We're waiting for you. Anything you need from me?"

"Uh yes, there's one more thing."

"Go ahead."

"The victim is Dr. Wyatt Barton."

An uncomfortable pause pervaded the airwaves. Dr. Moore couldn't respond until he was able to clear the gooey mass of dread that was now obstructing his own esophagus as if he had swallowed an apple whole with no saliva.

"Dr. Moore, did you receive the last transmission?"

"Affirmative, but my transmitter, I guess, went dead briefly. Is this Dr. Wyatt Barton of Premier Cardiology that you have?"

"Affirmative."

"Shit, get him here now!"

Nearly always calm under pressure, Moore was so shaken that he couldn't speak to the nurses when he sprinted to the trauma bay to receive the ambulance crew and his dying friend. It hadn't been twenty minutes since the chief of the emergency department called him, angry that his friend Wyatt was not answering his calls and wanting Moore to get him immediately with whatever means were necessary. Ironically, because his decision to call the police was for a different reason, they were able to deliver Wyatt to the hospital as ordered—unfortunately not for his delinquent call duties, but as a trauma patient. Dr. Moore never figured he had to also give instructions to bring him in alive. He just told the police to bring him now.

Katrina Anderson, a new nursing-school graduate, relished her assignment on the trauma team, and like everyone else in the emergency department that night, was fully aware that Dr. Barton was now being wheeled full speed down the hallways to the trauma bay. While she sprinted with the gurney from the ambulance entrance, she held her strength as best she could, but when she touched his pale, nearly lifeless hand she had to look away to hide her emotions and remain professional. She didn't know him very well, but remembered his kindness when he'd helped her interpret EKG's when she was just starting out, and that he always had a smile and a joke for her when she seemed stressed. The realization that she might lose Wyatt as a valuable medical team member began to make her more nauseated than the smell of the drunk's vomit in the next room. She released his hand when nearly twenty hospital personnel from various departments greeted the gurney that flew into trauma bay one, then ran to the nearest restroom and hurled from the stress.

Dr. Paul Duncan was the trauma surgeon on duty who ordered the immediate transfusion of typed blood. He needed to order CT scans to examine the damaged organs, but he quickly realized that they were losing Wyatt, and his only hope was immediate surgery after he was stabilized as much as possible. After a quick ultrasound and physical examination, Dr. Duncan confirmed that Wyatt's breath sounds were absent on the right side so he inserted a large chest tube into his chest cavity, with an immediate gush of air and blood, effectively allowing the lung to re-expand and capture precious life-giving oxygen. His blood pressure increased slightly after this procedure, but he remained in shock and was losing blood fast. Duncan thought it was possibly from a lacerated liver or abdominal vessel. He had no signs of head or neck injury but cervical CT scans would be accomplished later, if he survived.

While the anesthesiologist deftly placed a right internal jugular vein intravenous line to allow large volume blood transfusions, the OR staff efficiently prepped Wyatt for surgery. The respiratory therapist yelled out the blood gas results to Dr. Duncan, who then commanded, "He has a severe lactic acidosis from shock and blood loss. Give him one ampule of sodium bicarbonate. Start a bicarbonate drip, and damn it, where the hell is my blood? If you can't give him cross-matched blood give him type-specific blood now and stay ahead of his blood needs, people!" Duncan bumped into one of the ten medical personnel in the room, nearly falling to the floor, slippery from Wyatt's spilled blood.

"Anyone in this room not doing something specific needs to get the hell out of here and out of my way!"

Duncan requested the operating room charge nurse to call Dr. John Branson, his partner, to come in and provide surgical assistance. Duncan's face nearly matched the color of Wyatt's bloody body. He refused to show his stress to the staff watching him, and his hand remained steady and his actions confident. Obviously, Wyatt's chances for survival with severe hemorrhage and probably superimposed infectious shock from possible rupture of the colon were low at this point unless Duncan was able to stop the bleeding and the inevitable cascade of multiple organ failure. After the anesthesiologist put Wyatt to sleep, he gave Duncan a warning. "His blood pressure is tanking again, Paul. I'm starting Neo-Synephrine to raise it up if I can."

"Do what you have to do, then tell me later after you do it. Scalpel, please."

Wyatt Barton, M.D., was still alive but just barely, while his love, Marta, lay sleeping peacefully in bed unaware of the night's bloody events.

CHAPTER 35

While the medics raced Wyatt to the St. Anthony's Hospital emergency department, the two officers involved remained on the scene at his house. After determining that the scene was secure with no further threats to life, they made an initial assessment of the crime scene itself and then called headquarters and asked them to page the homicide detective on call:

"Yeah, this is Farmer. I hope you have a damn good reason for waking me up!"

"This is Bill Jenkins from sector two. I'm on the scene of a shooting in the home of a local cardiologist. He's not deceased, but he is now in the hospital, don't know if he'll make it."

"What's your initial assessment?"

"Not sure what to make of it, Gordon. Don't know if it was an accident, botched suicide attempt, or a home intruder that got caught in the act."

A seasoned veteran of police work, Gordon Farmer started out as a patrol officer, and after receiving commendations for bravery and exemplary work, he advanced up the ranks and was now the chief homicide detective in Evanston. He was exhausted, having stayed up all night the previous night to prepare for a court appearance on a financial crime case he had solved. He really didn't need another botched suicide attempt to deal with right now, but while he drove to the scene, he automatically gave orders to the officer in rote fashion with a concern to protect the scene for the legal proceedings.

"Where's the weapon?"

"12-gauge home protector about six feet from where I found the victim."

"How did you get the call?"

"Dispatch sent me to the location to find the doc since he wasn't responding to the emergency department at St. Anthony's, I guess. Apparently he's a busy cardiologist when he's on call. When I arrived, I saw the front picture window broken and a blood trail on the floor either leading to him or maybe leading away, I couldn't tell. Took some lead to his upper abdomen but I couldn't tell what kind of round it was. There wasn't any birdshot in him, though. Still alive when they scooped him up."

"Any family?"

"Not in the house."

"Why was the gun so far away from the victim? Did you move it?"

"Hell no, I didn't touch anything but the victim and as you can see, his blood's all over my uniform."

"Yeah you look like you've been through a war. Secure the scene and have Carl help you put crime tape around the house, trees, and utility poles and don't let anyone near that house. Don't touch anything and please minimize any disruption to the scene. I'm worried that those hose draggers can fuck up the scene when they barge in like they usually do. Oh yeah, and I need you to log in the names of everyone who comes to enter the scene, whoever it is, I don't care."

"Got it."

Gordon knew that doctors don't usually screw up their own suicides because they know how to make it successful, and while this could be a botched robbery and the doctor surprised the perp, it could be something else entirely. While typing out a warrant, his mind chewed on the possibilities.

"I'm calling out the crime lab to the scene while I go find the on-call judge to get the warrant signed. Don't let the lab guys get in till I get the warrant signed. Got it?"

"Done."

It was three am and Gordon drove to the station to obtain the appropriate paperwork supporting the warrant, and he learned that Judge Parillo owned the duty that day.

Parillo stumbled to the door in his silver bathrobe, and the hair that remained on the sides of his bald pate was sticking almost straight out. Despite his bleary eyes, he listened intently to Gordon's description of the events of earlier that evening, and then reviewed and signed the warrant. The judge then asked Gordon to raise his right hand and swear that the facts presented were true. Gordon did so, and then signed the affidavit and the judge signed the warrant. He thanked him, the judge went back to bed, and Gordon sped off to the scene to start the investigation, calling to tell Jenkins to go ahead and let the crime lab in.

Gordon arrived on the scene wearing an unbuttoned navy blazer, khaki cuffed slacks, and a plain burgundy tie topped with a partially tied Windsor knot at the neck. His Smith-and-Wesson nine mm was holstered over his left shoulder, hidden by his blazer, but available for crossfire when needed. The crime lab was already in action, photographing the bedroom and the blood on the floor and the foyer, Audi in the garage, shotgun on the floor, and everything else they could think of. They made a video recording of the entire inside of the house, basement, and garage as well as the exterior of the house, including a view from the street and the neighbor's vantage point on each side.

He briefly wondered whether Wyatt's wound was self-inflicted or from a smaller round from the perpetrator. He knew that it would be difficult to shoot yourself in the abdomen with a shotgun to begin with, and unlikely you would survive. No way this was a botched suicide attempt. There was a blood trail in the foyer leading away from the shattered window, then towards the front door. No, the intruder shot Wyatt, no question. But was this a robbery attempt and Wyatt caught the intruder by surprise and hit him with his shotgun? He would have his team check the walls and the bed for any rounds to take to the ballistics lab.

"I want fingerprints taken on the shotgun, and look for footprints both inside and outside. If you find any footprints outside in the dirt, make a cast. I want DNA samples of the blood both in the bedroom and from the blood trail in the foyer and the front window using strict protocol. Comb the area outside for cigarette butts, gum, blood stains, and anything else you can find."

"What the hell you think we are, Gordon, amateurs?" said the crime lab leader.

"No, but this is my case and my ass if we screw up, and that won't happen on my watch. And by the way, has anyone checked the license plates, registration, and serial numbers of the Audi in the garage?"

"Hadn't thought of that, Gordon."

"Figures. While you're at it, take fingerprints and DNA samples both inside and outside the car."

Wyatt had two neighbors close to his house in the cul-de-sac: one to the west and one to the east. The remainder of the short street had empty lots, not yet sold. Gordon knocked on the front door of the house on the west side and a man answered.

"Hello, this is Detective Farmer of the Evanston Police Department. Do you have a few moments to talk to me?"

"Sure but I need to leave for work in 15 minutes. Is this about something happening last night next door?"

"Yes sir, it is. Did you hear or see anything last night?"

"Well yes, my wife and I were awakened by the flashing ambulance lights outside Wyatt's house. We went out to our front porch and saw them taking someone out in a stretcher. We didn't know if it was Wyatt or someone else."

"Did you hear any gunshots?"

"Are you kidding? Gunshots?"

"No, I'm not."

"Well, no I didn't."

"Would you be kind enough to get your wife so that I can talk to her as well?"

By that time, his wife was at his side, listening intently, and she immediately related that she did not hear any gunshots either. Gordon then turned his attention back to her husband.

"Did you see any suspicious cars coming to Dr. Barton's house last night?"

"Well, no, but we were inside all night celebrating my wife's birthday."

"Okay, so tell me; did you—I mean do you—know Dr. Barton very well?"

The couple took turns describing their relationship to Wyatt. Basically they would talk a little about landscaping and such during the summer when they were out in the yard, but they didn't know much about him. They knew he was divorced and his wife and kids no longer lived with him. Throughout the conversation, the wife made the majority of the responses, with the husband nodding.

"Did he have any friends?"

"We would see occasional cars over there but didn't take much notice of them. No consistency. He was a private man, and I am sure very busy at the hospital, because we would see him come home late at night or odd hours. It seemed that his kids never visited him anymore after the divorce, though. Seemed strange. We looked for them but never saw them again."

"Thank you for your time. Here's my card, and call me if you have anything more to add."

"Is he all right? You mentioned gunfire. Did he get shot?"

"There was a shooting, but I can't comment on anything else. Have a good day."

Gordon couldn't get a response from the neighbor's house on the east side of Wyatt's place. He would try them later. His mind quickly switched to his next move on the case. It became clear to him that while the lab people were analyzing the scene, his next move would be to go to the hospital, which he'd already made sure was locked down in the ICU. For security reasons, Wyatt's name was listed as John Hemstrom. Hopefully if Wyatt recovered he could talk to him himself, but that appeared doubtful in the present situation considering the life-threatening nature of his wounds. Either way, he was sure some of the doctors and nurses could fill him in on what was going on in the doc's life before the shooting. Right now, he needed to get a large double-shot black eye from Starbucks or he wouldn't be worth a damn the rest of the day.

CHAPTER 36

80 mm systolic plummeted to 60, forcing the anesthesiologist to stabilize Wyatt's blood pressure immediately. After five liters of intravenous fluids and five units of blood, his blood pressure slowly crept back up to the still-precarious pressure of 80, forcing him to inject the pressor agent Neo-Synephrine into Wyatt's veins to maintain adequate systemic pressure and finally allowing Dr. Branson to make his incision and start the dangerous surgery.

Dr. Branson swiftly entered the abdominal cavity and located the bullet entrance wound at the right flank, and the abdominal cavity was a sea of vision-obscuring blood. Wyatt was in shock from severe and potentially fatal bleeding. Branson figured there was at least a liver laceration, but he was hoping that the vena cava was not also perforated. Trauma surgeons know that the most common cause of death after abdominal injury is liver trauma due to the size and location as well as the large blood supply and capacity of the liver. A vena cava rupture would cause massive blood loss and the need for large volumes of blood transfusions. Dr. Branson's breathing became visibly less stressed when he saw his partner, Paul Duncan, scrubbing in to assist.

"Thanks, Paul, we got a bleeder here and I need your hands in here with me."

"No problem, what do we have?"

"Shit, Paul. Looks like we got active bleeding from a through and through perforation of the inferior vena cava about three cm above the renal veins. The right lobe of the liver is lacerated also and bleeding like hell."

Without discussion, Duncan packed the bleeding liver while Branson isolated and clamped the bleeding vessels. Gushing blood made vision challenging and messy for the vascular repair, but Dr. Branson was the most skilled vascular trauma surgeon in the city, if not the state, and everyone in the room felt comfortable with his skills, no matter how grave the present situation was.

"Paul, looks like the common hepatic duct is transected. I'm concentrating on repairing the vena cava. Could you complete the exploration of the abdomen for me?"

"Got it."

With his foot tapping more frequently now, the nurses knew the anesthesiologist was increasingly jittery. Wyatt's blood pressure plummeted once again to the 60's with heart rate dropping into the 50's. His voice shot up to a high pitch, but no one cared.

"Damn it, John, we're losing him! How close are you to getting this controlled? I've got him on maximum Neo-Synephrine and I've got the eighth unit of blood running in wide open. Got any other bleeders?"

"Yeah, I found it. Hepatic vein laceration too. Working on it. Hold your pants on."

Eventually the two surgeons successfully gained control of the bleeding and repaired the vessel lacerations. Wyatt's blood pressure rose as did his heart rate simultaneously, allowing the anesthesiologist's foot tapping to slow down from a 100-meter sprint to a gentle mile jog in the park.

Duncan repaired the hepatic duct laceration, then notified Dr. Branson of another problem.

"Looks like the right adrenal gland is fractured, but I can take care of it. I ran the bowel and no evidence of rupture of the colon or other organs that I can see."

"Time to stabilize the blood pressure for a while, since the vessels are repaired. I don't think he can tolerate much more of this anesthesia." The surgeons took a several-minute breather to allow more blood transfusions while blood gases, hematocrit, and chemistry labs were drawn so that they could correct as much as possible medically. They both continued to explore the rest of the abdominal cavity and couldn't find any more injuries.

"How much blood have we given?" Dr. Branson asked the anesthesiologist.

"Ten units of packed cells, a pack of platelets, and six units of fresh frozen plasma."

"That's a ton of blood product, but I'm not surprised. What's his crit and gases?"

"Crit is up to 30 so we're good there, and the potassium is a little high because he's acidotic from the shock. I'll treat the potassium and give him some bicarb."

Dr. Branson felt relieved that Wyatt's six-hour surgery was a success and he'd survived the operation itself, but he worried about whether he would survive postoperatively in the ICU. His concern now was that Wyatt might develop severe lung injury from the massive transfusions, the blood in the chest from the gunshot wound, and therefore a prolonged run on the ventilator machine to support his breathing. Multiple organs could potentially fail after major trauma such as this, so he called in the critical care specialist, Dr. Kurt Owens, to help him during his time on life support in the ICU, and Dr. Owens met Branson when they wheeled Wyatt into the Intensive Care Unit.

"Thanks for your help, Kurt. We've got ourselves a mess here and it's going to be a rough ride for Wyatt, I'm afraid."

"Yeah looks like it, but I'm impressed that you brought the cowboy back!"

"Well, I don't know. It was rough, but he survived surgery. Lots of bleeding, ruptured vena cava and lacerated liver, hepatic vein and hepatic duct with a fractured adrenal gland. Thankfully no bowel perforation though. I'm leaving his ICU care up to you, but call me anytime."

"Okay, John, I'll take over from here."

Drs. Branson and Duncan both walked out to the intensive-care waiting room to talk to Wyatt's family. Or at least what was left of his family. In the waiting room were his partner, Charley Bennett, Katherine, and Marta. Branson asked the trio who was the closest family member, and Bennett replied that there was no immediate family here. Katherine glared at Bennett, then blurted out that she was the ex-wife and that the kids were at home studying for exams, but she would represent the family. Marta squirmed nervously when she heard that, and the tension in the room was like a fuse lit on a stick of explosives in front of a group of tied-up hostages. To avoid a confrontation Branson described the surgery to all three parties in attendance, how Wyatt was close to death, but was now on the ventilator for life support in the ICU. He told them that the next twenty-four hours would be critical to evaluate his prognosis. He was far from safely recovered and multiple postoperative complications could arise.

"Thanks, Dr. Branson, for your skilled efforts to save my Wyatt," Marta said softly. "Tell me, what complications could happen?"

"He may develop a severe lung injury called ARDS from the massive transfusions, kidney failure from the shock, and low blood pressure as well as severe infections."

Marta's face turned pale and her lips quivered after she heard the words. She shook both surgeons' hands warmly, thanked them, then sat down with tears in her eyes. She briefly looked coldly at Katherine, who turned her head.

"Who's going to be the intensivist taking care of him, John?" asked Bennett.

"Kurt Owens. I briefed him on the case and he's up in the ICU with him now."

"Good, Owens has an excellent group and he's in good hands. Thanks, John and Paul, for everything you've done in surgery, we appreciate your skills," said Bennett.

"That's what we do. We thought we were going to lose him, but it wasn't his time yet, at least not in the operating room," said Duncan.

"Wyatt's a damn good cardiologist and a good man. I would go to war for him," said Branson.

"You two already went to war tonight," said Bennett.

Quiet during the waiting-room conversation with the doctors, tears rolled down Katherine's cheeks while she snuck furtive glimpses at Marta's diamond engagement ring. Bennett hugged Marta and asked that they both pray for him and his recovery. Bennett was aware of Wyatt's suffering during the brutal divorce and attacks by Katherine impugning his character with lies and bizarre accusations. He looked at the two women and asked, "I know this is difficult, but do either of you know if Wyatt had a living will or whether he assigned a medical power of attorney?"

"Yes," said Marta. "He made me his medical POA and I have his living will."

"Wow, that was quick, you foreign gold digger!" said Katherine.

Bennett turned to Katherine with disgust. "Katherine, that's enough. We're all in stress, and it's time for you to act like an adult." His stern statement effectively zipped Katherine's mouth, an unusual occurrence.

He continued without emotion. "I hope these papers won't be needed, but it's good that he had the foresight to take care of these things. Let's not worry about these issues now because God willing, he will survive."

Katherine stared at Marta, then got up and walked out of the waiting room while dabbing her eyes with tissues.

Bennett stopped her before she reached the door. "Out of respect for Wyatt, I don't want you visiting him in the hospital. You aren't his medical POA and he needs peace—in fact, we all do."

"Well, fine. I always loved that man and now you're telling me that he wanted me not to visit his deathbed? That sounds typical of him, selfish as always. Since when did he ever care about the kids? In fact, you know what he did to..."

"That's enough, Katherine, we don't want to hear about it. Time for you to go, and don't come back."

Katherine's eyes sunk as dark as the Marianas abyss when she walked out of the room like a general in retreat. She would visit her ex-husband and no one would stop her. After several hours, Bennett left, but Marta stayed in Wyatt's room, holding his hand when she was given time alone with him by the nursing staff.

"Can he hear me or talk to me?" Marta asked the ICU nurse.

"He's sedated from anesthesia, and even if we were to allow him to awaken, it won't be for a long time, and the breathing tube in his trachea won't allow him to talk. If he does awaken, we'll keep him sedated with narcotics and sedatives for his comfort."

"I understand. I'll stay until visiting hours are over. Here's my cell phone number and work number. Call me if there are any changes in his condition."

Marta held Wyatt's hand and stayed at his bedside, never leaving his side until forced to leave due to the end of visiting hours. She didn't allow the tears to flow until she arrived home, falling to her bed.

CHAPTER 37

Gordon's priority now turned to interviewing the family and medical professionals who were close to Wyatt so that he could learn more about his life, career, friends, enemies—anyone who could shed light on him as a person and professional. The crime lab information would take time. Convinced this was clearly an attack on the doctor at his home, Gordon's visit to the ICU charge nurse resulted in a green light to come into his room and talk to whomever he needed to, as long as it didn't interfere with patient care.

When he entered Wyatt's room, it seemed to be controlled chaos. He had an endotracheal tube protruding from his gaping mouth, which the nurse said allowed the ventilator machine to breathe for him, a smaller flexible tube in his nose for aspiration of stomach contents, large IV's in his neck providing fluids, nutrition, antibiotics, and what the nurse said were pressor agents. These were medications such as norepinephrine that were needed to keep his blood pressure out of the shock range. He required heavy sedation and was unable to communicate. The nurse on shift he was talking to at that time was Brenda, and also in the room was Amy Adams, RN.

"Excuse me, ladies. I'm Detective Farmer from the Evanston Police Department. May I ask your names and what your function is here?"

"Sure, my name is Amy Adams. I used to work with Wyatt, I mean Dr. Barton, in the cardiac catheterization lab, but now I work as a visiting nurse."

"And I'm Brenda Connor. I'm his nurse for this shift."

"Nice to meet you two. I'm sure this is a shock for the staff here at the hospital since he worked here."

"That's putting it mildly. We're kinda walking around in a daze. This is just horrible," said Brenda. "Please excuse me though; I have to go get some medications for him." She walked out of the room. Brenda and the staff had also given Wyatt extra privacy by not allowing anyone in but close family and a limited number of essential staff, and of course, Detective Farmer.

"I hear that Dr. Barton was well liked in the hospital as a person, but also as a respected cardiologist. How well did you know him, Amy?"

"I worked with him when he came to the emergency department and also when I joined the cardiac catheterization lab team a few years later."

"I see. So what was your relationship to him? Did you know him on a personal basis, or just professionally?"

"Oh, professionally only. But I must admit he was a funny man to talk to when he worked. It seemed that no matter how much stress we were under, he would keep things light to help us through difficult times. I remember several cardiac arrests I was involved with as he supervised the code, and he was always smooth and confident, and never broke a sweat, even though we all knew he was shouldering the responsibility."

"I see that you respected him."

She smiled. "Yes, in fact one time I remember that he was trying to intubate someone's trachea because they couldn't breathe. There was no pulmonologist or anesthesiologist to help, and the emergency room physician struggled because the blood in the airway obstructed his view, so he asked Dr. Barton to assist. He smiled calmly even though he had only one minute to accomplish what no one else could, asked for a special GlideScope, even though he wasn't familiar with the equipment, and accomplished the task! He knew he had to be successful or the patient would die. Wyatt, I mean Dr. Barton, worked well under pressure, but didn't want to show us that he was nervous.

But he always made us feel important and respected, rarely raising his voice. Good doctor, but he had his moments though."

Gordon knew that Wyatt was divorced, but he wanted to ask Amy about his personal life just to see what she knew, or admitted.

"Amy, was Dr. Barton married or have children?"

"Don't know about his kids, but he was divorced. I mean *is* divorced. Seems none of us here in the hospital know anything about his kids, but we have heard a few things about his ex."

"How do you know he was divorced?"

"Mr. Farmer, the first thing that a single woman notices is usually the lack of a wedding band, which I'm sure others also noticed he didn't have as well. That isn't always the case, though, as you know."

"Of course," Gordon chuckled. "But what do you mean 'others'?"

"Well, we single ladies notice these things, and the hospital is actually a powerful gossip machine."

"I see. Did you know of anyone in the hospital who dated him or met him socially after the divorce?"

"No. We would talk about it amongst ourselves because we were curious, but we didn't hear of him dating anyone here in the hospital, and clearly, he kept his social life close to the vest. He keeps things professional, but he's fun to be around. I'm single and available, and would've gone out with him in a minute, but he never asked. He didn't have a reputation as a playboy though, if that's what you're asking."

"No, that wasn't what I was asking but I get it. Thanks for your time, you've been quite helpful."

"No problem, I hope you figure out who shot him. This is just so sad for us here at the hospital."

Just then, Marta walked into the room. She locked eyes with Amy first, recognizing her face from the desperate car chase incident months before.

Farmer observed the two women staring at each other coldly for a few prolonged seconds, then introduced himself to the new visitor.

"Hello, I'm Detective Gordon Farmer from the Evanston Police Department."

"Pleased to meet you, Detective," said Marta.

Farmer studied the two women's faces, then asked, "I take it you two ladies have met before?"

"Yes, Detective, we have, but just in passing, I guess you could say," said Marta.

Amy turned her head away from the detective and Marta and just stared at Wyatt, observing the multiple tubes coming out of his body. "Detective Farmer, you must find the monster who did this to the man I love, and I'll do anything to help you. Here's my cell phone number, office number, and e-mail address. Please find this evil person, please!" Her lips trembled and finally she allowed herself to break down and the tears flowed.

"Maybe he was depressed, and he tried to kill himself, Detective," said Amy.

"No way!" said Marta. "He was happy the night before and he gave me an engagement ring. No, this was an attempt on his life by somebody."

"You ladies have your opinions and I appreciate that, but I'm in charge of this investigation and I deal only with facts, not guesswork."

Nurse Brenda came back to the room to hang some intravenous medications for Wyatt. She listened to the conversation at the bedside and decided to contribute her opinion as well.

"We're definitely rooting for you, Detective Farmer."

"Nice meeting you three ladies, and Amy, I would like to have your phone number too because I'll need to ask you some more questions as well."

"No problem, Detective, I'll be completely available to you to provide whatever information you think would be helpful for this case."

He looked at Marta and Amy and observed that Marta looked him straight in the eyes, but Amy's eyes darted back and forth from Wyatt to Marta, then Farmer. "I'll be in touch with both you ladies to talk in more detail soon."

CHAPTER 38

Katherine Barton received the first formal interview in Detective Farmer's office at the police station. She presented herself with a determined walk and a courteous smile, and her red hair contrasted well with her silky white blouse and tan skirt. They sat in a dedicated interview room in the department, with stark surroundings, primarily composed of black steel chairs that screeched against the floor when pulled up to the cold metal desk. Behind Farmer was a one-way mirror used for observation of the interviews and video documentation of the meeting.

"Would you like me to get you some coffee or a soda, Katherine?"

"Sure. With cream, that would be nice."

Farmer watched while Katherine sipped her coffee. "How long were you and Wyatt married?"

"Fifteen years. We divorced four years ago when Colby was sixteen and Spencer was eighteen, but were separated over a year before then."

"I see. And are the two kids in college now?"

"Yes, and I'm so proud of them. They're both good students. Spencer is in his last year of pre-law at the University of Illinois and Colby is a sophomore at Northwestern. They're good kids and close brothers."

"Were they close with their father?"

"No, unfortunately, they've had no contact with him the last five years. He seems to have just walked away from us. Well no, he abandoned his family. It's too bad. He's missed so much with his boys during their early teen years, and you know it's amazing how much they've grown without him there."

"That is unfortunate, yes. Must've been hard on you to see that. But tell me what you mean by 'abandonment.' Did he just walk away?"

"Yeah, kinda. He did pay his alimony and it was always on time, but he never called us or tried to help with home repairs, car issues, or problems the boys faced as growing teenagers. He was rude and uncaring, it seemed. It was difficult for the three of us to understand. I tried my best to..."

"I really have my doubts he walked away. Did your ex-husband have any enemies that you know of, or individuals that may have wished him harm?"

Katherine folded her arms tightly, sighed, then answered. "Well you know I'm sure he had affairs, so maybe it could've been a jealous husband of a wife he was cheating with, I don't know. But that's a scary thought, isn't it, Detective?"

"Did you have evidence that he had affairs?"

"No, not really, but it all seemed..."

"Tell me, did you have any other men when you were married to Wyatt?"

Katherine's eyes widened as if stretched by retractors. "Of course not! I was with my precious children twenty-four/seven and adultery is a sin. I always loved him; he just never seemed to give love to me back. But despite that, I pray that he recovers, for the children's sake."

"How 'bout you tell me who Mark Thompson is and why he recently filed a restraining order on you?"

"Don't know the man."

Farmer grew tired of the junk spewing from Katherine's mouth. "You're lying. Tell me then, where were you the night of November 15?"

"I figured you would ask that. Always the ex-wife, huh? Well, I was with my wonderful children of course. They came home from college and we went to a movie, then they stayed with me that night. If you want, you can call them if you need verification of my whereabouts."

"I will. And one more thing. Are your alimony payments finished with Wyatt?"

"Why would you ask that?"

"I ask these things because I'm a detective investigating this case, and I advise you, Ms. Barton, to answer the questions without providing me with interference. I ask the questions, you don't, and you damn well better answer. Do you understand me clearly now?"

"Yes, Detective, I understand, and no, I still have a year of alimony payments due from Wyatt, but I'm worried this will be a financial burden on me now that he's not working."

"Oh, I'm sorry to hear that. Well, thank you for your time, and I wish you a good day. Is it okay if I call you if I have any further questions?"

"Sure, no problem. I hope you find the person who did this to Wyatt. It's just a senseless crime and it breaks my heart for the kids."

"Don't worry. We'll figure it out soon enough."

Farmer sat in his chair for about thirty minutes, thinking and reviewing his notes after Katherine left. *She's a pathological liar, plays a good victim, and I don't believe any of her shit.*

CHAPTER 39

Wyatt survived the shooting and the surgery was technically successful, but he continued to struggle with his recovery on the ventilator in the intensive-care unit. Because of the massive blood transfusions that he required during his initial resuscitation, he developed severe injury to his lungs. After one week with the tube in his trachea exiting from his mouth, his physicians could not successfully remove him from the life-support machines without causing respiratory distress. This necessitated putting a tracheotomy tube through an incision below his voice box in order to avoid damaging his vocal cords because of the tube extending outside his mouth down to his windpipe.

The nurses worried about keeping him sedated on the ventilator machine due to his agitation. They couldn't tell whether it was caused by pain or delirium from the medications themselves. They wanted him to be as comfortable as possible despite being tied to a bed twenty-four hours a day with tubes stuck in nearly every orifice and completely unable to communicate even if he was coherent. But it was important not to oversedate him with medications because then it was difficult to observe him breathe spontaneously with the machine switched to minimal support.

On Wyatt's eighth hospital day, the night nurse called the doctor on call.

"Hello, this is Susan from St. Anthony's ICU. Wyatt is agitated and pulling on his restraints constantly despite our medications. What do you suggest? I'm afraid he might pull out some of his tubes and IV's."

"We're trying to minimize his sedatives so we can try to wean him from the ventilator tomorrow morning. Each day we have to try. If you need to for his safety, you can increase his propofol and add a fentanyl drip."

"Okay. Thanks. I'll do my best."

Susan watched him struggle, kicking his legs with his eyes wide open. He had a terrified look. She secured four-point restraints to both arms and legs, but he was too strong and they seemed to be giving way. She called for a male nurse to come assist her and hold him down because of his wild thrashing.

"It almost looks like he's having a nightmare," said the male nurse. "You know it seems like we'll never know if these patients are experiencing severe pain or some kind of emotional trauma inside their brain. But in the end, we have to treat them as if it's pain to ease their comfort."

Spencer and Colby were locked in a metal cage on the deck of a chartered fishing boat that was sinking. They screamed for help. "Dad, help us. We need you. Help us please!" Wyatt saw them from shore and swam out to them as fast as he could. He crawled up to the deck and found the boys locked in their cage. Katherine stood in front of them laughing, holding the key. He lunged for the key, but she threw it out into the ocean, then she jumped off the boat. The kids screamed desperately. "Dad, we're sorry we were so mean to you. We were wrong. Please help us."

"Don't worry, my sons, I'll save you!" Desperately, he grabbed a tire iron and gradually pried away the iron bars with all his strength while trying to save his sons before the water gushed in over their heads and it was too late.

The nurse quickly pushed the high-dose sedatives into Wyatt's veins, and he stopped thrashing within a few minutes.

"He looks calmer now. Wow. That was intense," said Susan.

"Yeah, he's amazingly strong for a man who's been through so much. I still wonder, though, what was bothering him. It seemed that he was in a life-or-death struggle. I guess we'll never know."

At his dorm room desk, staring blankly at his physics text, he began pilfering through his lower desk drawer. He pulled out a family photo album and quickly flipped past the photos of his mother to a page where there was a picture of himself with his dad; he was proudly handing him the trophy for most valuable baseball player. Colby stared at it for a long time then swallowed hard, but his esophagus didn't want to cooperate anymore.

CHAPTER 40

"Thank you for coming, Marta," Detective Farmer said, escorting her to the interview room. "May I get you something to drink?"

"No thanks. Perhaps some bottled water if you have some."

Farmer pulled out his notebook and pen. "So tell me, how long have you known Dr. Barton?"

"I've known him about two years."

"I see you're wearing a diamond ring. I assume that's from him?"

She beamed and looked down at the ring. "Yes, he gave it to me the night before he was shot, after I accepted his marriage proposal. It was an amazing surprise and a wonderful night."

"That must've been quite a shock when you received a call the next day that he was in surgery after a shooting."

"A shock for anyone close to him, yes, but to the woman who was to marry him, it was devastating. This is a man who has gone through hell from his ex-wife and kids for no reason except that he married the wrong woman, a woman he didn't know."

"I know about his bizarre family situation and I've seen cases of what they call Parental Alienation Syndrome, but this, without question, is the granddaddy of all of them! Marta, you must've been an angel sent from heaven for him."

"Yes, he needed a friend, and thank God we found each other. I worried about his health and his future stability, but I saw that he was a good quality man. He finally removed himself from his family fishbowl and began to see reality, and that reality was not based on his ex-wife's or kids' view of the world. I could see that he accepted that he could no longer save his kids from Katherine, and that he needed to go on with his life. And the last year or so, he seemed much happier and I think he had finally resumed the life he was meant to have before Katherine."

Farmer caressed his whiskered chin in deep thought. "Most women would not have stayed with a man that long, considering the stressful position he was in. He was lucky to have you."

"Perhaps. But then I'm lucky to have him."

"Marta, I saw some tension between you and Amy when I met you two at Wyatt's bedside the other day. Can you explain why that is?"

"It was scary. I was on a dinner date with Wyatt a while back, and she apparently was stalking us, driving around his house. When we left the house she followed us down the road in her car, swerving and trying to—I don't know—knock us off the road? She yelled at Wyatt, then she drove up to my side, the passenger side, and yelled at me, 'You're fucking my man. Stay away from him!' But you know, it shocks me how nasty some American women are. Thankfully we were able to get away from her uninjured. I also had someone trying to spy on my house and maybe trying to break in, I don't know for sure. I called Wyatt and he came over and chased this person off my property. I don't know who it was, but he said, 'she ran like a girl.' Of course, I have no idea if that was Amy outside my house but I have my suspicions."

"Did Wyatt have any other people in his life, that you know of, that may be considered enemies?"

"I don't know. He was involved in a bogus malpractice suit, which involved two brothers, Gavin and Blake Flanagan, who for some reason have animosity towards Wyatt and they believed their father died because of Wyatt's cardiac catheterization, but this was found to be false."

"I've already reviewed the malpractice case. Did you know these brothers?"

"Um, I must admit I dated Gavin several times I guess."

"And then it ended, just like that?"

"Kinda. He was a gentleman and everything, but he wasn't my

type. He kept calling me several times a week after that, though. Seems he was infatuated with me but too aggressive for my comfort."

"Interesting you were dating a powerful man who filed suit against your fiancé for malpractice. That makes things more complicated, I think."

"Well, yes. But Gavin was before Wyatt."

"And Blake?"

"I didn't know him, but saw him at the Heart Ball along with his brother and Amy. Wyatt was the featured speaker there, he asked me to the dance, but I had already said yes to Gavin."

"Who was Wyatt's date then?"

"Amy Adams."

"That's interesting. Quite a complicated jungle of tangled relationships. I'm very appreciative of your time, and I know you want to get back to work and to visit Wyatt at the hospital."

"Yes, thank you, Detective Farmer. I worry about him so much."

"And one more thing. We've found out that you have a significant amount of financial debt. Did you see Wyatt as a way out?"

Marta glared at him and smiled comfortably. "If that was my goal, I would've chosen Gavin."

CHAPTER 41

Bridgett, the nurse on duty, alertly stopped the boys before she allowed them entry to Wyatt's room. "Who are you two?"

"Oh, hey, I'm Spencer Barton and this is my brother Colby." Spencer looked over at his father who was unconscious on life support. "We're his sons."

"Nice to meet you." She then took them over to the police guard sitting outside the room on sentry duty and he approved of their I.D.'s and let them in. "I'm sure this is difficult to see your father this way, but do you have any questions for me?"

"How's he doing?" asked Spencer.

"Well, it's been nine days that he's been on life support. He's recovered from the gunshot wounds and his damaged lungs may be ready for us to start weaning him from the breathing machine. He's a really strong man to be doing so well."

"That's great," said Colby.

"Yeah, cool," said Spencer.

"Is he in pain?" asked Colby.

"We monitor his facial expressions and his vital signs and then give him morphine when needed to ease the pain."

"Will he recognize us if we talk to him?" asked Colby.

"I'm not sure; he doesn't always follow commands predictably and is not completely alert yet. But you can try."

"Hey Dad, it's Colby."

Wyatt's eyes opened and he stared at Colby, then at Spencer standing next to Colby, but there was no clear recognition in his eyes. "Squeeze my hand if you recognize me."

Wyatt provided a viselike squeeze. Colby had to struggle to remove his hand.

"Spence, do you want to talk to him too?"

"Nah, that's okay. He's tired and sedated. Let's let him rest. We have to go soon."

After their brief visit, the two boys left his room and they walked down the hospital corridor, passing by Marta who had taken a break from her beside vigil and was now returning to his ICU room. The two boys stared at her for a while, and she looked at them and said "Hi," but they kept walking.

Marta knew what Wyatt's sons looked like from the pictures before the divorce he kept displayed in various locations of his house.

"Yes," said Bridgett, "those were his sons, Spencer and Colby. They signed in for a fifteen-minute visit. Seemed a little short to me, but they're young college kids. They've got a lot on their minds."

It was Amy Adams' turn to be interviewed by Detective Farmer.

"Anything I can do to help find Wyatt's attacker, I'll be happy to do," she told him. "It was probably a robbery, don't you think?"

"Interesting you would say that, but it's too premature to determine at this point in the investigation."

"Of course."

"We talked before at the hospital, Amy, and I just had a few more questions for you. Tell me, did you have a love interest in Dr. Barton?"

She displayed a calm demeanor, steady voice, and answered without hesitation. "As I told you before, Detective, he's an attractive man and a successful, respected cardiologist. Lots of single women were probably interested in him."

"That's not what I asked. Did *you* have a romantic relationship with him?"

"No. Wish I had one, though. I cooked some steaks for him after work one night, and we enjoyed a cup of coffee on another occasion but that's it."

"So no further social contacts with him outside the hospital?"

"No."

"The doc filed a harassment complaint against you a few months before the shooting. In his complaint, he stated that you were driving in an unsafe way next to him, trying to force him and his passenger, Marta, off the road. What was that about?"

"I have no idea why he would accuse me of that. Strange. Maybe Marta convinced him to file a false claim because of her jealousy of me, I don't know. Either way, there were no witnesses and the police didn't come to the scene. Completely false claim and I'm surprised that he would do that."

"Interesting. How do you know there were no witnesses if you weren't there?"

"Well um, I don't know but it seems unlikely."

"Whatever. So you mention this Marta lady. Tell me how you met her."

"We met at the Heart Ball benefit dance. I was Wyatt's date and she came with someone else."

"I thought you said you had no other social contact with him."

"Forgot about the dance, Detective. But I guess that doesn't count."

"Do you know of anyone who might have had animosity towards him, you know, an enemy?"

"Well, there are the Flanagan brothers. I'm sure you're aware they're sons of the late Sean Flanagan, whom Wyatt tried to save during a cardiac catheterization, but he died. The sons took it personally, and tried to file suit against Wyatt, but the judge dismissed the case quickly when it was obvious there was no evidence of wrongdoing."

Farmer gave no indication that he knew of the malpractice case and the brothers. "Do you know the two sons?"

"Not Gavin so much. But I have dated his brother, Blake."

Farmer scratched his head with this additional twist. "What can you tell me about him?"

"He's a Marine sniper scout instructor, tough guy type, you know. But I think he carries a chip on his shoulder and has made it clear to me he can't stand Wyatt."

"Did he ever tell you he wanted to cause him physical harm?"

"No, he didn't. Our relationship was you know, mostly physical."

He smiled. "Are you and Blake seeing each other on a steady basis?"

"No. Heavens no. Just some brief encounters, if you know what I mean."

"One more thing, Amy. Where were you on Saturday night, November 15, when Dr. Barton was shot?"

Amy paused for a few seconds, then answered. "I was at a sick patient's house providing in-home nursing. That's sure a lot less stressful than the cath lab."

"You quit your hospital job because of Wyatt and the alleged car chase situation, didn't you?"

Amy smirked and understood the detective's methods to trip her up. "As I said, there was no chase thing with him, and I just wanted a job change that was less stressful. I think you would understand that, Detective."

He closed his notebook with a slam. "That's all I have and thanks for your time, Amy. I may call you again if I need more information. I advise you not to leave town until this investigation is over."

Amy smiled graciously. "Any time, Detective. I think Wyatt is a wonderful man and doctor, and I'll do anything to help you find the shooter."

"Of course, but I have one more question for you. I have an emergency department record in my possession from October 18 that shows you were treated for a significant amount of lacerations on your arms, even needed a few stitches. Care to elaborate?"

"That's easy, Detective. I have a large rose garden and I tripped and fell into a row of them while I was pruning them."

Yeah, downtown condos in the city have plenty of rose gardens.

After she left, he thought about the interviews so far, and it certainly seemed to him to be quite a complicated group of characters involved with Wyatt. But clearly, there was a lot of lying going on and the stories weren't adding up. He knew Amy was lying through her pretty smile and so was Katherine. But what were their motives for lying?

CHAPTER 42

Dr. Wyatt Barton passed day ten on life support, and Dr. Kurt Owens stood at his bedside. Wyatt was finally awake and alert, following commands, interacting with the staff. When asked if he was ready to have the ventilator machine removed, he responded with the thumbs-up signal. Dr. Owens ordered the respiratory therapist to remove the machine that was connected by plastic tubing to Wyatt's tracheostomy tube, and he was successfully liberated from life support. Multiple nurses, aides, Marta, and even Dr. Bennett stood by the bedside and clapped for Wyatt because of this major success. Dr. Bennett and Owens discussed his case while Marta listened attentively.

"I originally thought the chance of his surviving this was less than ten percent, but you know he's a stubborn son of a bitch, and that's why he survived this," said Dr. Bennett.

"No question. Without a strong will to survive, he wouldn't have made it. But he has a long road ahead. His muscles are weak and he'll need a ton of rehab, both here and at home once he gets there," said Dr. Owens.

"Dr. Owens, when will he be able to talk?" asked Marta. "It seems he's so frustrated that he can't speak because of that tracheostomy tube."

"We'll deflate the cuff around his tracheostomy tube, and put a gauze pad over the end of the tube and see if he can talk. Then after about a week, if he shows he can stay off the machine, we'll remove the tracheostomy tube, and he should be able to talk quite well. In the meantime, he may require a Passy-Muir speaking valve to speak."

Dr. Owens told Wyatt what he was going to do, then deflated the tracheostomy tube cuff, covered the open end of the tube with a cotton dressing, then asked Wyatt to attempt to talk.

He tried several times, and then finally the first words in ten days came out slowly. "Marta—love you!"

She bent down to his bed, they kissed, and there were tears in both lovers' eyes. Even the nurses who watched had moist eyes. Several had to walk away. After several hours of smiling and laughter with Wyatt, the nurse asked Marta to leave for a while, so that they could start his physical therapy, and then eventual inpatient rehabilitation.

Before she left, he grabbed Marta's hand and spoke weakly while occluding his tracheostomy tube with the dressing. "How are my kids? Are they okay? Did they come to visit? What happened to me?"

"Yes honey, both boys came to visit yesterday. They both seem healthy. Why do you ask?"

Wyatt struggled to force enough air through the tracheostomy tube to allow his swollen vocal cords to produce a few more rare words. "Don't know. Horrible dream."

He smiled weakly at her, then looked away, gazing pensively out the window at the sun shining on the courtyard below; a sun that he had been perilously close to never seeing again.

"So Blake, thanks for coming to the station for an interview," said Farmer.

"No problem, Detective, am I a suspect?"

"Well, this case is wide open and we're just gathering facts, that's all. Everyone is a potential suspect. Relax, okay?"

Blake wore his civilian clothes—tight muscle shirt and jeans—but he seemed less intimidating without his Marine uniform and all the medals.

"I assume you know Dr. Wyatt Barton?"

"Yep."

"How do you know him, and what relationship do you have with him?"

"I met him at the Heart Ball last February. We were introduced."

"I see." *That Heart Ball seemed to be a bog of quicksand for Dr. Barton.* "And that's all?"

"Well, I guess. What else do you want to know?"

"Did you and your brother file a malpractice suit against him?"

"Yeah, but I don't see how that's important here."

"I'll ask the questions. You will respond. I can make it easy on you or tough. What do you prefer, Mr. Flanagan?"

"Easy as she goes, man."

"So you were not friends with him, obviously. Did you have any desire to do him harm after you lost the malpractice case?"

"Wow, that's pushing it, Detective. I'm impressed with your aggressive interview skills. But no, the court made its decision and my brother and I have gone on with our lives. More important things to worry about than that doctor."

"Do you know Amy Adams, RN?"

"Yeah, dated her a few times. Nice girl. She asked me to teach her how to protect herself with firearms, so I taught her at the firing range."

Farmer's eyes widened and he shifted forward in his chair. "That's nice of you. Was she a good shot?"

"Pretty good, but you know, I have high standards because of my profession."

"Of course. Anything else I need to know here?"

"Amy really liked this guy, and, you know, she wanted a relationship with him, and I believe he rejected her for another woman."

"Marta Liepa?"

"Yeah. She's been in a foul mood ever since she found out about their relationship, and she's been acting strange. I don't know, but seems she is one of those women who believes that if she can't have a man, then no one can. Maybe she had a score to settle with him. But you know, I don't really care about her much; she's a good lay and I don't need much else right now."

"Interesting you should say that, Blake, because she used the same words about you. She said you were a violent man who may have had a score to settle with Wyatt. And by the way, I heard your brother, Gavin, was dating Marta too."

"Figures she would say that. She's wrong. I don't have much else to say."

"One more thing. Do you have a solid alibi for where you were that Saturday night, November 15, when Dr. Barton was attacked?"

"Yeah, Quantico Marine base, a hell of a long way from Chicago."

"Okay, Blake. Thanks for coming to the station, and stay in town. I'm not done with you yet."

This guy is a real ass and he may or may not be telling the truth, but he has some dirt on him, and I'm going to watch every move he makes.

CHAPTER 43

"Gordon, I have some news you'll want to hear."

"Ah, yes, the phone call I've been waiting for from my favorite crime lab chief."

"I'm your only crime lab tech, Gordon," said Julie Carroll.

"Yeah, okay then, what do you have?"

"We've isolated two different blood types at the crime scene. We definitely have Dr. Barton's type A blood found in the bedroom and around the bed and some splattered on the walls. But we couldn't find hardly any of his blood outside the bedroom except for a few droplets on the floor that probably landed when they rushed him out on the gurney. All the other blood we found at the entrance of his bedroom, the foyer and around the shattered picture window, on shards of glass, and trailing outside in the grass. It is type AB."

"Good start, Julie. Do you have the CODIS DNA data match yet?"

"Don't buy the chicken farm yet, Gordon, because they could be ducks. It takes us a significant amount of time to prepare the DNA samples perfectly so that there will be no errors on our end."

"Yeah, go on."

"There's something else, Gordon. We found a slug in Barton's mattress. It was a through-and-through shot that exited his flank and penetrated the mattress. It's a .357 magnum slug. But the good news is some garbage man was emptying a dumpster about a mile down the road from Wyatt's house, and he said he saw a firearm fall out of a bag as he was emptying the dumpster into the trash truck. He thought that was unusual and brought it to us."

"What a good man. This is great news and certainly a stroke of luck! What did ballistics say?"

"We're lucky. The bullet came from this gun, a .357 magnum long nose. Fingerprints on the gun are degraded, but we're working on DNA. The garbage man was smart enough to keep his work gloves on when handling the weapon."

"Great work, Julie. Looks like we're making some progress."

"Yeah, thanks. We're pretty pumped here in the lab. I'll let you know when and if we're luckier yet to get a CODIS national DNA match."

"Damn right you'll let me know. I don't care if it's three am; call me."

The perp shot Wyatt and it appeared that Wyatt fired a wobbly shot off at the same time, injuring the perp. Gordon thought about the several potential assailants in this case. Katherine was obvious, but it was such a violent crime, that wasn't a slam dunk. Not only that, she still allegedly had alimony payments coming so she wouldn't want to shoot him and lose that money. What would she gain? She was probably not on his life insurance as an ex-wife, but that needed to be looked at. Then there was Blake. He was a violent man, and he was hiding something, big time. His brother Gavin was no Mr. Clean, but he wore a suit and tie, and wouldn't get his hands dirty. Clearly, he was jealous of Marta being in love with Wyatt. Did he hire a shooter? And then there was Amy. A rejected woman can sometimes be dangerous if she's unstable. She'd certainly shown some unstable behaviors. And she learned how to shoot from Blake? What was that about? And the bizarre chase scene with Marta and Wyatt? Maybe several were involved in some way. Hopefully, the DNA samples would yield an answer. In the meantime, it was time to put twenty-four-hour surveillance on Blake, Gavin, Amy, and Katherine. Nobody could leave town.

CHAPTER 44

"Hello Amy, it's Gavin."

"What the hell are you calling me for?"

"Nice greeting. I heard you implicated Blake and me with the detective during your interview. Probably not a smart move on your part."

"Oh really? You don't scare me, pretty boy. Never have. Where did you hear that bullshit, anyway?"

"I have my sources and snitches on my payroll all around town. You should know that by now. I suggest you stop badmouthing Blake and me if you know what's good for you. But I think you're doing this to deflect the attention away from you, because you're probably the one with blood on your hands. That's obvious."

"You're full of it and the hundred dollar bills you stuff up your ass for toilet paper are affecting your brain. You'll never know what I said. Why would I shoot him? I loved him and wanted him more than anyone else I could imagine. He was my future. A better man than most, and certainly better than you and your musclehead brother. I think you and Blake were involved, or maybe it was one of you alone. Maybe you, sitting around drinking martinis while some thug carried out your dirty work after receiving a garbage bag filled with cash. Am I getting warm, honey?"

"I'm done talking with you. I suggest you watch your step, Amy."

"Don't call me again, or I'll notify Farmer. Maybe I'll let him know that you're threatening me. That won't look too good for you, will it, Mistuh Havahd lawyer?"

Gavin's grey matter swirled in a turmoil like a washing machine on heavy-duty cycle. His people told him that Wyatt was still alive and maybe soon leaving the hospital. That meant he might be able to talk to the police. Would he be able to tell them what happened? Maybe Wyatt would implicate him somehow, even if he had no proof. Or his brother? What was his brother doing? He had to find out.

"Thank God you answered your phone!"

"Yeah, what d'ya want? I'm tired."

"You know this Barton thing. It's driving me crazy. I know you were interviewed. Am I next?"

"I don't know. I'm not the detective. You seem pretty nervous there, Gavin."

"I gotta ask..."

"Are you kidding me? You think I would tell you? You're a smart lawyer. Just think it through. Hell, everyone knows if I had shot him, it would've been between the eyes and he'd be six feet under. But what if I did? You gonna snitch on me? My only brother? By the way, you never got a chance to frame this guy with your stupid prostitute plan in his medical office, did you? So instead you took care of it in another way, didn't you?"

"You got to be kidding me, man. Do you think I became successful in life by being stupid? Listen, we need to stop this accusation mind game and stop communicating with each other. No more phones, text messages, or personal meetings, okay? We're suspects under surveillance. Don't inflate their suspicions any more."

"Got it. But just for the record, the success you're referring to in life is money, and you inherited that from Dad. Either way, I think everything's going to be all right for us, Gavin. Get some sleep. This detective is a dumbshit anyway. He's got no idea what's going on."

CHAPTER 45

Wyatt had one more day left during his stay on the rehabilitation unit of St. Anthony's hospital. After removal of his tracheostomy tube, his speech was intelligible but still hoarse due to irritation from the tubes in his airway and esophagus for so long.

He walked slowly, doing two flights of stairs with some mild heavy breathing, and the physical therapists and occupational therapists recommended that he go home without assistance. The staff was amazed at his quick recovery from his near fatal experience and prolonged immobility while on the ventilator machine. But that was Wyatt Barton, the cowboy. Marta was often by his side, and when she was gone at night, he missed her, wrote her love letters on his laptop, and e-mailed them to her. On his last day on the rehab ward, Detective Farmer had permission to interview him. Wyatt's doctor said he was strong enough for any interview and his mind was sharp as ever.

"Dr. Barton, I'm Detective Gordon Farmer. Pleased to meet you." He tried not to stare at Wyatt's eyebrow scar.

"Likewise, Gordon. Marta told me about you. She's impressed with your detective skills, and she's happy that you're investigating this case."

"Dr. Barton, I'm sure you've got a lot of pieces missing from the time surrounding the attack on your life, but can you tell me what you do know?"

"Of course, I'll try."

"Do you remember anything at all about that night? Anything in the hours before or during the attack itself?"

"Maybe, some captive images are coming back in small pieces. I definitely remember smiling all night because I had asked Marta to marry me the night before at dinner, and she accepted. She accepted my ring, and I felt free and happy. It was like I was floating on a calm sea with sunshine bathing me with soothing warmth, despite being on call that night. Seem to remember that it was kind of a noisy night from the wind, and I wasn't receiving any phone calls from the hospital. That was unusual, but I didn't think too much about it."

"Sounds like a nice beginning to the night. Do you remember anything else?"

"I remember a loud crash, and I leaped out of bed. I figured it was an intruder, because I had some training in that regard. I immediately grabbed my shotgun under my bed, pumped the action but couldn't find my glasses, saw a vague shape, took aim in the direction of a moving blob, and that's all I remember, except for pain. Excruciating pain. Then I felt complete whiteness. It was a calm feeling and that bright light, you know, people describe who have near-death experiences. I saw it. I wanted to follow the light up to its source but someone or something told me, 'No, don't follow it, keep fighting.'"

"Interesting. Well that's more than I thought you'd remember. Do you think you had enemies, or anyone you believe might want to harm you?"

"Obviously we both agree it was attempted murder."

"I'm pretty sure."

"I don't know. It's kinda bizarre. There are two brothers, Gavin and Blake Flanagan. I bet you've already heard the story before."

"Right, but tell me what you experienced."

"Seems Gavin was extremely jealous that Marta had rejected him for me. Seemed a little out of the ordinary, and his bitterness worsened after he also lost the bogus malpractice suit against me, despite all the money I'm sure he spent on it. Interestingly, his brother, as you know, is a Marine whose muscles inadequately compensate for his brain vacuum. For some reason, he had it out for me too, and he made the mistake of attacking me in the bathroom of the Heart Ball."

"Really? Now that is new information. This Heart Ball sounds like some type of war zone. He obviously didn't tell me that."

"No, not surprising that he wouldn't. Anyway, he thought he was tough, but I took him down quickly to the floor and neutralized him. I think he was embarrassed, since he was in his Marine dress uniform and others were watching, but I told him in no uncertain terms he was to stay away from me, forever, or I wouldn't be so gentle with him next time."

"Apparently he has poor judgment, and can't control his temper. Not a good move against a Krav Maga expert."

"Precisely. Must've mistakenly thought I was some kind of wussy doc, I guess."

"Anyone else you can think of?"

"Well, of course, there's always the crazy ex-wife, right?"

"Right and from what I've gathered she was a handful. But the problem I have with that scenario is that the two of you still have kids in college although they are estranged in a peculiar way, and you're still paying her alimony payments, so it would not be in her best interest to do violence to you."

"What alimony payments? Is that what she told you?"

"Well, yeah that's what she said."

"My alimony payments terminated two months before the shooting."

Gordon looked at Wyatt in cold silence. He'd caught Katherine in another lie.

"She's a master manipulator and liar. Hell, she could teach a course on how to lie effectively to the CIA interrogation service, and they would be better for it. In fact, it's more likely that her broomstick she rides will eventually get tired of the load and drive her into the ground. You know, burial by broomstick."

"I get the picture. Wyatt, I imagine as a physician you had a large life-insurance policy on yourself. Who was the beneficiary?"

"I took Katherine and the kids off as beneficiaries after they threw so much hatred at me for no reason, wrongly accusing me of abuse, abandonment of the kids, and of course, complete destruction of the free world. I won't tolerate that, even from my children. They need to live with their words and actions. Marta is the new beneficiary even though we're not married yet."

"Okay, thanks for clearing that up. Does Marta know she's a beneficiary on your life-insurance policy?"

"You know I don't remember if I told her. Anyway, Katherine is a piece of work, a real devil woman, but I really don't think she would do this. She likes herself too much and needs me desperately as a punching bag to show the kids how bad I am and apparently continue to be. No, she needs me. I'm just happy I have had enough self-control not to murder her. Just kidding of course."

"Yeah, I get it, Wyatt. But please get me a copy of the life-insurance policy with Marta's name as beneficiary."

"Why, you certainly aren't suggesting…"

"All your contacts are possible suspects. What about this Amy Adams?"

"She's a nurse at the hospital and I worked with her. Attractive and smart."

"I know, I interviewed her."

"Well, she may have been attracted to me I guess, but I wasn't interested. Sure, she was pretty, but I don't date women I work with, and what's more, I'd just met Marta. Then bizarre things started to happen. I found someone at Marta's house trying to break in or maybe snoop on her. I ran after the person, and I know it was a woman. Doesn't prove it was Amy, but it's strange. However, sometime later, Amy chased Marta and me in a car while we were driving to dinner, swearing at us as loud as she could and giving us the finger. I thought she would force us off the road. I think she quit the hospital and took another job after that, but that's all I remember of her. It was damn scary. Almost like she snapped."

"Strange behavior from a woman who seems to have a calm demeanor. That's the same story Marta gave me almost to the word. And one more question, Wyatt. What did you mean you had some 'training' to prepare you for the attack that night? Just curious."

"I taught Krav Maga to some special forces units at various bases across the country, and at the same time, they reciprocated with some weapons training for me and a few other things."

"What other things?"

"I'm not at liberty to go into my military training right now, I hope you'll understand."

"Thanks for your time, Wyatt. I wish you the best and hopefully better luck in the future."

"I can't wait to go home tomorrow and be with my Marta. I've been given a second chance on life, and I've achieved one of my goals: finding the woman I love completely and unconditionally, and she loves me the same way."

"May I ask what your other goal is?"

"The goal that seems impossible for me to achieve, yet continues to occupy an empty space in my heart: reconciliation with the sons I love. Few men have lost all contact with their children, while they are still alive, like I have. I hate to say this but if they were dead, at least I would have a closure that although horrible, I could understand. But this in some ways is just as brutal as the alternative. Parents who have lost their children to death, continue to grieve for them forever, but I believe I grieve just as much. You see? Hope for an impossible goal can be a brutal quest. I've lost so much over too many years. They've chosen their life path and they will have to live with it without my intervention to guide and protect them anymore. But at the same time, as their father, I will never give up hope for them."

CHAPTER 46

"I'm following him now into the subdivision. He's driving forty in a twenty-five mile per hour speed limit and I'm going to pull him over."

"I don't want you pulling him over for a damn speeding ticket. Just follow him from a safe distance and see what he's up to. Stay far enough away so he doesn't get suspicious. I think this guy's dangerous."

"Yeah, Gordon. I'll keep you informed."

"If he's doing anything suspicious, call for backup before you arrest him. If there's nothing to pick him up for, then stay away. I want us to document what he's doing. Got it?"

"Copy."

Blake Flanagan drove his red corvette around the various streets of Chicago, and then went north to Evanston. The officer tried to follow at a distance that was close enough to keep him in sight, but far enough away not to cause suspicion. Too many twists, turns, and quick accelerations. He was struggling to keep up, and his unmarked Ford proved no match for the Vette. He lost him.

"Adam 10, lost contact with the suspect. Await further instructions."

Gordon stopped using his police radio and went to his cell phone. "Shit, Greg. Not much we can do now. Let's hang tight. Amy, Gavin, and Katherine are all at home tonight so Blake is the only one mobile. He sure as hell isn't on a joyride at three in the morning. I'm alerting Evanston police Bolo for the Vette."

Wyatt finished reading the last month's issue of *The Journal of the American College of Cardiology*, then tossed the journal on the stone floor where it scattered with multiple other half-read journals with dog-eared place markers. He was finally at home in the black leather chair in his study, plaid boxer shorts, T-shirt, and white tube socks. He gently rubbed his long semicircular scar that tracked almost across his whole abdomen, just below his right rib cage. His surgeon told him he would have pain for months. Pleased that his mind was back in gear, he went to bed early so he could make rounds at the hospital for the first time in two months.

He had to call her before bed, his usual ritual that he looked forward to every night. He walked to the bedroom on the first floor in the back of the house so he could call her while he was lying in bed. The bedroom walls had been repainted, the stone floors cleaned, and the bed replaced since the shooting. There were no traces of the previous carnage in his bedroom. Wyatt didn't fear the bedroom, because he knew he couldn't be attacked twice and he had his trusty twelve gauge as well as a state-of-the-art alarm system that this time, he made sure he turned on before bed. "*Face the fear head on so the fear won't consume you.*"

"Hello, love. Wish you were here with me. I need to feel your lips stuck to mine."

"Oh Wyatt, you're so nice to me. What would I do without you?"

"Well, thankfully you don't have to worry about that anymore. Are you in bed, cuddly and warm?"

"Oh yes. But I could be warmer. Need a nice handsome cardiologist with blue eyes to keep me toasty and happy. Know anybody that fits that description?"

"Yes, as a matter of fact I do. I know him well, and he's ready and willing to serve as your human hot-water bottle."

"I love you, Wyatt."

"Love you too. See you tomorrow for coffee if I have a few free minutes. I think my partners will kill me with work tomorrow, but I don't care. I want to work so badly I can taste it. Good night, sweetie."

Blake drove around the neighborhood in Evanston making four laps around the circumference, each time slowing down to about five miles per hour in front of Wyatt's house so that the engine noise was muffled. Finally, on the fifth lap, he pulled off into a wooded lot, about four houses away from Wyatt's place, hiding his car behind the trees so it couldn't be seen from the road. He wore black cargo pants, a black sweatshirt, and a plain black baseball cap with no logo, but he didn't wear face camouflage. He sat in his car for thirty minutes, constantly looking at his watch and listening for noises outside while his window was rolled down. Although he'd mastered recon techniques during his Marine training prior to sniper school, he had never done recon in a nice subdivision in Evanston, Illinois, inhabited by doctors, lawyers, businesspersons, and dogs.

With my training, no one will catch me, and Barton will be quivering with fear in his bedroom. Scare the hell out of the pussy doc so he might just pee his pants thinking he's going to be shot again. Nobody does what he did to me at the dance and gets away with it. I'll play with his mind so he'll never feel safe and never sleep. Red spray paint on the side of his house: "Eyes on you." Satisfied that he was not being followed or watched, he exited the car and ran quietly through the yards. He saw that the house to the west of Wyatt's had no fence between the two back yards, but the house to the east had a fenced backyard, probably with a dog. He crouched behind some bushes in the west neighbor's yard, and when he thought the time was right he made his move.

Wyatt heard the neighbor's dog bark with a peculiar howl that seemed unusual. Instinctively he jumped out of his new Sleep Number bed and immediately put his glasses on, pumped the action on his shotgun and chambered a shell, now looking out his bedroom window in his shorts. He saw nothing, but had a sickening feeling in his gut; his eyes dilated as wide as an owl's in the darkness, about to capture his prey. He was hyper-vigilant about noises that were slightly out of the ordinary or inappropriate. He could feel his pulse pounding incessantly on the cold steel of his weapon, sensing danger while knowing how to calm his fear. His Special Forces friends had pounded that into him. No way was he staying in his bedroom this time. *This can't be happening again! If he's coming back to finish the job, he's got some hot lead to eat first.* He figured the perp would probably try to enter the house from the lower level in the back of the house where he could enter, then hide. If the guy stayed in the house, despite the alarm going on, then it would be a shootout. If it's the same guy, he wouldn't break the window the same way to gain entry.

He looked out through a small hole in his shutters and studied the bushes adjacent to his house, looking for subtle movement patterns. The illumination provided by the moonlight showed him that the north wind was blowing the tiny branches to the south, but his trained eyes detected a few branches leaning awkwardly to the north in the dense shrubbery. That was all he needed to act. He then quietly called 911.

"This is Dr. Wyatt Barton. 3614 Sunnyside Lane. I have a trespasser on my property. I need the police now. I'm going outside."

"We're dispatching the police to your location now. Do not go outside! Stay in your home, sir."

"Did that before. Didn't work." He hung up.

Wyatt slipped out the garage service door, still in his shorts and T-shirt, now with laces tied tight on his Nike running shoes so that he could sprint if needed. He slowly walked to the back where he previously saw the movement in the bushes, knowing he had the advantage of knowing his property, and how to avoid the noisy gravel and stay on the grass. The full moon provided plenty of illumination and he was thankful it was at his back, just like the scene he remembered from the movie *The Outlaw Josey Wales*, only it wasn't the sun and he didn't have Josey's perfect aim. But then he didn't need to with a 12-gauge shotgun. He saw movement and immediately aimed the barrel of the shotgun at the man's leg.

"Get down on the ground, face down, and don't move!"

"What the h..."

"You heard me. Down on your face, you piece of shit, or I'll blow your tiny head off."

Blake did as he was told. Immediately.

Wyatt pulled out his hospital penlight from the back pocket of his shorts and shined it into the man's face.

"Well whattdya know. It's little Blakey Flanagan again! Tell me, Blakey, what are you doing in my backyard at almost four am, crouching in the bushes like you're playing hide-and-seek? You've proven once again that you're a poor excuse for a man, let alone a Marine. You're dumber than a piece of shit."

"I don't have anything to say to you, Barton."

Just then, the Evanston police arrived with Detective Farmer.

"Put the gun down, Wyatt," said Farmer. "We've got this under control."

He wouldn't put it down. He kept aiming it at Blake's trembling head.

"Wyatt. I said put it down now!"

He put the shotgun on the ground and the officers removed his weapon. They frisked Blake and found a can of spray paint in his gun holster, but no weapon.

"So tell me, Blake, what are you doing in this man's backyard, carrying a can of spray paint, a few hours before daylight?" said Farmer.

Blake said nothing.

"I can tell you what he's doing, Gordon. He's pissed because I took him to the ground when he tried to attack me like a coward at the Heart Ball, then he unsuccessfully tried to kill me a few months ago.

Now he's here trying to finish the job he couldn't complete. What were you going to do, spray me to death with paint? Too bad I found you, huh Blakey boy? You made me sick when I first met you, and now I just think you're a slithering night crawler playing in the mud because you can't face the light of day. Get him off my property, Detective."

Blake did not acknowledge Wyatt. "I was going to a late-night party but seemed to have lost my way. These fancy-ass houses all look the same, you know."

"What's the name of the owners of the house who had a party you were invited to?" asked Farmer.

"That's all I have to say to you until I get a lawyer."

The officers handcuffed Blake, read him his Miranda rights, walked him to the car, and took off for the police station.

Wyatt went into his house; his pulse rate hammered hard enough to make his incision bounce along the edges that hadn't quite healed. The liquor cabinet was beckoning him like a long-lost friend. He hesitated, thought about the smooth bourbon for a moment, then walked away and went to the refrigerator to splash some cold orange juice down his parched esophagus. He told himself never again would he put himself in a dangerous position because of alcohol. He was alive and he was his own master. He had to call Marta. "Honey, you won't believe what just happened!"

CHAPTER 47

Amy yearned to call Wyatt and congratulate him on his recovery, but she knew it wouldn't look very good in the grand scheme of things. *Especially after I chased him around town with that bitch in the car with him and snooped around her house. Got to learn to control myself and my anger. Farmer's got his eyes on me.* She sat in her La-Z-Boy chair while she drank cold beer out of a bottle and stared at her pink cell phone, highlighted Wyatt's number from the directory, and almost pushed "call" several times then thought better of it. She hated the thought of Marta and her man together. *That foreign slut doesn't deserve him. Only I deserve him.*

E. David Carson worried about his boss, Gavin, and was grateful that he finally agreed to meet in his office to talk. He was a good friend of Gavin's late father Sean, who gave him the breaks he needed to become financially successful at his firm. He cared about Gavin, especially when he saw him distracted and not coming to work more than once a week. The accountants were telling him there was a large amount of money missing from the books. He needed an explanation and asked him to come to his office and sit in front of his desk so he could look him in the eyes. He felt safe behind his massive mahogany desk with gold-plated desk lamps and walls adorned with stuffed antelope and bear heads from his previous hunting trips.

"Hey David, what's the pressing issue? You want me to give you some more vacation time to travel to the islands to look at the pretty girls while they laugh at your gut? I think you're better off going on safaris in Africa because you'd have to point a gun at the beach girls to get them into your bed."

"Funny. No, Gavin, I was just worried about you. You don't seem yourself lately. What's going on?"

"Ah, yes, you're trying to be a substitute father figure. I understand. Don't worry about me; everything's fine. The firm continues to flourish, and we get more and more clients in nearly every department every month."

"Maybe so, but the accountants tell me that there's fifty thousand dollars not accounted for on the books. Do you know anything about that, Gavin?"

Gavin gazed furtively out the window behind David's massive desk. "I don't know what you're talking about, but my guess is it's just a little math error somewhere. Our bean counters will figure it out soon enough; I'm not worried. Lighten up a little, David. Life's good for you. Enjoy what my father created for you."

"Yeah, okay, but the bean counters tell me they tried to talk to you, but you've been unavailable the last few months, and that's unusual for you. You're not worried about the Barton trial are you? I mean, you don't have anything to worry about there, do you? Or is it Blake you're worried about?"

"Hell you know I always have to worry about my little brother. He's a hothead and needs to be reined in sometimes. That's my job. Honestly, I don't give a shit for this quack and have better things to do with my time than worry about him. He stole my girl; she doesn't answer my calls anymore, and he may or may not have been able to save my dad. I don't know anymore. Unfortunately, he survived a botched home-invasion shooting, but no, your insinuation is clear. I wasn't involved. I've got a brain. You know better than that."

David thoughtfully caressed the pure gray goatee neatly trimmed on his chin. "Yes, of course, Gavin. I never thought you were involved, but I do want you to get back to business here. The company needs you."

"Thanks for the lecture, and don't worry about me, David. Have a good day."

Wyatt kept his picture albums and mementos stored in a closet in the basement. He didn't like going downstairs because the stepping and braking action necessary for walking downstairs stretched his taut surgical incision, but in a way, he welcomed the physical pain—it reminded him that he was definitely alive and that his muscles needed the workout. It was time for winter maintenance downstairs, and on the way to the furnace room, he walked by the basement wall shelving system he'd built, glancing briefly at all the storage boxes marked with a felt-tip marker with their contents. He knew what was in the two boxes in the center of the wall without reading the label: all the baby pictures, vacation photos at Disney World and the Bahamas, photos of the boys with baseball and soccer trophies, pictures with Santa Claus, and the smiles while they opened their gifts at the holidays with their grandparents. He remembered all of those precious images, but he kept them locked deep inside his soul and physically hidden from his sight, protected from the light of day, and the clutches of his fragile heart. He'd refused to look at them over the years of separation and alienation because it was too painful to bring the memories back with actual images. He continued walking to the furnace room, installed new filters in the furnace, checked the sump pump backup system, and brought in the garden hoses curled semi-neatly on the deck to avoid the winter freeze. On his way back to the stairs, he glanced at the wall of boxes and he felt his strength tumble down a black hole. He walked over to the boxes labeled "kids" and opened each one, poring over the pictures reflecting a previous life of hope and happiness. The memories pulsed back, flooding the melancholy in like a tidal wave, crushing him momentarily and then sucking him back out to sea with the undertow of loss. But he didn't allow himself to be buried too long in the darkness. He woke up out of his reverie and realized that now they sure didn't worry about him and in fact, he believed over the years that his sons likely no longer cared if he lived or died.

Several years after the divorce, the social worker advised him to block all e-mails and change his phone number from Katherine and the boys, due to their easy access to him and the destructive words from them that he took to heart, and he knew she was right. After he left the basement, he walked briskly out to the mailbox at the end of his long driveway, enjoying the fall colors of yellow and red leaves on the trees blowing and falling from the crisp wind. He was calm now, and the lack of hateful communication gave him an inner peace.

He opened the creaky metal mailbox and found a letter with "Dr. Wyatt Barton" printed by a computer as well as a return address, which looked real but he couldn't figure out who it was from. He knew better, but opened it anyway. It was a letter from Katherine, desperate to make contact with him, and this was the only way she felt she could accomplish it now. She enclosed pictures of the boys at multiple Christmas parties with her and her new boyfriend, photos at their high school graduations and various other events that Wyatt had missed over the years due to the hate she'd injected into his kids' souls. It was clearly designed to show him how happy the three of them appeared to be without him, and that he was missing out on such a wonderful family over the years.

Dear Wyatt: I thought you would enjoy these pictures of the boys. I'm so proud of them for doing so good in school and growing up to be such fine young men. We are all so happy. Too bad you've chosen not to be a part of us. We're so happy. Katherine.

Wyatt was much stronger now. He knew nothing about the boys and their lives, and certainly if they were so happy why would she care to spend the time doing these manipulations after all these years? She had the kids wrapped around her finger and a new honey who likely wouldn't approve of these behaviors. Previously, the pain of it all would have thrown Wyatt into a deep abyss, but now he protected himself. She still thought she could push the knife in deeper. She didn't realize that her knife was no longer a sharp dagger, but a rubber toy knife or a Twizzler's licorice stick that bent on impact to his chest, no longer penetrating to his heart.

He walked to the garbage can in the garage, tore up the pictures, and threw them away with her stupid letter.

CHAPTER 48

Potato chip packages, pop cans, and McDonald's bags littered the floor around the apartment and on the cheap card table in the kitchen; Spencer Barton banished himself to immerse his mind in intense study for the upcoming LSAT. He was oblivious to most of his surroundings while he studied, and he told Lisa that he wouldn't be available at all that weekend to meet her, but he would make it up to her soon. He did, however, make himself available to Jerry. He needed some speed.

"Hey Spence, great to hear from you! Funny you should call, though. Brock was asking if I'd heard from you. Guess he worries about you."

"Been busy, you know, studying and keeping my honey happy. Who's Brock?"

"I'm surprised you forgot about him already. I introduced you two at my party and he's kind of a guy you don't forget very easily."

"Oh yeah, he said any friend of yours is a friend of his. I remember."

"So tell me, Mr. Clean Future Lawyer, looks like Lisa has her claws in you and you don't mind at all, do you?"

"Well, maybe. But sometimes I think about what things will be like when I'm in law school. We like to spend time together and all that, but maybe I'm not ready for commitment yet. Need some quick meaningless encounters with some hotties when the need arises."

"There you go, selfish Spencer. That's why I like you. You're good for my business. Which reminds me; I've noticed you're not buying any shit from me lately. Your mommy cut your money pipeline off?"

"No, she'd never do that. She always gives me what I want without questions because well, she thinks I'm everything, you know. I just tell her I need to buy some new suits for law school interviews or I need money for a Kaplan law review course or something like that. She bagged a large wad from my jerk father after the divorce. I certainly don't mind taking the selfish bastard's money. She's an honest woman, but she did tell me that my father didn't pay her alimony very consistently, but when I think about it, that's probably not possible with all her lavish spending."

"Now I know you're the selfish one, Spence. Previously you told me he abandoned you and gave her no money, and now the story is changed? You're a damn momma's boy, that's for sure. But you're a good customer, so who cares."

"Whatever. I need some amphetamines, maybe some Adderall or Ritalin so I can ace this test coming up."

"You got the green, I got some good shit for ya. By the way, you need any downers for when you want to come down off your high?"

"Good idea. Maybe about twenty Oxycontins would be good. I'll bring you the cash tonight."

"Great. By the way, congrats are in order. I saw on the news that your old man was released from the hospital. Amazing that he recovered from that attack, don't you think?"

"Yeah, 'amazing' probably isn't the right word. Maybe 'lucky as hell' is more appropriate."

"I'll see you tonight, Spence. Bring fifteen hundred."

Colby enjoyed coming home to Momma for dinner on the weekends. The food was, well, Mom's cooking; much better than dorm-room pizza. However, it seemed to him that the conversations over the years always seemed to be about Wyatt and how well Spencer was doing, and how many law schools were interested in him.

"Colby, I wanted to tell you the good news that your father was released from the hospital."

"Yeah, I know. It was all over the news. 'Respected cardiologist makes miracle recovery.'"

"You're not thinking of going to visit him, are you? If so, that blond of his will put up a wall against us I'm sure. She's probably the one who destroyed our family."

"Are you sure, Mom? That kind of stuff doesn't matter to me anymore, and I think I'm gonna call him. It's been years since we talked, and maybe it's time now that he's apparently home and recovering."

"You know I always wanted you and Spencer to have a relationship with him and I never stopped you, but be careful. You know he rarely seemed to care about our wonderful family, and it was horrible how he abandoned us. All he cared about was his three 'W's': work, women, and wodka. And now you want to call him after all that?"

"I've been thinking about this for a while. Seems that's the junk you've been pounding into our brains for years, Mom, and I accepted it before without question. I've been thinking about this and you know there's another side to this, and he is my father. I'm tired of this crap you keep throwing at us, and it's making me sick."

"I can't believe you're talking to me like that, Colby! After all I've done for you over the years—protecting you, feeding you, making your holidays nice, and shuttling you to and from school and sports events. I love you and Spencer, and I don't want your father to hurt you two anymore. I've always been there for you boys 24/7 since you were babies."

Colby put on his jacket and walked towards the door while she continued talking. "Goodbye, Mom; thanks for the nice dinner. I need to go back to my dorm to study." *It's time that I think about doing the right things now, and make my own decisions without her warped interpretation of reality.*

CHAPTER 49

Marta drove to Wyatt's house to enjoy a cookout he told her he was preparing for her on his deck, overlooking the colorful autumn trees in a wooded nature preserve. She had enjoyed the natural setting when they sat on the deck before, in the summer, when he cooked hamburgers for her, the American meal she learned to love when he introduced it to her when they first met. They preferred salmon, but the grilled-out taste of the hamburger adorned with mayonnaise, mustard pickles, and sometimes onions was hard to resist on occasion. She told him not to bother with all that since he was still weak from the shooting, but she knew he was too stubborn to admit that, so she went with it. Her flaxen hair blew back and forth during the drive with her sunroof open, and each male driver whom she passed nearly broke his neck staring at her. It was an unavoidable and innate behavior imprinted on men, she thought. She appreciated the attention, but didn't seek it. Right now she wanted to spend every moment she could with Wyatt, the love she'd almost lost. She was not going to let go of her miracle man.

Wyatt had smooth jazz playing and cleaned the house as best a man could do in the circumstances. He had to take a break every ten minutes or so because his endurance was still lacking after the shooting. After preparing the table with a vase of red roses, he opened a bottle of ten-year-old Chateau Franc Mayne and poured two glasses to allow the elegant wine to breathe. He was in control of his desire for alcohol now; he threw out all his scotch and bourbon that had previously held him captive. On occasion, he would enjoy a glass or two of fine red wine, but that was now all he would allow himself. Today, he would enjoy it with his woman. Life was too precious, and the trauma he'd endured taught him that lesson well. He knew he was lucky during the malpractice case that no one pursued the drinking issue, even though he knew he wasn't impaired at all; the beer had been washed out of his system well before the surgery, and the case had nothing to do with the medical facts. Theoretically it could've brought him down, and he was not going to let the bottle destroy him.

Every day after he left the hospital, he made sure he saw Marta for dinner or at least coffee at Starbucks, and it seemed he could never get enough of her. He knew she felt the same. When she stayed over, he wouldn't wash the pillowcase she slept on; the scent of her lingering perfume filled him with an enduring image of her beauty, her smile, and her angelic soul. It reminded him of the diamond he'd nearly lost, but now he had life, and Marta, the love of his life, back. He would not erase her voice messages, but would play them back several times per week, just to drink in the sultry sound of her accent and her feminine voice filled with life and confidence. When she finally walked into his house, he held her tight and wouldn't let her out of his arms, loosening them slightly to kiss her soft lips and then releasing them to tenderly float his fingers through her soft hair.

"Well Wyatt, after that kiss, I don't think eating dinner is my highest priority."

She pulled him towards her, wrapping her dainty hands around his neck, and kissed him back with a passion that only soul mates understand. They remained silent, eyes fixed upon each other and bodies held close, until Wyatt broke away briefly to pour her a glass of Bordeaux. She sipped and he sipped, and they laughed and enjoyed the wine mostly by kisses that shared wine-soaked lips. He took her free hand and led her to his bedroom that he prepared with candlelight earlier. At the foot of the bed, he held her wine glass but his lips remained on hers, and then gently explored her supple neck, allowing her hand to loosen his belt while he gently explored her legs under her skirt, delicately touching every bit of feminine paradise possible.

His pants fell to the ground, followed quickly by her skirt. He took her glass away and they fell tangled together onto the bed. He worshipped her body with gentle touches in sensitive spots, listening to her helpless moans and inhaling her feminine scent, playing all the parts of her eager body as if they were instruments in a symphony orchestra; he conducted her feminine orchestra to a blissful perfection that they both existed to experience with multiple resounding encores.

She fell asleep with her head on his chest, and Wyatt remained awake, holding her lovely head, deep in calm but clear thought.

I know some day I will again touch the hearts of my sons that have been stolen by their borderline mother and hear their laughter that I once enjoyed and share our lives as father and sons again. I will not forget my Boogie and Bubba.

CHAPTER 50

Farmer figured Blake was the most likely suspect. He possessed a motive, though inappropriate, the means, and the opportunity. However, it didn't add up completely, and Farmer hoped he would make some progress during his second interrogation of Blake. He needed solid evidence from the shooting, though. The two men sat in the middle of the stark interrogation room at the police station. A video camera in the far corner of the room recorded the conversation, and the grey metal office table where they were sitting held an ashtray, a book of matches, and two water bottles. This time, though, he turned the room heat up to 85 degrees to make Blake uncomfortable.

"So, Blake, tell me what were you doing in Dr. Barton's yard last night?"

"Like I said, I was going to a party and got lost. Sure is hot in here, Detective."

"Feels fine to me. Hard to believe a Marine sniper scout instructor, highly trained in land navigation at night, camouflage, and surveillance would make such a simple mistake. I don't believe you."

"That's your problem, Detective, not mine. You don't have anything on me."

"No, it's your problem. You're now the prime suspect. I think you were trying to harass Dr. Barton, probably going to spray paint his house to intimidate him or scare him after all he's been through." Gordon couldn't help but chuckle. "Problem is, looks like he scared the hell out of you instead."

"Got nothin' more to say to you, Detective. I'm not your man. I'm not going to hide the fact that I can't stand the guy. But if I really wanted to kill this doc, I would've done it the right way the first time.

You can try to charge me with trespassing if you want, Gordon, but I caused no damage and had no weapon. Either way, my brother Gavin will get me off because you have no case. You know that, Gordon."

"Oh, that's clever. Bring Gavin into it now. That's perfect for my case. Mr. Pretty Boy with a Harvard education and his enforcer brother. Right?"

"All you can charge me with is maybe just trespassing on private property. No big deal 'cause that won't stick and you know it. You're going to release me today, or Gavin and his team will have your ass for interrogating me without a lawyer. Either way, I have a right to make a call, so let me make my call now."

"You talk big for a man with no brains, Blake. Were you aware that the sentence for attempted murder is up to 40 years? And while you think about that, your brother is a person of interest too. He's just smarter than you are. Yeah, go ahead and make your call. Here's the phone."

Blake called Gavin on his cell. "Farmer's got me here at the station, accusing me of trespassing at Barton's house."

"You're a certified idiot. What the hell were you doing, and is he there listening to this conversation?"

"Yeah, he's sitting right here."

"Okay. Ask him to leave for a few minutes while you talk to your lawyer."

"Detective, may I have a few minutes in private with my lawyer?"

Farmer smirked. "Go to hell."

The brothers resumed their conversation while Farmer waited and watched. "So, Shit for Brains, tell me what you were doing in Barton's yard."

"Surprised he was able to sneak up on me, considering my training, you know. The guy's pretty slick for some reason I can't figure out. He's got some training or something. But I just wanted to plant fear into his mind so he couldn't sleep anymore. So I wanted to spray paint 'eyes on you' on the side of his house, but damned if he didn't catch me and point the barrel of a twelve gauge at me. I could've taken him down if I'd wanted to, though, but decided against it to avoid violence."

"Bullshit. You're dumber than a jackass. Why can't you just leave the guy alone? You know by now this is no average doc and you can't mess with him. Not only that, they're investigating the case and both of us are potential suspects. So tell me, did you have a weapon and did you cause any damage to the property?"

"No weapon. I knew that would be a problem, and no, I caused no damage."

"Good. One more thing. Were there any 'no trespassing signs' on his property or did Barton give you a warning that entry to his property was forbidden?"

"You got to be kidding. Shit no."

"Okay then. You were lost, there were no signs that said 'no trespassing,' and you were not warned to stay off the property. They have no case of criminal trespassing to real property. I'll come down and he'll drop the charges."

Farmer reentered the interrogation room and sat across the table from Blake, who hung up as soon as he entered the room. Just then, Farmer's cell phone rang and he stepped out of the room so Blake wouldn't hear.

"Julie, there better be a good reason for you calling me in the middle of interrogating our charming Marine."

"Yes, as a matter of fact you'll find this interesting. I called Blake's commanding officer at Quantico and his alibi is solid. He was at Quantico supervising night maneuvers for the sniper candidates when Wyatt was shot. He has a solid alibi. The other piece of information is that I checked court records on the divorce and Katherine was lying. As Wyatt said, the hefty alimony payments he sent to her were finished two months prior to the shooting. She was no longer receiving money from him."

"Interesting. I'm going to have to let Blake go for now. He won't be charged with anything, and yes, I knew Katherine was lying. She's got skills, but so do I. Is there anything else you want to tell me, Julie?"

"Yeah, I saved the best for last."

"The CODIS database produced a match?"

"You got it. The blood samples we found in Wyatt's house from the window glass shards and foyer floor produced a match and we may have a fingerprint match on the gun the garbage man found. We have an exact DNA match from an ex-con named Brock Lawson."

"Brock Lawson? Who the hell is that? He sure wasn't on our radar screen."

"Served time for possession and armed robbery at the state pen in Springfield. Got his DNA recorded from his last bust."

"Any last known location for this guy?"

"Seems to have been involved in the drug scene again according to our street sources, but he's been quiet last few years. Hasn't been seen locally, but he's been seen in Champaign though, probably trying to hook some students if he can. He's easy to spot. He's a six-five white guy with red hair and dagger tattoos on the back of each hand with the business end pointing out. Last worked as a bouncer at a club here in town, but he's been clean as a politician kissing babies since he left the slammer."

"Julie, I want you to issue a national BOLO on Brock Lawson with his physical description and last known location. He's probably long since left the state and he's hiding in some smelly rat hole."

"I'm all over it, Gordon. The chase for the real perp is on."

Gordon spent the rest of the day feverishly searching for information on Lawson. Did he have a connection to Barton, or was this a robbery? Nothing was stolen. Did it have something to do with drugs? What was the motive? He obtained Lawson's prison records from Springfield and San Quentin and interviewed his last employer at the bar where he was a bouncer. Seems he did his job, was punctual, and didn't get in trouble after his parole was over. He had no family and was never married, but he drove a red Porsche 911 registered in Illinois. It was late in the evening after he was able to find basic information on Lawson, and it was now time to call Wyatt.

"Hello, Dr. Barton? It's Gordon Farmer."

"Hello, Detective. How may I help you? Do you need some more information?"

"Well no, but I have some information you will be interested in. We have a DNA match from the blood in your house with a man named Brock Lawson and I've released Blake Flanagan."

"Are you kidding me? Where in the world did you find him?"

"My same reaction when I heard it. We're not sure about what his motive is or what his connection to you is, but there's a nationwide manhunt out for him now."

"Are you sure about this? It just doesn't seem to make sense and it's weird. I don't know a Brock Lawson and can't remember a patient by that name either."

"Check your patient database to see if he's in there and let me know if you find out anything, Wyatt. We'll find him, you can bet on that. All the police departments and the FBI have a BOLO on him and I'll let you know when he's captured."

"What's a BOLO?"

"It's an acronym for 'Be On the Look Out.' It's information sent nationwide to law-enforcement agencies regarding his physical characteristics and last known location. Quite effective in finding the vermin stupid enough to venture out into the light of day. By the way, Wyatt, did you ever keep medications or narcotic pain pills in your house? You know, like for supplies when you went on your medical mission trips?"

"I never stored any of that in my house. Medical supplies are available through the usual volunteer organizations with strict monitoring of any controlled substances by the state pharmaceutical board."

"Figured. Had to ask. You probably guessed why. This guy's into the drug scene and may have wanted some drugs to sell. I've got to get back to work now, but I want you to get to your office and check your patient database to see if you had ever had him as a patient. By the way, he's a six-foot-five Caucasian and has dagger tattoos on the back of his hands."

"I'll check, Gordon, but that's the kind of guy I damn well would remember forever if he was a patient. Good luck and find this asshole and bring him to justice."

"You can bet on it, Wyatt."

CHAPTER 51

After a week of waiting, Gordon Farmer received a call from the Tucumcari, New Mexico, police department that they had a subject in custody that fit the description of Brock Lawson, distributed on the national BOLO.

His Porsche 911 was now yellow and he had a stolen New Mexico plate. He was staying at a Super 8 Motel and the front desk clerk told Gordon she was alarmed when she saw this tall guy with nasty tattoos walking with a cane and called her friend at the police department, who then matched her description of him from the BOLO. The Evanston Police Department extradited Brock Lawson the next day and after he was booked, cleaned up, and fed, Farmer began the interrogation. He positioned two detectives planted behind the one-way mirrors and the videotape hummed in the corner of the interrogation room. Lawson sat at the gray metal table with his left foot on top, cane tapping on the table while looking up at the camera and purposely picking his nose and smiling. Gordon walked down the long corridor slowly, thinking about the highest profile case he'd investigated, and stopping to drink from the chewing gum decorated water fountain midway down and trying to collect his thoughts before meeting with the violent shooter.

"Brock, I'm Detective Gordon Farmer, and I need to ask you some questions. Glass of water, coffee?"

"Nice of you to ask but no thanks. I've been through this shit before."

"I know. We've reviewed your arrest records. You were sentenced to do time for possession and selling heroin and for armed robbery. You're a menace to society and it's too bad they didn't lock you up forever."

"Well Mr. Detective, I expected the 'good cop bad cop' routine, but it looks like you're just doin' the bad cop stuff all by your lonesome. You must be quite a tough guy. They call you Dirty Harry?"

Farmer stared at him, especially the daggers on his hands. He couldn't stand guys like Lawson. Selling drugs to young kids and pulling guns on helpless women store clerks just to get a wad of cash. And now, he planned on making sure he went away for a long time for shooting Wyatt. It wouldn't be murder one since Wyatt survived, but he faced a long prison sentence especially with all his priors. Hopefully the court system wouldn't make any mistakes. But Farmer took a gamble that this guy had been on the run ever since the shooting, and although there was TV and media everywhere, the Wyatt Barton case just wasn't national news. He would take advantage of the fact that maybe Lawson was not aware that Wyatt survived the attack and would therefore try to scare him; the arrest is for first-degree murder, not attempted murder.

He finally broke off his stare. "So tell me, how long you been walking with a cane?"

"Oh, not long. Fell off a step and twisted my knee about a year ago and it's never been the same. I just probably need some knee surgery but I hate doctors."

"Our sources say they saw you working as a bouncer in Champaign four months ago, walking well and throwing troublemakers out of the bar with ease. Seems that doesn't jibe with what you just said."

"Sometimes you ignore the pain when the adrenaline pumps, ya know. Anyway, what are you going to charge me with, Detective? There was no dope in my car. Ain't robbed anyone since I got out of the pen. Been a model citizen. A regular John-Boy Walton."

"Murder one," said Farmer firmly.

"What? You got to be shittin' me!"

"Does the name Dr. Wyatt Barton ring a bell?"

"Like I said, I stay away from doctors, and no, I don't remember a dude by that name. And I'm done talking with you, Farmer. I need a lawyer."

"Damn right you do. I'll get you a court-appointed attorney unless you can pay for one yourself."

"Don't worry; I've got a nasty shark to call. He's smart as hell and he'll take care of this mess, but believe me, I can afford his expensive ass."

"Interesting that you have money to throw at a lawyer, but you don't have a job. I think your next job will be to clean your prison toilet cell with your only toothbrush for the rest of your life, or maybe you'll get the death penalty. I don't know. Depends on the judge."

The silence thundered throughout the room. Lawson constantly ran his dagger-inked hands through his red-matted hair, and then nervously stroked his sandpaper chin. Then he smiled, showing his methamphetamine-blackened teeth. "You got the wrong man."

"No I don't. It's solid. Got your DNA all over his house and fingerprints on the murder weapon. Dr. Barton shot you in the leg and you bled in his house. That's why you limp and need a cane. Your lawyer has Mount Everest to climb, so I want you to speak up about why you were in that house and if there was anything or anyone else involved. Could be you start moving your mouth with some words that are true and maybe your sentence will be less if the information pans out. Might even save your life."

"I got nothing more to say to you. Take me back to the cell and give me the phone to call my lawyer."

"No problem. But I suggest you think about what I said with every remaining brain cell you have that hasn't been incinerated by meth and heroin."

Wyatt typed on his office computer late that night searching the database for patients that might have the name Brock Lawson. He found some women patients named Lawson and the only male name was Tom, but he was five feet five inches tall. He just couldn't fathom why this guy would be in his house trying to shoot him if there was no robbery. He tried to think of a patient or a family that became angry with him for something, but he came up short. It seemed that now when practicing medicine, you could stay up all night and save a patient's life, but some could still be angry with you if you looked at them the wrong way. It was an entitlement society, that's for sure. All he could think of was Blake and Gavin Flanagan. However, what was their relationship to this Lawson guy, if any? His cell phone rang and the caller ID read "unknown," but he picked it up anyway because he thought it might be Detective Farmer.

"Dad? It's Colby."

He hadn't heard the word 'Dad' in so many years he couldn't count. Colby's voice was so deep and manly now; it was almost as foreign to him as a telemarketer's. Wyatt's breath obstructed just below his larynx, and air wouldn't start flowing again until he finally forced a deep breath with his diaphragm and was able to utter "Hello, Colby. It's been a long time." Wyatt prepared himself to receive another onslaught of searing vitriol from his son that he had heard so many times, but would no longer tolerate. He was ready to end the conversation immediately if the hate from his selfish youngest son again showed its ugly head to him.

"Yes, it has."

Wyatt knew that the kids didn't have his new cell phone number since he changed it due to the abusive messages he'd previously read and agonized over. But he didn't ask how Colby was able to obtain it. Maybe someone from the office gave it out, but it didn't matter. It had been a little more than five years since he and Colby had a pleasant conversation not dominated by hateful words from his son. Even longer from Spencer. The dark chasm remained between father and his youngest son, and it was impossible for either of them to jump the painful crevasse in a single bound.

"I heard you were at Northwestern. Are you doing okay in school?"

"Yeah, doing well. Thanks. The reason I called was that I wanted to say that it's amazing that you survived the shooting and I'm happy you did. Spencer and I visited you when you were in the ICU but you were unconscious."

"Thanks for the visitation and the call, Colby. So tell me, how is—"

"Well I have to go now and study. Take care."

"Take care, Colby."

Wyatt put the cell phone down, paced quickly around the house like a runner getting warmed up to stand at the starting line before the race starts. The hateful words never came from his son's mouth. His breathing transformed to a heave followed by a wheeze rather than a real breath. He tried to slow his breathing down by prolonging his expiration with pursed lips. It worked finally. The phone call lasted forty-five seconds but to Wyatt, it was equivalent to successfully accomplishing the trek to base camp of Mount Everest without a guide. It's a long way from the top, but it is a beginning. It was the tiny step he'd carried hope for during the years of brutal estrangement from the children he loved. His knees crumbled and he fell to the floor and buried his head in his hands on the couch.

CHAPTER 52

Brock Lawson sat on the edge of the cot in his jail cell, his orange jumpsuit nearly matching his hair and patchwork goatee. He passed the time away rolling up lint-balls and making high-arcing 3-point shots into the toilet in the middle of the cell.

"Mr. Lawson, I've got a visitor for you," said the burly guard. "Says he's your lawyer."

The guard brought Charles Kingston, Brock's longtime lawyer, to the bars in front of his cell, and when he recognized his lawyer, he immediately jumped up to greet him.

"Thanks for coming, Chuck. Knew you would."

"Yeah, cavalry always comes to the rescue."

The guard let Kingston into the cell, then locked it and told the two men they only had thirty minutes before he would ask Kingston to leave.

Brock slid to the end of his cot, allowing Kingston to sit on the opposite end. Although Kingston was a good eight inches shorter than Lawson was, his size around the belly was at least eight inches more and the cot creaked, nearly sinking to the floor when he sat down. He was bald with bushy eyebrows that curled at the ends, and looked like the Pillsbury doughboy.

"They charged me with murder, Chuck! I got no idea what they're talking about. I ain't killed no one."

"No, as far as I know you didn't, at least with this case. Dr. Barton is alive and well. That was just the detective's ploy—to get you to think Barton died so you could squeal like a little girl. Guess you didn't fall for it."

"What do you mean 'fall for it'? There wasn't no murder, and so there ain't nothing to—"

"Let's get to the point, Brock. I've known you for a long time, and I've represented you when no one else would. You've served time and you're dirty as coal in a mud pit. Now, I'm the only one who can help you, so you've only got now, I guess, 20 minutes to tell me what happened, because they have the stuff on you. That includes a DNA match, fingerprints on the gun, and your kneecap's been blown apart. Only thing is, they don't have a motive yet. If you don't come clean with me, you're going away for a long time now, probably die in prison due to your priors. And by the way, if you don't wire to my account $10,000 by tomorrow, I won't represent you."

"That's what I've always liked about you, Chuck. You're kind and gentle, working for the common man."

"Right. I'm not your friend and you're certainly not even close to a common man. I don't do volunteer work, and I'm your only hope right now. So start singing to your audience of one."

Lawson's face lost its energy and his smile faded. "Don't know who this Wyatt Barton is and I didn't shoot him."

"That's your response? Even with the DNA match and fingerprints and gun ballistics?"

"Yeah. I'm not scared of that shit. Forensics can be beaten in court."

"Maybe, but unlikely in this case. Better ask for a court-appointed attorney." Kingston walked away to the front of the cell, called the guard, and just before he walked into the corridor, Lawson called out.

"Wait, Chuck. I've got to tell you something."

"So. What? You want to talk now?"

"Yeah. Hey Guard, please let Mr. Kingston back in." The guard let him back in and Brock told his story.

"I broke into Dr. Barton's home and shot him."

"Of course you did. But why?"

"I had some debts to pay and I was trying to stay away from pushing dope for a while. So, someone made me a business deal."

"No, don't tell me you were..."

"Yeah, a dude paid me some good cash to shoot the guy, with a bonus if I killed him."

"You know, Brock, you're quite a gift to humanity. Lucky for you this doc didn't die, but it was close. So tell me who the co-conspirator was."

"I didn't want to kill him anyway. I purposely missed the vital organs and tried to wound him."

"He almost died from this little wound you gave him, Brock. Who paid you the money?"

"You need to tell me if I cop a plea and give this guy to the prosecutor whether I can get a lesser sentence."

"Probably your only chance, but we'll have to talk to the state's attorney and then present it to the judge and they'll have to check your story out extensively. So who was it, Mr. Songbird?"

"I need some water first because this whole thing is weird."

"No you don't. We've got five minutes left. Tell me who it is so I can try to cut your sentence down with the judge."

"Spencer Barton."

Kingston's eyes widened, heard it completely, thought he recognized the name, but had to ask for confirmation. "Who?"

"Spencer Barton, the doc's oldest son."

CHAPTER 53

T. Randolph Connor prosecuted hundreds of criminal cases out of the state's attorney's office in Chicago. Armed robbery, felony assault, rape, murder, and attempted murder were the most common cases for him. He didn't mind coming to jail cells to meet the alleged perpetrators of crimes because he knew it gave him an up-close view into the psyche of the accused. He was six foot three, wearing a three-piece black silk suit. He had black hair and distinguished gray on the sideburns. When he walked down the jail corridors, his stride was so long that he covered the ground quickly and with purpose. Few people could keep up with him.

At the guard station, he met Charles Kingston; they shook hands and both men were escorted into Brock Lawson's cell by the guard. Lawson stood up and shook Connor's hand; the power of Brock's baseball-mitt-sized hands nearly crushed Connor's hand, an appendage that Connor was told in the past was substantial as well. He gazed at Lawson's dagger tattoos and knew immediately that this guy knew the criminal justice system quite well.

"Thanks for agreeing to meet us and discuss my client's plea, Randy," said Kingston.

"I'm here to listen. Let's get to business, shall we?" He looked at Lawson, studying his facial expression, and saw that it was devoid of any spirituality or inspiration. "I've read the case and I'm prepared to prosecute you for the attempted murder of Dr. Wyatt Barton. Do you understand that, Mr. Lawson?"

"Yes sir, I do."

"Now, Charles, I need you to tell me what your client's plea is—I only have fifteen minutes so you need to make it as succinct as possible."

Kingston knew it was his time to shine, and he was already $10,000 richer, having checked for the bank wire that Lawson arranged. "My client is prepared to admit to the crime of attempted murder. However, he will offer the name of a co-conspirator who hired him for the job on the condition that he receive a lesser sentence."

"I see. And why would I want to accept that plea?"

"We can give you the name and the evidence against the man who masterminded the crime, and not only will justice be served, but you'll probably receive a commendation from the state, and accolades from the press for solving the case, further bolstering your career; probably put you on a fast track to the governor's seat in Springfield. Oh and by the way, who's the judge presiding the case?"

"Kennedy. And he doesn't look favorably on people with multiple priors, especially when committed with a firearm."

"Understood. Will you help us out here and accept our plea or take the risks in court of me beating you on Mr. Lawson's behalf?"

"I'll see what I can do. I am not exactly sympathetic to your client, and I wouldn't shed a tear if he stayed in prison for life. However, if I recommend this to Judge Kennedy, you'll hear from us to appear before him. Now give me the name of the co-conspirator."

"No, sorry we won't until you guarantee a plea deal with us. Then you get the name and information."

"It doesn't work that way, hotshot. You tell me the name and the information now, because I need to corroborate your story. If I can't corroborate it, then there's no deal. Got it?"

Kingston knew he was in a corner and had no choice. He knew Connor was right and doing due diligence. "Spencer Barton, the victim's oldest son. He's a senior in pre-law at U. of I."

"You've got to be kidding me! You expect me to believe this crap? His son orders a hit on his father, the doctor? You're living in a fantasy world if you think this play will save your client."

Lawson finally broke his silence. "Yeah, ain't that a fucked-up family?"

"Connor, you go do what you have to do and I imagine eventually the producers of the TV show *Snapped* will be calling you," said Kingston.

Connor left and Kingston remained with Lawson for a few minutes more. "I think he'll do it, Brock, and it's your only hope."

"I know."

CHAPTER 54

Suzie Perkins was 75 years old and in for her yearly exam. She followed up with Wyatt at least once a year since she had a mild heart attack 10 years ago when her husband died. She sat on the edge of the exam table, and Wyatt took her blood pressure and pulse, listened to her heart and lungs, felt her ankles for edema, then helped her get down to a comfortable chair to talk.

"Dr. Barton, why don't doctors wear white coats anymore? Used to be so common, but then I do like that you wear that blue shirt; it matches your eyes. That tie doesn't go with that shirt, though."

Wyatt laughed aloud. "Thanks for your honesty, Suzie. No, I don't like wearing white coats in the office, but I do wear scrubs and a white coat when I'm at the hospital."

"I see; so how do I sound, Dr. Barton?"

"Your heart is doing well. Keep up your exercise program and diet, keep taking your statin drugs and beta blockers, and I'll see you in a year. As always you know what symptoms to look for in the meantime, and call me if you have problems."

"Yes, honey, I will."

His phone rang and he excused himself from Suzie and walked into the hallway to answer.

"Hello, Dr. Barton, it's Detective Farmer, do you have a few minutes to talk?"

As soon as he heard Farmer's voice, adrenaline surged throughout his body in anticipation of the news he expected to hear.

"Hi Gordon. I'm in between patients right now and I have a few minutes. By the way, I came up zero on patients in my practice named Brock Lawson. What do you have for me?"

"Well there's been some new information on the case that I thought you needed to know."

"Great. I bet you've already figured out the story on this Lawson guy and you're going to nail the idiot and put him in prison for the rest of his life for what he attempted to do to me."

"Yes, but not exactly, Wyatt."

"What do you mean, 'not exactly'?"

"Are you sitting or standing?"

"Standing outside a patient exam room in the hallway. Why?"

"I need you to go to your private office and sit down at your desk now."

Wyatt walked down the hallway to his private office, wondering what could be so dreadful that he had to be sitting. Was Marta hurt? Did they drop the charges for lack of evidence? When he entered his office, he was met by his office assistant who said, "Dr. Barton, Mrs. Krueger has been waiting 30 minutes. Just wanted to make you aware."

"Just a minute. I've got to finish this phone call."

He closed the door, took a deep breath, and picked up the phone. "Go ahead; I'm sitting at my desk now."

"Okay. Brock Lawson had a co-conspirator."

"Interesting. You mean there were two devils in the house that night?"

"No, Lawson shot you himself, alone, but someone paid him to do it."

"What kind of loony asshole would pay him to kill me?"

"Now I want you to take three deep breaths, Wyatt, before I tell you this because I don't think you'll be ready."

"I've been through so much that I could never have imagined, I doubt that anything could hurt me now."

"Okay, then. Maybe you're ready for this because I sure wasn't. It was your son Spencer who paid him $20,000 to shoot you with the intent to kill. Brock confessed and we arrested your son today."

There was a lengthy pause while the words registered in Wyatt's brain.

The phone went dead.

"Are you there? Dr. Barton? Pick up the phone!"

CHAPTER 55

Marta called Wyatt five times on his cell the whole afternoon when he should've been in his office but was unable to connect. When she called the office, they told her that he left early because of an emergency, and they had no other details to share with her. After six hours, her worry for him forced her to drive to his house to see if he was okay. She had a key and went straight into his house where she found him sitting out on the deck, staring off into the woods, with a cup of coffee and a jar of peanuts on the deck table in front of him.

"Wyatt, I've been worried about you! Why didn't you answer my calls? Thank God you're okay, or at least it looks like you're physically okay."

Wyatt looked at her, smiled weakly, and she saw the faraway look outlined by red in his previously sky blue eyes. He possessed no words for her.

"What happened to you? The office told me you canceled all your afternoon patients for an emergency. You never do that. What was the emergency?" Are you sick or injured?"

Wyatt continued to stare off at the eagle's nest far off in the tall pines behind his house. Somehow he felt jealous of the eagle, a proud bird soaring high over the earth, seeing everything from afar, and enjoying the solitude of strength without having to lower himself to participate in the mundane activities on the ground. He swooped to the dirty earth only when he needed to get a meal.

"I'm not physically hurt. It was my little Bubba. My Bubba wanted me dead!"

"Who's Bubba and what did he do?" She held his hand tight, a hand that she never saw trembling before.

"This is difficult for me to say, but Detective Farmer called me this morning."

"And..."

"They arrested Spencer."

"Why?"

"Seems the guy who shot me, Brock Lawson, named him as the one who paid him to shoot me. They arrested Spencer."

"Oh my loving God!" Marta's previously rosy skin suddenly turned pasty. She put her arm around Wyatt and held him tightly and they both stared out into the woods together, stunned with the horrible turn of events. She knew that it must be true due to the devastation she saw in Wyatt's eyes. After about fifteen minutes of silence, Marta got up and went inside, opened the kitchen liquor cabinet, and poured two glasses of bourbon and brought them and the bottle out to the deck, putting Wyatt's glass in front of him on the table. She took a healthy gulp, but Wyatt pushed the glass away.

"Thanks Marta, it's damn tempting, but although this is a difficult time that in the past would've been soothed at least temporarily from alcohol, I've learned to avoid alcohol during stress, and it no longer controls me. I've conquered that demon at least."

"Suit yourself, Wyatt. But I need it. You know she's an evil bitch, Wyatt."

He got up, took the glass of bourbon, poured the alcohol into Marta's now empty glass, and hurled his glass out into the woods as high and far as he could. He listened while it fell gently through the branches, but didn't break when it hit the ground softened by a cushion of pine needles. Unsatisfied, he grabbed the whole bottle of bourbon and hurled it as far as he could, and this time he heard it smash into a pile of rocks.

"Yeah, she's actually Satan incarnate who lured my sons to the dark side that only she knows so well. That psycho bitch will rot in hell for what she did to those boys."

Judge F. Ransom Kennedy's chambers had two walls packed with law references that saturated the room with a smell of musty paper and scholarly journals. A laptop computer sat to his left on his desk, and a framed picture of his wife, three children, and six grandchildren at a Christmas get-together occupied the right corner of his desk. He kept his Glock 9 mm loaded, easily reachable in a drawer under his desk. In front of his desk for all to see was an elongated wooden piece that had the inscription "Forget the buck; this is the end of the line." Charles Kingston sat in front of the judge to his left, Brock Lawson in the middle, and Randolph Connor sat to his right. Lawson wore handcuffs, ankle shackles, and an orange jumpsuit. Two armed guards provided security at the door.

Kennedy didn't bother with introductions or formalities and when he saw that everyone was seated, he looked directly at Lawson. "I've read the case and your plea of guilty to the charge of attempted murder. I have some questions to ask you, Mr. Lawson."

"Go ahead, sir."

"Now, is your plea voluntary?"

"Yes, Your Honor, it is."

"Have you spoken to counsel, and this is still your plea?"

Brock looked at Kingston, saw him acknowledge with a nod, then answered. "Yes, Your Honor, it is."

"Very well. It's time for you to recite to me exactly what happened. I want to know the name of the victim, the location of the crime, details of the shooting, what weapon was used, and how much payment you received."

"Yeah well the victim was, or I mean is, Dr. Wyatt Barton, and the location was his home on Sunnyside Lane in Evanston. I broke into his house through the front window, went to his bedroom, and shot him. He fired at me simultaneously and some buckshot busted up my right kneecap, but I was able to escape without being seen. I used a .357 magnum revolver. As far as the payment, I received $10,000 in cash from Mr. Spencer Barton up front, then another $10,000 after I shot him."

"That was a helluva bold and brazen attack on an innocent man, a man who saves lives in this city every day. Do you have any idea in that pea brain of yours what it means to contribute positively to society, Mr. Lawson? And also, do you have any idea how lucky you are that he didn't die?"

"Yes, Your Honor, to both questions. I really had second thoughts after I entered the house about killing him for his son, but things got out of hand and I could've shot him in the head, but I purposely aimed to the side, hoping to hit his leg."

"Whatever. From what I hear, the guy's a good shot when he's not half-asleep without glasses on. You're lucky he didn't put you six feet under."

Kennedy scratched the top of his nose, wiped his forehead, and then said, "Let me advise you, Mr. Lawson, that there is no appeal. Do you understand?"

"Yes, Your Honor."

He looked at Kingston and then Connor, satisfied that it was a legitimate plea. "I will notify you of your sentence within a week or less through your attorney, Mr. Lawson. My decision will be based on the severity of the crime, recommendations from the state's attorney, your prior record, and of course, the information you have given us as part of your plea with regard to the man who hired you. You can all leave now, except Mr. Connor."

After the others left, the judge poured some coffee for Connor, they both slurped a few sips in the silence, then Kennedy asked Connor his recommendation.

"Judge, you need to know that I've corroborated this information he's told you. However, as you know, an attempt to commit first-degree murder while armed with a firearm in this state is a Class X felony that adds 15 years to the prison term, which is no less than 20 years and no more than 80 years. This guy has priors with armed robbery and drug distribution and so he's a menace to society. Because of the plea, I recommend we knock off the extra 15 years because of the firearm and give him the minimum of 20 years."

The judge thought for a while then said, "I want to give the scum the maximum allowable by the state, 80 years, but he did plea and name a co-conspirator. Therefore, I'll give him 25 years with no parole and he'll be lucky to receive my warm kindness. Now, I expect you to file charges on Spencer Barton for solicitation of murder for hire, and let's get a court date on the docket for this troubled young man."

CHAPTER 56

"This is the Cook County Jail. I need to speak to a Ms. Katherine Barton please."

"Speaking."

"Is Spencer Barton your son?"

"Yes he is. What's happened to him?"

"He's been arrested and is now a resident of the Cook County Jail. You are allowed…"

"Why is my little boy in jail? He didn't do anything wrong. There has to be a mistake. Is this a practical joke or something? Please tell me this is a mistake!"

"Ms. Barton, your son is arrested and is in jail. You are welcome to visit him during the day and the visiting hours are 11am to 12 noon, then again from 2 pm to 3 pm."

"What are the charges?"

"I can't give you those over the phone. You can discuss the charges with your son when you visit with him. Thank you and have a good day."

Katherine jumped into the car and sped to the jail. She didn't put makeup on or even check to see that she closed the garage door. She went through the metal detectors at the jail entrance, signed in to the family visitation roster, and took a seat in the family waiting room until she was called to go in to see Spencer. She arrived at 9 am and preferred to sit in the waiting room until visiting hours began at 11 am so she could see him immediately. She thought about what could possibly have happened. Is there something she didn't know about Spencer? Did he get mixed up with the wrong crowd at college? She always made sure she talked to him as much as possible about his life, his friends, and his loves. He was her firstborn, and the son she hoped would have unlimited potential in life, and she was there for him always to give love and support. After all, he didn't have a father figure for almost half his life now.

"Ms. Barton, we're ready for you to meet your son."

The deputy led her to the secure visiting room, where she saw Spencer, dressed in orange, sitting in a chair in a cubicle, protected by bulletproof and soundproof glass. She looked into his eyes and saw nothing but blank redness.

"Just pick up the two-way telecom phone and you can speak to him. You have thirty minutes. When you hear the buzzer, your time is up and we'll escort you out."

"That's not much time for me to have with my baby! I need more time!"

The deputy shook his head and walked away.

"Spencer, my baby, what happened! I love you. Speak to me please."

"Nothing to say, Mom. I'm here, and you aren't."

"What do you mean by that?"

"Just what I said, Katherine. You see the obvious, so accept it."

"I can't believe you called me Katherine for the first time in your life. You always called me Mommy or Mom. Please call me Mom from now on."

"Katherine, it's over."

"No it's not over, my son. What did they arrest you for?"

"Solicitation for murder."

"Impossible. You know it. Who framed you for this? It's got to be a mistake, right? Who is the alleged murder victim?"

"He is still alive. He survived."

"Who was it?"

Spencer stared at her now, his eyes showing an accelerating fire that she had never seen before. His voice began to crack during his struggle to answer her.

"Wyatt."

"Wyatt who?"

"Who is the only Wyatt you know? The man you used to tell me was my ex-father who didn't love us. The man you said cared only about his alcohol and other women. The man you said told you he wanted to abort me as a fetus. Do I need to go on, Katherine?"

"Well, no of course, but I never..."

"Shut up. I don't want to hear your shit anymore."

Katherine's face turned icy grey. "Did you do it, Spence?"

He wouldn't answer, looked at his watch then back at her with a quiet disgust. He wanted this over and motioned to the deputy that he was done.

"No Spence, not yet. We're not done! I love you so much! You're going to be fine and this false arrest won't stick. Don't worry about it. We'll get you a good lawyer. In fact, you're going to be a great lawyer someday and you'll get married and have a great family, and I can't wait to be a grandma. I'm so proud of you and for your future."

"It's over, Katherine. I'll never go to law school, and I'll never have a family and it's all because of you! He choked up and started losing control, but he had to get the words out. "You are my biological mother, but what scares me is that I now realize that you are the she-devil incarnate. The definition of evil, and your lies and hateful stories against Dad I heard over the years make me sick now. You have destroyed me and also Colby, but I hope Colby can recover. I'm sorry it took so long for me to see this, but now I do. No, I don't love you, and I care nothing about you."

Spencer got up to leave, but he still had the communication phone in his hand.

"No Spence, my baby. Everything's okay. You don't understand, I love you so much, and I know you don't mean those words you said, you're just under stress. Are you on drugs?"

He put the phone to his mouth and made one last statement to his mother. "You are nothing to me, and your life is meaningless. You've destroyed me and lost me, and you've lost Colby too. I'm sorry I was so blind."

"No please! I can't lose my kids or I'll kill myself!"

The deputy escorted him back to his cell and never looked back.

CHAPTER 57

Two months later, the trial of The People of Illinois vs. Spencer Barton was about to begin. The winter cold descended in full force on Chicago, blustery winds whipping people's scarves and red skin until they came in off South California Avenue into the warmth of the Criminal Court Building. Randolph Connor chose his best prosecutor, Julie Harrison, for the case, and Jerry Mangioni, an experienced defense attorney who spent half the year representing clients in New York, represented the accused, Spencer Barton. He was expensive, but Wyatt decided he would help pay for Spencer's defense, because he felt that was the only way to get to the truth, and a fair trial. He still had a father's desperate hope that this would all end well, and that his own progeny could not have possibly done this crime. He had to hear the truth himself though, no matter how it hurt. Marta sat with him in the middle of the defense side, six rows back, and three rows in front of them were Colby and his mother Katherine.

The gallery overflowed with people from the community who were lucky enough to be allowed in, including newspaper reporters, TV news journalists, and producers from the TV show *Snapped* and *Law and Order*. Clearly, the case had gone national with its bizarre drama.

Ms. Harrison started her opening statement by first looking directly at each juror. She occasionally played with her long brown hair that reached her mid back, and her business suit wrapped innocently around her feminine curves despite her attempts to find the most conservative outfit possible. But she had to wear heels and they made her feel powerful, and thus could easily prey upon the enraptured men on the jury. "I know it's difficult to serve on a jury trial, and I appreciate the time you have given out of your lives. However, you need to know that service to your community and fellow citizens is an honor. During this trial you will hear evidence that the accused, Mr. Spencer Barton, did, in fact, willfully hire, and subsequently pay cash to a ruthless killer for the express purpose of murdering his father, Dr. Wyatt Barton."

She paused for dramatic effect and listened to the hushed murmurs in the crowd. "Fortunately, Dr. Barton survived, due to the miraculous work by his colleagues at the hospital who were able to save his life. However, his life is forever changed. Yes, he is back at work as a cardiologist, but he will continue to wonder what went wrong with his family, and the son that he loved. You will hear from the defense evidence that may dissuade you from listening to the facts in this case, hoping to work on your sympathy for the young man and the life that he has yet to live. However, I ask you to stay strong, listen to the facts, and decide the case, not with emotion, but with truth, and if you do that, you will find Spencer Barton guilty of solicitation of murder for hire, a class X felony in the state of Illinois. That is all, Your Honor."

"The court will now hear the opening statement by the defense," said Judge Kennedy.

Mr. Mangioni rose up from the defense side, walked slowly to the jury, and smiled. He was short and round with gray hair on the sides of his bald head, with several strands of hair crossing from one side to the other as if they were desperate holdouts from falling off. But his eyes were deep dark brown, and they knew how to pierce into the eyes of the jurors and then directly into their hearts.

"Ladies and gentleman of the jury. I'm sure you found Ms. Harrison's opening statement quite eloquent and dramatic. However, words, no matter how well they are presented, cannot produce evidence if it is not there. During this trial, you will find no evidence beyond the shadow of doubt that the defendant, Mr. Spencer Barton, did in fact know the man who shot his father. You will learn that the shooter is a drug pusher who spent much of his adolescent years in juvenile detention, and a significant amount of his adult life in and out of prison. You'll see Spencer Barton as a gentle, bright young man whose goal in life was to build a career in business law, and was already accepted at Harvard and Yale law schools. You will determine him to be innocent of a charge that has been fabricated by the shooter to protect himself. Thank you for your time and thank you, Your Honor."

Julie Harrison presented her first witness, Dr. Wyatt Barton. When he entered the witness stand all eyes were fixed on him, studying him to see if he had a limp or any physical signs of the shooting. Instead, what they saw was the athletic walk of a confident man, dressed in a black sport coat, grey dress slacks, and a red and blue tie. He completed the swearing in and avoided looking out in the gallery except when he needed to find the comforting smile of Marta.

"Dr. Barton, do you remember the night of November 15, one year ago?" said Ms. Harrison.

"Some pieces I do, but certainly there are blank spots."

"Go on, tell us what you remember."

"I came home that night in a good mood. My fiancée had accepted my engagement ring the night before, and I enjoyed a good day at the hospital, helping a pregnant woman who was suffering from a complex heart condition. It was a good day. I remember a loud crash in the front of the house, and fell to the floor, grabbed my gun, and fired, but then all I remember is pain and trying to reach the phone, then all went black."

"So, I take it that you had no inclination that you had enemies or that anyone had made a threat to your life?"

Wyatt hesitated. He knew where this was going and he would go ahead and say it. He took a deep breath and felt an inner strength that carried him through. "I'm estranged from my children and haven't had any relationship with them in well over five years after the divorce from my ex-wife. There were times that my ex-wife has threatened me and also has threatened to kill the kids if I didn't return to the marriage home."

There was a collective gasp from the audience, and Colby and Spencer both looked at their mother with a look of astonishment. Wyatt saw and heard it all, and his mind was as clear as a fresh mountain stream.

Mangioni flinched a little in his chair, but didn't object. He was ready, but allowed Wyatt to continue because it might help his case.

"Go on, Dr. Barton. What did she threaten you with?"

"Well, she also said she would kill me if she couldn't have me and would file charges of physical and sexual abuse against me with regard to the children if I didn't come back to her."

"Seems to me, Dr. Barton, that this threat is not conducive to bringing a man back to rekindle a relationship, don't you agree?"

"Absolutely."

"And don't you think, Dr. Barton, that if you were as bad as she said you were, most rational women would not want you back?"

"Ms. Harrison, I don't know where you're going with this but I want you to change your line of questioning," said Judge Kennedy.

"Yes, Your Honor. Did you ever abuse your kids, Dr. Barton?"

Wyatt didn't move a muscle. "Never."

"Why do you think she never pressed charges against you if you were such a bad man, Dr. Barton?"

"Because she tried to manipulate me with lies and threats."

"Did you have any proof that she stated she wanted to kill you?"

"Well, yes, I did record the conversation but the quality was so poor it wasn't audible."

"Did Katherine ever make any attempt to physically attack you?"

"Yes, one time she tried to run over my feet at my office garage with the kids inside the car. She said I was wearing nice shoes after the divorce and that she believed the only reason I did that was to pick up women."

"Any other time?"

"After we separated before the divorce was finalized, she found me with my friend in the car and she followed us all around town, tried to run us off the road, driving erratically and yelling at us while we were driving."

"Go on. Were you or your passenger injured?"

"No. I was able to drive through town and eventually lost her."

"You said the kids were in her car during this chase?"

"Yes, unfortunately. It was late at night and it was a school night yet she had them out with her, looking for me and hoping to make me look bad in their eyes. That was her usual behavior."

"Did you tell anyone about this incident, or the police?"

"No sir, I did not."

"Thank you, Dr. Barton. Your Honor, I'm ready for my next witness."

Wyatt stepped down, glanced briefly at Spencer in the front row, and he looked away. He hoped to gain eye contact with his son, but to no avail.

"Your Honor, I would like to call Dr. Randy Turner to the stand."

"Dr. Turner, how do you know Dr. Barton?"

"I'm a PhD forensic psychologist and I was hired at the request of the divorce judge to evaluate the family due to the estrangement and accusations that had been made by Mrs. Barton."

"I see. And how did you proceed with your evaluation, Dr. Turner?"

"Separate psychological evaluations of the family, including psychological testing, intelligence testing, and interviewing."

"And what was your conclusion after your evaluation, Dr. Turner?"

"There was absolutely no evidence of abuse in any way by Dr. Barton and that he was a decent father who loved his kids. It was the worst case of parental alienation I had ever seen in my practice, and my goal was somehow to get father and children back together because they needed him in their lives."

"And were you successful in that endeavor, Dr. Turner?"

"No, unfortunately."

"Why do you think that is?"

"Katherine Barton clearly has severe Borderline Personality Disorder and had deeply indoctrinated the boys against their father, so that they would feed her insecurities about her own self and give her love and attention at the expense of the father. The children were taught to believe that their father was horrible, and he suffered from their brutal hatred."

"Your Honor, I have one last witness."

"Proceed, Ms. Harrison."

"I would like to call Mr. Jerry Thompson to the stand."

Jerry Thompson glanced at Spencer while walking to the stand, but unlike his previous encounters with his drug client, he didn't smile. He wore a khaki blazer covering a white t-shirt and straight-legged jeans.

"Please tell the court how you know Mr. Barton."

"He's a friend of mine from college; we're both studying to get into law school."

"Did you socialize?"

"Spencer is damn smart, so he helped me to get some good grades. I paid him back by introducing him to friends at parties."

"Were there drugs at your parties?"

"I object," said Mangioni.

"Sustained."

"Let me rephrase. Did you ever engage in any business relationships with Mr. Barton?"

"What do you mean?"

"Did you ever exchange money for services between the two of you?"

"Yes."

"Would you please elaborate for the court?"

"He did a lot for me, you know, and well, he needed to stay up to study so I helped him stay up."

"And how did you accomplish that, Mr. Thompson?"

"Well you know, occasional speed, sometimes coke and..."

"Objection, Your Honor."

"You can proceed, Ms. Harrison."

"Did he pay you well?"

"Yes, and usually on time."

"Tell me then, where does a college student get that kind of money, Mr. Thompson?"

Jerry looked at Spencer and the two locked eyes for a few seconds. "He told me he got it from his mom. Said his dad gave her a lot in the divorce and that he deserved his dad's money. Said he told his mom he needed money for various things, I don't know."

"Did he say anything about his dad?"

"Yeah, he used some foul words against him, said he was selfish and was a bad father and wasn't good for his mom and stuff like that."

"Did you believe him?"

"Didn't care much, just whether I would get paid. But I wondered what planet he was on."

"I have no further witnesses, Your Honor."

An eerie silence pervaded the courtroom gallery and no words were heard, just occasional coughs and sneezes. Kennedy wanted to proceed on with haste and try to resolve the case as quickly as possible. Wyatt lost the strength to listen. He fidgeted and looked up to the ceiling, trying to avoid eye contact with Spencer. Marta held his hand stronger and stronger, never letting go. "Mr. Mangioni, you may call your witnesses."

He called Brock Lawson.

"Mr. Lawson, did you shoot Dr. Barton in his home on November 15, one year ago?"

"Yes, I did."

"Would you please tell the court the events of that evening?"

"Yeah well, I was hired to shoot Dr. Barton by the guy there,

Spencer. He paid me $10,000 cash up front, and then a second $10,000 wired to my account the day after he was shot.

"Do you deny that you have served time for armed robbery and drug distribution?"

"No, sir. But I don't do..."

"Please answer the question."

"You were looking for drugs in Dr. Barton's house that night to fuel your habit, Mr. Lawson, hoping that he had some narcotics stored there for his medical mission work he did, right?"

"I don't do narcs, sir, and no, I was there to do the job I was paid to do."

"Why are your teeth black and in disarray?"

"Objection, Your Honor," said Harrison. "Mr. Lawson's dental hygiene has nothing to do with this case."

"Overruled. You may continue your response, Mr. Lawson."

"I've been known to do some meth and a little smack too, but I was clean that night. Had to be. Meth blackens teeth, everyone knows that."

Mangioni showed his frustration. He believed he'd established that Lawson was an unreliable druggy who may have been in a drug-fueled craze that night. But he knew he needed to put Spencer on the stand. Spencer was a clean kid, and he knew he would save himself and therefore his life. He would say what he told him to say. Therefore, he called Spencer to the stand to seal the deal of a nice kid who got into the wrong crowd.

"Spencer, where did you meet Brock Lawson?"

He hesitated, looked down at his feet, and then answered. "He was a friend of Jerry Thompson's whom I met at a party."

"I see, and did you know him very well?"

"No not really, but he's a man you can't forget and a man that could..."

"Just answer the question, Spencer."

Shocked by the forcefulness of the questioning, Spencer's eyes widened with fear. He thought Mangioni was on his side, but the tension forced him to tremble; ever since Jerry testified and brought his secret life out of the closet, he knew he couldn't hide anymore.

"I didn't know him very well."

"You were an honor student, accepted at Harvard as well as Yale law. Were you excited for your future?"

"Yes. Very much."

"And you had a girlfriend too, right?"

"Yes, that's right."

"I would find it hard to believe that you would hire Mr. Lawson, a drug pusher and user with a criminal record, to shoot and kill your father with all the bright future you had ahead of you, is that right?"

Spencer's silence clearly displayed his discomfort. He quivered. His lips trembled and he couldn't speak. The courtroom was like a funeral home; all you could hear were soft breaths interspersed with sighs. Spencer looked at Katherine, and she stared at him like cold steel.

"Would you like a glass of water before you answer, Mr. Barton?"

The clerk handed Spencer a glass of water, and he chugged the whole thing down, gulping as if it was the last drink he would ever have. He glared coldly at his mother. "Yes, I paid Brock Lawson to shoot my father, and I did that because my mother told me on many previous occasions that she wanted him dead, and that he ruined us as a family, rejecting her as his wife. She said she would've killed him if she knew how, but she didn't know how."

Mangioni knew it was over now. "Spencer, is this really what you wanted to say, or are you saying this out of stress to protect someone else, like your mother?"

Spencer finally looked at his father in the gallery and the tears streamed down his face. "Yes, I hired Brock Lawson to shoot my father, and I did this because I saw that my mother was so sad, and she said she wished he was dead and that she loved me. I believed that is what she wanted me to do." He looked at Wyatt forlornly. "I'm sorry, Dad; please forgive me for my sin against you."

Wyatt looked at him. Father and son were finally communicating, although too late. Wyatt clutched his chest and leaned forward to his knees, his hands desperately trying to remove the black anvil that crushed his heart against his backbone. Marta tried to soothe him, but the only words he could utter were "My little Bubba. My Bubba is gone."

Cuffed and shackled, the bailiff led Spencer out of the courtroom with Katherine following right behind, her head fixed straight ahead, never looking at the faces of so many watching her from the gallery. Wyatt, Colby, and Marta turned in unison, staring at Spencer and Katherine as they exited quietly from the side of the stunned courtroom.

"I'll call you soon, Dad," said Colby. "We need to get together for dinner or something."

Wyatt smiled warmly. "I'd love that, Son. Drive safe."

CHAPTER 58

Brock Lawson went to prison to serve his 25-year sentence without parole and Spencer Barton received the much heavier sentence of 40 years in prison because the state found him guilty of solicitation of murder for hire and actually made the decision to pay Brock Lawson for his services. It was obvious that he did this to make his mother happy by following what he thought were her wishes, but despite the brainwashing he clearly didn't have to go through with it. He would be released from prison at the age of sixty-two, and the judicial system couldn't prosecute Katherine as a separate trial just on Spencer's testimony about why he did it.

Two days after the trial, the neighbors found Katherine's body in her car in the garage, motor running, with a sock stuffed into the tailpipe. She didn't leave a note. The funeral home director found it odd that only her neighbor, her newest boyfriend, and her sisters attended the wake.

When Spencer had been in prison for over a year, Wyatt finally felt that he had to visit him.

The prison guard walked up to Spencer's cell and gave him the news. "You have a visitor waiting for you in the family reception area. I'll take you down there, but you only have fifteen minutes."

Spencer jumped up. "Really? Who is it?"

"Don't know, man, I'm just the messenger. Guess you'll find out." He put hand and leg cuffs on Spencer and escorted him to the family waiting area. "Now remember the rules: no swearing, spitting, or exchange of contraband or bodily fluids. I'll search you afterwards anyway."

"Don't worry about me. I can't wait to see who it is. Maybe it's Lisa, my girlfriend."

"You told me she broke up with you the day you were convicted. Hell, she needs a life and she ain't waitin' for your sorry ass, that's for damn sure."

"Yeah. I was just hoping for some type of miracle I guess."

Wyatt and Marta sat on cheap plastic chairs on the visitor's side of the heavy glass-partitioned family contact area. The prisoner stopped in his tracks when he saw his dad and stared at him, unsure of what to do next.

Wyatt quietly motioned to Spencer to take a seat. It had been nine years since Wyatt had talked to his son face to face, although in this case their faces were separated by bulletproof glass. So much in life had changed since then. However, all Wyatt could see when he looked at Spencer's sad blue eyes were the fond memories of the young child, laughing and playing with his proud daddy. To Wyatt, Spencer was young, handsome, and athletic, but still his little boy. "Hello, Son. Are you doing okay? Are you healthy?"

Spencer looked at him without emotion. "Yeah, Dad, I'm healthy as could be expected I guess. Thanks for coming; I really didn't think you would ever come here after all that's..."

"I know, Spencer. Of course. But we're here. Marta and I got married after the trial and I wanted you to see her, the love I was lucky to find to spend the rest of my life with."

Marta and Spencer looked at each other and smiled. "She's beautiful, Dad. You've done well and I am happy for you at long last."

The two men just looked at each other peacefully, examining each other, searching deeply for answers that just weren't there. "Dad, I am so deeply sorry for what I did and for all the years I forced us to be apart because of my stupid blind marching to Mom's orders. I realize now that what Colby and I did to you, the harmful words of hatred and rejection, were inappropriate and selfish, to say the least. I only wish

I had all those years back, to do it over, and well, I thank God you are actually alive. I need your forgiveness but it seems inappropriate to ask."

"Thanks for those words, Spencer, I never thought I would hear them." He looked at Marta lovingly. "Yes, thank God I'm alive."

Once again, there was silence. The only sounds were muffled conversations from the other visitors while they laughed and smiled with their families. Spencer looked down to his feet most of the time, and sometimes around the room. Wyatt constantly looked at his son's dejected eyes, never flinching, soaking it all in.

"Spencer, Marta and I are going back home now. However, I need to tell you something before I go, and I want you to remember it as long as you live. I love you, my son, and always will, and I forgive you for all that you have done. May God be with you."

The tears flowed freely for all three of them, and after a few minutes, the guard took Spencer back to his cell.

REFERENCES

1. *I Hate You Don't Leave Me*. Kreisman, J., Straus, H. Avon Books. 1989.

2. Jorgensen, C. "Disturbed Sense of Identity in Borderline Personality Disorder." *Journal of Personality Disorders*. 20(6). 618–644, 2006.

3. Barnow, S. "Individual Characteristics, Familial Experience, and Psychopathology in Children of Mothers with Borderline Personality Disorder." *Journal of the American Academy of Child and Adolescent Psychiatry*. 45(8): 965–72, 2006.

CPSIA information can be obtained at www.ICGtesting.com
Printed in the USA
LVOW05s0619020514

384181LV00001B/18/P

9 781478 729846